MR JONES

MR JONES

ALEX WOOLF

i
n

Indie Novella

First published in Great Britain in 2022 by Indie Novella Ltd.

INDIE NOVELLA www.indienovella.co.uk

Edited for Indie Novella by Emily De Vogele and Matthew Gowans

A CIP catalogue record for this title is available from the British Library

Paperback ISBN 978 1 739 95992 0

Printed and bound by Clays Ltd in the United Kingdom.

Indie Novella is committed to a sustainable future for our readers and the world in which we live. All paper used are natural, renewable and sustainable products.

For Maya

PART I

18 JUNE – 13 JULY 2018

1

MONDAY 18 JUNE 2018

IMOGEN IS KICKING at something poking out of the ground with the tip of her shiny black shoe. It looks like a curved stick, bleached and dry from the sun.

"What is it, Midge?" I ask her.

"It won't come out," she says, now pulling at it with small, insistent fingers.

"It's probably a root," I tell her, pointing at the nearby oak. "Come on, or we'll be late for school."

She finally relents and totters after me, lurching slightly under the weight of her bag. We walk the narrow path that twists through the little park. It's not even nine yet, and the sun is already warm. My back is damp with sweat. The grass is very long, iridescent under its glitter of dew. There's a look of neglect. Here and there are dandelions gone to seed.

I open the gate for my daughter and we enter Leafy Wood Lane, a long, curving avenue of giant mock-Tudor dwellings. I'm grateful for the shade from the heavy, overhanging branches. We tread the uneven paving between the bushes and mossy walls. The air is ripe and gently buzzing. Trees cast deep, slumbering shadows over the pale tarmac. Huge houses peep at us from behind their security gates and foliage.

Imogen stops to examine a slug. She crouches, prodding at it with a twig. The plump, greasy mollusc writhes from the touch. I feel the sickly weight of that extra slice of toast and peanut butter in my stomach.

"Come on, Midge!" I bark at her, too harshly. "We can't keep stopping like this."

My voice cuts through the sleepy air like something jagged. She looks up, startled, perhaps a little scared by my tone. I swallow some bile, and wish I could swallow back my words. I want to explain to her about time, how easily it can slip away from us, but what's the use? What would she understand? Only that Daddy's upset and it's her fault. Imogen runs towards me, lips pressed tight, her honey-coloured hair already escaping the clips I hurriedly applied before we left home.

"Sorry Daddy."

I put my arm around her tiny shoulders, feeling the frilled sleeve of her summer dress beneath my fingers.

"It's okay." I give her shoulder a squeeze. It's my way of saying sorry.

We continue at Imogen-pace down the long curve of the avenue. I can hear someone behind us. I shuffle my girl to one side to let the person past. But the footsteps continue with the same plodding gait.

"It's Mr Jones," says Imogen. The muscle in her upper arm stiffens slightly.

The footsteps stop. When I glance back, there's no one there.

"Mr Jones must have gone into his house," I tell her.

We reach the main road opposite East Halsted Primary School. Other uniformed kids are milling around there with their mums or dads. We're not late – we're *never* late, however much I think we're going to be. Rose, the elderly lollipop lady, grins at us. "Morning," I say to her as I do every morning.

"Morning," she half laughs, same as always.

At the gate, I kiss my girl goodbye, and she runs off with her friend, already deep in conversation.

I stand there, smiling inanely, basking somewhat in the warmth and a little parental pride, nodding at another parent I know by sight.

On my way back through Turnwood Park, I see a little girl about the same age as Imogen, watching me from the slope above the path. She has a dirty, naked doll clutched in one hand. I wonder why she's not in school. Where are her parents? She looks clean enough – pink Hello Kitty T-shirt and blue jeans, combed brown hair – not a runaway. Home-schooled, probably. Still, something doesn't fit. Why is she here in the park on her own? I smile at her. "Are you okay?" I ask.

She stares back at me, but doesn't speak. Her hand pulls and twists at the bald head of her doll. With a dull pop, the plastic head comes off. I start slowly towards her, moving off the path and up the bank of long grass. As I do so, she turns and starts to wander away, going further up the slope towards the corner of the park. By the time I reach her, she's disappeared into some bushes. I push aside some leaves and peer into the shady corner. There's no sign of her, but I see a fence behind the bushes, leaning under the weight of a gnarled and twisted apple tree. The fence, marking the rear border of a house backing onto the park, has a couple of broken slats, which the girl must have crawled through.

I stand there for a moment, unsure what to do. Should I ring the doorbell of the house, just to make sure the parents are there and okay? I decide against it, hating the idea of being thought a busybody. She's probably fine. A little lonely perhaps, but fine. These are good family homes around here. Loving families. A nice neighbourhood.

Returning to the path, my foot hits something half-hidden in the long grass, making me stagger. It's that curved root that Imogen was pulling at earlier. Looking at it more closely, I see that it's about four or five inches long and doesn't actually look much like a tree root – too thin and curved. As I'm studying it, the soil moves very slightly around its base. Something is pushing its way up to the surface. I watch, revolted, as the soil crumbles around it and a pair of tiny antennae break through and wave blindly in the air. A small black beetle proceeds to lever itself out of the earth and climb up the sticklike protrusion. I get another attack of bile, watching the insect open its wing case and wheel clumsily away through the air.

When I get home I take a couple of Pepto-Bismol to settle my stomach and try to do some work. My client, Mrs Mattinson of Pine Walk, has a sagging floor in her hallway. I was over there yesterday, taking photos and measurements, inspecting the beams and floor joists in the basement. It didn't take me long to spot the problem. Groundwater infiltration was rotting the support posts. There was also a lively carpenter ant infestation in the main beam. The client was hoping for repair, but I had to recommend replacement. It will mean putting in temporary jack posts and beams. I told her it would take a while as it's an old house, and we'll have to jack it up slowly to avoid causing cracks and stress – maybe a turn or two a month to be safe. She wasn't happy, said she was going to seek a second opinion, but asked me to go ahead and quote anyway. I'll have to calculate the load before I can determine the size and type of lumber we'll need. It's a straightforward maths problem, but I'm finding it hard to concentrate.

I keep thinking about that little girl and the root thing and the beetle. Something's nudging at the edges of my memory – a story I read about, maybe a year ago in the local advertiser. A young girl went missing, not far from here, in Halsted Town. There was a big search, then nothing. The story died. I guess her body was never found.

I make myself a coffee, and while I'm waiting for the kettle to boil, something else comes back to me, something Imogen said this morning: "It's Mr Jones" she said, and then the muscle in her arm twitched. Mr Jones, the little girl, the way she pulled the head off that doll, the thin curved stick that looked like – like a rib... Forgetting my coffee, I go out to the shed in the back garden and grab a rusty garden trowel.

There's no one in Turnwood Park when I get there, apart from a couple of pensioners over by the pond. They ignore me as I get down on my knees beneath the oak tree. I have to dig quite deep around the thing, taking care not to break it or any other evidence there may be down there. Before I've even got it out of the ground, there's no doubt in my mind what it is. It's a rib, and it could easily have belonged to a child. There's nothing else buried with it in the soil apart from actual tree roots. No other bones. There are gnaw marks in the rib. Must have got detached from the rest of the body, carried here, then buried by a fox or dog. It could have been buried here unnoticed for a year, easy – since the time the girl disappeared. Then with all the hot weather recently, the oak got thirsty, sucked the moisture from the soil, caused a little subsidence, and the rib got exposed. But where's the rest of her? I glance at the pond. Then I look the other way, up the bank towards the far corner of the park where the shadows always seem to gather. My gaze eventually comes to rest on the overgrown bush and the broken fence.

"Who's Mr Jones?" I ask Imogen when I pick her up from school that afternoon.

"I'm not scared of him," she said, skipping away from me.

I chase after her and grab her, steering her towards the zebra crossing. I can feel her ribcage beneath her thin summer dress.

"Good afternoon," I smile at Rose.

"Afternoon," she chuckles.

"Who *is* scared of him, Midge?" I ask my girl once we've crossed the road.

"Scared of who?"

"Mr Jones."

She shrugs. "It's just stories. That's what I tell Aisha and Theodora."

"What's just stories?" I persist.

"Mr Jones will come up behind you when you're not looking, and he'll grab you. That's what Harriet from 6b says."

2

"IT'S GONE," says Imogen, staring at the hole where her little stick used to be. "Now it's a hole."

We're passing through Turnwood Park.

"Come on," I tell her. "I've got some nice juicy cherries at home."

"Maybe it's a mouse hole," she suggests.

I feel a delicate prickling of the hairs on my arms and neck. Instinctively, I turn towards the shadowy corner of the park, with its tangled bush and broken fence. I half expect to see the girl there again. I almost hope she's there, thinking it would be an opportunity to introduce her to Imogen. But when I see she isn't, I actually feel relieved – I don't know why. Still, a feeling of being watched won't leave me. I imagine her crouched there on the other side of the fence, spying on us through the gap.

I drag Imogen from the hole and back to the path.

"I think Mummy took the stick," she says, after blowing out a cherry stone.

We're sitting in the kitchen. My hand shakes very slightly as I place the discarded stone in the bowl on the table between us. It's been several months since she's mentioned her mum. I was starting to hope, maybe, she was getting over her.

"She must have seen me trying to get it out," Imogen nods to herself. "She took it because she wants to give it to me for my birthday present, all wrapped up."

I enclose her small hand in mine and look at her cherry-stained face. "Midge," I say.

"Yes Daddy?"

"Mummy's gone. She's not coming back."

Her bright eyes harden. She sticks out her jaw in the way Susan, her mother, used to. "I don't think you're right, Daddy. Granny says she disappeared. Maybe a witch made her invisible and that's why we can't see her. But she can see *us*. So if I find the stick all wrapped up, then I know it will be from Mummy. That's how I'll know."

I wipe her cheek with a paper towel. "Speaking of Granny, I'm going to have to take you over there now."

"Why?"

"Daddy's on a deadline this afternoon. I can't be disturbed. Now go get yourself cleaned up."

We arrive at the front gate of my mother's pebbledash-rendered house on the southern curve of Oakfield Crescent. Imogen races up to the front door. Granny's there within a minute of the door chime, a big welcoming smile on her face. She and Dad moved here ten years ago. It's only a few minutes' walk from our house, so we could be on hand in an emergency. He died two years later. As far as Imogen knows, Granny has always lived here, and lived here alone. Immersed as I am in my daughter's life, I've started to see things in the same way. "Mum" has morphed into "Granny", at least when I'm talking to Imogen, and somehow this is where she's always been. There's a familiar smell of cigarettes and turpentine wafting from her as she opens the door.

After hugging her granny, Imogen asks if she can go straight to the studio.

"It's all set up and waiting for you, dear," my mother tells her. "Today, we're going to paint flowers."

Imogen runs through the hall into the kitchen-dining room and out through the open French windows to one of her favourite places in the world – Granny's garden studio.

"Do you want a cup of tea before you go?" my mother asks me.

"Better not, I'm on a deadline."

"Everything okay, love?"

"Yeah, fine," I say automatically, before adding: "Midge mentioned her mum again today."

Mum frowns and nods. "Yes, she occasionally talks about her to me."

"She says you told her she'd disappeared."

"Well it's true. I think it's important to be as honest as we can be..."

I purse my lips, try to breathe calmly through my nostrils. "She's seven. In her world *disappear* conjures up magic spells and fairy tales. You've given her hope. I don't think that's a good idea."

"Come and sit down a moment. Let's talk about this."

"I really don't have time," I say, but I follow her anyway, into the large kitchen-diner.

Her fingers, stained with green paint, fish a cigarette from her cardigan pocket, and she spends an age lighting it from the stove. "We don't know what happened to her Ben. She may come back, you never know."

Mum sits down at the table, pushing out a chair for me with her foot, encouraging me to sit down.

I sit, but can't relax. A queasy impatience rises in my throat, an acid taste of cherries. "It's been ten months." I feel the need to remind her of this, because she talks sometimes as if Susan's only been gone a week. "Do you think I haven't explored every possible avenue? We have to accept that she's gone!"

But I can see from the way Mum's brown eyes dance that she doesn't accept that. "What about Devon?" she asks.

I let out a tired breath. The county that has recently become a synonym for despair in my vocabulary. "Will you leave it alone Mum? She's not in Devon. She's not anywhere."

"She mentioned it didn't she? Just before she disappeared."

If there's a straw anywhere, my mother will clutch at it. Three, maybe four days before Susan disappeared, I was in the corridor outside our bedroom about to come in, when I heard her in there talking to someone on the phone. "I can't *wait* till Devon," she said, with the emphasis on "wait", as you might when anticipating a holiday.

My mother taps ash into an ashtray shaped like a fish with a large mouth. "Why didn't you ask her about it? About what she meant?"

"I didn't know it was significant at the time, did I? I didn't know she was about to..."

The truth was I didn't know a whole lot about Susan by that stage, although I kidded myself we were okay, or *would* be okay – that we were still in a bad patch following my discovery of Susan's affair. So when I heard *Devon*, I made a decision to ignore it, convinced myself it was unimportant – or that I'd misheard her. There's no point now wishing I'd gone in there, grabbed the phone from her cheek and demanded to know what was going on. You can't live your life in retrospect.

"She may still come back Ben. Miracles do sometimes happen."

Nor can you live your life in hope. That's maybe worse. My patience, already a thread drawn tight between white knuckles, snaps. "Believe what you like Mum, but please don't talk about it to Imogen or me. I'm serious! You've got to shut up about miracles because it's stopping us from moving on. It's as if you want to keep us in a state of limbo, and I'm sick of it!"

She looks startled, tries to interrupt, but I shout her down, laying out the facts for her, bashing the heel of my right hand against the fingers of my left for emphasis: "*No* communication! *No* ransom note! *No* sightings. What are we supposed to think? She may not have loved *me*, but she definitely loved Midge. Are you telling me she would voluntarily abandon her own daughter? Are you telling me..."

Imogen reappears from the garden, and that silences me. My voice was probably loud enough to be heard as she was coming up the path. I just pray she didn't understand what I was saying.

"What's wrong Daddy?" Imogen is clutching a paintbrush and holding it to her chest, as if for protection.

"It's alright Midge," says her granny. "Daddy's just a little upset." She crushes her fag and stands up. "Let's go paint, shall we?"

Her grimace of sorrow and sympathy, which she flashes at me before leaving, makes me feel ashamed. I move to the French window and watch them walk down the path to the studio. Mum has her arm around Imogen's shoulders. I want to go and apologise, hug them both. But they've formed their own self-contained little unit now. I listen to their exchange and it's so odd I have to smile.

"Why did you come back, dear? Didn't you like the flowers I picked?"

"It's not that, it's your painting Granny. The one on the easel."

"Oh, that's an abstract. Just a bit of swirly nonsense. It's not meant to be anything."

"But it *is* something Granny. I looked at it and I saw a face. An extremely ugly face."

"Nonsense Midge. I never paint anything ugly."

The rib is in a polythene bag on top of the wardrobe in my room. When I get back home, I take it down and turn the thing over in my hands, thinking. The phone rings. Still holding the rib, I go through to my study and pick up.

It's Mrs Mattinson of the sagging floor. She wants to know why we can't just reinforce the existing support posts. I tell her the problem isn't just that they're rotting, but that her basement has a dirt floor and the concrete poured around the post bases simply isn't strong enough. The entire hallway floor is in danger of collapse if we don't install new posts with concrete pads and footings that will spread the load. At the same time we'll need to replace the main beam, which is riddled with carpenter ant holes. She asks me when she can have the quote and I promise her she'll have it by 5pm.

I put the phone down and go on examining the bone. It's small and delicate, smooth and gleaming like ivory beneath the grey patina caused by its long immersion in the soil. It has a thick, knobbly end where it connected to the girl's spine, then a long, graceful, sweeping curve, flat in section. The other end is abrupt, but with a slightly flared shape. For a second, I shudder with the knowledge that Imogen has a bone exactly like this one inside her – probably this very size.

I regret my outburst in my mother's kitchen. The thought of it scares and disgusts me, as if I'd conjured some horrid, slimy monster out of my guts and deposited it there in that sanctified space. I wonder why I get so riled by Mum when she talks about the possibility of Susan being alive.

In a battered contacts book, I find the number I'm after and key it into my phone.

"Geoff Gunnell, Roxwell Forensic Services. How can I help?"

"Geoff," I say on hearing the nasal, estuary English greeting. "It's Ben. Ben Rose."

"Ben!" His voice warms up. "Wow, it's been ages. How are you doing?"

"Okay. You?"

"Can't complain. I cannot grumble sir. Listen, I've been meaning to give you a tinkle for ages. How've you been?"

I don't want to get into a heart-to-heart right now with Geoff. We go back a long way – all the way back to Miss Absil's reception class at East Halsted Primary, where we bonded over a mutual love of Scalextric and Jaffa Cakes and an antipathy to football. We were best mates all through primary school and the first couple of years of secondary, both of us stereotypical nerds, who would get a kick out of referring to sugar by its chemical formula $C_{12}H_{22}O_{11}$, and building model steam turbines for science fairs. But then, aged thirteen, I discovered acid house music and girls, while Geoff just went on being a nerd.

"I'm doing okay, Geoff. Listen, I have something I'd like you to check out."

"What is it old friend? How may I be of service?"

"It's better if I just show you. Can we meet?"

"Of course we can. Bien sur! How about this evening at Ye Olde Pear Tree."

Geoff pronounces the pub name phonetically. In many ways, he's still thirteen years old. I can tell he's angling to turn this into a social thing – Geoff isn't married, and doesn't have many friends. Life, for him, revolves around work and his pet degus.

"I can't leave Midge alone I'm afraid, Geoff. How about I come over to your office tomorrow morning?"

"There's Harriet from 6b." Imogen points out a tall girl with prominent teeth. We follow Harriet and her mother through the school gates, past the kitchen outlet pipes belching their nauseating fug of cheap bolognese sauce and chip fat, and into the playground.

"Excuse me," I say to the mother, trotting slightly to catch up with her.

Imogen tugs at my sleeve. "Daddy, please don't," she begs.

The sharp-nosed woman turns. "Yes?"

"Would you mind very much if I ask your daughter a question?"

"What is it? What's she done now?" She turns on Harriet. "What've you done now?"

Harriet stares at her mum, then at me, like a startled, buck-toothed rabbit. "Nuffing, Mum."

"She's done nothing wrong," I assure the mother. "It's just that she mentioned something to my daughter, and I'd quite like to ask her about it."

"Da-ad!" snivels my mortified Midge. I give her shoulder a calming squeeze, and direct my attention towards Harriet. "You mentioned a Mr Jones. According to my daughter, you said to her, 'Mr Jones will come up behind you when you're not looking, and he'll grab you.' Did I get that right?"

Harriet continues to stare at me for a moment before nodding dumbly.

"It's just stories, though," says Imogen quickly. "She didn't mean to scare us or anything, did you Harriet?"

Harriet swiftly shakes her head, still staring at me.

"Were you scaring the younger ones?" says Mrs Harriet, frowning at her daughter, nostrils wide like two gun barrels.

"No, Mum! Honest! It was just stupid stories, like she said. I didn't scare no one."

I break in: "It's alright, I'm not accusing your daughter of anything, I'm simply interested in finding out where the story originally came from. I want to know who Mr Jones is."

"Well?" says Mrs Harriet. "You heard the man? Who is Mr Jones?"

The bell clangs raucously, marking the start of the school day.

We all go on staring at Harriet, even Imogen, as the other children mill past us, heading towards their classrooms.

3

TUESDAY 19 JUNE 2018

I'M in fine spirits as I steer my silver Renault Megane towards Geoff Gunnell's office in North Halsted. I'm playing New Order at extravagant volume and thumping the steering wheel like a drum. I'm happy because Mrs Mattinson has seen reason. She's accepted my quote, and I've arranged with the contractor to start work in her basement next week.

The smile leaves my face though, and the sound of 'True Faith' fades from my head, as I pull into the car park of the industrial estate off the A108. The breeze hits me like a sharp slap as I get out of the car. The paper-white sky is gently luminous. A Tesco bag skitters along, until it is caught on the wing mirror of a Mazda. In my hand I'm carrying part of a little girl.

The reception of Roxwell Forensic Services has a dusty fake ficus plant and stained carpets. The plump woman at the desk runs some fingers through her blond-highlighted hair as she waits for the phone to pick up. "Mr Gunnell will be out shortly," she informs me before turning back to her screen. I drop into a boxlike fake leather sofa. The rib, in its see-through plastic bag, I've stowed in my pocket. After five minutes, I'm starting to wonder if Geoff is deliberately punishing me for rebuffing his pub suggestion. I'm almost tempted to pick up one of the slim, glossy brochures on the IKEA coffee table just to pass some time, but then I hear the squeak of the double door, and through it lumbers Mr Gunnell in his thin-collared lab coat. His broad, pockmarked face widens into a grin and he clasps my hand. "Benjamin. Binyamin. Benny. So good to see you sir. How's Midge? How's your mother?"

"They're fine thanks Geoff. And how are the degus?"

"Basil died. Liver disease. I know. Tragic." He puts up a hand as if to brush off any expressions of sympathy that I might have been thinking of extending. "Thank you Ben, but it's okay, I'm fine. He had a good innings. And I've still got Button and Boo."

The grin returns, and his hand is now on my arm as if he's scared I might flee. "Let's sit. Let's sit right here, Ben, and you can tell me all about whatever it is I'm going to help you with."

He releases me and we sit down. I check the receptionist is still playing Solitaire with her computer, then remove the rib from its bag and hand it to him. "I want to know, Geoff: did this come from a child?"

He twirls it back and forth a few times between thumb and forefinger. Then he knocks it with his knuckle. Then he flexes it gently, making its curved shape bend. I'm watching this performance intently, like I might that of a conjurer.

"What you've got here, Ben," he says after a while, "– what you've got yourself here, is a *côte de porc*."

"A what?"

"Granted it's seen better days."

"Sorry, I don't understand..."

"*Costata di maiale* Ben. *Schweienerippe*. It's a pig rib, old man."

I feel a tug inside me, and something starts to drain, as if a plug's been pulled.

He's still twirling it like a bloody majorette with her baton. I want to slap it out of his hand.

"Where did you find it?" he asks.

"Half buried in a park near where I live."

"My guess is it was probably stolen from a bin by a fox." The rib is back in his palm now, and he's running a thumb down its rough, pearl-grey surface. "Look here, you can see the tooth marks where it's been gnawed."

The grin, when he looks up at me, is mellower. "Hey, it's an easy mistake to make old friend. Pig ribs look a lot like human ones – something you may care to think about next time you're tucking into a rack of juicy ones smothered in barbecue sauce. But they're denser, see." He tapped it again. "Sounds sort of like ceramic, doesn't it? Cows, sheep and pigs have to get up as soon as they're born to avoid predators, so their bone has to be laid down fast and it has to be tough. Our bones take longer to form and build strength. They have a different kind of structure. I can show you in the lab, if you like. I'll saw a bit of this off and show you under the microscope..."

"No, that's okay, Geoff. I believe you."

I stand up, just wanting to be gone. I'm surprised to be feeling this disappointed. This ought to be good news...

"Sure you won't stay for a coffee? It's from the machine but it's actually quite drinkable."

"Thanks, but I ought to be going."

"What about this?" he asks, still twirling the rib like a demented drummer. "I can dispose of it for you if you like."

I think of Imogen... *So if I find the stick all wrapped up, then I know it will be from Mummy. That's how I'll know.*

"No, that's alright," I say. "I'll take it."

I'm not going to wrap it up and give it to her – that would be insane. But neither do I want it meeting its end in some anonymous industrial incinerator. I'll find my own way of disposing of it.

Or so I say to myself as I recross the car park and climb back into the Renault. I switch on the engine and start reversing out of the parking space. The rib is back on the passenger seat next to me. Now it's just a pig bone I no longer feel the need to respect it with a polythene shroud.

On my way to pick up Imogen, I find myself thinking about the girl, Harriet, and the expression on her face just before she ran away from us this morning. The blush on her cheeks had been pure shame, and her lips had twitched, as if trying and failing to conjure words to explain herself. She'd been caught out scaring the younger kids with made-up stories about the mythical Mr Jones. That was certainly the conclusion reached by her mother, who after Harriet had fled from us, swore to me that she would "get the truth out of her, don't you worry". But shame hadn't been all of it. There had been something else, too. Those pale blue eyes of hers hadn't shifted about with the evasiveness of a liar. They had been hard yet fragile, like two little beads of frozen rain, gaping into the empty space between her mother's head and mine, seeing something there that no one else could – consequences, perhaps, of confessing what she knew about Mr Jones.

I'm in Turnwood Park now, on the narrow concrete ribbon that winds me through the lush, unkempt grass and fading dandelions. I'm squinting slightly from the sun, and the world has turned a hazy gold. The wind has eased and the air is dense and still. The only movement is caused by clouds of tiny insects, hovering and glittering in their nauseating abundance. I can see them swarming above the pond, its surface clogged with dense mats of pale green algae. Wherever I turn, there's no escaping nature's ugly and wasteful fecundity. I don't remember the park ever falling into such a state before. I should write to the council. We need a team of unemployed youths out here, armed with strimmers and long poles. But no sooner does the righteous anger boil up than it fades. It's too hot to entertain any mood for more than a few seconds. My shirt is damp, my shoes tight.

The path loops its way through the fleeting shade of the oak tree. There's the little hole I dug – was it yesterday or the day before? And further up the slope, in the shaded corner of the park, is the snarl of overgrown bushes where I spotted that strange little girl, the doll decapitator. My eyes are drawn there again now, as they are every time I pass this patch – it's become a regular feature of my landscape, like the oak tree or the pond, like Sid the big ginger cat who's become a sort of mascot for our road. Only this shabby corner doesn't bring on warm, fluffy feelings the way Sid does. I'm drawn to it not out of a desire to see the girl again; the opposite if anything. It feels closer to a duty, a need to keep watch. She's there again now, I'm sure of it. I can't see her, but I'm aware of her, like an extra sensitivity in my skin. She's secreted herself behind the broken fence, watching me through the gap. I can picture her observing my slow, meandering progress.

Without really meaning to, I find myself wandering from the path into the long, hairy fronds that whisper against my ankles. I climb to the top of the slope where the grass is even taller and snaked about with half-hidden brambles that I must crush underfoot before they trip me. There isn't time for this, I realise. Imogen will be out soon. I picture her alone with her teacher, the last child in the playground.

An ancient apple tree growing in the strange girl's garden

leans heavily against the fence. Its limbs, like crooked, arthritic arms, hang into the park, displaying their diseased and withered leaves. The tree casts the fence area into a shade that appears stygian to my dazzled eyes. I can see nothing in there, but I can sense her close, can almost hear her breathing. My foot treads on something harder than turf. I look down and glimpse, down near the roots of the grass, a dirty pink bulb, like a fat, poisonous fungus. I jerk my foot away, and cringe when I see two black holes in its surface, which look like eyes.

They *are* eyes.

And beneath them is a pert bump of a nose and a small mouth, lips half open like hungry flower petals. Baby lips, belonging, I realise, to the girl's discarded doll head – baby lips that are supposed to arouse in little girls a desire to nurture, to mother. Feed me milk, they'd say if they could – but positioned beneath the black, hollow eyes, set in that bald, filthy, severed head, the lips seem to express a different kind of hunger. They drag me down until I'm on my knees. Feed me, they say. Come closer, don't be shy.

The head moves.

I leap backwards as if stung, and collapse on my backside in the long grass. Heart wild in my chest, bramble thorns ripping the skin of my elbow, I take a shuddering breath and force my gaze back towards the doll head. It's motionless now, but this doesn't weaken my conviction that I did just see it move. I study it, unblinking, as decades ago I would anxiously scrutinise the shadow on my bedroom ceiling, not daring to close my eyes even for a second, for fear that it would come to life.

But then I blink – I have to – and I immediately wish I hadn't. For I see that something has started to change in the doll's face. I can't explain it, but the expression has altered, even though the features remain plastic and still. A twinkle has appeared deep in one of its black eyes. The lips haven't moved, yet the face seems to be smiling. The eye is definitely twinkling, and now it swells into something blackly fleshy and glistening. As I watch, the eye continues to grow, pushing out from the confines of its socket. Am I really seeing this?

I start edging backwards, pulling my foot away from the head. The eye, or whatever it is I'm seeing, is now growing hairs, or maybe legs. They're waving about in blind, agitated motions. It's a blind eye, feeling its way into the world. It moves like silk, like black honey, flowing out of the socket with horrible fluidity, pouring down the cheek. And now I can see it has a long body. And legs, hundreds of them.

I start to breathe again, deep, wheezing, grateful breaths. It's horrible – but at least it's explainable. I can start to feel the world once more – the sweat, the stinging pain in my elbow, the grass tickling my back – and its familiarity makes me sob with relief. What I'm looking at is a creature, a grotesquely long and fat creature, but still, just a creature, extricating itself from the eye socket. I have not fallen over some previously unsuspected edge of this world into a place where doll heads move and smile and twinkle their eyes at you.

The crawling thing slides over the doll's sweet little *feed me!* lips. It's a centipede of some kind – far too big to be native. It probably came over here in a crate of exotic fruit, hatched out in someone's kitchen and escaped. You hear of these stories sometimes. It has evil-looking pincers at its front end, and I'm forced to retreat further as it drops off the chin and starts squirming through the jungle of knee-high grass towards me.

4

"DADDY. You were late! You forgot about me!"

I observe Imogen's quivering lower lip, the accusing jut of her jaw, and I'm reminded so much of Susan it's painful.

She delivers this little diatribe once we're outside the school gates, having maintained a dignified silence while I picked her up from the office and mumbled my apologies to the teacher. Now I must apologise again.

"I'm so sorry, Midge. Daddy got caught up with work. It'll never happen again, I promise."

"I was waiting and waiting. I was the last one."

"I know, I *know*. I'm sorry."

I'm still shaken up after the encounter with the doll head and the centipede. Reentry into the normal, everyday environments of street and school have served, if anything, to accentuate the weird otherworldiness of that incident. Did I really just see a centipede of Amazon rainforest proportions in our local park? It reinforces my suspicions that the park is running out of control. Not only has its pond degenerated into a primordial swamp, its vegetation is now wild and thick enough to create a habitat for exotic lifeforms. The overheated summer, toxins released into the air, or leaching into the water supply – whatever the cause, nature is on the rampage here in the heart of suburbia, and no one seems to have noticed but me.

"Daddy, why are we going this way today?"

Without even noticing, I've taken the long way home, bypassing Turnwood Park and negotiating instead the warren of small sleepy roads that border it – roads that are barely visited, save by their elderly residents and their cats.

"I just feel like it, sweetie." I turn my attention to her, mainly as a way of escaping my own morbid thoughts. "How was your day?"

"Fine."

"Did you learn anything?"

"Yeah."

She stops to stroke a black cat, basking on top of a wide pillar at the edge of a driveway. Her fingers get lost in the hot thick silk of its fur. The cat purrs contentedly. I wonder if it and its kind are enjoying the bonanza of new wildlife in the park.

"Harriet kept away from us today," says Imogen.

"Really?"

"I think you scared her."

"I only wanted to know the truth about Mr –"

"I know, Daddy. But it's just stories. She didn't mean to scare us."

"Are you sure it's just stories?"

Imogen squints up at me, then shakes her head.

"You're not sure?"

She doesn't answer. Her attention is back on the cat.

"Midge, I need to know. Are the stories true or not?"

"I think... *may-be*... the stories are true."

"Mr Jones *does* exist?"

She nods. "But he's invisible, like Mummy. That's why we didn't see him that time when he was right behind us." Her fingers splay as she smooths the cat's tail, and her voice drops to a whisper. "Sometimes he wears a mask, when he wants to be seen. But under the mask there's nothing there."

The doll head with its hollow black eyes floats into my brain.

"I'm not scared of him, though," says Imogen. "Sometimes I *want* him to grab me, because maybe he'll take me to see Mummy."

I pull her to her feet almost roughly, making her gasp.

"You know you must never talk to strangers, don't you Midge?"

I can hear the tightness in my voice. The anger I've tried to lock away is rattling its chains.

Her lower lip wobbles. "Yes Daddy."

That evening, I sit on Imogen's bed and read to her. Piglet and Pooh have been surprised to discover that Eeyore's tail is, in fact, Owl's new bell-rope – something that Imogen already knew very well but doesn't seem to mind hearing about again and again. Christopher Robin has nailed the tail back in place and all is well again in the Hundred Acre Wood. I stand up and stretch. "Goodnight, Piglet."

"Daddy?"

"Yes?" I reply, knowing what's coming.

"How many days till my birthday?"

"Eighteen." I don't even need to work it out, as she asks me this every single day.

"Eighteen more breakfasts," she says. "Eighteen more

27

lunches. Eighteen more suppers. Eighteen more chapters of Winnie the Pooh."

It will be her first birthday since Susan disappeared. This one, I know, will feel very different. I'm determined to make it special.

"How many friends would you like to invite?"

"All the girls in my class."

"Oka-ay. And what would you like to do? Cinema? Go-Karting? Ice skating? Swimming with sharks?"

She giggles. "No, Daddy, I don't think that would be very safe. What if someone gets eaten?"

"You're right. Better cross that one off the list."

She ponders for a moment. "I think I'd like to do.... Pottery Dreams."

"Are you sure?"

Pottery Dreams is a café on the high street where children can paint pottery pieces – dinosaurs, gnomes, dragons and what have you. The staff then glaze and fire the little masterpieces and have them ready for collection a week later. I took Imogen there a while ago for one of her friends' parties and she really enjoyed herself. I'm pleased with the choice. It's a bit cheaper than some of the other options, and quite creative, too.

It's much later now. I'm on the sofa in the living room. I don't feel like watching the box, but I'm too restless for sleep. I pour myself a second glass of wine. What a strange day it's been, starting with that abortive trip to Geoff Gunnell's office. I'm quite surprised at my disappointment that my rib theory didn't pan out. Why did I invest so much expectation in that stupid bone? I think of Pooh and Piglet's hunt for imaginary monsters, the Woozle and the Heffalump. I think of Imogen's belief in the invisible Mr Jones and her invisible mummy. I am no better.

For now, the object of my dashed hopes lies in the bottom drawer of my desk – I haven't yet been able to bring myself to throw it away. It's been joined there by another object: the doll head. I don't know what possessed me to pick it up after the scare it gave me. *Evidence*, I told myself at the time. But evidence of what? Of the centipede? Of the girl? Of the fact that I'm not losing my mind?

I take a gulp of wine and listen to the pipes settling in the basement. Tonight it's a dull creak, like a door handle being slowly twisted open. Sometimes it can sound a bit like knocking. That's usually when Imogen makes me go and check there's no one else down there. I have a vague recollection of going down there earlier. Perhaps I did. I can't be sure.

I'm feeling lonelier than usual. On restless nights like these, I really miss Susan's presence next to me on the sofa. She had an infectious enthusiasm for whatever box set we were working our way through – whooping like a child whenever the hero was triumphant, or hiding her eyes and clutching my hand with painful tightness during the tense moments, demanding that I describe exactly what was going on on the screen. After long years of watching TV with someone who got so adorably gripped by everything, it's hard now to go back to watching alone – so I don't, much. Mostly I just watch the news, and kids' programmes with Imogen.

Funny that my mind returns to those happy little moments with Susan rather than the loneliness I experienced during our last months together. We'd stopped watching TV together by then. She was often out, or we went to bed at different times.

It's very rare for adults to just disappear without trace,

I remember the private detective, Gooberman, telling me this once.

No ransom note, no communication, no body. That's vanishingly rare, he said, immediately apologising for the pun.

I knew what he was hinting at: this wasn't a disappearance, it was an escape. Susan disappeared on purpose, changed her identity, rebooted her life somewhere else, most likely abroad. Or in Devon.

I can't wait *till Devon! That's what she said.*

The police never took the Devon angle seriously enough to commit major resources to it. The Missing Persons Unit was helpful in publicising the case – getting her mugshot seen by hoteliers and catering establishments in the south-west. The few reported sightings all turned out to be false.

You had problems, you and your missus, you admitted that yourself.

Well we certainly argued. But all couples argue, and I knew that wasn't what Gooberman was hinting at. He meant her online romance. It started about a year before Susan disappeared. She began coming to bed very late. She claimed she had to work. But when I passed by her study on my way to our bedroom and glimpsed her face in the light of the laptop screen, she often looked a little too flushed and excited for someone preparing lecture notes. Sometimes she'd continue on her phone in bed, while I pretended to sleep. One day in January 2017, around four months after this all started, I checked her Internet history and found the name of the guy she'd been sexting: Richard Landry. I found his photo, too. He looked younger than me – fitter, too. He looked like a yachtsman or a lumberjack. A big, handsome outdoorsman. I confronted her and she apologised and promised to end the relationship. To the best of my knowledge, she did.

So here's what I think: Susan wasn't evil, she was just an ordinary woman with ordinary wants and desires. She argued and laughed and lied and had fun; she strayed, once, but continued to love me, and she loved her daughter more than the world. She did not run away. One day, she was kidnapped by a lone psychopath, who probably raped her before killing her, then disposed of her body with such sick thoroughness (vats of acid always come to mind) that we could search from now until doomsday and never find a trace of her.

When I said this to the detective, he just shrugged and looked away – which is how most people react, because to most people the lone psychopath theory is the least likely possibility. They draw a different conclusion, which is that Susan ran away with a man – either Richard Landry or someone else. As for my mother, she subscribes to no theory, but prefers to see Susan's disappearance as an effect without a cause; a mystery that simply hangs there in the midst of our world, like an inexplicable patch of darkness, and which will go on hanging there until one day, God in His own good time will reveal the truth.

After draining my glass, I take myself to bed. It's a cruel universe that snuffs out a life at random and then presents it as a mystery to be solved.

5

12 SEPTEMBER 2016

RL: Hi.

SR: hello

RL: So this is strange isn't it? How does one begin? Probably not by using "one" as a pronoun! I suppose I should start by saying I liked your profile. That's got to be the traditional opener in this sort of scenario right? You can probably tell I'm new to this. But I really did like your profile. Obviously, or I wouldn't be here.

SR: thanks. I liked yours too. I'm also new to this btw, and quite nervous

RL: Me too, don't worry. Well let's see - checking that profile of yours again - so I've always wondered, what exactly is media studies and how do you teach it?

SR: do you mind if we don't talk about work or family stuff - that's exactly what I come on here to get away from

RL: Okay, no problem. Understandable. What would you rather talk about?

SR: what kind of sex do you like

RL: Oho, right down to it. Ah, well let me see. Huh. Pretty

normal sex I suppose. I've not tried anything too kinky or bizarre - yet. But I'm open to suggestions... What sort of sex do you like?

SR: maybe this was a mistake

RL: Hey, sorry if I'm boring. I was just being honest.

SR: no it's not you, it's this, it's me. I want to be here. I want to have a fling with someone but I don't know how to do it, not in text form. If we were in a bar or something having a drink maybe I'd feel more relaxed, but talking about intimate things with a stranger on here just sounds stupid

RL: I know what you mean, and it would be great to meet at some point, but it's difficult in my situation, as I'm sure it is in yours. We'd have to be very careful. I guess that's why people like us meet on sites like this.

SR: people like us. you mean the unhappily married

RL: I mean active adulterers, which is, I imagine, a fairly small subset of that group.

SR: I wish I could see you. it would be a lot easier doing this. I'm not a very texty person.

RL: I imagine it gets easier the more you do it. Why don't you try telling me something about yourself - avoiding the topics of work or family. And maybe sex as well. I don't want to come over as a prude, it just feels a little early in our acquaintance for that.

SR: you are a prude! and I don't know what else to talk about. suggest a topic

RL: Okay. How about fear. What scares you?

SR: I don't know - spiders? my daughter! what scares you

RL: Whatever's underneath.

SR: what do you mean by that!!!

RL: Sorry, that sounded weird, didn't it. I didn't mean to sound weird. I just meant anything that's underneath something else. You must have picked up a plant pot or a brick in the garden and found the underside crawling with woodlice. That sort of thing gives me goosebumps.

SR: yeah that sounds pretty yuck

RL: Graves, manhole covers, ponds covered in slime, even covered swimming pools. They all give me the willies.

RL: Not skirts though (joke!)

RL: You still there?

RL: Oh shit, was it something I said? Was it the skirts thing?

RL: Or willies?

SR: still here

RL: Thank god! I thought I'd lost you.

SR: you know what I'm most scared of

RL: What?

SR: being alone - I feel alone right now, even though my husband and daughter are here in the house, sometimes I think I'd just like to

RL: Like to what?

SR: don't know exactly. or maybe I'd rather not say. you seem nice. a bit weird but nice. I have to go now. let's do this again some time

RL: Sounds good to me. It was nice meeting you SR. Sweet dreams.

SR: goodnight

6

FRIDAY 22 JUNE 2018

"Daddy?"

"Yes?"

"How many days till my birthday?"

"Fifteen."

Note to self: must remember to pay deposit for Pottery Dreams.

"Fifteen more breakfasts, fifteen more–"

"Fourteen more breakfasts," I point out. "You've already had your breakfast this morning."

Rose, the lollipop lady, directs us across the road. We exchange good mornings.

"I have all the invitations in here," says Imogen, pointing at her bulging book bag. "I wrote them out last night."

"Goodness me, you're efficient!"

I wave goodbye to her at the school gate.

"Mr Rose," calls a sharp voice. I look up to see a woman barging towards me through a crowd of parents and kids moving the other way. It takes me a second to fix her as Harriet's mum. I'm surprised she knows my name – until I remember that I'm semi-famous around the school, or used to be, as 'the father of the girl whose mum disappeared'.

"Mr Rose."

I do wish I knew her name. The woman has a nose like a sparrow's beak, which she thrusts forward as if threatening to peck me with it. I feel a wash of sympathy for young Harriet.

"Yes, hello."

"I finally got the truth out of my daughter. She admitted to having been set upon by a man calling himself Mr Jones. It happened less than three weeks ago."

"What exactly did he do?"

"He walked up behind her and grabbed her."

"Good God!"

"Yes, exactly."

"And then?"

"Then he let her go and began talking to her."

"Why didn't she run away?"

"I asked her the same question. She said she was so surprised to see a man in a mask that –"

"He was wearing a mask?"

"Yes. Didn't I say? A panda mask. And he was dressed in a smart grey suit. It was only when he asked her if she would go for a walk with him that she finally came to her senses and ran."

"Where did this happen?"

"In the little park on the far side of Leafy Wood Lane. Turn-wood Park, is it? She was on her way to her piano lesson near there. Of course I've informed the police and the school. One can't be too careful, especially after what happened to the Parker girl last year. You live near there, don't you, Mr Rose?"

"Yes. Yes, I do."

"Well, you should warn your daughter not to go wandering about on her own, at least until this man has been apprehended.

I for one shall be *driving* Harriet to her piano lessons from now on."

I watch her strut away, and for a moment I find it hard to move. Blurry figures of parents flow around me, their babbling voices muffled as if underwater. I can picture it now, the park, with the fly swarms billowing above the stinking stagnant water; the sun hot and dazzling, yet everything somehow darker than usual, the shadows deeper and crawling with baroque forms of life that should never find their way into the light. And there is Mr Jones, walking slowly along the path. I see him as tall and slender, erect in posture and dressed in a businessman's suit, which makes his panda mask all the more incongruous.

I decide to return home through the park, feeling the need to reclaim it as a safe and normal recreation space, and not some mythical realm of demons. The western edge of the park – the Leafy Wood Lane end – is bordered by a railing, next to which a thick, tangled hawthorn hedge has been allowed to grow beyond head height, separating park and outside world as completely as a wall and rendering both invisible to each other. The only break in the hedge is a small and rusty gate about halfway along that opens reluctantly and with some squeaking. The hedge is encroaching above the gate on both sides, forming a leafy arch – though a far from welcoming one. The arch is no neatly pruned piece of topiary, but a crude collision of dense, thorny foliage that forces me to duck to avoid getting *punctuated* in the eye, as my dad used to say.

I close the rusty gate behind me, seeing it back onto its latch. The park looks empty, yet it isn't. I don't know how I know this, or how I'm not surprised to see her standing up there on the rise, exactly where she was last time. Surprised or not, I flinch. I can feel the click of my jawbone as it drops open. As before, her dark hair is clean and neatly brushed, with a pink band pulling it clear of her forehead. She's in the same pink Hello Kitty T-shirt and blue jeans with a pink butterfly design on one of the pockets. In her hand is the headless doll, looking even more filthy than before. She's standing in full sunlight, and the light turns her hair bright silver and casts a crisp, black shadow across the grass that submerges her up to the ankles.

The girl is facing the pond, so I'm seeing her at a slight angle. Even so, I know she's aware of me, aware of my smallest move-ment. I can't see her eyes, so bright is the nimbus of sun around her head, yet I sense her scrutiny as powerfully as I did the other day. It's not about her eyes, or the position of her head, it's about a sensation in my skin. I stand stock still by the gate, careful not to scare her with any sudden moves, mindful of how she ran away last time. The moment stretches on, silent but for the drone of the fly-laden air and the hiss of traffic a world away. A droplet of sweat trickles slowly down my back. Her stillness is unsettling – even more so than the wreck of the doll in her hand. I see that her fist is clamped very tightly around its leg – the only hint of tension in her otherwise quiescent pose.

"Hello," I say in a low, barely audible voice. I say it almost as an experiment, just to see what will happen.

Slowly she turns to face me. Her eyes grow bigger and her lips part.

"It's okay," I tell her. "I'm not going to hurt you. I just want to be sure you're okay."

Unthinkingly, I start edging towards her, off the path and up the grassy rise. Her face twitches, reminding me of the way the doll's head moved when it had the centipede inside it. The flesh of her cheeks seems almost to writhe as I approach. Then she turns and starts unhurriedly towards the top corner of the park. I follow her, forcing my way through the thicket of knee-high grass, brambles and ferns that infest this corner of the park – a natural barricade the girl seems to move through with ease. I have to warn her and her parents about Mr Jones. They need to know that she can't hang out on her own in the park when there's a predator on the loose. However fast I go, she always remains several paces ahead of me, and I watch her disappear once again into the shadows of the bushes growing in the top corner.

I push through the bushes to the fence. The apple tree's twisted limbs welcome me into their shadow. The ground here is sludgy underfoot. I can feel the pulpy, putrid remains of last year's crop of diseased apples bursting beneath my feet, releasing a hot steam of rank decay. My buttocks tighten at a memory of that oversize centipede ejaculating itself from the doll's eye. It must be around here somewhere. I can picture it now, flowing through the undergrowth towards me, slipping up my trouser leg. A delirious tremor nuzzles my skin. I stop and hastily push the hems of my trousers into my socks. Grimacing, I push on to the fence and squat down so I can peer through the gap made by the broken slat.

I'm surprised to see a wilderness as unruly as the one I've just hacked through. What must have once been lawn is now a forest of inflorescent grass, tall dead stalks and cactus-sized weeds and thistles giving onto a jungly mass of trees and bushes at the back. On the other side, the lawn-forest laps the edges of a ruined patio, its slate-grey and terracotta slabs cracked, askew and fringed with weeds. As for the house, the windows are dark and smashed, the brickwork crumbling like cake and stitched with dry moss. Rooftiles are missing, exposing the trusses beneath. The back door is dangling from one hinge, and by its step is a heap of junk: rusted poles, corrugated fibreglass sheeting, a rusty sink unit, a stained mattress.

No one can live here – no one can have lived here for years.

There's no sign of the girl, yet I feel her presence denser than ever in my sweat. She's watching me through one of those dark, smashed windows, or from behind that dilapidated shed peeping above the lawn-forest like a piece of boat wreckage on a wild sea.

I struggle to imagine her making this hideous place her home. A feral child could live here, perhaps – a kid who's escaped from her parents. It can happen, I suppose, even in respectable, middle-class neighbourhoods. But this girl is clean cut – she doesn't fit the image of a runaway or truant.

I flick a wasp away from my face and call out to her. Only the insects reply. The gap is too small for me to crawl through, and the prospect is not tempting. There's a sweet stink of corruption – of death – about the place. I feel sorry for anyone desperate enough to make it their home. What can she be escaping from to regard this as preferable?

Back at home, I sit at my desk trawling the local news sites and neighbourhood forums for any reports of recent abductions, disappearances or assaults. I can't find anything. The Forest Estate has been quiet for several weeks, if the newspapers are to be believed. People are more worried about the heatwave and its effect on their gardens than who might be coming for their children. Harriet's mum might be able to shake things up – she has the personality for it. But how seriously will they take her? Man in panda mask grabs little girl – it's a great opening. But then what? He lets her go, suggests they go for a walk, then she runs away. With no witnesses on hand to back her up, it sounds too bizarre to be believed. Even Imogen called it "just stories" at first, before changing her mind and deciding it was true. But what does "true" even mean to the average seven-year-old? In her version, the man behind the mask is invisible.

I'm struck by the need to do something, to take steps. I should complain about the park and the abominable state it's in, and register concern about the little girl who may be living rough in the derelict property bordering it. But there's no point in just phoning the council. I should gather evidence first – take a few photos, maybe even one of that Amazonian centipede, if I can find it. As for the girl, a photo wouldn't be enough. No one would believe, from the look of her, that such a well-groomed child could live in that place. I'd need someone to actually come along and do a proper search of the property and the garden – preferably a team of people dressed in white coveralls, rubber gloves and face masks.

But was she really there? How? In that stinking dump? Back here in the normal, everyday environs of my study, it seems impossible, and I'm starting to wonder if I imagined it.

I found the doll's head, didn't I? There's evidence!

I pull open the bottom drawer, needing to see it physically, to reassure myself.

The doll's head is there alright, staring emptily at me. The rib, however, is gone.

"Have you been in my study recently, Midge?"

"No, Daddy."

"Are you sure?"

"Yes. You told me not to go in there, so I don't."

"It's just that something in there has gone missing."

"Well it wasn't me," says Imogen emphatically.

We're walking up the long curve of Leafy Wood Lane, on the

journey back from school. Imogen is dragging a stick along a brick wall, dislodging the moss that's growing in the cracks. The stick isn't the rib – I've checked to make sure.

"It must have been Ellie," she says, referring to our cleaner. "Ellie's always moving things. I can never find anything after Ellie's been."

"It can't have been Ellie," I explain to her, "because Ellie doesn't clean my study. The only person who ever goes into my study is me."

"Well then," says Imogen, stopping to dig out a large wedge of moss, "it must have been Mummy."

7

SATURDAY 7 JULY 2018

TODAY IS Imogen's big day, and I'm feeling stressed at the prospect of being *in loco parentis* for fourteen over-excited, sugar-crazed girls, wishing, not for the first time, that practical, no-nonsense Susan was around to help organise things. I say girls, but actually one of them is a boy. He's a new kid at the school, and Imogen has very sweetly taken him under her wing. Even so, she hadn't actually planned to invite him until her class teacher stepped in a few days ago and asked me if I wouldn't mind, as so far Imogen is his only friend.

Imogen and I arrive at Pottery Dreams ten minutes early. The room is dominated by a large pine table covered in protective paper, with fourteen places, each with its own set of brushes and jar of water. In the middle of the table are a couple of trays containing tubes of brightly coloured paint. Shelves lining the right-hand wall are filled with white, unpainted pottery objects of almost everything imaginable, from mythical beasts to musical instruments. At the back of the room is a counter with a kitchen behind it. I hand the birthday cake to the manager, a jolly lady with red hair called Becca. She makes me a cup of tea and pours Imogen some orange juice, then shows me the food boxes she's prepared for each child: sandwiches, carrot sticks, crisps, chocolate and fruit. "Not a turkey twizzler in sight," she laughs. Her motherly nature is a comfort. Things can't slide too far into chaos so long as she's around. Imogen, cheeks flushed with anticipation, gives me a tour of the shelves, pointing out her favourite pieces.

The guests start arriving – mums, sometimes dads, with their excited daughters bearing colourfully packaged gifts. Imogen's face lights up when she sees the presents and her friends, and the children immediately plunge into intense and animated conversation, most of which I can barely understand. I recognise them all, of course, from countless school-gate encounters. There is Antonia: tall and angular, able to trump everyone with the volume of her voice and the endless things she's willing to speak and laugh about. And here is Kate, small and shy, but with shining eyes and endearing smile, gazing up at Antonia with a look of pure devotion. And there are Aisha and Theodora, who form an unbreakable triumvirate with Imogen. All three of them are talking almost without stopping for breath, about whatever latest fad is currently blowing through their universe, be it a Disney film or a method of weaving rubber bands into bracelets.

Imogen receives the gifts with fluttering, wide-eyed excitement, and I remind her to say thank-you before taking them from her and piling them up on a table in the corner. Parents leave as quickly as they can, and a familiar anxiety steals over me – one I always get when left alone with large numbers of kids. Happily, Becca has a loud and commanding voice. Between us, we manage to shepherd the children to their places around the table. There is some awkwardness about who should sit next to Imogen, which is ultimately resolved by the birthday girl herself, who promises that she will come and sit next to Lura and Tabitha later, *after* she's sat with Aisha and Theodora. The jilted girls appear to accept this, and I smile with pride at my daughter's display of Solomonic wisdom.

Last to arrive is the little boy, Alex, accompanied by his flustered mother, who apologises profusely for their lateness, and then launches into a long explanation about how he'd had a sleepover at the house of a friend from his former school and the friend's dad had been late delivering him back and hadn't given him enough breakfast, and then she couldn't find the venue and when she found it there was *literally* no parking within three hundred yards and Alex's asthma, which has got worse since she and his dad separated, meant that she couldn't risk letting him become breathless or agitated, so they'd had to walk. I try to break in several times to tell her that it really doesn't matter, but she won't be interrupted.

In fact, she's only about five minutes late and the kids haven't even started on their painting projects. Still, I find myself strangely touched by the woman's contrition, a rare emotion among the parents I've had dealings with, and also by her belief in the importance of punctuality – again, quite rare these days.

I show Alex to his place, while Becca goes and fetches some pottery items from the shelves. Alex is a shy boy, I can see that instantly, and he looks especially intimidated by being thrust into the midst of a bunch of girls. He finds himself between two who completely ignore him and go on talking to their neighbours on the other side.

"Have you ever painted pottery before?" I ask him.

He looks up at me and shakes his head. He's small with dark hair and big, soulful eyes.

"This is his first time," says his mum, who seems calmer now. "But he likes art, don't you Alex?" She studies the display shelves. "Fantastic, isn't it? Here, Alex, what about this one?" She picks up a large gnome.

"Um, that comes with a higher price tag," says Becca gently. "For birthday parties we offer smaller items."

"Oh, I am sorry!" apologises the mother, blushing.

Becca hands around the pieces. Antonia predictably objects to the cat she's been offered, and wants a dog instead. Kate immediately decides she wants a dog, too. Aisha and Imogen choose baby dragons, Lura and Tabitha opt for bunny rabbits, Theodora settles for a teddy bear, while Holly, a girl who likes to think herself a bit mad, decides to paint a hamburger, and this starts a trend among the other girls for food items. Alex rejects everything cute or food-related and goes for a T-Rex.

Pretty soon, the kids are engrossed in their work, and the volume level noticeably drops – with the exception of Antonia, for whom silence is simply an invitation to make herself better heard. When she isn't demanding different colours of paint from Becca, she's showing her friends the progress she's made, or passing comments on their efforts, or talking about the puppy her dad has promised her.

Alex's mum has decided not to leave like the other parents, and instead has taken up a position by Alex. She's squatting by his chair, chatting to him quietly as he works. The boy barely acknowledges her, his focus entirely on the daubs of dark green paint coming off his brush. And yet I'm sure he's comforted by her presence. But is this a good thing? Shouldn't she be encouraging him to integrate with the other children? Hovering there by his side, she's giving him no incentive to try and make friends. In fact I'm beginning to think the whole idea of Alex coming to the party was misguided, and maybe his mum has realised this. Imogen may have taken a liking to him, but she's surrounded by her established clique, many of whom she's known since nursery school, and there can't be many eight-year-olds with the maturity to know how to be inclusive towards a stranger in such a gathering. Alex would be better off making progress in small steps: play dates with individual friends, for example, rather than subjecting him to this scary, all-girl affair.

Thinking that maybe I could help out by inviting Alex on a play date, I approach his mum. I want to lever her away from Alex so I can make my offer without him overhearing – just in case she says no and this causes trouble between them. So I sidle over and ask her if she'd like a cup of tea.

She glances up. "That would be lovely. Thanks."

"How do you take it?"

"Just milk, no sugar."

She makes no move to leave her son.

Becca has her hands busy with the other kids, principally with finding new colours for Antonia's rainbow-hued dog, so I enter the little kitchen and make the tea. When I hand the mug to Alex's mum, she thanks me with a smile, then goes back to murmuring encouraging words to her son.

I wonder why I feel disappointed that I can't budge her from her son's side. Is it genuine concern for Alex, or a desire for some normal, everyday chitchat with another adult? Or could it be something else again? I have to question my motives sometimes because they aren't always entirely clear to me. I seem able quite often to form desires or make decisions without even knowing why.

The woman made reference to the fact that she and Alex's dad separated. I registered that, didn't I? I also registered that she's quite attractive, with sandy brown hair that falls appealingly around her shoulders. Right now she has her back to me and I can't quite remember her face, only that it's oval-shaped and she has an appealing smile when she stops looking strained and anxious. While pretending to observe the children's progress, I study what I can see of her. Now that I have the chance to look more closely, I can see that her hair is not that lustrous but a bit wispy and dry, and there are some greys among the brown. Her jeans reveal shapely hips and legs. The soles of her sandalled feet are pink and weathered and peeling in places. Her upper arms are chubby and quite pale, and she has a long silver scar on the underside of her forearm. Her waist sags over the belt of her jeans. She's leaning forward slightly, encouraging Alex to try a different colour for the dinosaur's eyes. I wonder if she has a man in her life.

The pottery projects are done. Some of them are lovely, others less so, but in the language we reserve for children, there are no words for "inferior", "rotten" or "third-rate". Instead we say things like "colourful", "original", "inventive", or, in the case of "mad" Holly's pink and blue hamburger, "zany". Imogen's isn't the best, though I feel a strong urge to tell her that it is.

The pottery is cleared away and placed on another table for drying, and the lunch boxes are distributed. For the next twenty minutes I'm preoccupied with serving water and orange squash and making sure everyone's happy. Becca reassures Alex's mum that there are no nuts in the food – nuts, apparently, can trigger an asthma attack. When everyone's eaten their fill of sandwiches, crisps and chocolate, and we've tried and mostly failed to get them to eat up their carrots and fruit, Becca, Alex's mum and I clear the table. Then I light the candles on the cake. It's a rectangular slab of sponge covered in white icing, decorated with sugar flowers and edged with piped pink icing, with the words *Happy Birthday Imogin* written in more piped pink icing on top. The baker offered me a twenty per cent discount when I pointed out the spelling mistake.

Imogen giggles at the way her name has been spelled, as I knew she would, even while warning the baker it might just ruin her day. She blows out the candles and everyone sings Happy Birthday, then I set to work cutting the cake, while Becca and Alex's mum distribute the slices to the kids. Soon afterwards, the parents start arriving and it's time to swap pleasantries and give out party bags. The fired and glazed pieces will be ready for collection in a week, Becca informs us. In no time the room has emptied and the high-pitched chatter of girls fades to an echo in my head.

"Thank you so much!" Alex's mum says to me as I hand the boy his party bag. "He really enjoyed himself today."

"Are you sure? I felt a bit for him as he doesn't really know anyone yet."

"Oh, he was fine," she says. "And I'm sorry again for being late."

I like the way she speaks – forthright and without hesitation, with every consonant enunciated. Her voice is low, pleasant on the ear. What's more, she *is* attractive, and oddly familiar. I suppose I must have seen her at the school gates.

I make the invitation quickly, before she slips away: "If Alex ever fancies coming over to ours for a play date, he'd be very welcome."

"Oh, that's so kind!" Delightful little wrinkles appear around her eyes as she smiles. "Alex really likes Imogen. Why don't we swap numbers?" She takes a phone out of her bag and I recite my number to her, watching as her slender fingers move across the keypad.

"I'm Ben Rose, by the way."

She looks up, and this time her smile has a slightly different quality. "Amy Parker. Pleased to meet you."

"Keep note of who gave you what so we can send them thank-you notes," I say to Imogen when we get home. I place the presents in a pile on the living room carpet and get ready with pen and paper. It's like watching a young shark on its first feeding frenzy as she rips into the wrapping and holds aloft each gift for a few seconds of bright-eyed delight before diving in for another one. The room is soon a mess of torn paper and brightly packaged toys and games. I write as fast as I can: Nail Varnish Kit – Lura; Bookmark Dictionary – Antonia; Brainbox Game – Theodora; Doodle Socks – Aisha; Native American Bead Loom – Kate; City of Zombies Maths Game – Holly; Design Your Own Glitter Dress – Priyanka; Shamballa Fire Jewellery – Josie; Rainbow Loom Kit – Ajani; another Rainbow Loom Kit – Diara. There are more, but I can't keep up. She's about to open the final gift – a long, thin, slightly bent thing, poorly wrapped.

"Hold on, hold on," I say. "Who sent you the Talking Alarm Clock'?

"Alex."

"The Remote Control Tarantula?"

"Tabitha."

"The Glitter Butterflies?"

"Tia."

I scratch my head, puzzled. "That's everyone. There shouldn't be any more presents."

Imogen shakes the last one. "Well there is."

"Open it," I say quietly, my stomach tightening. I recognise the wrapping paper.

The paper falls to the carpet and the rib drops into her hand. Imogen utters a laugh of ecstatic surprise.

"It's from Mummy! I knew she wouldn't forget!"

I'm in Turnwood Park, standing by the gate. The sun is beating down, and I'm sweating. The girl is there, dressed as she always is. She's standing perfectly still, staring at the path in front of her. Without warning, she turns to face me. Her eyes widen and her lips part. Her jaw drops so that her mouth forms a long black oval of... I'm not sure what. Surprise? Anger? Her mouth seems unnaturally extended, as if she's dislocated her jaw and the skin of her cheeks has stretched like elastic. I can see something twitching in the dark cavity of her mouth. Her tongue? But it seems alive, not part of her. There is a suggestion of writhing insect legs in there – pincers.

My eyes open to darkness. For a second I don't know where I am or what's going on. Then I feel the sheets and pillow beneath me, damp with my sweat. I start to breathe. I'm in bed. Thank God! It was only a dream. Even so, the image of the girl isn't leaving me. I can still see her mouth dropping into that horribly elongated oval, and the giant centipede inside it.

I lie there as my sweat leaks into the bedclothes. I wipe my face with the sheet. It's so hot. The windows are open and I'm naked beneath a single sheet, but it's still unbearable. The image of the girl gradually fades, yet I can't relax. Sleep is so far away, I might as well get up. There's pain in that restlessness – and guilt. What's that from? Oh yes. Imogen. I got angry with her today. On her birthday of all days, I made her cry. It was that damn rib. She kept on insisting that Susan gave it to her. No matter what I said, no matter what I threatened her with, she wouldn't admit that she'd stolen it from my desk and wrapped it up herself.

"Look at this," I said to her, holding up the discarded wrapping paper. "This is our wrapping paper. It's from the roll I keep above the cupboard in the laundry room. You did this."

"I didn't Daddy," she cried, her voice cracking, her eyes by now twinkling with tears.

I took a deep breath and tried to restore some calm and rationality. "Why do you insist on doing this? Mummy's gone, I keep on telling you. Is it because of what Granny said about her disappearing? You know that what she meant to say is that she's dead."

Imogen stuck out her jaw when I said that, and hung her head, so her fringe covered most of her face. She muttered something that I failed to catch.

"What did you say?"

Her lip trembled, but she didn't speak, just got up from the sofa and walked slowly to the door.

"Midge? What is it?"

She looked at me, her face now full of defiance. "She isn't dead!" she screamed. "Granny knows it. I know it. It's only you who doesn't know it!"

Then she marched out of the room, slamming the door behind her.

Later, I went upstairs and stood outside her door and asked if she wanted some supper, but I got no response.

"Sorry for shouting, Midge. It's just..."

Then I heard her sobbing.

I opened the door. She was curled up on her bed with the rib – the filthy old pig's rib – clutched in her fist.

"Hey," I said softly, approaching her.

"Go away pl-please, Daddy," she said between sobs, and I could sense the rising hysteria in her voice.

"I just wanted to –"

She sat up. Her face had turned bright red. "It was my birthday today!" she screamed. "I prayed and prayed that Mummy would send me the stick. I wanted it more than all the presents in the world. I don't even care about my other presents. You can send them all back if you want. I just wanted Mummy to remember me on my birthday, and she *did* and I was so *happy*. But now you've..." She collapsed back onto her pillow. "You've spoiled everything."

I stood there in the middle of her room, stunned and devastated. Eventually I found my voice and mumbled an apology, told her I'd be downstairs if she needed anything. Then I quietly left.

I didn't see her again tonight. She didn't even come and ask me for a chapter of Winnie the Pooh. I guess she fell sleep.

8

MONDAY 9 JULY 2018

TODAY, I'm in the offices of Halsted Borough Council – Environmental Services Department, seated opposite the man in charge of parks administration. Mr Terrence Raynerson has a smart blue carpet and white walls dotted with pictures of parks. He's a small man with a grey complexion, a slate-coloured comb-over and thick-lensed glasses. Mr Raynerson has no lips, and he gapes at me from the other side of his ultra-smooth, wood-effect desk with a strange sort of gecko-smile. He looks like he's lived his entire life under a rock.

"This is about Turnwood Park, isn't it, Mr Rose? I took a look at those photos you sent me..."

"Good."

"...And I'm not sure what the problem is. The park does not look in any way run down or overgrown."

It's my turn to gape. "Are you serious?"

"Yes."

"But what about the pond? It's become a filthy swamp." I've got my phone out now, and I'm pointing at the picture on the screen.

"It's got a bit of algae," says Mr Raynerson. "It happens to many ponds in the summer, especially during hot spells. It's perfectly normal. We'll send in a maintenance team in the next few weeks to clear the worst of it, maybe put in some bags of barley straw if the budget allows. It's not a swamp, Mr Rose."

"Clearly you're not seeing what I'm seeing," I say to him, directing him again towards the photo. "The surface is virtually yellow!" But I suppose its revolting state cannot fully be appreciated on the phone's small screen. "Perhaps if you were to visit the park yourself, Mr Raynerson, you'd see what I mean..."

Mr Raynerson stares at me patiently through his bottle-lensed glasses. He doesn't look as if he's ever seen sunlight, let alone visited a park.

"Well what about the unmown grass then?" I say, flicking through the other photos. "And the weeds and the ferns and the brambles? Look at the state of it!"

"I think you're exaggerating, Mr Rose," says Mr Raynerson, barely bothering to glance at what I'm showing him. "It may not be the most manicured of parks, but then Turnwood never has been. It's always tended towards the, uh, 'bucolic'. That's part of its charm. According to our surveys, residents enjoy the diversity of our parks and gardens. If you want well-cut lawns and flowerbeds, may I suggest you visit Halsted Town Park. It recently received a Green Flag Award for outstanding cleanliness."

"I don't care about the town park!" A fleck of spit flies out of my mouth and lands on his powder-blue carpet. My ears are thundering, my shoulders tightening. *Bucolic!* What utter shit! Why won't he look at my photographs? "I'm talking about my *local* park, which my daughter and I have to walk through every day. Did you know, I saw a ten-inch-long centipede in there the other day?"

"Yes, you mentioned the centipede. Did you manage to photograph it?"

"No. But I can promise you I saw it. The place is turning into a jungle. I wouldn't be surprised to see a caiman coming out of that swamp."

"Then perhaps you ought to be alerting Mr David Attenborough in that case." The edges of his lipless mouth twist upwards into an expression of mirth. I can imagine him repeating this little gem to Mrs Terrence Raynerson over dinner this evening.

I glare at him coldly until his face turns back to normal.

"Mr Rose," he says to me, raising his elbows and folding his fingers into each other like a grotesque praying mantis, "we have sixty-seven public parks in this borough, forty-eight playing pitches and sports facilities, forty-two allotment sites, fourteen cemeteries and churchyards, forty-five children's play areas and two hundred and eighty hectares of native woodlands and grasslands, not to mention numerous river and canalsides and urban green spaces, all of which have to be maintained out of a budget that has suffered severe cuts in recent years. Despite this, the latest public service satisfaction survey records a seventy-three per cent satisfaction score. I assure you that Halsted Council is committed to making open spaces places for everyone, delivering high-quality, sustainable open spaces for the future and protecting and managing the exceptional quality and diversity of Halsted's open spaces. Now I've checked through the files for the past five years and not a single person has complained about Turnwood Park except you. But if you feel so strongly about it, may I suggest that you start a petition. If you manage to gather enough signatures to demonstrate that there is a community-wide concern about this park, we'd be far more likely to take your complaint seriously."

Susan, who began her working life in local journalism, back

when that was still a viable career option, once explained to me the defensive strategy deployed by most institutions when faced with a complaint: First, ignore the issue at hand. Second, blandly restate policy. Third, isolate the complainant. Fourth, make vaguely reassuring noises that don't actually commit you to anything.

I rise from my chair, already knowing that I'm wasting my time with Mr Jobsworth Raynerson. "Thanks, I'll bear that in mind," I tell him with all the disdain I can muster.

"By the way," I say, on my way out, "a girl was attacked in that park a few weeks ago."

"Not my department," says Mr Raynerson, not even bothering to look away from his computer screen. "Try the police."

"And there may be a young runaway living in an abandoned house on its border."

"Again, not my department. Goodbye Mr Rose."

～

"Hello, is that Ben?"

"Yes."

"Hi. It's Amy here. Alex's mum."

"Oh, hi!" I can hear my voice rise by several semitones.

"Alex has been asking if Imogen would like to come over for a play date one afternoon this week."

"Yeah, that would be great! Now let me see... she's got karate this afternoon, choir practice on Wednesday, drama on Thursday, tennis on Friday. She's free tomorrow though. How about that?"

"Yes, that would be fine. Alex doesn't have much in the way of after-school activities."

"You live in Daintree Gardens, don't you? – so Imogen was telling me..."

"That's right."

And then a light bulb goes on in my head.

"Tell you what, why don't you and Alex come here instead? We're in Cedarwood Grove, which is kind of on the way to yours, so it would make sense if you stop off here on your way back from school."

"Oh," she says, and I can sense her hesitation.

"I'll make sure I don't give him anything with nuts in it," I tell her, guessing that's what's on her mind.

"No, it's not that. I mean I'm sure you wouldn't. It's just that I don't want you to think that I..." For once, this forthright woman seemed lost for words.

"You?" I prompted.

"What I'm trying to say is that I genuinely thought that it would be nice if Imogen came here. I wasn't in any way fishing for an invitation."

"I know you weren't," I tell her.

"As long as you know that, I'd be delighted to accept your offer. We can all walk back together from school tomorrow, if you like."

"Perfect!"

9

THURSDAY 3 JULY 2003

ROY LOVED THE HOUSE, and was greatly obliged to his uncle for lending it to him for the summer. It was spacious to a fault. The Edwardians who built the place were clearly civilised geezers. There was stained glass in the front door window, and fancy floor tiles in the hallway. The kitchen was easily his favourite spot. It was south-facing, with sumptuous windows letting in huge wodges of light from the back garden.

This would be his writing room, he decided. There was easy access to kettle, snack cupboard and fridge, and it was as quiet as a grave, but for the melodious tweetings of birds drifting in through the open window. The kitchen table – a big, rough slab of birch – provided acres of space for his laptop, coffee cup and reference books. Yes, this was certainly a splendacious location for a writer. And after five long years of reviewing the literary efforts of others – if *literary* wasn't too pompous a word to describe horror novels – here was a chance to prove that he was worthy of joining their ranks. He had the tools. He'd studied the craft, had read the masters – Lovecraft, Stoker, Shelley, Poe,

Jackson et al – and even penned a few of his own spooky yarns, one of which earned him an honourable mention in *Gore Monthly*'s annual contest for new writers. Now the time had come to attempt the big one – the novel.

He'd given himself the summer – eight weeks – to complete the first draft. There would be no distractions – no phone or email. If he managed to write four pages a day, even allowing for a break at weekends, he'd end up with 160 pages. In other words, a bloody novel!

The only snag, the one grotesquely mutated fly in the ointment – which he acknowledged while eyeing the blank page of the Word document on his laptop screen – was that he didn't yet know what story he wanted to write. None of the plot ideas he'd jotted down before coming here seemed, on reflection, quite big, bad or scary enough for a reputation-making debut in such a competitive field. He tried not to let this worry him unduly. The right idea, like the vampire, would come to him if he invited it in. It was probably at this very moment festering in his subconscious ready to emerge once ripe, if not putrescent.

In the meantime, he busied himself thinking about fonts and formatting. He arranged and rearranged his reference books. He made himself a coffee, and spent ten minutes looking for a mat to put beneath his cup so it wouldn't damage the table. He burned through quite a bit of time this way waiting for the big idea to reveal itself, but the blank page on his laptop screen only seemed to grow blanker each time he looked at it.

Maybe it was this place, Roy speculated. It was too bloody perfect, and so tranquil it was intimidating. If he was back in his cramped bedsit in West Halsted with the traffic noises outside and that baby screaming its head off next door, he might even be clacking away on his keyboard by now, his head a steaming cauldron of blood-chilling ideas – if that was possible, thermodynamically speaking. It was a sobering thought. What the horror imagination needed, he realised, was some kind of impetus. It needed to be agitated by something, shocked into life like Frankenstein's monster. This place was just too damn serene. So out he went in search of an impetus.

10

TUESDAY 10 JULY 2018

IT'S THE FOLLOWING AFTERNOON, and Amy and I are walking slowly up a sun-dappled Leafy Wood Lane. The birds are singing. Alex and Imogen are a few paces in front, heads bent close, deep in conversation.

"So, you're a builder, is that right?" Amy asks me.

"A structural engineer."

She laughs – an odd, disconcerting reaction. Mostly, I get blank or bored faces.

"What is that exactly?"

"I make sure buildings are safe and structurally sound. These days I mainly work on old houses – failing beams and lintels, that sort of thing. There's been a big surge in subsidence cases during this dry spell we're having. The lack of moisture makes the ground shrink, causing buildings to move and crack."

I half expect her to pipe up at this point with her own tale of a worrisome wall or ceiling crack – almost everyone around here has one. Instead, she says: "Do they have structural engineers of the soul, do you think?"

It's my turn to laugh, though not entirely comfortably.

"What do *you* do?" I ask.

"I'm a voice actor – though not a busy one these days. I may go back to it when Alex is more settled. Right now I'm completely devoted to taking care of him."

Her devotion is all too apparent. While we're talking, her attention continually flickers back towards her son like a nurse bee darting protectively towards its larva. I wonder if her protectiveness might be one cause of Alex's social problems.

"What sort of voice acting do you do?"

"Adverts, radio dramas, video games, audiobooks, dubbing, anything I'm offered really."

"I can imagine you get lots of work – or did. Your voice is..." I hesitate. An extravagant compliment at this stage might sound creepy. "You have a very nice voice."

"Thank you."

"Have you done anything I may have heard of?"

"Paint and confectionary ads are probably the most high-profile. Nothing too glamorous I'm afraid."

We reach the top of Leafy Wood Lane, and Imogen's hand is on the gate leading into Turnwood Park. "Not today, Midge," I quickly tell her.

"Why not?" Amy asks.

"The park's a real dump. I wouldn't want to inflict it on you."

"Oh, but it looks lovely," says Amy, peering under the hawthorn hedge to see past the gate.

"You think so?" I'm surprised – disappointed.

"Please can we go through the park Daddy?"

I shrug and nod, pretending I'm unbothered.

Imogen opens the gate and we make our way along the winding grey path, a slender ribbon of sanity increasingly encroached upon by the chaos on either side. One day soon, even the path will disappear.

"Don't you find it romantic?" Amy remarks. "A little patch of wilderness hidden away in the midst of these ordinary suburban streets?"

"I've never thought of it that way." I'm keeping my eyes fixed on the path ahead, determined to avoid a sighting of the mysterious girl. After the nightmare I had, I'm hoping never to lay eyes on her again.

"And there's no one around but us," says Amy, "which makes it all the more like a place out of fantasy."

"Like a fairy garden," says the treacherous Imogen.

"Yes, exactly!"

I glance at the putrid pond and wonder what kind of gross and slimy fairy would choose to make this her garden.

"It's so much nicer than the park near us, where the teenagers come to snog each other and smoke dope. I can never take Alex there after about six o'clock."

I'm thinking: *Give me a teenager any day over an eight-year-old with a giant caterpillar in her mouth.*

Back at the house, Imogen takes Alex upstairs to play in her bedroom. Amy and I stand in the hallway watching them disappear round the bend in the staircase.

"Your daughter is so lovely," says Amy, who has something in her eye – probably a dandelion seed from her beloved fairy garden – and is dabbing it with a tissue.

"Alex is pretty charming, too – once you get to know him."

"He didn't used to be so shy," she says, a touch defensively.

"Tea?" I offer, leading her through to the kitchen.

"Thanks. Just milk, no sugar."

"I know."

Two mugs side by side on the clean, empty counter. Teabags in. Teaspoons at the ready. I'm glad I spruced the place up a bit this morning in anticipation of their visit.

Over the sound of the kettle: "I suppose the divorce hit him hard."

"It did. That and other things. It's been a tough year."

She takes a seat at the dining table, leans an elbow there and pushes up her hair with her hand. I can see her scar clearly: it runs from just above her wrist to near her elbow. She seems melancholy, yet unwilling to talk about what's bothering her. I don't feel I know her well enough to probe.

Instead I point out the fox in our garden, asleep in the shade of the trampoline. "That's the cub. His mum's probably in their den under our decking. She'll be out hunting later."

Amy watches it, blowing gently on her tea.

"I for one am glad that Alex and Imogen are friends," I tell her. "There's a kind of Berlin Wall that exists between boys and girls at that age. Good for them to have breached it."

"I hope it hasn't damaged Imogen's status among her friends, reaching out to the class pariah."

"Alex is no pariah. Give him time. He'll find his feet."

She glances up at me, a small smile breaking out unexpectedly. "Why don't we go upstairs and spy on them?"

"Are you kidding?"

"No. Actually..." She drops her head, and raises her eyes at me in a look of faux contrition. "Okay, confession time: I quite often listen in on Alex when he's playing by himself."

Again I find myself wondering about her relationship with her son – she seems over-involved.

"Don't you think kids should be allowed their privacy?"

She laughs, a hint of mockery in her eyes. "Are you telling me you've never snooped on Imogen?"

"No, of course I haven't!"

This makes her flinch, almost as if I've struck her. "You said that with some venom! I'm sorry, I didn't mean any offence."

Surprised at my own touchiness, I find myself apologising back.

Amy stands up. "Well, do you want to give it a try?" Without waiting for me to make up my mind, she walks out of the kitchen towards the stairs.

I'm disconcerted, perhaps a little peeved that she prefers spying on her son to spending time with me. On the other hand, I don't want to come over all priggish. I follow her up the stairs. At the top, I silently indicate Imogen's bedroom door. Bending our heads close, we can hear their muffled voices on the other side.

It feels oddly yet pleasantly intimate, standing next to Amy like this, facing each other, our heads close, our eyes with nothing to look at but each other. I can smell the tea on her breath, and her perfume – a familiar scent I can't put a name to but know very well – and watch the subtle changes in her face as she listens to their talk. She smiles at something Alex says, and because she's looking at me, the smile seems for me, and I reciprocate. She suppresses a giggle, her eyes still locked to mine, alive with amusement, and the illicit nature of what we're up to, the importance of not getting caught, adds to a tension that feels almost sexual.

It takes me back to a day, maybe a quarter of a century ago, when Susan was still just a friend of a friend. We were in our early twenties, spending Christmas at her parents' house, playing sardines with her much younger cousins. It was Susan's turn to hide, and I was the first to find her, in her mother's wardrobe. We had to wait there for ages, just the two of us, in the lavender-scented darkness, amid all those silky dresses. God was smiling on me that day, or else the younger cousins were lousy seekers. Susan and I stood there within kissing distance for long minutes, suppressing our giggles, as well as more powerful urges – because we didn't want to be found, least of all by Susan's boyfriend who was also some-where in the house. We managed to restrain ourselves, and it would be many years before we actually got together. Still, I reckon it all kicked off that afternoon in her mother's wardrobe.

And maybe something's kicking off right now between me and Amy, though it could all be in my head. I have a strong sense of her body standing close to mine – can almost feel her in my arms. It would take only the smallest movement on my part to make that happen. I wonder how she'd react. Of course I'm not going to try anything. She's the parent of a schoolfriend – probably seeing someone. And I have baggage of my own. Susan's presence hangs heavily in this house, including on this upstairs landing. I can almost smell her sometimes. I'm not over her, may never be, and this is no time to contemplate starting anything new. But I do like those wrinkles around Amy's eyes when she smiles.

I'm not really listening to what they're saying, just observing the effects on her face, so am taken by surprise when her smile suddenly vanishes. The wrinkles transfer to her forehead and her face stiffens. At first I think she's upset with me – that she's somehow read my thoughts. But that can't be it, because she's not even looking at me anymore. Her ear is cocked to the door. I lean closer and overhear Alex saying: "My sister's there too, in the invisible world. She's there with your mum."

Then Imogen: "Mr Jones took your sister to give to my mummy for company, because she's a girl like me. He couldn't take me because that would make my daddy very sad. But sometimes I wish Mr Jones would take me because then I could see my mummy again."

I clench up inside. I'm about to go in and put a stop to this nonsense, but there's pressure on my arm. Amy's hand is there. I look at her: pale, eyes wide, her head shaking at me.

"I think Mummy's happy with your sister," says Imogen blithely, "but she would definitely prefer me."

"Will my sister ever come back from the invisible world?" asks Alex.

"Maybe she will," says Imogen. "Maybe they'll both come back one day, when Mr Jones gets tired of them."

Amy's beckoning me to follow her. She's heading back towards the stairs. My hand is still on the doorknob. I'm still half thinking I should go in, but then Amy comes back and drags me away from the door. She hisses in my ear: "we need to talk."

Back in the kitchen, my tea is lukewarm between my cupped hands. I'm frowning at the tablecloth, still of a mind to stride back upstairs and rebuke Imogen for infecting young Alex with her poisonous and scary fantasies.

Amy is sitting next to me, knees close together, sandalled feet hooked around the strut of the chair. "I'm sorry to hear about your wife," she says quietly.

"Yeah, and I'm sorry for *your* loss... When did your daughter, um...?"

"Die? I don't know. She disappeared a year ago."

This jerks me out of my self-absorption, and suddenly I'm no longer thinking about Imogen and what she said. *The girl who disappeared a year ago.* Disparate memories start sliding into place, aligning themselves to form a single image.

"Your daughter is Stephanie Parker." Her barely perceptible nod tells me I'm right. "Oh my God, I'm so sorry."

She makes a dry chuckle in her throat. "Like I said, it's been a tough year. Losing Steph. I don't think there's any bottom to it – the pain I mean. I just keep falling and falling. I rarely sleep, even now." She shrugs and tries to smile. "There you go."

"Amy I really am so sorry…"

She's in some place I can't begin to reach, her dry, pink eyes staring. She whispers, "It's too much for a mother to bear. I wanted to kill myself. I very nearly did." She shows me the scar on her forearm: "It felt so good for a moment, watching the blood come out, and that bright pain that eclipsed everything. I felt at peace for the first time, watching my life flowing away downstream. My friend Ronnie found me, luckily. She called an ambulance. When I came to, I began to think more sanely, about the fact that I still had a child. We came up with a story, pretended it was an accident so they wouldn't section me, so they wouldn't take Alex away."

"How did it happen? I mean how did she disappear?"

Amy looks at the fox cub asleep beneath the trampoline. She speaks as if reciting the story from memory: "It was an afternoon a lot like this one, warm and bright. Alex was on a play date. My husband was working. I'd promised Steph I'd take her into Halsted Town to buy some new shoes. Then I thought maybe I'd treat us both to a cream tea. We were in the multi-storey car park. I left her in the car and went to buy a ticket. The guy in front of me was having a problem with the machine. He kept keying in his registration, but it wouldn't recognise his vehicle. It was so aggravating. Still, I couldn't have been gone more than three or four minutes. Five at the very most. I could have gone and checked on her, but I didn't want to lose my place in the qu…"

She stops, and it's as though sharp glass has pierced the skin of her cheeks.

"When you got back, she was gone?"

She nods.

I can picture the car park. I've been there dozens of times with Imogen, and before that with her mother as well. It's a bare place of concrete ramps and squealing, echoing tyres. I fear it because of the way the cars sometimes come at you fast around corners. But I've never thought of it as a place of monsters.

Amy's expression is glazed. This must be endlessly trodden ground for her, the span of her mental prison cell, a memory that's been worn to the bone. How many times must she have tortured herself with the counterfactuals? What if they hadn't gone out that day? What if she'd parked somewhere else? What if she'd taken her with to buy the ticket?

"I remember there was a big search. It was in all the papers."

"Yeah, and I gave press conferences on the national news. But nothing came of it. Not a sodding dicky bird. But that doesn't stop you hoping. It's the worst kind of drug hope is, because you cling to it even as it eats away at your heart. You hope with every knock at the door or phone call or if you spot a similar-looking girl in the street. It never leaves you alone. Even now I still look around for her whenever I'm in Halsted Town, still watch the news every day for a story about a missing child showing up somewhere. I've driven the police mad with all my phone calls and emails, but I can't help it. I drove my husband mad, too. It wasn't enough that he had to cope with losing a daughter, he had to cope with a crazy wife as well. He left in the end. Just walked out one day. I don't blame him. He couldn't understand what I was going through. A man can't feel like a woman can, like a mother can."

This jars with me. "If something like that happened to me,

I'd probably go mad, too... It must have been hard, living in that house, surrounded by all those memories."

"You can't escape them," says Amy, "but you kind of don't want to either. After my husband left, I sold the house in West Halsted and moved here. And you know, I packed up all her clothes and toys and took them with. Ronnie told me to get rid of them, but I couldn't ever do that. It's all I have left of her. I know in my heart that she's not coming back. They never do, not after this much time. But I still can't stop believing that one day she might, and that I'll be able to give her back her old bike and her dresses, even though she'd be too big for them now."

The ceiling above us creaks. Faintly, I can hear Imogen's voice raised in excitement. I'm glad they've moved onto livelier games.

"How did Alex cope?" I ask Amy.

"Well, you've seen him. He was a normal, outgoing kid before it happened. And he loved Steph to bits. There's only a year between them. When she disappeared, he retreated into himself. Developed asthma. I don't know if the two things are related. It might have been anxiety because he thought he was losing me as well."

Again, she looks at the fox cub. "He's the only reason why I'm still living. He's what gets me out of bed each morning, and keeps me going through the day. I had to take him out of his old school because he was getting bullied. Can you imagine that? Bullying a kid who's lost his sister? Sometimes I can't understand people." Her eyes are welling up again. I put my hand on hers. It feels like a natural thing to do.

My job is to calculate loads and stresses – how much a structure can take before it cracks. There are physical and mathematical laws governing such things. Looking at Amy I see someone shattered by her loss, who has somehow continued to live in defiance of everything – even her own desire not to. If there were mathematical laws governing the human heart, she'd have broken them.

"I'm glad he's found Imogen," she sniffs. "I like that they've created this invisible world where your wife and Steph can live together and keep each other company. Children need their own coping mechanisms, just like we do."

"Maybe," I say gruffly, removing my hand. "But I don't like that Mr Jones is there as well."

"Why's that?"

"A girl in Year Six was nearly abducted about six weeks ago by a masked man calling himself by that name."

"Oh, I heard about that. He was wearing a panda mask or something?"

I nod. "It happened in Turnwood Park, which is uncomfortably close to here."

"Did it *really* happen though? There've been some doubts cast on the girl's story. Her mum forced it out of her apparently. It doesn't really ring true anyway. I mean a panda mask? It's too bizarre! And the girl was on her own with him in the park, yet he just let her go. It doesn't sound very likely. I wouldn't worry too much about that. Kids make things up all the time. They create their own worlds." She blinks and dabs at a tear with her tissue. "Sorry for going on just now. I never planned on telling you any of this – it's such a difficult thing to put on people, especially someone you hardly know – but the kids sort of forced my hand. What about you though? When did your wife pass away?"

11

───────────

AFTER AMY and Alex have gone home, I run a bath for Imogen, then sit on the toilet seat and watch her as she plays in the foam.

"Did you have a nice time with Alex this afternoon?" I ask.

"Yes."

She's pushing a yellow plastic duck through tall icebergs of white froth.

"What kinds of games did you play?"

"We played with the remote control tarantula, and then we played City of Zombies, which I won."

"What did you talk about with him?"

"Nothing... I don't really remember."

She pushes the duck right inside the bubbles, so it disappears. Then she slowly raises it into the air. The foam clings to its upper surfaces, from beak to tail, giving it a comical appearance.

"It looks like Ducky has got caught in the snow," I smile.

"Ducky disappeared," she says solemnly. "And then he came back."

I pour some wine into a glass and settle down on the sofa. The pipes in the basement boiler room are creaking and tapping contentedly as the hot water cools. Imogen is asleep upstairs. Earlier, Winnie the Pooh accidentally discovered the North Pole while trying to save little Roo from drowning.

When did your wife pass away?

"Well, as it happens..."

I told Amy the story the way I always tell it, with the same words, and I'm no longer even sure how true it is. If you tell a story often enough, at some point the story becomes the truth and the truth becomes the story.

It was one Monday, last September. Susan, who lectured in media studies at Halsted College, had no courses to teach that day, so she was at home when I took Imogen to school, and she was still there when I got back at 9.15. We must have had breakfast together. Did we argue? I can't remember, but we probably did. We fought most mornings, or bickered. It could have been about anything: the messy state of the house, about Imogen, about money – but it was really always about the same thing, which was Susan's growing absence from my life.

One could say she started fading long before she actually disappeared. When I forced her to break off her online flirtation with Richard Landry, she started going out in the evenings – to the gym, to her classes, to her reading group – anything but spend time with me. She remained a devoted mother, helping Imogen with her work, reading to her, playing with her. But when Imogen went to bed, Susan would mostly do her own thing.

Then there was the *Devon* remark – the phone call I overheard as I was approaching our bedroom that afternoon three or four days before she vanished. *I can't* wait *till Devon.* I can hear her saying it now – there was emotion in it, longing almost, though who could say if it was genuine? Susan could be quite melodramatic at times.

On the morning she disappeared, we had breakfast together and I'm sure I grumbled about something – most likely the lack of food in the house, which probably set her off on her usual sermon: she was the main breadwinner now – had been since I'd gone freelance – therefore shopping for food was my responsibility. And while I was about it, I could lend a hand with the washing and ironing, too, at which point I'd indignantly remind her that I keep the kitchen and bathroom clean, not to mention do all the cooking and babysitting. I guess I went upstairs to my study at about 9.45. Soon after that, I heard the front door open and close with a bang, and that was it. She was gone.

It's an unsatisfying story. That much is obvious from the frustrated looks on the faces of everyone I tell it to. It's unsatisfying because it contains so little. There's no smoking gun in there to support the theory that everyone but me believes: that Susan left me for another man. Yet the determined will always see what they want to see in the facts. Perhaps the argument was worse than I remembered. Some even found evidence in the slammed front door. Most intriguing of all, for those who insist on being intrigued, was *Devon. Devon*, they insist, is the key to everything. Clearly, she's started a new life with her West-Country lover. They don't say this last bit, but I'm sure that's what everyone believes.

Personally, I don't read significance into any of it – there was nothing remarkable about her behaviour that morning. As for *Devon*, it was probably a mishearing of *seven*, as in seven o'clock, when 'The One Show' was on. I checked in the schedules and on Friday 6 September they interviewed Antonio Banderas – Susan had always had a thing for him.

Amy was the first person to agree with my lone psychopath theory. "You knew Susan best," she said simply. Though the *Devon* thing might just be a clue, she had to admit. "Intrigue," she murmured. "Mystery. That's all you need."

"What I need is closure," I said.

"You and me both," she sighed. "I hate having to live all the time between hope and despair. It's so exhausting. Sometimes I just want them to find her body. I'd like a grave to put flowers on."

Then she muttered something about it being fate, her and Alex meeting me and Imogen.

"Do you believe in that?" I let my scepticism show.

She shrugged. "I'm not sure, but it's quite a coincidence, don't you think? Our stories are so similar. I like Imogen's idea of an invisible world. It seems to capture the... the sort of in-between state that Steph and Susan exist in. They're here somehow, and yet they're not, like invisible people. I think she's very wise, your daughter, and I'm sure she's helping Alex."

I grunted. "Not if she's encouraging him to believe that his sister might come back one day."

"Is that so different from telling a child about Santa Claus, or Heaven?"

And now I'm staring into the lees of my wine and reflecting on this woman, Amy, and my evolving perceptions of her. For just a moment this afternoon, outside Imogen's room, I'd begun trem-blingly to imagine her as a lover. Then, like a hologram shifting to a new angle, everything changed and a different Amy came into view: I saw the lesions, the burns, the deep wounds. It was hard to look at her when she talked about what she'd been through. The tears seemed to bleed from her eyes.

12

WEDNESDAY 11 JULY 2018

I'M in Imogen's bedroom tidying up after her playdate with Alex. She was unusually quiet on the walk to school this morning, and I sense the possibility of a rift opening up between us. Perhaps she's keeping her thoughts to herself, scared that I might get angry. I need to learn to stay calm with her and not let my anxieties show too much. I suppose I may need to take Amy's advice and embrace this idea of an invisible world, or pretend to – so long as she doesn't imagine people can ever return from there. And I don't want her thinking Mr Jones inhabits it either – just in case the panda-faced paedophile really does show up one day and she's tempted to go off with him.

I've packed the remote-controlled tarantula and the City of Zombies game back into her games cupboard and am just about to close the cupboard door when I catch sight of the rib. It's sitting on the third shelf from the bottom, in front of the Glitter Butterflies. She's balanced it so that only the central part of the rib is in contact with the shelf while the two ends curve upwards. I stare at it for a while, then reach out with my finger and push down one side so that it touches the surface of the shelf. I let go and it bounces back up. The bone seesaws for a while before returning to equilibrium.

I pick the ugly thing up and run my fingers over its rough, gnawed surface, wondering what could have possessed Imogen to think her mother would send her *this* as a present. Why couldn't she have fixed on a more attractive or hygienic object for her fantasies? As I'm staring at it, I notice something peeping out of one end – something white. It's the furled edge of a piece of paper. Using the nails of my thumb and forefinger, I manage to get a grip on the millimetre or so of exposed paper, and pull. A small, tightly rolled sheet emerges from a hollow that's been dug into the spongy interior of the bone. To judge from the width of the scroll, the hollow must be around three and a half inches deep.

Breathless and suddenly very cold, I unfurl the small square sheet of paper. Written in blue biro in Susan's distinctive hand are the following words:

Dear Midge, I'm safe, don't worry. I wish I could come and see you. But Mr Jones won't let me. If you want to write back to me, just put a note in the stick where you found this one. Leave it under the big oak tree in the park. Please don't tell Daddy about this or Mr Jones will get angry. Let's just make it our little secret. I love you Midge. Write soon. Mummy. xxx

I stare at the note for a long time, reading it over and over again until my eyes start to water and the words get blurry. My mind feels torn, as if by a whirlwind, with competing thoughts and explanations dragging me in different directions. Did Imogen write this? Did she copy Susan's handwriting? Or could it be real? Is Susan alive somewhere, held by this madman – this Mr Jones? Does that mean he's real then, this demon? Could Mr Jones be my 'lone psychopath'?

No. It's impossible. Susan can't be alive. Not after I spent nearly a whole year searching for her – even hiring a private detective after the official search petered out. This has to be Imogen's work. The girl is crazy and precocious enough to do something like this. I can imagine her spending hour after hour in her room, practising her mum's handwriting...

...or Mr Jones will get angry.

I'm trying to unravel my daughter's mind here – what would drive her to write something like that. Mr Jones is, as far as I can work out, the bogeyman at her school – the supernatural demon that haunts all their nightmares. So why would she imagine her mother held captive by him? Maybe because it's the only way she can explain the fact that her mother has never come back. She's woven a fantasy to make sense of the mystery that haunts her life: Mummy loves her, so why hasn't she returned? It must be because she's being held captive by Mr Jones. It makes me sad – and strangely proud – to think of the painstaking lengths Imogen has gone to heal the wound of her mother's absence.

Please don't tell Daddy about this...

So I've been cast as a threat to the scheme. She's sure I'll trash her fantasy as soon as I find out about it, so she's got "Mummy" to tell her to keep it a secret from me.

Please don't tell Daddy about this...

It crushes me to imagine Imogen writing those words. For the first time in her life, she's deliberately excluding me from something that's important to her. I no longer have her complete trust.

*If you want to write back to me, just put a note in the stick where
you found this one. Leave it under the big oak tree in the park.*

Does this mean she's planning on keeping this correspon-
dence going? What should I do? Talk to her? But what can I say?
If I give it my blessing, she'll think I believe it's true. And if I
don't, then I'll just be playing my preassigned role of fantasy-
trasher. Both alternatives are bad. Best to say nothing. I suppose
there's no real harm in a kid fantasising about corresponding
with her missing mum – though I don't relish the idea of her
going up to the park on her own, in case Mr Jones turns out to
be real.

Trembling just a little, I roll up the paper and, with difficulty,
slide it back inside the rib. Then I put the rib back on the shelf
in its former position.

～

"Can I go for a ride on my bike, Daddy?"

I turn from the multi-perspective 3D model on my computer
screen. She's standing there in the doorway of my study. Late
afternoon light slips through the window blinds, exposing hints
of deep russet in her dark blonde hair. It's a charming mess, her
hair, with plaits like frayed ropes – I struggle every day with it.
The girl misses a mother's touch.

I picked her up an hour ago from choir practice. She had a
snack, then disappeared into her room. I'm certain she must
have spent that time composing a reply to the note sent by
"Mummy", and now she plans to plant it in the park.

Her expression is innocent, disturbingly so. *How soon they
learn the ways of deceit!* Part of me wants to confront her about
this and end the charade. I could admit that I found the note,
tell her that I know she's sad about Mummy, but really it's time

to stop with these games. It's time to move on. I could do that and watch the bitterness and misery distort my daughter's beautiful face and know that I was the cause. Or, to hell with it, I could suggest we go bury her reply together – grace this delusion of hers with an adult stamp of authority. In one moment of weakness and folly, I could reverse all the months I've spent trying to get her to accept the fact of her mother's death.

I could do either of those things, or I could do nothing...

"Sure, sweetie," I say to her. "Just up and down the pavement outside the house, yeah. No crossing any roads."

"Could I go over to Aisha's? See if she wants to play?"

Aisha lives in Oakfield Crescent, just around the corner from here. Oakfield Crescent curves around Turnwood Park and gives access to its eastern entrance. I guess Imogen is planning to inter the bone in the park before backtracking to Aisha's house, or maybe she's even hoping to involve her friend in her little game. She's been to Aisha's on her own before, so I can't very well say no.

It's not difficult following Imogen. I wait behind the hedge by our front gate until she's a good twenty yards away. Then I slip out onto the pavement and walk after her. Oakfield Crescent is at the end of our road – less than two hundred yards from our door. By the time I get to the corner, I know my hunch was correct: she's cycled straight past Aisha's house and is speeding towards the park.

From the park gate, I watch her beneath the oak tree, pushing the rib into the soil, her bike left sprawled on the bank just above the path. Then she gets to her feet, wipes dirt from her knees and picks up her bike. Before she can raise her head and catch sight of me, I turn around and trot back along Oakfield Crescent.

So my girl's a fantasist. As Amy said, children need their coping strategies, just like we all do. I suppose there's no real harm... I'm putting the key into the lock of our front door when another thought strikes me, far more frightening than anything I've considered so far: what if she *is* in communication with someone, but it's not Susan? What if some paedophilic predator has got wind of Imogen's vulnerability and is posing as Susan – grooming her for a meeting? It's such a sick idea that at first I dismiss it, but then I stop what I'm doing and a deep coldness seeps through me. Immediately, I start running back the way I came. Fear gives me energy. Despite my lack of fitness, I'm hardly out of breath by the time I reach Aisha's house. Imogen's bike isn't in the front garden. She must have taken it into the house I tell myself, trying to keep the panic from spilling over. I ring the doorbell. *Please, please let her be here.*

Aisha's mum, Nita, answers. She seems surprised. "Hello, Ben. How're things?"

"Did Midge visit by any chance?" I ask her.

Her face clouds. "No, she's not been here..."

And now the panic starts like a twitching monster. I don't even wait to say goodbye. She's still speaking as I sprint towards the park. Sid, the ginger cat, is lounging on a wall near the alley leading to the park. He assesses my panic with a cool depth of understanding. He's seen her. Sid knows every damn thing. I run down the alley, wrench open the gate and start along the path, searching for a flash of chrome or white paint through the trees. But the park is empty.

"Midge!"

There's a flapping above me as some pigeons take off in fright at the sharp snap of my voice.

I slow down when I reach the oak tree. To my left, the swamp glistens like something putrefying in the heat. I don't even want to look there. My eyes home in on the rib, its white tip sticking out of the earth where Imogen buried it not five minutes ago.

"Midge! Where are you?"

I glance at the distant gate leading to Leafy Wood Lane. But she would never have gone down there on her own. There are no other paths in the park – nowhere else to go.

Could someone have been lying in wait for her while she was burying the rib?

My heart nearly stops at the idea. I think of Stephanie, left alone for four minutes. I push my hand hard against my teeth, more frightened than I've ever been in my life.

"Midge! For God's sake!"

Her bike had lain here, on the bank. I can see indentations in the grey dust from the pedal, from one of the wheels. I search for other patterns or wheel marks, anything to tell me where she went. I go down on my knees, scouring the earth with my eyes, begging it to yield up its clues. There's nothing in the dust: just the tiny marks left by birds and squirrels, a nest of ants, a disturbed stone.

I scramble further up the bank, closer to where the rib is buried, and that's where I see it: a thin tyre track. It disappears after less than a yard into the long grass. I look up, mentally tracing the line she would have followed, based on that brief track. It leads up to the shadow-dimmed corner of the park – a place of tangled bushes, a diseased apple tree and a broken fence: the derelict house.

"Ben?"

I turn around. Nita is standing there. For one beautiful second I think it's Imogen standing next to her – but then I see it's Aisha, and I'm thrust back inside my heart-crushing hell of fear.

"Have you any idea where she might be?" Nita asks.

I shake my head and start a stumbling run towards the derelict house. I blunder through the bushes, breaking free of brambles that try and catch at my shoelaces, tramping down the macerated flesh of mouldy apples. I hear mother and daughter behind me as I reach the broken fence. Dry, brittle wood splinters as I force my shoulders and body through into the rank lushness of the garden.

"Midge!" I scream.

Silence.

A soft rustle of leaves.

"Yes Daddy?"

"Oh my God!"

I half trip as I rush to her. She's standing in some bushes where the lawn-forest meets an impenetrable mass of vegetation at the rear of the garden. Her face turns pale and frightened as I approach. *Oh Christ, what must I look like?* Does she think I'm going to hurt her? I stumble to a halt in front of her and fold her in my arms. "Midge, you must never..." My voice cracks.

"Never what?"

"You said you were going to Aisha's house. Why did you come here?"

"I'm sorry." She sounds pained, breathless. "Daddy, you're holding too tight."

I let go of her. "Why did you come here, Midge?"

She frowns. Her gaze is wandering all over the place as if trying to think of an excuse.

Then she smiles.

"I met somebody."

"You..." I gasp. My tongue almost gets trapped in my throat. "Midge, how many times have I...?"

"Not a grown-up." She gives me a look as if *I'm* the one acting like a child. "I would never ever go anywhere with a grown-up stranger. But this was a girl, Daddy. She was my age I think. She invited me here." Imogen gestures around her. "This is where she lives."

I stare at her, unable to speak.

Nita comes over and crouches by Imogen, taking her hand. "No one lives here, Midge. This is a deserted house. No one's lived here for years."

"Did you really see a girl living here?" asks Aisha.

"Yes," giggles Imogen. She's wearing a look of serene amusement, which I don't like at all.

"Then where is she now?" asks Nita.

Imogen glances about. "Oh, she's gone now. You lot frightened her away."

Something cold and dead curls up in my stomach when I hear this. I don't want to ask the next question, but I have to: "What was the girl wearing, sweetie?"

Nita looks at me, puzzled, but Imogen doesn't even pause: "She was wearing a Hello Kitty T-shirt and jeans with butterflies."

13

SATURDAY 12 JULY 2003

THE SUN SLAMMED down its heat on Roy. It was merciless. Why did he have to choose the warmest bloody summer since records began to write his masterpiece? He sat in the miserly shade of the oak tree, leaning back against the corrugations of its mighty trunk, licking the sweat trickles from his upper lip. He'd have retreated to his uncle's house, only there was something about this park that drew him like a moth to a moth-killing flame. He'd discovered it on his very first day, when he went out in search of an impetus for his imagination. He didn't find one (an impetus, that was) and still hadn't, but he found this park right at the foot of his garden. He knew straight off that it was exactly the sort of place where an impetus might be found, if one was to be found at all.

The park was horribly disorientating. Everything about it was off-kilter and strange. It had no describable shape, no centre or focal point. There were weird slopes and dips, and a path through its middle that meandered to no purpose but its own twisted logic. The park was magnificently neglected – clearly hadn't felt the blade of a mower, strimmer or chainsaw in years. The uncollected leaves of a hundred autumns formed a layer of dust and loam from which sprang weeds and wild shrubs – goldenrod, chokeberry, butterfly bush and spotted laurel – many of which sported picturesque diseases. Most dreadful of all was the pond, or the mire as Roy liked to think of it. Apart from a few waterlilies and a stand of despondent rushes, it was entirely coated in a thick veil of pallid green slimeweed. Roy was looking at it now from his vantage beneath the oak, and a more baleful stretch of water in all of Halsted he could not imagine.

Roy had been living in his uncle's house for a full week now – a week in which not a word had been written in anger – and he was starting to fret. He'd set himself a target of four pages a day, blithely assuming that when he got here, the ideas would start to flow. Now he had just seven weeks left to write his masterpiece. After that, his self-imposed sabbatical would have to end. Reviews needed writing, because bills needed paying. This was his one chance, and if he didn't start soon, he might as well jack the whole thing in and go back home.

With an effort, he levered himself to his feet and stretched out his arms like a preacher. He stared at the park, and nothing met his gaze. "This is it," he bellowed. "I'm leaving tomorrow. Show me what you've got. I know you have a story for me. I can smell it, taste it. I just can't see it." His words fell into the empty air. The park wasn't listening. It was persisting, as it always would, in its unheeding slumber, and he would leave it, in puzzlement and frustration, to resume his small life.

He lowered his arms and started to wipe a salty droplet of sweat from his eye, then stopped, hand frozen in mid-swipe. He blinked, but kept his gaze locked on the pond. Something had moved down there, as sure as daylight. He'd seen a tremor beneath the sickly film of green. What could possibly be alive underneath that suffocating mat? Another movement, and a zipline of fear ran straight up him from his balls to his throat. Something was climbing out of the pond.

14

WEDNESDAY 11 JULY 2018

MY MOTHER SMILES AT IMOGEN. "We'll have fun, won't we, Midge? We can make pancakes. And afterwards we can play a round or two of rummy. Now why don't you go to the kitchen and take out everything we need. I'll be with you in a minute."

"Thanks so much Mum," I say, as Imogen trots off.

We're seated in the parlour, as she insists on calling the living room. Mum deposits ash from her cigarette into her fish ashtray. "Now what's going on Ben?"

"It's a work thing," I lie. "I have to see a client with a bad case of cavity wall tie corrosion. It's going to take a while. I'll need to take lots of photos and measurements. He can only do this evening unfortunately. Sorry for the short notice."

"Don't worry. That's what I'm here for." She lowers her voice. "How's Midge been lately? Still talking about her mum?"

I nod tiredly. "It would really help if you could speak to her about that. Tell her Mummy's in Heaven now. She won't listen to me."

"I can't tell her something I don't believe Ben. I still think

Susan might be alive, and I'll go on thinking it until I'm shown proof that she isn't."

I grind my teeth but say nothing, because Imogen has come back into the hallway. "I like your painting Granny."

"Oh that," Mum laughs. "I got tired of working on it and not getting anywhere, so I've decided to call it finished. Come in and look, Ben, if you have time."

The abstract, or "bit of swirly nonsense", as Mum once called it, is propped against the kitchen wall. It looks like a perfectly normal painting that has been stabbed and then twisted like spaghetti around a fork, dragging all the elements towards a spiralling vortex near the top left. It's a clever effect, because you can almost recognize objects in there, like the vague shapes of a stork, a fish and a water lily, but they're so stretched and distorted that it's hard to be sure. I make polite noises, but find it hard to look at for more than a few minutes because of the predominant colour: a listless, pallid green with hints of grey. I don't know why she chose such a colour. It makes me think of death.

"There's a face in there, can't you see?" says Imogen. She points to an area near the top, close to the vortex. "Granny can't see it but you can, can't you Daddy?"

I suppose I *can* just about see something that's possibly a face with a gaping, froglike mouth and a pair of round, jelly-like eyes that seem to be dripping out of their sockets. But the whole painting gives me such a queasy feeling, I have to look away before I can be sure I saw anything.

"I don't know sweetie."

"It's a bad, bad face," says Imogen. "I don't want to think about it tonight."

"I still don't see it," says Granny.

I leave them studying the painting and head back home. From the cupboard in the laundry room, I grab a flashlight, a roll of string, some tent pegs, a wooden mallet, a sleeping bag and a penknife, and dump them in a rucksack. Then I go to the kitchen and make myself a thermos flask of coffee. I place this, together with a bar of chocolate, in the rucksack, before heading out into the evening.

The air is warm and heavy. A faint breeze carries scents of rose, lilac and new-mown grass. The sky is pale purple, deepening to copper-coloured clouds above the steeple of a nearby church. When I reach the park, the atmosphere seems to thicken. As soon as I close the rusty gate, the air nestles closer and more densely against my skin. The prevailing odour is of something earthy and ancient. As I suspected, there are no people around. Whatever Amy and Mr Raymerson from the council may say, people instinctively steer clear of this place.

I hurry straight over to the oak tree and uproot Imogen's half-buried rib. I want to check that "Mummy" hasn't already sent her a reply. With some difficulty, I claw the paper note out of the hollow in the bone. The message is from Imogen – I recognise her careful, flowery writing.

Good! That means "Mummy" hasn't been yet. My plan may yet work…

Dear Mummy. I was so happy to get the stick for my present. Thank you! It was lovely to recieve your note, so hear I am writing back to you like you asked. I havent told Daddy, but I think he is suspicius. I hope you are safe. I don't want Mr Jones to hurt you. When can you come back? I miss you. Love your Midge xxx

. . .

My hand is shaking as I read this, and the light is dim beneath the tree, so it's a struggle to figure out the words. But when I take them in, I start to seethe. The thought of a stranger beguiling a confused and grieving girl with these lies, setting her against her own father – it's too much! I wipe my eyes and sniff away a tear. After scrolling it up again, I stuff the paper back inside the rib and replant it in the soil. Again I think of Imogen smiling so confidently in that overgrown garden today – how quickly she'd forgotten all my warnings about talking to strangers.

But this was a girl, Daddy. She was my age I think. She invited me here.

A girl! That girl! Just the thought of her is enough to make me start shaking again. She must be working for Mr Jones. He knows that children wouldn't go with him – they're too well-trained these days. So he's enlisted the help of someone their own age. What a diabolical idea! What a perversion of innocence! He probably looks after the waif, keeps her looking smart and tidy, so she seems like any ordinary girl. God knows what else he makes her do for him...

I must get on with my plan. Fifteen yards further up the bank, almost completely shrouded in long grass, is a fallen tree. It's in an advanced state of decomposition, with moss and fungal growths covering most of its surface. Next to the tree is a flattish area and this is where I empty out my rucksack, rolling out the sleeping bag and placing the coffee and chocolate within easy reach.

I return to the oak tree, armed with mallet, tent pegs and string. The dusty grey earth beneath the tree is granite-dry and it's hard work banging in the metal tent pegs. They have to be driven in far enough to be firmly embedded, yet with at least a couple of inches of their shafts showing above the earth. I arrange them in a rough circle of about five yards diameter around the rib, then thread the string around their bent necks. The string needs to be tight enough to trip up an unwary foot, and it takes me further minutes of adjustment to ensure that it is. As I work, I cast frequent glances towards the upper corner of the park with its broken fence leading to the suspected hideout of Mr Jones. There's no sign of any activity over there, from girl or man. I can only hope that neither of them are watching.

When I've completed the tripwire to my satisfaction, I keep hold of what remains of the ball of string and let it pay out behind me as I clamber back up the bank. Seating myself half inside my sleeping bag, I use the penknife to cut the string and then tie one end of it around my left wrist, making sure it remains reasonably tight. Now there's no chance of me sleeping through "Mummy" when she comes to retrieve the rib. All that's left to do is lean back against the deadwood log and wait. There's still no sign of life from the top corner of the park. My penknife remains close to my right hip, ready for use as a weapon, should "Mummy" turn out to be dangerous.

By this time, most of the remaining light has leaked from the sky. A scattering of stars have appeared. Lights from nearby houses sneak through the bushy ramparts at the park's perimeter, laying a cloudy sheen on patches of grass and seeming to press all else deeper into shadow. The surface of the swamp glistens like pale, unhealthy skin. I can smell it from here, a dank, sulphurous reek of flowers gone bad. As I watch, the surface trembles as something shifts beneath the algae. I wonder what could possibly be alive under there.

Long minutes go by and the world gets slowly darker. Soon, the only light is the ghostly milk that seeps in from the surrounding houses and a thin, ethereal glow from the sickle moon. As the darkness closes around me, so do the first doubts. When I conceived this plan earlier this afternoon, it seemed the obvious thing to do. I had no proof of anything, only a fear in my gut that something was wrong, which wouldn't have impressed the authorities. So I decided to act on my own: I had to take steps to protect my daughter, which meant confronting the predator, this Mr Jones, whoever he may be.

But crouched here, now, in the full darkness, with all the soft rustlings in the undergrowth, I'm starting to wonder if maybe I've done a mad thing. I'm a structural engineer, not a fighter. I have no self-defence skills. What would I do if Mr Jones turns out to be a psycho killer with an axe? I should have brought the big kitchen knife at least. Perhaps I could run home and get it now. But what if he comes when I'm gone? He'll trip up on the string and then he'll know I'm onto him, so he'll get sneakier, and probably more dangerous. Everything depends on catching him tonight.

So I stay put, sleeping bag snugged around me, sipping my coffee with trembling lips. The night is not quiet. By God, it's a cacophony. From all around me come muted creepings, swishes, sighs, drones, whistles, creaks and whirrs. They come from the trees and from the ground and from the log behind me. I think of the insects and grubs living in that decaying timber, the woodlice, the millipedes, the beetles and their larvae, the flies and their maggots. The whole thing's alive. It's a city, that log, as rich and teeming as the great metropolis to the south. Something touches my bare arm, soft and sticky. I bash at it with a fist, spilling coffee on my shirt.

The park is rotting. Witness those diseased apples bursting beneath my feet, the slimy, festering pond. And decay breeds and nurtures its own life forms, an ecosystem of tiny clammy, viscid things that move in slime and eat death and then pupate into flying horrors in such numbers that they thicken the air with their vibrating wings. And in the steaming heart of this necropolis is me – in time I'll no doubt provide it with another home. Fungal spores will sprout from my toes. Maggots will spontaneously generate from my flesh.

Sounds creep into my ear like treacle flowing thickly on dry leaves, and furry whisperings on bark, the whine of a tiny winged vampire. My shoulder writhes against the side of my head.

A breath.

I tighten up.

That sounded human, and very close.

Tossing away my coffee cup, I fumble for the penknife. The string is taut from my wrist to the tripwire. I'm waiting for a tug. *Where's the flashlight?* I need three hands. I grab it with my knife hand, my thumb seeking out the recessed button but not yet pushing it. The night noises go on around me with their tiny skitterings and scratchings, but I'm filtering all that out now, bracing myself for something bigger – a footstep, the snap of a twig.

Instead I hear a small, frightened sound, a kind of gasp.

Something curls up inside me at this sound, so tender, sweet and scared. A little girl. Here in the night, in this place. It can't be. The spit turns sour in my mouth. I can't form words. What am I hearing?

It must be his minion. He's sent her here to do his bidding: to pick up the note. I shouldn't be scared, I should be angry. My eyes pick out a shape up there on the slope, near the broken fence. It's her, in her usual spot. A small figure, perfectly still. I can almost see the mangled doll in her hand.

I stand up too quickly, struggling for balance. I start towards her. My legs are heavy and I find it hard to disentangle my feet from the clutches of weeds and brambles. Her eyes, staring at me, are big, too big. Her face and body twists as I approach.

"I'm not going to hurt you!" I try to say, but my mouth seems made of brittle elastic – it sounds, even to me, like indecipherable grunting.

Then I see her properly, and I stop. The "big eyes" are dark, circular bruises that extend from eyebrow to cheek. Her mouth is bleeding. There are more bruises on her arms. Her body is contorted because she's been beaten. She can barely stand.

When I see this, I start shouting. I don't know what I'm saying, or if they're even words. Rage seizes me, it boils up from my chest, and I fall to my knees and scream. Then my eyes open – and I understand that all this time, they've been closed.

It's dark, too dark to see anything. I'm bent forward in a sitting position with the log against my back. My mouth is hanging open, my mind still juddering with that image of the beaten-up little girl. I look back to where I thought I'd seen her. Nothing disturbs the darkness there. Relief brings a flood of air back into my lungs.

I have no idea how long I was asleep, or what I missed. A big chunk of time seems to have slipped away from me. I feel around with my hand until I locate the flashlight in the grass next to me. Flicking it on, its pale beam lights up the trees. I sweep it across the park. Everything is motionless in its white tunnel. Ghost-shapes of trees and bushes rush into view, then vanish. The place seems bigger in the dark, like a forest. I try to scan more slowly, my heart pounding at the thought of what I might catch in the roving beam. There's something out there, or it feels that way. I have to force myself to turn the light on the top corner, by the derelict house. My flesh crawls at the thought that I might see the girl up there, headless doll in hand, watching me.

But there's no one.

I move the torch more urgently now: along the path, down by the pond, under the tree. No signs of activity anywhere. My mind is playing tricks again. It's only a park, just a short distance from my home. My torchlight lingers beneath the tree. At first I'm not sure why. Then I notice that something's changed down there. The rib looks different.

Using the log, I lever myself upright. My muscles feel stiff and sore. I have to stamp my feet to get the blood circulating. I must have been sitting asleep in that position for hours. Down the slope I stumble. Dislodged earth and dust crumbles around me, some of it pouring into the tops of my shoes. Under the tree, I bathe the ground in the hard, scientific glare of my light. The trip wire is undisturbed and the rib still protruding from the ground, but leaning at a more acute angle than it was when I placed it there earlier. Whether this is the work of gravity or a small animal or something else is anyone's guess. But it looks... tampered with.

Part of me doesn't want to look, as I reach down and pull the rib from the earth. Cradling the light in the crook of my elbow, I tug the note from its hollow. It's awkward, fumbling with the note while keeping the light in the right position. In the end I have to seat myself cross-legged on the ground with the torch balanced on my thigh so I can unroll the tightly curled paper with both hands. Inside I'm pleading: *let it be Imogen's message...*

It isn't. The note is a new one, in Susan's handwriting, and the sight is like a stab in the eyes.

Dear Midge, Daddy is watching for me. Did you tell him that we were writing to each other? Daddy should know that if Mr Jones catches him or anyone else watching for me, he will get angry. If Daddy tells the police about any of this, Mr Jones will get super angry. He might do something bad to Daddy or even to you. For your own safety, we'd better stop writing. At least for now. I'm sorry princess. Stay strong and brave for me. And keep believing that one day we can be together again. I love you. Mummy xxx

I hear myself groan as I read these words. My fingers tighten around the edges of the note. Every part of me wants to rip it up and burn the scraps, then snap the rib into a thousand pieces and hurl the whole lot into the pond. I feel an overwhelming need to purge my life, and Imogen's, of this evil, psychotic contamination. Who does this Jones bastard think he is, playing these sick games with us? I'm about to crush the note into my fist when I stop.

This is evidence.

I need to prove to the world that we are being menaced by someone, and this note will help me do that. What's more, there may be fingerprints on it, DNA, human traces of one kind or other that could help identify the creep. A strange sort of chuckle bursts from my throat. This note could be Jonesie's first big mistake.

15

THURSDAY 12 JULY 2018

"STANDARD CHEAP BIRO OLD MAN," says Geoff Gunnell, peering at the note through a magnifying glass. "Your basic ten-pee ballpoint. And the paper it's written on is bog standard supermarket stationery. *Papier ordinaire.* There's nothing much to be gleaned from this."

We're in his cramped office, a messy little annexe to his lab. He's seated at his desk, calm and methodical, serene in the halo of his spot lamp. I'm standing over him, waiting impatiently for the science.

"DNA?" I ask plaintively.

He shakes his head. "Not unless it was written in blood or saliva."

He turns to the other document I've handed him – a yellowing sheet containing some notes jotted down by Susan during a phone conversation with a builder about five years ago. "I'm not exactly a trained graphologist, but I can immediately see the similarities in the handwriting. Look at that *a* and the *g*. It's got the same looping style. It's a good imitation – if that's what it is."

"What do you mean, *if that's what it is*?"

Geoff raises his pockmarked face. I'm aware that my hands are gripping the edge of his desk and make an effort to relax.

"I mean if it's not genuine," he clarifies.

"How *could* it be genuine? Are you suggesting Susan wrote this?"

"Well, it's a possibility old man."

"No," I shake my head as if trying to evade an annoying mosquito. "Susan's dead. I searched for her, don't you remember? This is just some sick bastard playing a game with me."

Geoff shrugs, and hands both sheets back to me. "You should take this to the police my friend," he says. "Let the *gendarmes* do their job."

"Didn't you read the note? He's threatening to hurt Midge if I go to the police."

"They'll offer you both protection."

I shake my head. I don't tell Geoff this, but I'm scared – scared of what Jones might be capable of.

"You seem stressed, Ben," says Geoff. He's looking at the coffee stain on my pink shirt – residue of last night's shenanigans in Turnwood Park. "This Mr Jones thing is getting to you. I don't know if you're thinking straight."

"Do me a favour, Geoff," I say, handing the note back to him. "Keep this. Check it for fingerprints. Double check the ink. You never know. You might find something. Bill me for your time."

I leave him there, holding the paper distractedly, and hurry out of his office.

~

"Daddy, can't we go the park way today?"

We're at the top of Leafy Wood Lane, coming back from her drama club. Imogen has her hand on the park gate.

"Why do you want to go that way?" I ask her innocently.

"I like the park," she says. "It's more fun than just walking past houses."

I purse my lips. It's time. I've been building up to this. "Midge, we need to talk."

I have no idea what will happen next – what she will do, what I will say to her. All I know is that we have to do this, and do it now.

I take the rib out of my pocket and show it to her.

Her eyes go big as she comprehends it in my hand. She makes a noise like a gulp mixed with the beginning of the word *you.*

"You found the stick," she says breathlessly. Keeping her eyes on the thing, she inclines her body very slightly to her right, peering around my thumb, trying surreptitiously to ascertain if the note is still in its hollow.

She blinks and swallows when she sees it's empty.

"I found the note, too," I tell her.

At last her gaze drifts upwards to meet mine. Her eyes are watery, but fierce.

"You shouldn't have," she says. "It was none of your business."

"It *is* my business, Midge. Everything about you is my business."

"It was between me and Mummy! Mummy told me not to tell you." Then she falters. Her jaw trembles. "But you don't even believe that Mummy's alive."

I put my hand on her shoulder and feel the warm flocculence of her hair between my fingers. "I know that you believe it."

She pulls herself free and goes marching off down the pavement, away from me and the park. "You think I wrote that letter," she fires over her shoulder. "Well I didn't!"

"I know you didn't."

She stops, and slowly turns to face me.

"The spelling's too good for a start."

"So then you *do* believe Mummy's alive."

Light, as from a distant galaxy, starts to warm her face.

"I never said that."

Her smile, only half-formed, stills and trembles, a dewdrop gathering on the edge of a petal.

"Someone else wrote that note, sweetie. It wasn't Mummy. I think it was Mr Jones."

The smile cuts out.

"No," she says. "You're wrong, Daddy. Mr Jones is keeping Mummy prisoner, but Mummy wrote the letter. She wanted me to know that she loves me."

I go towards her, but Imogen backs away, her face now tight with dread.

"She told me not to tell you, but now you know! Mr Jones will be angry! He might *hurt* Mummy..."

Imogen suddenly freezes. Shoulders hunched, head darting towards the park, like a stalked animal. "Quick!" she hisses. "Give it to me. He might not have seen us." She scampers up and yanks the rib from my scarcely resisting grasp.

Her expression is steadier now, full of furtive resolution. I'm riveted by her performance, no longer able to think like an adult, a father, as she slowly raises a finger to her lips and fixes me with a grim stare.

"Our secret," she whispers. "Tell... no one."

~

Imogen is in bed. The rib is back on the shelf in her wardrobe. I'm downstairs on the sofa with my wine. There's a nature programme on the box – a crewcut, barrel-chested man and his camera crew are on the trail of some rare predator, hacking their way through vegetation. The pipes are settling in the basement – quietly rattling and knocking like woodpeckers deep in the forest.

My talk didn't go well. Midge is as hard to reach as ever, bottled up in her own world – a world where Mummy lives and loves her and Daddy is persona non grata. Tomorrow I will go to the derelict house. That has to be Jones's hideout. I've put it off for too long. I'll break in through the back and search it, shine a light on all this pernicious nonsense and put an end to it.

And if Jones is waiting there for me with a knife? What then? I think again about what Geoff said. It's tempting just to put all this in the hands of the police. But can I trust them to take me seriously? To act competently and with sufficient urgency? There's something about those notes, the way they were written. I sense I'm up against a fierce and calculating intelligence. He knows I won't risk my daughter's life. He's successfully isolated me, and if I'm going to confront him, I'll have to do it alone.

I'm thinking about me and Mr Jones, likening myself just a little to Crewcut on the screen, hacking his way through the jungle with his machete, when the phone rings.

I hook the receiver between my shoulder and cheek, and press the mute button on the television remote.

"Hello."

"Hello, Ben. It's Amy."

"Amy." I sit up straighter. "How are you?"

"I'm... not good."

"What's wrong?"

"Nothing, it's just..." I can hear her breathing deeply, struggling for calm. "It's coming up to the anniversary of Steph's disappearance... I don't know if I want to mark it – part of me wants it to be just another day. But I don't think I can just ignore it. So Alex and I have agreed we'll light a candle, and we'll say a little prayer. I'm not religious but... I have to do something. For Alex as much as for myself."

"Of course."

"I'm sorry."

"What do you mean?"

"Laying all this on you. I barely know you."

"It's fine, don't worry." I try to clear my head and get my tongue working. "I mean I'm glad to, you know, be someone you feel you can talk to. Like you said, our stories aren't so different. So I... I'm guessing it makes it easier for me to imagine what you've been through, to empathise, kind of thing."

"Yes," she says quietly.

A lone pipe is pounding a dull beat beneath the floorboards. On the screen, Crewcut is examining a pile of animal dung.

"So..." I can't think what to say next – just trying to fill up the silence. I don't believe in God or an afterlife, and nor, it seems, does Amy. There are no easy words of comfort. "So I think it's good that you're thinking about her, remembering her. That's got to be a good thing."

She doesn't reply.

"Amy, are you okay?"

"Yes."

She doesn't sound okay.

"Is there anything I can do?"

"Ben, would you have dinner with me one night? At a restaurant. My treat."

My mind flounders at this. I clear my throat and say "Really?" And then: "Sure. Why not? I'm sure we can find someone to... Where would you like to go?"

"I don't mind," she says. "Do you like Lebanese food?"

"Sure."

"There's a place on the high street called Tabaxa. It's supposed to be good. Are you free tomorrow evening?"

Tomorrow is Friday.

"Yes," I say immediately. "My mother can look after Midge. Alex, too, if you want."

"I can't put her to that sort of trouble," she objects, though not too strenuously.

"It's no trouble. Two kids are always easier than one – especially as they get on so well. They could even have a sleepover."

"I couldn't possibly..."

And then we're into the practical kind of conversation that all parents engage in at moments like these – sleeping bags, food preferences, drop-off and pick-up arrangements – the strangeness and the thrill of Amy's unexpected invitation and what it might imply is for the moment put to one side.

As soon as we end the conversation, I'm on the phone to my mother. I'd promised Amy that she'd be alright with all this, but I couldn't know that for certain. She might have plans.

As it turns out, she's free, and happy to look after the children – but when I tell her it's a "kind of date," she hesitates. "Is it serious, Ben?" she asks.

"No," I laugh. "I hardly know her."

"Be careful," she says. "You're still married, remember."

"No, I'm not," I tell her firmly.

16

FRIDAY 13 JULY 2018

"ARE you going to marry Alex's mummy?" Imogen asks me the following morning, after I mention our evening plans.

"No, of course not," I snort.

"Then why are you going to a restaurant with her?"

We're walking down Leafy Wood Lane on the way to school. As usual, she only has half her mind on our conversation. The rest of it is flitting about, attracted by whatever's just flashed upon her retina, be it a swaggering cat or the flight of a ladybird.

"Sometimes friends go out for meals," I tell her. "It's nothing serious."

"You mean men and ladies can be friends?"

"Of course."

"But what if you have some wine? You might get drunk and start kissing each other."

I stop and stare at Imogen, who is currently observing a line of ants weave their way around the roots of an old tree.

"What on earth are you talking about?" I ask her. "How do you know about getting drunk and kissing?"

Imogen giggles at my surprise. "Antonia told us that's what

happens. She spied on her big brother once when he was watching television with his girlfriend, and they drank wine and then they kissed." Then her smile fades and her nostrils flare. "I don't want you to do that with Alex's mummy," she says. "If you do, I will have to tell Mummy."

I turn away from her and carry on walking down the road, my shoulders stiff, my cheeks hot. I'm too confused and angry to speak. Her little footsteps come trotting up behind me. I feel her hand slipping into my palm.

"Don't be angry Daddy," she says. "I won't tell her if you don't want me to."

I turn to her, and can't prevent a harshness from permeating my voice. "You will not use that stick to speak to Mummy any more. Do you hear me, Imogen?"

Her lower lip wobbles, and her eyes become liquid. I'd used her grown-up name – something I hardly ever did.

Then she frees her hand and runs away down the long crescent of pavement.

"Midge!" I call. "Midge, I'm sorry!"

But she doesn't stop running.

I'm wearing my pink shirt – the one still bearing the coffee stain from my night in the park. The collar is fraying – it's at the end of its days, so I don't care if I ruin it. I'm also in my oldest, baddest jeans, a pair of dirty Birkenstock boots and tough, canvas gardening gloves. Thus armoured, I yank open the back door of the derelict house. The one remaining hinge pops, and I fling the door behind me onto the patio with a loud clatter. I'm announcing my presence. Whoever's in here should know the game is up. In my right hand is a sharp kitchen knife. I step inside, take the torch from my pocket and switch it on. There's enough dusty sunlight coming through the windows to see most of the room, but I immediately arrow the bright beam into the corners, illuminating the permanently shadowed spaces. If Jones or the girl are there, I want to see them before they see me. There's no one there though, just rubble, crumbling plaster, exposed brick and broken furniture. The smell is foul – mildew and rotten upholstery, and behind that, faint yet distinct, the sour-sweet stench of old meat.

Carefully, my eyes on swivelling stalks, I move into another room. My soles scrape audibly on the filthy tiles, but I don't care. I want them to know I'm here. There's a dining table in the middle of the room with fancy curved legs, laid as if for a meal with fine crockery on a tablecloth and a tall glass jug with a neck like a swan – all coated in a grey skin of dust. A heavy dresser squats against the wall, ornamental swirls carved deep into its oak, topped by a mottled oval mirror. The walls are densely patterned with mustard wallpaper, blotched with dark green mould and peeling away at the corners. Everywhere there's the smell of cold and musty neglect, and that hint of something sweet and rancid.

In the kitchen next door I find another level of foulness: pans on the counter caked with burned-on grease, stagnant black water in the sink, crusty old cloths, and a fridge and cooker like relics raised from an ancient sunken ship. No one sane or fully human can have lived here in recent times. Wiping dust and sweat from my face, I pass along a short corridor into the entrance hall and flash my torch on a steep hill of carpeted stairs. There's light filtering through from somewhere above where the roof must have partly collapsed to judge from the piles of debris everywhere. Years of rainfall have blackened the carpet and rotted the timbers beneath, causing a deep sag halfway up the staircase. In my long experience of inspecting old houses, I've never seen anything slide this far into ruin.

On the far side of the hallway, someone has splashed words in dark red paint on the faded wallpaper: I WILL COME FOR THE ONE YOU LOVE THE MOST. The message has been slapped on in a careless frenzy, with paint dribbles sliding off the ends of some of the letters. A blind rage impelled the hand that did that, and it shakes me. Who is this ONE? Please let it not be Susan. Next to this graffiti is a half-closed door. The room beyond is dark and the death-stench is, I think, emanating from there. Upstairs is inaccessible. If they're anywhere in this house, they're in that room.

I have to do this – for Imogen even more than for myself. I think of those notes from "Mummy" and have visions of finding a madman in there, scribbling away in a corner. I try to ready myself inside, shaking my limbs and flexing my muscles. They'll be waiting for me – they've heard me coming. I tighten my grip on the knife. Before my fears can take control, I quickly stride across the hallway and kick the door hard with the underside of my foot.

It crashes open with a satisfying loudness and suddenness. The smell is foul, and my ears are filled with the mind-numbing drone of flies. My torch slashes at the darkness, exposing a large desk by a curtained window. With each jerk of my wrist, more is revealed in monochrome flashes: an overturned armchair, a low table, a fireplace, a filthy old bed in the corner, some discarded beer bottles – but no human presence, just that flat insect hum.

Yet I feel watched. As in the park, it's like a creeping sensation in my skin. There's an intelligence in the room, observing my every movement, crouching just out of sight in the shadows. Something instinctive and possibly fearful. The girl?

My torch falls on something lying on the bed. I can't yet

make out what it is, but I can guess from the shape. I take a step closer, and the stench hits me like a faceful of warm, rank meat. I press the back of my knife-holding hand to my nose. There's a human figure lying there. Flies swarm around the blue-white flesh covered with open wounds like glistening black mouths. My whole body feels tight as my torchbeam travels slowly upwards from the feet and legs. Let this not be Susan. Let this not be Susan!

I take in the face, and it's a man, and I can breathe again. He has a grey, dishevelled beard and the cracked, leathery face of a destitute. The poor bastard probably crawled in here for the night and died. His hand is up by his ear, as if trying to listen for something. Two of the fingers are missing.

Something growls – a low, menacing rumble from deep in the shadows next to the bed. I stumble backwards into the door behind me, hitting my head and nearly dropping the torch. Steadying myself, I shine the beam into the gloom to the left of the mattress and it reflects back twin pinpricks of light. A pair of eyes – wary and hostile – watching me. I can make out the furry muzzle, ears and snarling teeth of a dog. It looks feral, angry and scared by my presence. Hastily, I back out of the room and close the door.

17

THURSDAY 16 SEPTEMBER 2004

ROY WAS IMPRESSED with the plumber. Who wouldn't be? He was like a man from the future, towering above him with his six-inch smile and helmet of black hair, and enough blue overall to clad a Christmas tree.

"Your name is Luke?" Roy asked.

"Correct!" beamed the demigod, as if this was the answer to the final question on *Who Wants to be a Millionaire?* "Now what seems to be the problem?"

"My sink is blocked."

"Then take me there."

Roy led him through the entrance hall to the kitchen and the offending sink. The man set down his tool box, knelt on the linoleum floor and athletically inserted his enormous frame, face up, into the pipework.

"I'll leave you to it," said Roy, returning to the sitting room and his laptop.

"What are you writing?" asked the plumber after a moment, his deep voice emerging muffled from inside the cupboard.

"Editing my novel."

"You've written a novel?"

"You bet I have! And now the editor wants changes, which is what I'm working on at the minute. It's a right pain in the tits, if I'm honest."

"You don't like the changes?" The plumber grunted with the effort of unscrewing something.

"It's not that. They're decent changes, and they'll make it a better book. But compared to writing the thing, this is like digging through sludge."

"I've dug through plenty of sludge in my time, and worse," said the plumber.

Roy laughed heartily at this.

"Your P-trap is full of gunk my friend. What the devil have you been pouring down your sink?"

"Stuff I clearly shouldn't have."

"I hope you're more careful with the words you pour into that machine of yours."

Roy laughed again. He decided he liked Luke the plumber.

"What's it about then, your novel?" came the giant's muffled voice.

"It was inspired by something that happened to me last summer. I was in the garden of a manor house belonging to a wealthy friend. He invited me to summer there – me and my girlfriend of the time." The lie flowed and expanded into his mind to become its own highly detailed world – sometimes he forgot he was even doing it. "Something happened one day while I was on my own, walking by the ornamental pond. It scared the living shit out of me. I wrote the first draft in just seven weeks. It was like a long scream. Ninety-six thousand words. Looking back, I'm not sure how I did it. That July and August were blistering hot, as you'll remember. I was in some kind of fever I think – a mix of blind terror and exhilaration. It's hard to describe. I don't remember eating or sleeping very much. My friend thought I was sick. Threatened to call for a doctor. I just called for more paper and ink."

"And your girlfriend?"

"My...? Oh, she couldn't cope. We broke up."

"I'm sorry to hear it... So what happened to you? In the garden?"

"I saw something. Something that couldn't be. A monster I suppose you could call it. It climbed right out of the pond. It fucking spoke to me."

The plumber whacked the last of the gunk into the bin. "I don't believe in monsters in ponds. The only true monsters are human beings, in my opinion."

"That may be true."

"Are you sure this happened? You could have been dreaming? Maybe your friend was right. Maybe you *were* sick."

"Of course that's possible. But the point is, I believed it at the time. Whatever happened or didn't happen, it was the spark for this book."

"Well that's a good thing. And I congratulate you on your achievement."

"Thanks."

Luke finished refitting the P-trap and washed his hands. "I could never imagine writing a book. But my sister Jean, she's the clever one in the family. She LOVES books! I think you two would get along."

"Perhaps we could meet up?" smiled Roy. "The three of us. I don't mean to be forward but – I enjoy talking to you."

The plumber launched a smile big enough to fill the room. "Why yes, perhaps we could. But business first. I will email you my invoice."

18

FRIDAY 13 JULY 2018

IT'S EVENING NOW, and Amy and I are seated opposite each other on red-cushioned seats in the pink chandelier glow of Tabaxa. There are Moorish arches, wall mosaics, linen tablecloths and tuxedoed waiters. A male Arabic singer warbles sentimentally from hidden speakers. The place is about half-full.

We're served with dips – hoummos, labné, grilled aubergine and tahini purée – and pitta bread. We order a bottle of white wine.

Amy studies the menu, her gaze flickering every now and then towards me. Last time I saw those grey eyes of hers, they were dry and empty. Tonight they're quick with nervous amusement. She's put on a little make-up – a casual touch of lipstick and mascara – deliberately casual, perhaps. She's wearing a simple, sleeveless black dress with semi-transparent fabric around the cleavage area. And scent – that pleasant and familiar one I can't quite put a name to. She seems determined, for tonight at least, to banish all signs of her grief. Almost. The long silver scar is visible on her forearm.

I don't tell her about my day when she asks – about finding

the half-eaten body of a tramp and the scary dog, and the hours spent at the police station waiting to give a statement before being quizzed suspiciously about what I'd been doing in a derelict house in the first place, and how I was forced to make up a story about being on a scouting expedition for spare parts to support my DIY habit: door handles, pipework, that sort of thing, maybe even a radiator I could recondition.

I don't say any of this to Amy, not wishing to cast a morbid shadow over our evening before it's even got started. Also, to be honest, I'm struggling to fix some parts of today in my memory. I may have experienced one or two things that I now can't remember. This happens to me occasionally.

Instead, I pretend I had a quiet, normal day, and she says her day was pretty quiet, too.

"Thank you for this," she says. "I don't know what you must think of me."

I lean forward slightly. "To be honest, I'm flattered."

"Why?"

"It's not every day an old geezer like me gets asked out to dinner by a beautiful woman."

"I'm hardly that," she says, blushing a little and returning her attention to the menu. "And you do yourself down. You're not that old. Do you like vegetarian food? The vegetarian mezze is very good here."

Reluctantly, I drop my eyes and examine the choices in front of me. They all look appetizing, typically Mediterranean dishes. Deep-fried pastry parcels filled with mixed cheese and herbs. Grilled halloumi. Vine leaves filled with parsley, mint, tomatoes, onions and rice. "It all sounds fantastic," I say.

"Good," she says, letting the tip of her tongue caress her top lip. It's a gesture I've not seen her make before – thoughtful, and also sensual.

Her behaviour, as well as the effort she's made with her appearance, seems at odds with her mood on the phone last night, and I'm starting to wonder what I'm here for – am I just some friendly company to get her through this terrible anniversary, or something more than that.

"Are you a vegetarian?" I ask.

She shakes her head. "No, but I like this food."

I watch a waiter serve up a tray to another table, containing bowls of colourful vegetables, deep-fried patties and creamy sauces. I get a wave of hunger.

"It feels good being here with you," I say impulsively.

"Oh," she says, looking surprised. "I'm glad."

I take a nerve-stiffening sip of wine and ask her the question that's been wheeling around my mind ever since we got here: "So why am I here tonight?"

She laughs. With Amy, laughter is an autonomic response, seeming to act almost like chaff, deflecting all incoming enquiries.

"Why do you feel the need to ask such direct questions?" she says, her eyes dancing with amusement.

This throws me.

She sees my confusion, and relents. "I needed some company. I'm an attention-seeker. Always have been. And you're a good listener, Ben."

A darker look enters her eyes – a look she's done her best to conceal so far tonight – and she's no longer seeing me. "Right now, I'm a fugitive."

"What do you mean?"

The pain has leached the colour from her face like a fast-acting disease. "I can't tell you what it's like. Whenever I look at my son, or when I go into Steph's room and my mind starts down that track again. Sometimes I just need to forget about all that for a while. I need to fill myself with a different kind of experience."

"I understand that. But don't you have friends or family who can help you?"

"I have a couple of close friends, and they've been great. Family, not so much. My sister and I aren't close. My parents have retired to Spain."

She cradles her wine reflectively, and its ring of pale light dances in the shadows of her cheeks. I listen to her talk about her friends. Ronnie – short, I guess, for Veronica – is hard-headed and practical, great at giving advice and being support-ive. Amber is fun-loving, good for a night out, but can be flighty and irresponsible. It's clear she loves them both, and they've been there for her through the bleakest times. Along with Alex, she says, they saved her life this past year.

Our order – kibbé la'kteen, warak inab, falafel, sambousek and grilled halloumi – arrives, attractively arranged and garnished with salad on little white plates.

She tells me about Alex and the progress he's making, and the setbacks. When she asks about Imogen, I admit that the girl misses her mother, but I don't say anything about the rib, the messages or the incident in the derelict garden. I'm starting to realise that this evening is just as much an escape for me as it is for her. I need a break from myself and my obsessive fears about Mr Jones. Also, I want to impress this woman – I want her to think me sane, at least. I don't want to scare her off with mad tales about spending nights in the local park, or afternoons breaking into derelict houses.

"What do you do when you're not working or being a dad?" Amy asks at one point.

The question throws me. I realise I should have a hobby. That's what's wrong with my life. I should take up the piano.

"Nothing," I admit.

I think of my lapsed gym membership. The silent blue water in the pool. All the unswum lengths.

"Are you happy with your life?"

Dumbly, I shake my head.

"How could you improve it?"

I almost feel like admitting everything then – the mess, the fear, the rib, the sightings of strange girls in the park.

"Do you ever feel lonely?" she asks.

"Sometimes," I say after a moment. My mouth feels dry. I notice my glass is empty, and so is the bottle. I try to catch the eye of a waiter so I can order some more. The waiter sees me and starts towards our table. I glance at Amy and notice she's looking sad again, drawn in upon herself, and I start to wonder whether all these questions weren't really aimed at herself.

With the second bottle, things get easier. A mellow glow settles around us, and it's not just the soft lighting. It's in her cheeks and her eyes, which dance with the same wry amusement as they did when we first arrived.

"I watch a lot of American serials," she admits with a giggle. "Anything with romance or zombies works for me. You know, hearts getting broken or eaten."

I laugh at that one. "Well, I suppose all is fair in love and gore."

She opens her mouth in delight. "Did you just make that up?"

"It's the sort of thing my Dad might have said. He was always mangling his sayings. Like, I don't know, *absence makes the hair grow blonder. Mud is thicker than water. Don't bite off more than you can spew.* Stuff like that."

Amy claps her hands and laughs. "He'd just come out with those things?"

"Yeah, I could never be sure if he meant them, or if it was accidental. When he and Mum were courting, as they called it, and she was hesitating about going all the way with him, he said to her, *Good things come to those who mate*. She said that somehow that was enough to convince her."

As our plates are cleared from the table, we shift minutely closer to each other, our hands within touching distance. Her eyes more often seek out mine, and she gets bolder at holding my gaze as she laughs or smiles. We're enclosed in a bubble-like moment and nothing exists but us and this, right here.

"You remind me a little bit of the lead actor," she says, referring to one of her favourite serials. "You've got the same rugged looks."

"Is that good? Is rugged good?"

She nods. "Rugged *is* good. Are you sure you're not him?"

"Pretty sure... Isn't he the one with the drug problem?"

"No, sex addiction. He has a thing for male prostitutes, so I've heard."

"Well that *must* be me then."

She laughs delightedly, even though she'd virtually gift-wrapped the line for me.

With a dour smile, I run with it. "I really couldn't get through an evening without at least a couple of male prostitutes."

She almost snorts her wine. "I'll bet you couldn't... So how do you cope then with that blonde cowgirl throwing herself at you each week?" – referring to the show's co-star.

"I just close my eyes and think about..."

"About what you got up to last night in the local public convenience?" Amy suggests.

"No."

"What then?" She raises her head almost challengingly, looking me in the eye.

"About you," I tell her.

Her head tilts, a mist of puzzlement obscuring her smile. She sets down her wine. "Are we still joking around here?"

"I don't know. Are we?" I start stroking her hand, just sliding my finger gently over the ridge of her knuckle.

Her fingers entwine themselves tightly in mine. Her eyes are empty, like kissing eyes. Then she blinks, and she's looking at me properly again, her face serious, like someone taking stock of something. She withdraws her hand. "I'm not sure this is a good idea." Her voice is deeper now, more authoritative – it's her audiobook voice. "I'm not saying I don't want to. I asked you out this evening because I like you. But I have to be careful."

"Careful about what?"

"About my motivations. I'm not in a good place. I don't trust myself."

I shake my head, trying but failing to understand.

"Sometimes," she says, "I find I can escape from the pain by losing myself in the arms of someone else. I was feeling very low when I called you. But I can't afford to go with this impulse, not this time. If you were a stranger – but you're not. You're the father of my son's only schoolfriend. Maybe you and I can be friends, too, hopefully. I don't want to do anything that might jeopardise any of that, do you understand?"

"Of course," I say, and I do. But still I can't help feeling disappointed, and my disappointment comes tinged with envy for all the strangers she's been apparently enjoying meaningless sex with. After all I've been through recently, I could have done with some meaningless sex – except that with Amy, I know that it could never be just that.

～

One hour later, I'm sitting on the sofa in Amy's front room. She's in the kitchen sorting out the coffee. She lives in a small 1930s semi with lots of very appealing clutter. There are mismatched cushions and throws, none of which match the rug or the sofa, and family photos and childish drawings crowding the wall. There's an overstuffed bookcase, and yet more books, as well as LP records, Lego bricks and toy cars littering the floor. If I didn't like Amy before – in fact, if I'd never set eyes on her – I think I would like her for this room alone.

She was full of apologies for the mess when we came in, and when I told her it was beautiful, she presumed I must be drunk. But I insisted it was beautiful because it was a reflection of her and Alex, or some such nonsense, which only confirmed her in her presumption.

I'm here for coffee and that, genuinely, is all. It's no euphemism for anything else, as Amy made abundantly clear when she invited me back. Her house happened to lie between mine and the bus-stop, and it made sense for us to have a nightcap here rather than spend more money at the restaurant. Even so, some schoolboyish, alcohol-fuelled part of me is holding out hope that something could still happen between us tonight. I can hear Imogen in my head saying: *But what if you have some wine? You might get drunk and start kissing each other.* This makes me smile, until I remember the threat that followed: *I don't want you to do that. If you do, I will have to tell Mummy.*

Amy hands me my coffee and sits down next to me. It's a small, lime-coloured sofa – the kind that folds out into a bed, no doubt for when her drinking buddy Amber is staying over. The smallness means our knees are almost touching.

"Thank you for tonight," she says. "I really enjoyed myself. I felt I said way too much. Are you hot? It is quite hot, isn't it?"

I murmur that I'm okay, but she's already on her feet,

opening the curtain and pushing the latch on the window. The night breeze is warm and carries with it the residue of a neighbour's barbecue. A lone streetlight gleams on the roof of a car. In the distance a siren wails.

She returns to the sofa, putting a little more distance between us this time. Curling snugly into its interior, she brings her knees up and rests her cup on them, as she probably does every evening in front of the television.

"I think," she says, "I revealed more to you tonight than I normally do to people. It's not just the questions you ask, you're also a very good listener. You don't jump in all the time the way people do. That's so unusual."

"I was interested in what you had to say. You're quite compelling."

"My questions were a deflection," she says. "I'm not used to talking about myself. I don't like it. My job is basically to give a voice to others, whether it's a company advertising its products or an author telling a story. I'm much more comfortable being a ventriloquist."

"What about when you're with your friends?"

"Ronnie does most of the talking when we're together. I'll tell her something vague like how I sometimes feel lonely, and then off she goes giving me fantastic advice that I never follow. I do love her for that. Amber and I get drunk, dance and talk about men. In their own ways, they both help me escape my problems, not confront them."

"Maybe that's the answer," I suggest. "Ignore your problems and hope they go away."

This makes her laugh. With Amy, laughter kind of bubbles out of her like a mountain spring – an endless spring that keeps on giving. "What you're saying is we should sweep it all under the carpet. Keep those skeletons locked firmly in the closet where they belong."

"Exactly. A problem shared is a problem squared, as my old man used to say."

"Ignore your inner child."

"Absolutely! Lock him away. And whatever you do, please don't tell me how you feel."

We're both chuckling now. Her subversive sense of humour is infectious. But then I see something on her mantelpiece, and the laughter immediately dries in my throat.

She twists in her seat to follow my gaze, and she stops laughing, too.

As I get up and move closer to the framed photo, it feels like something slimy, something with pincers, has just crawled into my stomach and made its home there.

I can hear Amy behind me saying: "That's the last photo I have of her."

The girl is standing in a garden. The sun is shining on her neatly brushed dark hair, turning it silver. She's wearing a pink hair band, a pink Hello Kitty T-shirt and blue jeans with the pink butterfly design on the pocket. She has a doll in her hand – a clean doll with clothes on, and a head.

I pick up the photo. Amy says: "It was taken on the morning of 15th July last year – the day she disappeared."

PART II

14 – 17 JULY 2018

19

SATURDAY 14 JULY 2018

THE LIGHT WAKES ME, silver and sharp in my eyes. With a soft grunt, I turn over and smother my face in the bedding, trying to block out the day and the painful realisations that come washing back with it. For a few moments I manage it, floating in a sleepy sea of pure sensation. The light feels pleasantly warm on my shoulder. The sheets are snug and smell of home and sanctuary.

But the bad stuff soon breaks through again – the confusion, guilt and fear.

The girl in Turnwood Park, Mr Jones's minion, is Amy's daughter. I didn't say anything to Amy last night. I couldn't. It was all too much for me to process, let alone articulate. I was quite drunk and in a state of shock, and it would have sounded insane. Even at my most sober and eloquent, it would still have sounded insane. All I could do was compose my face into a normal expression and say something polite and sympathetic about the photo.

She saw through it, saw I was disturbed by something, asked me what was wrong. I should have told her, however crazy it sounded, but I'd spent the whole evening trying to be sane, and I wasn't going to spoil it by blurting out that I thought her daughter was living in a derelict house, forced to do the bidding of the local child molester.

I left soon afterwards. We said goodnight on her doorstep. It was an awkward, unsatisfying ending to our evening. I walked home, and the fresh air must have helped because I slept well last night, with no dreams that I can remember. And now it's Saturday, which is a relief – no rush to get Imogen ready for school. Mum will give her a big, leisurely breakfast. I won't need to roll up there before ten. For now I can lie here and try to make sense of it all, and the thing that's preoccupying me is the photo of Stephanie. It had to be the photo they used in the papers last year when she disappeared, being the most recent one, with her dressed in the clothes she'd been wearing when she vanished. I have no memory of it now, but I must have seen that photo, and maybe it lodged itself in my subconscious. So what I saw then, up on the rise, in the shadowy corner of the park, was that same photo, superimposed on reality. In other words it was a halluci- nation. What could have brought it on? All this talk of Mr Jones no doubt, my fears for Imogen's safety, combined with my revul- sion towards the park.

It makes sense because there's no way Stephanie Parker could really be living in that house. The police and forensic investigators were in there yesterday after I reported the tramp's body. If she *is* living there, they'll find her, or evidence of her, but they won't because she isn't there. It was a hallucination.

For a moment I actually feel relieved about this – and thankful I didn't say anything to Amy last night. Sense prevailed and I managed to shield her from my insanity.

But then I remember that Imogen saw the girl too. She described her exactly. There's no way my daughter can be having the same hallucination as me. Did she really see her, or was she reacting to something I'd said? Could I have said something to her about the girl without realising it? Maybe I've forgotten. I am getting forgetful.

All the same, the coincidence of Imogen's experience puts a tiny question mark on my hallucination theory, as does that filthy doll's head in my desk drawer. These things aren't enough by themselves to convince me to open up to Amy about this. I don't want to imagine the fresh torture it would bring her if it turns out I'm wrong. I'll need more evidence before I say anything. I need a photograph.

It's Saturday afternoon and we're in Turnwood Park. Heat ripples the air and beats down on my head. The unkempt grass, brown and gold, crackles like straw beneath my sandals. Imogen is climbing the big oak tree. I'm keeping watch for Stephanie Parker, my camera phone at the ready. Behind us there's another family – a mother and her two young boys. They're sitting on the bank of the primordial swamp that Mr Raynerson would probably describe as a sylvan pool. The boys are lobbing sticks onto the scummy green surface and watching them float away. They're shouting, and I wish they'd quiet down as the noise may be deterring Stephanie, if she exists, from making an appearance.

Imogen is exerting those playground muscles, pulling herself up with her arms and then swinging her feet up to get her body on top of the next branch. I've learned through long experience not to worry about her, or yell instructions. When a kid is concentrating like that, the last thing they need is an adult distracting them. She crawls along, feeling for the next sturdy branch to grab onto. It's terrifying watching her thin legs wobbling as she finds her footing on the bark. My face and neck are glazed with sweat. I can feel it running in narrow rivulets down my back.

Taking a steadying breath, I force myself to turn away, glancing once more towards the overgrown and shadowy corner of the park where the girl usually materialises. She isn't there. Down by the pond, the boys are using sticks to make holes in the green slime. I check on Imogen again, who's looking less precarious now, seated on a thick branch near the trunk with her legs dangling on either side. She was a bubbly chatterbox when I picked her up earlier, telling me about the banana bread she and Alex had baked the night before and showing me the picture she'd painted of her granny's fish-shaped ashtray. She appeared to have forgiven me for yesterday, or else forgotten our little disagreement, and she didn't ask if I'd kissed Alex's mummy. Thank heaven for the butterfly nature of the eight-year-old mind.

My head is starting to feel heavy – probably the wine I had at lunch. I sit down on the sun-warmed grass dappled by oak shadow. The shouts of the little boys blend serenely with the buzz of insects. My eyes are closing, and my arms folded on my knees make a pillow for my head.

I'm woken by a scream.

Imogen! Oh my God! Oh my God!

I leap to my feet and rush to her little figure lying beneath the tree, bawling her eyes out, her body contorted with pain.

"What is it my poor girl? Did you fall?"

Her mouth is a scream, her eyes staring up at me, her throat making tiny sucking breaths. "Da... Da... Dada..." She's clutching her knee.

"Let me look darling. Let me see."

"N... N... No!"

Gently but firmly, I prise away her hand to see the wound.

"Ohhh!" she cries when she sees the blood.

There's a lot of blood, but it doesn't look too serious, thank God. I take out my handkerchief and press it to the gash, cuddling her through her crying, and whispering to her: "Don't worry my darling. It's only a tiny cut. You'll be fine."

Inwardly I'm cursing myself. How could I fall asleep while my little girl was climbing a tree? What kind of father am I? At the same time I'm puzzled. She's been climbing trees since she was five – been up and down this one at least a dozen times – and never fallen before.

I wait for her hysteria to subside, for her sobs to soften and fall into a steadier rhythm. Then gently I start to probe. "What happened, Midge? What made you fall?"

The memory of this makes her start wailing again – she seems more scared than in pain. She tries to form the words she wants to say. "M... M..."

I wait patiently, rocking her, stroking her hair. "Take your time darling."

"M... M... M-Mi..." Her voice rises to a scream as she wrests back power over her voice. "M-Mister Jones! Mister Jones did it Daddy! He climbed up after me. I was s-so frightened! I crawled away from him, to the very end. And then he shook it really hard. He shook the branch I was on and I... I fell Daddy!" She collapses into renewed fits of wailing and sobbing, and I hold her tight to my chest waiting for the spasms of panic and terror to subside.

My stomach has turned to boiling slurry as I stare up into

the foliage of the great tree. I can't see anyone up there. I'm trembling, tense with fury, but also fear. Those words come back to me, the ones painted on the wall of the derelict house in blood-red paint: I WILL COME FOR THE ONE YOU LOVE THE MOST.

Trying to stay calm, I move her from my lap onto the earth. "Hold this," I tell her, and she clamps her hand onto the handkerchief. Then I rise and go closer, peering straight up the trunk. Nothing. Just a squirrel gnawing on an acorn. Mr Jones, if he was ever there, has gone.

Maybe that family by the pond witnessed something, but when I turn to look, they are no longer there. I return to Imogen, who is curled up on the ground, shivering like a wounded bird.

I remove the blood-soaked handkerchief. The cut, I'm pleased to see, is not too big, but it will need cleaning and bandaging.

"Let's go home," I say, picking her up.

She's so pale and unresisting, almost inert, all the joy and adventure of just moments ago gone out of her. I carry her as I did when she was little, chest to chest. She puts her arms around me and buries her head in my neck. I'm so sorry for her, so angry with myself I want to scream, but what she needs from me now is calm and reassurance.

I'm heading down the slope towards the path when I see it, sticking up out of the dry, earthen bank like a devil's horn – the rib.

"Midge?" I murmur as I glance around. The park is empty apart from us.

"Yes Daddy?" she replies sleepily. She's calmer now.

"Did you bring the stick with you to the park?"

"No Daddy. It's still in my wardrobe."

·   ·   ·

I take her home, where I dab warm water on the wound, washing away the blood. She screams when I spray TCP on it, but only for a second. Quietly, she watches me put on the bandage, wrapping it around and securing it with a safety pin. Then I treat the other, smaller cuts and bruises on her hands and elbow where she tried to break her fall.

"I'm scared Daddy."

I promise her she's safe now. "I'll call the police, and they'll catch him. But first I'll need you to give me a full description. You have to tell me exactly what happened and what he looked like. Do you think you can do that for me?"

She pushes a sweat-soaked strand of hair away from her face. "Yes, I think so."

I don't *want* to involve the police. The last note from Mr Jones warned me against doing that. But Jones has gone too far this time. He's attacked my daughter – could even have killed her.

"I know this is hard," I tell her. "I'm sure you just want to forget all about it. But the police will need to know everything if they're going to catch him. So you have to be brave and try and remember every detail, okay?"

"Okay Daddy."

Imogen tells me that she first became aware of him when she was sitting astride a branch – the position I remembered her being in just before I fell asleep. She looked down and saw him standing beneath the tree, staring up at her through the leaves. He was dressed, she said, very smartly in a suit and tie, and his face and head were covered by a panda mask – not a happy, smiley panda mask, but a serious and slightly scary one. It was made of plastic, she thought, and was all white except for the black ears and black patches around the eyes. "But I couldn't see anything through the eye holes Daddy. It was just like Harriet said: under the mask there's nothing there." For a moment, she stares past me at nothing, frozen by the horror of this thought.

She was so frightened, she said, that at first she couldn't move, couldn't even call out, because she knew this was Mr Jones. Then she remembered that this was the man who had stolen her mummy, and somehow she found her voice and started shouting at him: *Give me back my mummy! Give me back my mummy!* But he didn't say anything, and he didn't stop staring at her through those empty eye holes. After a while she gave up shouting and started to feel scared again. The park was so still and silent. She looked around and couldn't see me or the family by the pond, or even any ducks or squirrels. The whole park was empty, she said, except for her and Mr Jones. And then from somewhere she heard a sound like thunder, she said, and suddenly Mr Jones was clambering up the tree towards her. He climbed really fast and it made her so scared she couldn't move at first. But she forced herself to slide further along the branch, further and further along it to where it got all thin and bendy and couldn't support someone big like Mr Jones. She'd be safe there, she told herself. But when she got there, the branch began to tremble and shake as if she was in an earthquake, and she looked back and saw that Mr Jones was up in the tree, shaking the branch with all his might. She had to cling on for dear life as the world became blurry. She still couldn't see his eyes inside the mask but she had the feeling he was laughing – laughing while he was trying to kill her. At last he shook the branch so hard she lost her grip and fell, and landed in a terrible heap on the ground. She was in such pain, but the pain, she said, was nothing compared to how terrified she was.

Telling the story makes her cry again, and it's a while before I can ask her any further questions, and I have questions because so much of her story makes no sense.

"Midge," I say once she's calmed down again. "I was dozing in the shade of that tree, no more than twenty feet from the trunk. I could look up and see you there on your branch. Your shouting would have woken me for absolute sure. I don't understand how I didn't wake up."

"I don't understand either Daddy."

"The police are going to ask about that," I warn her. "They're going to look for holes in the story, and I'm afraid that's a hole. Another one is my disappearance. You said you looked around at one point and couldn't see me, but I was there, like I said, all along. The police won't understand that. Are you quite sure you didn't see me?"

"*Quite* sure yes. I think that maybe there were some leaves in the way."

I nod. "That may have been it. And then there's Mr Jones's disappearance. How soon after you fell out of the tree did I arrive?"

"About a few seconds."

"A few seconds. Well Mr Jones should still have been up there then, but he wasn't up there when I looked, and I really don't see how he could have climbed down and run away in just a few seconds."

"Are you saying you don't believe me Daddy?" Her eyes are big, her face flushed.

"Of course I believe you Midge. I'm just worried the police won't."

"So what shall we do?" she asks.

"Well the important thing is that we tell the police a story that makes sense. Otherwise they may not believe us and they won't agree to look for Mr Jones, and we wouldn't want that, would we?"

"No." She shakes her head.

"So if it's okay with you, we're going to have to make a few small adjustments to the story you told me, just so that it makes sense."

"What do you mean by adjustments?"

"Small changes."

"Do you mean we have to lie Daddy?"

20

THE STORY I prepare for the police isn't a lie exactly, but I do massage certain elements to make it sound more plausible while at the same time avoid appearing criminally negligent towards my own child. For one thing, I compress the timeframe. There's none of this staring business from Mr Jones, and she doesn't shout down at him. The first she sees of the man, he's already climbing up the tree towards her, and just seconds later, he's shaking the branch and she falls off. All of that activity, in my account, takes less than a minute. Where I add some time in is after she's fallen. In my version, she makes scarcely a whimper, and thus another full minute elapses before I wake up and go to her, giving Mr Jones time to make his escape.

What I'm doing here might seem, at first glance, self-serving and manipulative, but it's actually the opposite. I'm trying to make sure that Imogen is believed, that her story is taken seriously. I'm extracting what must, in fact, be the truth, or close to the truth, of what happened, from an account given to me by a panicked and terrified young girl. This was a serious crime against a child that took place in our local park, and I want to make sure it gets investigated.

Once I've got it all straight in my mind, I call Detective Constable Dave Adler, the officer I reported the dead tramp to yesterday. I tell him the story, my version of it, and when I finish, Adler wants to clarify a few details. "This happened in Turnwood Park you say?"

"Yes."

"At between three and three-thirty this afternoon?"

"That's right."

"*Busy* place, isn't it?"

"Sorry, what do you mean?"

"Well, that house where you reported the dead body yesterday – it backs onto Turnwood Park, doesn't it?"

"Yes, I see what you mean. But I don't see how the two things are connected. The tramp died of natural causes, right?"

"We're still looking into that."

"I just wonder if you can do something about finding this man."

"You say he was wearing a suit and a panda mask?"

"That's right." I tell him about the Mr Jones legend that has grown up at Imogen's school, and about her classmate, Harriet Glass (I found out her last name from Imogen), who was harrassed by this same masked man about a month ago.

"Harrassed?" queries Adler.

"He asked her if she'd go for a walk with him."

"And then?"

"Then she ran away."

"And I suppose there were no witnesses to that incident either?"

"No."

After a few more questions, Adler thanks me and says they'll look into it, but I don't feel reassured by his tone. I realise that what I've given him is pretty thin. All we have on Jones is the panda mask and the suit – nothing about his actual appearance – and only an eight-year-old's word that the incident took place at all. An eight year old who believes that *under the mask there's nothing there.*

"Do let me know if you remember anything else, Mr Rose," Adler says in closing. "Any little detail could be helpful."

He sounds bored, sceptical even. I should tell him about the notes in the pig rib. That would make him sit up and take notice. But I'm worried. The last bone message to Imogen was clear, if unspecific, in its warning: *If [Daddy] tells the police about any of this, Mr Jones will get super angry. He might do something bad to Daddy or even to you.*

"Mr Rose?"

I feel a pressure building behind the eyes, a powerless hatred for this man Jones. What kind of sick monster pretends to be a mother writing to her child with words designed to fill that child with fear? Words of faux childishness – *super angry... something bad* – the vagueness of it is both infantile and terrifying. I hate the power he has over us. I also fear it. I know the police can't do anything when so much of what he's doing to us leaves no physical trace.

The attack on Imogen today was, I realise now, a warning – probably a punishment for showing the note to Geoff Gunnell. So I have to assume Jones knows everything. He's so much more formidable than the sad pervert I originally took him for. Imogen described him as wearing a suit and tie. His notes are carefully crafted to appear written by Susan, not only imitating her handwriting but using terms of endearment she used to use, like *princess*. This is no ordinary man. He even contrived somehow to retrieve that rib from Imogen's wardrobe. I can only assume he's found some other way of communicating with her and told her to replant it in the park. The other possibility – that he gained access to our house – is too scary to contemplate. A man like that would have no difficulty tracking my phone calls. He could even be listening in right now.

"Mr Rose? Are you alright?"

I mustn't say any more to Adler. I've already said far too much. Jones will have his revenge – will do his *something bad* – unless I can quickly rectify my mistake. "Of course," I say, "she may have just imagined the whole thing. In fact I think that's what probably happened. My daughter has a vivid imagination. And this whole Mr Jones thing has made her extremely anxious."

"Are you now saying it didn't happen?" Adler sounds cross, but I don't care.

"I am, and I'm sorry to have wasted your time. I was worried at first, but now I've had a chance to think about it, now that I'm actually telling you about it, I realise how crazy it all sounds. I... Listen, I think she just had a fall and got confused."

I end the call with more fumbling apologies and put away my phone. This will have to be *my* fight. I feel a sudden, vertiginous terror at the prospect, which I try my best to suppress. I'll need to be practical and clear-headed. The first thing I must do is go back to the park and dig up the rib – but I can't leave Imogen alone, not even for ten minutes. She's currently in the playroom curled up on the sofa watching *Shaun the Sheep*, a show she used to watch regularly when she was younger. She's reverted to something nostalgic and safe, like a comfort blanket. I get that. But if I'm going to go out, I'll need to find her some company.

Mum, I know, will be giving an art lesson in her garden studio, as she does every Saturday, so I call up Nita, Aisha's mum. I explain that Imogen had a little accident this afternoon and is feeling a bit out of sorts and would she and Aisha like to come over for a while. Nita says she'd have loved to, but they have family visiting and can't leave them. Next I try Androulla, Theodora's mum, but only get voicemail. I'm running out of options, and curse my own laziness in not getting to know the mums of Imogen's other classmates. And that's when I remember Amy.

She answers on the third ring.

"Hello Ben." Her voice is strong yet mellow, like a BBC radio announcer. It reassures and relaxes me. From the background noises, I'm guessing she's somewhere crowded.

"Hi Amy. Sorry to bother you. Listen, Midge had a little accident today, she fell out of a tree and..."

"Oh my God, is she okay?"

"She's fine, but feeling somewhat fragile. Anyhow, something's come up and I have to pop out for a bit. I know this is asking a lot but is there any way you and Alex could come over and keep her company? I'll cook us all a meal when I get back – as a thank you."

"Wow. Okay. Yes, I'm sure we could manage that. Poor Midge! We're at the shops at the moment. We've bought a candle to light for our little ceremony tomorrow – to mark a year since... you know. And a cheesecake – it was Steph's favourite. We'll just finish up here and be round to yours for around five if that's okay?"

"That sounds great. Thank you so much."

Imogen doesn't respond when I inform her that Alex and his mum are coming over later, she just snuggles deeper into her cushion and continues watching her stop-motion ovine adventures.

With an hour to kill before Amy and Alex arrive, I do some

laundry, adding Imogen's shorts, which have some blood on them, to everything else. I notice my pink shirt in the pile – the one with the frayed collar and the coffee stain – and wonder if it's worth washing. After a second's hesitation, I chuck it in the bin.

The washing machine is doing its thing, and I'm feeling thirsty. I open the fridge and reach for a beer. Then I stop myself. I have to remain clear-headed. So I take out a diet cola instead and go out into the back garden. The heat is physical out here, like a dry weight pressing down on everything. I crack open the can and let the fizzy liquid cool my tongue and throat just before the sweetness hits. It lacks the sour hit of alcohol I so relish, but it's okay.

The lawn is brown and patchy after weeks without rain, clipped brutally short like the scalp of an American army recruit. There are no weeds anywhere. I'm not a gardener in the creative sense. I don't plant things. I see the garden as something wild and chaotic that needs taming. I like nature brought to heel – the sight of neat lawnmower stripes across a summer lawn or a well-ordered flower bed is what gives me pleasure. I hate the fecundity of spring, when everything comes at you at once, growing, leafing, flowering, strangling, sneaking up on you like the brambles that slide in under the fence from Mrs Gilbert's garden. Spring turns me into a swivel-eyed maniac armed with clippers and shears. I also hate the over-abundance of autumn, especially the rotting apples that fall on my decking from Mrs Gilbert's tree, attracting wasps. The one good thing about this drought is that it's killed off all possibility of new growth, leaving our garden looking like a well-manicured, beige desert.

We made a good gardening team, Susan and I, back in the day. I was the destroyer – weeding, mowing, dead-heading and pruning – while she was the grower and nurturer. "As you sow, so shall I reap," I said to her, or as Dad used to say to Mum when she badgered him to do the garden: "As you mow, so shall I sleep."

The garden bloomed under Susan's care. We had snowdrops, anemones, geraniums, lily of the valley, tulips, pansies – and those are just the ones I remember the names of. The only remaining evidence of her handiwork are the big, unkillable shrubs that dot the perimeter.

In the autumn of 2016, when we were going through a tough time, this garden became a kind of refuge for us. Susan was unemployed and stressed, while I was working all hours on a major project in Farringdon involving Crossrail and at the same time dealing with the fallout from the Macey suicide. Earlier that year I'd given evidence in court against a dodgy builder by the name of Thomas Macey. I had no qualms about exposing the cowboy, but that didn't make it any easier when the man took his own life just a few months later. This was followed by a two-month spate of abusive emails and letters directed at me from some anonymous source. He or she blamed my testimony for the suicide, and threatened all sorts of violence as a consequence. The police investigated it, questioned his family and friends, but were unable to identify the culprit.

So I, too, was stressed, not to say neglectful. We barely had a civil word to say to each other, and the house became a cold, barren place. Yet somehow it always felt different in the garden. We cooperated with each other, we made tea, we even shared the odd joke. I remember one September Sunday, the three of us raking leaves into huge piles and loading them by the armful into a wheelbarrow for composting. Imogen, then just five, dug a hole and filled it with water to make mud pies. Susan and I helped her, and we were like a family again.

The next day Susan and I were back to our old, cold, bickering selves. Was it the gardening that brought us together? I thought so at the time, but it might also have been something else. I worked out later, this was around the time Susan joined an extramarital dating site called confidential.com. She may even have met Richard Landry by then and was probably feeling guilty or loved up or both.

Richard Landry. How I despise that name.

Susan's relationship with Landry had been over for eight months by the time of her disappearance. It ended in January 2017 after I confronted her about it – at least that was when the Internet trail between them stopped – yet he was the only person I could think of who she might conceivably have decided to run away with, or who might have kidnapped her. In my most paranoid fantasies, it even occurred to me that he was the source of the disgusting messages I received after the Macey suicide, and killing Susan was his act of vengeance. So the police checked him out and they couldn't find him. They found plenty of Richard Landrys, but none that fitted the profile of the man Susan had been dating. He had no presence on social media. He'd vanished from the Web, as if he'd never existed. It seemed as if Susan had been dating a mirage.

21

SATURDAY 14 JULY 2018

MY PHONE STARTS TO RING. I check the screen to see who's calling. It's Geoff Gunnell.

"Hey Geoff."

"Ben!" he says in his over-friendly, nasal twang. "How goeth thou, me old mucker? *¿cómo estás?* Not so good? Well this might cheer you up. I may just have found something on that note you gave me."

"What have you found?"

"Marks."

"Karl or Groucho?"

"Karl or Groucho," chuckles Geoff. "That's very funny Ben! *Trés drôle!* No, I'm talking here about *pen* marks."

"You mean writing?"

"I mean a faint impression. A light indentation on the paper. This note must have been under another piece of paper, which someone wrote something on, and the marks from their biro have left an impression on this one. *Comprende?* It happens more often than you'd think."

"What does it say?"

"It's hard to make out, but I did a pencil rubbing on it. Looks like a telephone number. Have you got a pen and paper handy?"

"One minute." I return to the kitchen and rip a sheet and grab a pen from the magnetised shopping list pad on the fridge. "Okay, fire away."

"It looks like zero-seven-seven-zero-zero...nine I think, zero-zero-four...five-one. I'm pretty sure that's it."

I read it back to him, and he confirms those are the numbers as far as he can make out.

"Thanks Geoff. This is really helpful."

"No problemo old man. Drink sometime?"

"Definitely. I owe you a pint or three for this."

"How about Tuesday evening?"

"I'll have to see..."

I manage to end the call without actually committing a date to the diary. Standing there by the kitchen counter, I contemplate the numbers I've just scribbled down. I've left a space after the fifth digit, like you would with a phone number, and written like that it does look familiar. Could it be Susan's mobile? I check in my contacts list, and it isn't. I know I should just call it and see who picks up, but I hesitate. When you open a door, it's always best to know what's on the other side. What if Mr Jones answers? What will I say? I don't want to provoke him into another attack. On the other hand, I can't just cower in my house and do nothing. Either I investigate this or I turn the whole thing over to the police.

I press out the numbers. It *is* a phone number, and a live one. I can hear the ringing tone. After the second ring, someone answers. To my complete shock, it's Amy.

"Hi Ben, I'm just unloading the groceries now. We'll be with you in ten minutes..." When I don't immediately reply, she asks if everything's okay.

"I... Yes. Yes. Listen, um, don't worry about coming over."

"Oh. Are you sure? I really don't mind."

"No, it's alright. I've, uh, sorted things so I don't need to, you know, go out. But listen... thanks."

"Well, if you're sure..." She seems confused, which isn't surprising, given how crazy I must sound. She also seems deflated, probably disappointed for Alex, who no doubt got excited at the prospect of another playdate with Imogen so soon after the last one.

"Well give my best to Midge and I guess I'll see you at the school gates on Monday."

"Yes, see you then."

I click off, and try to regain control of my breathing. My response had been panicked, spontaneous, but probably correct. I can't have her come here until I've figured out what's going on. *What the hell is Amy's number doing on a note from Mr Jones? How can they be connected?*

Stephanie. It has to be.

Mr Jones took Stephanie.

I should tell Amy about this... But can I trust her? How inno-cent *is* she? What if she's involved with Jones? He has her number for pity's sake. I need to figure all this out.

My phone starts to ring, startling me. I look at it buzzing in my hand, suddenly fearing it. "Unknown Caller" the screen announces. *Mr Jones?* I feel him closing in, snaking towards me like the bramble beneath Mrs Gilbert's fence.

I rub sweat from my fingers and swipe to answer it. My voice sounds sharp and tight in my ears.

"Ben?" It's a woman speaking. "This is Andy. Theodora's mum."

"Oh!" I breathe out slowly.

"My son Nick walked off with my phone this morning – sorry about that! This is my husband's phone. Nick told me you called earlier. Something about Imogen. Is she okay?"

"Yes. Yes, she's okay. She had a little fall. Would you... Could you and Theo pop by for an hour or so to be with her? I just need to go out."

"Sure. We'll be over in five minutes."

"Thank you."

I put away my phone and stare out of the window at the baking lawn. "The world is normal... the world *is* normal." I murmur this like a mantra under my breath.

Near the back of the lawn, by the steps that lead to the decking, stands the circular trampoline with high protective netting – a birthday present for Imogen a year ago (the last birthday when she still had a mother). As I watch, the vixen creeps out from a hole in the side of the steps. Her red coat flashes momentarily in the sunlight before she slinks into the shade beneath the trampoline. Here she sits, scratching at her fleas.

I think of Amy and her sudden arrival with her son at the start of last term, in the middle of a school year. She's told me quite a lot about her life, but she's never explained to me why she moved here of all places, and why then. Why did she stay on at Imogen's party after all the other parents went home? And of all the kids in his class, why did Alex latch onto Imogen? Was he coached to befriend her by his mother?

Imogen loves watching the foxes. Granny, bless her, told her that the vixen had been sent here by Susan to watch over us, and that she reports back to her regularly. "If you get thin or unhappy, the fox is sure to tell your mummy, so make sure you eat well and keep smiling."

What can I say? Mum will come out with these ridiculous

fantasies, and Imogen keeps swallowing them. I suppose if it results in Imogen eating healthily and staying positive, I can't complain too much.

The doorbell chimes and I go and let in Androulla and Theodora. Andy has brought half a watermelon with her, which I accept with gratitude. I take it into the kitchen and start slicing it while the visitors go and check up on Imogen. Now I wish I'd warned her they were coming instead of Alex and Amy. She might say something tactless. But I'm reassured by the low, friendly murmurs coming from the playroom. I don't think Imogen has committed any serious faux pas.

The watermelon's cold, dark pink flesh is tempting. I pick up a slice and crush it in my mouth, letting its juicy sweetness explode on my tongue. Once it's all sliced up, I put it on a serving plate and take it through to the playroom, together with a roll of kitchen towel.

I find Imogen sitting up in the middle of the sofa with Theo and Androulla seated on either side of her. The TV screen has been paused with the farmer character from Shaun the Sheep caught in mid-tantrum. Imogen's telling them about her fall, about the panda-masked Mr Jones shaking the branch, and they're both listening, slack-jawed.

My whole body tightens. *I am so stupid!* I should have told her that this has to be a secret.

Androulla looks up at me, her round face furrowed with concern. "You've called the police I assume?"

I put the plate down on the low table in front of them. I have a second or two to work out how to play this. Any hesitation and she'll see straight through me. I bite my lip briefly, then force out a big grin. "Have you been making up stories again, Midge? Are you telling them stories about Mr Jones?"

Imogen stares at me, blinking, her lips trembling, tears brimming once more at the corners of her eyes. Maybe more than at any previous moment in my life, I hate myself. I've betrayed my daughter, mocked her, discredited her in front of her friend.

"Anyone for watermelon?" I say with ferocious geniality.

22

SATURDAY 2 OCTOBER 2005

AP: Hi. Is that Roy Parker?

RP: It depends. Do I owe you money?

AP: No, it's nothing like that.

RP: Then are you trying to sell me something? Legal services? Credit cards? Sex? God? I'm not interested. I can't afford it, and the devil's already put a down payment on my soul.

AP: Mr Parker, this is Amy Price. I've been commissioned to narrate the audio version of your book.

RP: Oh bloody hell, that's a relief! I suppose with a voice as nice as yours it was either going to be a sales call or... that you're narrating the audio of my book. Of course, that makes sense. Pleased to make your acquaintance. And sorry for everything I just said. Can we start again?

AP: It's quite alright. I'm the one who should be apologising for disturbing you on your weekend.

RP: I'm a freelance writer. Remind me what a weekend is again? And hell's bells, did I really just accuse you of trying to sell me sex?

AP: Among other things. But it was the God bit I found most objectionable. Do I sound like a Jehovah's Witness to you?

RP: Not at all. And you don't sound like a prostitute either. I think I was just in shock. I don't get many phone calls and when I do they're generally bad news.

AP: Well I hope this one won't be.

RP: We'll see about that shall we? What can I do for you today, Amy?

AP: I was hoping you might be able to help me with the pronunciation of some of the names in the second half of your book – the part when Clare and Richard start investigating monster legends around the world. Specifically –

RP: Can I stop you there?

AP: Of course. What is it?

RP: I don't have a clue about any of that. I'm a creature of the written word, so pronunciation of names isn't something I've ever had to worry about. I'm just happy if I can spell the damn things right. All that monster legend stuff came out of too many hours spent in the British Library.

AP: Oh, but...

RP: But what?

AP: In that interview you gave on local radio a few weeks ago, you said the book was inspired by an experience you had in an Australian billabong, when you saw a bunyip. In the book you call it the... Hang on, I've got it here, the *mi-hi-rung paring-mal*.

RP: That's all true, all true. I had that experience. But the details of the name and stuff came out of a reference book... Hey, do you mind me saying, I'm quite surprised you got the job of reading my book.

AP: Oh, why's that?

RP: Don't get me wrong, I'm sure you'll do a splendacious

job, but the main character in my book is a man, so...

AP: So you thought they'd choose a man to do the reading?

RP: Is that disgustingly sexist?

AP: No, I don't think so. It's the way it usually goes. Men tend to narrate books with male leads, and women narrate ones with female leads. I was quite surprised they gave it to me too. They probably liked my audition tape. I worked ever so hard on it. I wanted the gig, Roy – do you mind if I call you Roy?

RP: Of course not. Why did you want it, Amy?

AP: Because I loved the book!

RP: Really! That's wonderful. By the way, you have no idea how close I came to ignoring this call. I'm now very glad I didn't! So you were saying you loved the book...

AP: I did! I could hear the characters in my head as I read it, and I knew exactly how their voices should sound. Luckily, the publishers agreed.

RP: You could hear the characters? That's fascinating. Usually people say they can *see* the characters.

AP: I've always been more of an audio girl. Growing up, I preferred radio to TV. These days I love listening to podcasts. Have you heard of podcasts?

RP: No, never have. So tell me, how did you imagine the character of Richard?

AP: To me he sounded – *a bit like this.*

RP: Hey that's him to a tee! You know you're not half talented.

AP: Thanks! I just hope I do your book justice.

RP: I'm sure you will. Listen, it was lovely talking with you Amy. Maybe I'll catch you at the launch party next month?

AP: I don't think I'm invited. Unless, if you don't mind, perhaps you could...

RP: Say no more. I'm onto it.

23

SATURDAY 14 JULY 2018

As Theodora takes a slice, Androulla continues to stare at me. She looks suspicious. I meet her eyes, still wearing my terrible grin. "Midge had a little fall," I tell her. "She was climbing a tree and she fell. She hasn't lost her imagination though, right?"

Imogen rises from the sofa, squeezing herself between Androulla's knees and the table, and runs from the room. I can hear her sobs in the entrance hall.

I excuse myself and go to her, try to put my arms around her, but she wriggles away and scoots upstairs. Before I can catch up to her, she slams her bedroom door shut.

I knock. "Midge," I say gently. "I'm so sorry. The police told me to keep this all hush hush. I should have told you. They don't want Mr Jones knowing we're onto him, so we can't tell anyone about this, do you understand?"

No reply.

I open the door. She's lying on the bed, her face almost covered by her pillow. "Go away!" she moans.

"I'm really sorry my darling. I hated doing that to you, but they can't know. No one can know."

I come and sit down on the bed, put my hand on her shoulder, but she shrugs me off. Then she turns on me, all the hurt inside her distorting her face. "You didn't even call the police, did you Daddy? *Did* you?!"

"Of course I did sweetheart. They're looking for him now."

The lies, they come so easily, it scares me.

She was silent a while. Then she mumbled, "I don't want to play with Theodora. I just want to be on my own."

"Okay. I understand."

I leave her and return downstairs.

I apologise to Androulla. "She's in a strange mood today. I think it may be delayed grief over losing her mum. Sometimes these things come out in funny ways."

"That's okay." She seems stiff with me, distrustful.

"I'm sorry for dragging you over here on your Saturday. It turns out Midge just wants to be alone. Sorry Theo. She'll be back to her usual cheery self on Monday, I'm sure of it."

"We can stay a bit longer if you still need to go out," says Androulla.

"That's very kind of you. I'll be as quick as I can. Fifteen minutes tops. Please help yourself to tea, coffee, biscuits, orange juice."

"We'll be fine, Ben. Just do what you have to do."

I grab the trowel from the garden shed and head out into the sweltering street. I feel truly terrible for what I just did to Imogen. But trying to redirect this useless weight of guilt into anger at Jones doesn't work. Right now I can only see my daughter's anguished, tear-filled stare.

Damn this heat! My polo shirt, freshly donned after lunch, has quickly become damp and clingy. Cedarwood Grove, my leafy suburban street, resembles an arid New Mexico highway. I half expect to see tumbleweed rolling between the dusty cars. Turnwood Park is empty, abandoned by all wildlife except, I'm assuming, lizards, rattlesnakes and scorpions. I walk quickly to the oak tree and there, beneath the bank, I see the narrow tip of the rib protruding through the parched white soil of the bank. At first, digging with the trowel is like chipping at concrete. But the soil gradually cracks and then crumbles around the bone and I'm able to tug it out of the ground. Blowing away the dust, I find, at the bottom end, the fine, scrunched edge of a tiny paper scroll. I glance up the bank towards the bushes at the corner of the park and the derelict house. I've no doubt he's watching me, and I don't care. I don't think he cares either. In a way, these messages are aimed not at Imogen, but at me – always have been. What he doesn't want is me sharing them with anyone else. Using my fingernails like tweezers, I coax out the tightly furled scroll. Then I sit down on the bank, in the shade of the oak, and open it. The message is, once again, in blue biro, in the same, casual, looping style characteristic of Susan, but smaller, and it fills both sides.

Dear Midge, (it begins) *I'm living close to you. Sometimes I watch you go to school. But I can't speak to you. Mr Jones won't let me. Mr Jones says Daddy is being naughty. He's sticking his nose into things that aren't his business. But I'm starting to think he's only pretending to be angry with Daddy. I'm starting to think Daddy and Mr Jones are actually secret friends. And they worked together to take me away from you. If I try to leave here, I'm frightened they'll catch me and hurt me really badly. So I must stay where I am. But I so want to see you Midge. I have a plan for how we can meet. Turn over the page to see how...*

. . .

Mr Jones goes out every afternoon at four o'clock. If you come to the wild garden behind the bushes in the top corner of the park on Monday at four o'clock, I'll be waiting there for you. We won't have long. Maybe five minutes at most. But at least we'll be able to see each other and talk. You'll have to skip karate. But you can miss one lesson to see your Mummy, can't you Midge? Just whatever you do, don't tell Daddy about this. If Daddy hears about it, he'll tell Mr Jones and Mr Jones will hurt me. Remember, four o'clock on Monday. I can't wait to see you princess. I love you. Mummy xxx

For a long time I can only sit there on the bank and stare at the paper, blood pounding in my head, my breath a quiet rasp in the silence. I can feel a trickle of sweat on my forehead and let it drip into my eyes. My eyes are blurry and sore. I reach up and wipe them, so I can read it again. The words are just as depraved the second time. What game is he playing now? First I was the blunderer who had to be kept in ignorance. Now I'm the villain and co-conspirator, in league with Mr Jones. He's driving her away from me, tempting her into his lair, into the wild garden. He wants her. His audacity astounds me, but so does his stupidity. Did he not foresee I would read this – that there's no way on God's Earth that I will ever let Imogen anywhere near that garden again?

I can only conclude that this, as I initially suspected, was meant for me, and I should read it as a statement of intent, a demonstration of his ambition. He'll do this, he wants me to think, he'll take Imogen from me, and he'll do so by a means and at a time of his own choosing.

There's a gurgling sound from the swamp. Looking up, I see

a ripple spread across the thick carpet of algae, and I feel a wave of nausea at the thought of life in that cesspit. Then my eye is caught by something glittering at the bottom of the bank. It looks like spinning glass. Looking closer, I see, on the path, a dragonfly and a hornet locked in a deadly embrace. The dragonfly's wings flutter madly as its legs grapple with the giant wasp, and its long, thin, colourful abdomen lies bent on the tarmac. The hornet is feeding on its neck, while injecting it with sting after sting, until the dragonfly's wings flap only weakly and then fall still.

24

I CRUSH the note into a tight ball and shove it in my pocket, planning to destroy it later. I no longer care about its value as evidence, only that Imogen must never see it. Then I look at the pig bone in my hand – Imogen's stick. In a fit of anger, I grip it tightly at both ends and break it in two. It makes a satisfyingly dry crack. I hurl the two halves into the swamp. They land with soft plops on the dense green mat and float there. There will be no more messages, no more secret communications. I will go to the garden at four o'clock on Monday and heaven help Mr Jones when I find him.

I walk out of the park and into Oakfield Crescent, and barge straight into someone coming the other way. Jolted sharply out of my thoughts, I mumble an apology before hurrying on. As I open the front door of my house, I catch Androulla coming down the stairs. This immediately causes me to tense up. "What's going on?" I ask, wiping sweat from my face with the back of my wrist.

She stops about five steps from the bottom. Her demeanour is smooth, unruffled. "I wanted to speak with Midge alone," she says. "She told me everything. Why did you tell her to keep her story a secret?"

I know inside that I'm not calm, that I shouldn't react – I'm overheated, and still in shock from that note – but I can't help myself. "You really shouldn't have done that!" I yell at her. "This is none of your business!"

"I'm sorry," says Androulla in a tone that tells me she absolutely isn't, "but if someone attacked your daughter in a public park, that *is* my business. If there's a crazy person going around in a panda mask hurting children, that's *everyone's* business and you need to alert the police. If you won't, then I will."

"You shouldn't," I say more quietly and through gritted teeth. "You really shouldn't. If you do, you'll regret it. We'll all regret it."

Her smooth round face seems to inflate, like a sail caught by a strong breeze. "Is that supposed to be some sort of threat?"

"No. Just a warning."

She hurries down the remaining steps, calling for her daughter. "Theo! Come along now, we're leaving!" Her voice is high and shrill. Theodora, recognising its tone and alarmed by it, immediately trots out of the playroom into the entrance hall. Without a glance in my direction, Androulla squeezes Theo's shoes onto her feet and opens the front door. She turns and looks at me with a baffled shake of the head as if she's caught me in the middle of some despicable act – as if I myself was the panda-masked branch-shaker. Then she ushers her daughter out of the door and leaves.

I feel a tightness in my throat that spreads through my neck and skull. I can't let her do this. Mr Jones will be angry. He'll think I told her, and then he'll come after Imogen. Those words on the wall flash at me like a neon sign, *I WILL COME FOR THE ONE YOU LOVE THE MOST*. I reach towards the door, wanting to open it, wanting to go after her, but a dizziness makes me stagger. My head feels heavy with clouds.

"Daddy! Daddy! Wake up! I'm hungry."

I open my eyes. I'm in the entrance hall, sitting on the floor by the shoe rack. Imogen is standing over me, shaking my shoulder.

"Hey sweetie," I say croakily. "What's the time?"

"Tea time," she says. "I've been very patient, but I can't wait any longer because now I'm just too hungry."

I glance at my watch. It's nearly half past seven. *What the hell just happened? Where did my mind go for the last two hours?*

I stretch and stand up, staggering slightly so that I have to use the wall for support. "Sorry Midge. Daddy must have been tired. What would you like to eat?"

"Egg-fried rice with cucumber."

"Okay. Let's see what I can rustle up."

We head for the kitchen. The back door is still open from earlier when I went into the garden. The cooler evening air is pleasant, so I leave it. After putting the kettle on, I check the fridge. There are a couple of eggs. The cucumber is nearly finished but there's enough for three or four slices, which is the most she'll ever eat anyway.

Imogen is sitting at the dining table by the open door, reading *How To Train Your Dragon* by Cressida Cowell. Her dark blonde hair, free of its weekday ponytail, curls messily around her face. Tufts of it are ruffled by the breeze. She seems calm now. I don't know if she's forgiven me – I doubt it. But she craves peace above all right now, and food, and I'm only too eager to offer her both. Imogen has always hated arguments and fighting.

When Susan and I quarrelled, she'd cry and run to her room. And her laughter tended to be what coaxed us to patch things up. We'd hear the uncontainable delight of that sound emanating from the playroom or the garden, and we'd be drawn to it from our separate parts of the house like shadow-dwellers beguiled by the sun.

The boiled kettle water is poured into the pan. Once it's bubbling I shake in a load of arborio rice – too much, but I know I can give her the rest tomorrow for lunch. Imogen can never have enough rice. I feel a deep well of love for my daughter, and a determination to protect her from all the madness that's currently encircling us. Mr Jones, Susan, Amy, Androulla. Each, in their own way, poses a threat. In the end it's just me and Midge against the world. I'm the only one she can really trust.

I wonder what happened to me just now in the entrance hall. A two-hour blackout? That's worrying. Should I go and see a doctor? I don't feel ill. In fact I feel fine now that the last of the grogginess has worn off. I can only assume it was a combination of heat stroke and stress from Imogen's accident and my clashes with her and Androulla, not to mention reading that awful message. I feel in my pocket for the scrunched up paper. It's still there, nestling at the bottom. I'll throw it away later.

When the rice feels soft between my teeth, I strain it and pour half into a frying pan where it sizzles in the hot oil. I crack an egg into it and mix it up in the fluffy, sticky grains.

"Daddy?"

"What is it sweetie?"

"Will the police find Mr Jones?"

"I'm sure they will."

"And will they find Mummy?"

I dodge this one by ignoring it, scooping the eggy rice onto a plate next to the slices of cucumber and serving it up. "I miss your mother, Midge," I tell her over the sound of water filling up a glass. "I miss her every day. I want her back, just like you do. But we can't always get what we want in life. The important thing, my darling, is that you have me, and I have you. We've got each other and nothing's going to change that."

I place the glass on the table next to her food, which she's already tucking into. She eats while I tidy up, wrapping and refrigerating the remains of Androulla's watermelon and the unused rice, loading the dishwasher. It's been an awful day, one of the worst I can remember since Susan disappeared. Even so, it's left me with an odd sort of hope. Jones has shown his hand today, shown what he's capable of, and now I have a better idea of what I'm up against. I also know I can't trust anyone but myself. And that, in a way, is liberating.

25

WEDNESDAY 19 OCTOBER 2011

ROY SNEAKED into Ye Olde Pear Tree in the furtive manner of a politician entering a brothel. He slid into the armchair near the brick hearth. His beer was already waiting for him on the small, circular, oak table. He picked it up and took a deep swallow, relishing the rich, malty flavour. The brother and sister, seated opposite, watched him, their expressions quite dissimilar in the red light from the embers. Compassion furrowed the face of Luke. His older sister Jean, on the other hand, appeared dispassionate and curious.

"I shouldn't be here," Roy said. "If Amy knew..."

"Amy doesn't need to know," said Jean, her voice as sharp as a bitten crisp.

"A man needs a break once in a while," said Luke. "You'll be a better dad for it."

Roy glowered. "What pair of bloody geniuses decided to have two kids one year apart. Oh wait, it was us!"

"You didn't decide," smiled Luke. "It was a happy accident. And now you have two beautiful, bouncing babies."

"What we have are two insatiable little psychopaths. If they don't need cleaning at one end, they need feeding at the other. The boy's got colic and nappy rash. The girl's always putting filthy stuff from the floor into her mouth. They wake up at all hours, crying out of hunger, teething pains or just to piss me off."

"It can't all be bad," said Luke. "There are good times, too, right? Like when they smile at you and when they curl their little hand around your finger."

"I would sell a kidney for a decent night's kip," muttered Roy.

"How's the new book going?" asked Jean.

Roy forced a laugh. "That's a joke, right? You remember my agent dropped me after the failure of my first one? So these days Amy refers to the new novel as my 'hobby'. She says I should focus on paid work because we need the money. Any writing I do is basically theft. I'm stealing time out of my working day, and hence food out of my babies' mouths. She doesn't say that, but that's what she's thinking." He took another long pull of his beer. "Who am I kidding anyway? I'm not a writer. Not any more."

"It doesn't have to be this way," said Jean.

Roy tilted his head and stared at her, a hank of fringe flopped over one eye. "You what?"

"You always have a choice, Roy, about how you want to live."

"Oh right, yeah. Just walk out on my responsibilities you mean?"

Jean's expression didn't waver. "It's always an option. You could go and spend some time in your friend's castle, for example. You might find some inspiration. We could even come too, if you like."

Roy flicked his head, as if trying to dislodge a fly. "I've lost touch with him."

"Roy would never do that," said Luke, slurping the last of his pint. "You're a family man at heart, aren't you Roy?"

"A family man," murmured Roy absently, his eyes still lingering on Jean. His mind began to drift. He thought about that summer eight years ago. A lifetime ago. The blind terror he felt when he saw what he thought he saw – what he *did* see! – coming out of that swamp. The exhilaration of the feverish weeks that followed in his uncle's kitchen. Terror and exhilaration of such intensity that all he had experienced since seemed like a vanilla daydream.

He snapped out of it and got to his feet. "I'll get another round in. Then I have to head back."

26

SUNDAY 15 JULY 2018

THERE ARE jobs I ought to do around the house, like fixing the bolt on the side alley gate and doing something about the noisy pipes in the basement, but I don't want to be inside today. I want to go out somewhere with Imogen. I feel very strongly that we both need a change of scene. I also want to show old Jonesie that we're fine, we're happy, and he's not going to destroy us. Tomorrow at four o'clock, after dropping Imogen at karate, I'll go over to the wild garden and meet with him, or he can play the coward and stay away and that's fine, too. Either way, I'll get the measure of him and he'll get the measure of me.

After Imogen went to bed last night, I read the note one more time before burning it in the garden. It troubles me that he's captured Susan's style so well – that slightly infantile tone she always used to adopt when speaking to Imogen – and that he's sufficiently aware of Imogen's schedule to know the time of her karate class. His deep familiarity with her life terrifies me, and I know that's what he wants. He wants me to believe that he's watching us, that he has power over us. This is why I have to try and act normally and without fear – and why it's important I take Imogen on an outing today. I don't care where we go, so long as it's somewhere fun and distracting.

When I consult her for ideas at breakfast, she immediately says Paramount Wildlife Park. The last time we went there was two summers ago, when we were a trio. It was a pretty magical day, at least that's my recollection of it, despite the crowds and the queues. I hadn't consciously avoided going back there since Susan disappeared, but now Imogen suggests it, the idea of a return visit feels oddly inappropriate, even shameful, like stepping on a memory. It also feels like exactly the right thing to do.

So I book tickets online and we brush our teeth. Imogen spends a typical age choosing what T-shirt to team with her grey leggings, eventually opting for the white one with the rainbow design. Then we climb into our silver Renault Megane, and both let out a sigh at the already unbreathable heat. The electrics are screwed and only the front passenger's window still opens. Still, departing Halsted, and joining the A108 heading out of London, feels liberating. We've spent far too long festering in the confines of the Forest Estate. After leaving the main road, we drive along a tediously long and twisting road, with Imogen constantly asking if we're nearly there yet, before we eventually arrive at the grand arch of Paramount Park, with its cheerful, anthropomorphic tiger, elephant and giraffe.

I park the car and we get out, and Imogen runs on ahead, with only a slight limp differentiating her from the dozen or so other kids converging on the entrance. Who would have guessed that eighteen hours earlier she'd been shaken out of a tree by a madman in a panda mask?

The first place we visit, almost as a religious rite, is the petting zoo. She takes her seat in a big circle with the other children. With pride I observe her waiting patiently to be handed an infant rabbit. Her eyes, riveted on the animals in other children's laps, are the only hint of her mounting excitement. Finally, an assistant hands her a small grey rabbit, and she strokes its long ears with such instinctive tenderness that the baby lagomorph almost instantly falls asleep. Not so the poor creatures in some of the other children's rougher, more vigorous hands. I've seen this before, her natural way with animals – it's something I remember Susan and I both remarking on last time we were here. An almost physical pang arrives with the memory. I want so much to be able to share this moment with Susan. Instead I take photos and smile and wave whenever Midge catches my eye.

Outside the petting zoo, a lady wearing a large badge and a bright smile is collecting money to save the red squirrel. Imogen asks if she can put some money in the collection bucket, but I don't have any change and, still smarting from the cost of the entry ticket, would prefer not to contribute a whole fiver. I hurry her on past with a cheery, "Let's go see the animals!"

Imogen enjoys pointing out the zebras and tapirs, the camels and the deer. I read out the signs and tell her their names and history. She barely listens, but she's happy and distracted and it feels like a weight's been lifted from both of us, even if it's only temporary. She wants to see the big cats, literally drags me there. The enclosures look too small to my eyes and the beasts we can see appear apathetic or restless. The white lion has flies in its eyes; the tiger paces back and forth with manic regularity by our viewing window. I see a bone on the concrete – pink with the remains of flesh, and I think of the dry snap of the rib yesterday.

Imogen leads us to the reptile house, sited in a replica of a South-East Asian temple, and we move from the baking brightness of an English heatwave to the sultry gloom of a rainforest understorey. A giant coiled snake in a glass box shows all the liveliness of a heap of car tyres. A bearded dragon watches us, its mouth agape, tongue flickering, its empty black eye staring at me like a primordial psychopath. Mammals, I get. But with these things, the gap between us and them is simply too wide to be bridged. I don't even want to know their state of mind, just as I don't want to know what slithers at the bottom of the swamp in Turnwood Park.

There are non-reptiles there, too: molluscs and amphibians that move and breathe through their own slime; eight-leggers with fur; armoured six-leggers that hiss. I think of the monstrous centipede fighting its way out of a doll's eye, and wonder again at the grotesque fecundity of life. Imogen laps it all up, dashing from one glass box to another. I make friends with a wrinkled tortoise that looks at least a thousand years old.

We eat lunch at the Safari Cafe, at a table by the window. Imogen has a lunchbox containing a cheese sarnie, crisps, a granny smith apple and an orange juice. I have a just-about-edible tuna nicoise. Imogen's excitedly reciting facts she's picked up. Tarantulas, I learn, can temporarily blind you if they flick their hairs in your eyes. Cockroaches can apparently survive being frozen and microwaved.

"That'll be your tea tonight then Midge!"

"Earrgghhh!" She pushes me away.

We're both giggling, and I'm thinking this is it. This is us. We're indestructible, like cockroaches. The world can do what it likes, but we'll survive. Then, right out of the blue, she says: "Do you know Mr Jones, Daddy?"

"Hm?"

"Mr Jones. Mummy says you know him. She says you two are friends."

I say nothing, just slowly put down my plastic fork and look at her. She's eating her crisps, selecting each one with care as one might a tray of individually prepared delicacies, before placing it in her mouth.

I'm thinking about my actions yesterday – what I actually did. I screwed up that message into a tiny ball, placed it deep inside my pocket, then last night I burned it. There's no way Imogen could have known about it or seen it. There were the two missing hours of course, when I was lying unconscious in the entrance hall, but what could have induced her to search me? And why, if she found the note, did she screw it up again and return it to my pocket?

"How do you know she said that?" I quietly ask.

"She wrote to me again," says Imogen, carefully choosing another crisp.

The cafe is busy and its noises fill the air around us: kids running about, chairs scraping, the loud bark of an adult telling off a child. Outside the window: a thump of pigeon wings. None of it's real though. It doesn't feel like we've gone anywhere today. We're back there in the little park at the end of our road, just me and Imogen. I can almost smell the swamp.

"How did she write to you Midge?"

"In a letter. I found it in my stick this morning."

"In your *stick*? This *morning*?"

"Yes."

"And where is your stick?"

She raises her head from her crisps and looks at me in a puzzled sort of way. A lock of honey-blond hair has fallen across her forehead. In the sunlight I can see auburn in there – hints of Susan.

"It's in my wardrobe Daddy, where I put it."

Another rib. Another note. So Jones was taking no chances. He wanted to make sure the message got to her, one way or another. But how did he get into the house? This thought frightens me more than any other.

I swallow and lick my lips, trying to suppress any sign of fear or dismay. "Midge, if your mother thinks that, she's wrong. I don't know Mr Jones and he's not my friend."

Imogen nodded once and went back to her crisps.

"Do you have the letter?" I ask her. "Can I see it?"

She shakes her head. "It's private Daddy. It's just between me and Mummy."

"The thing is, Midge, and I know we've spoken about this before, but I don't think it's Mummy who's writing to you..."

"It *is* Mummy!"

"And whatever she's saying to you, whatever she's asking you to do, I don't think you should do it because it's not her and..."

"It *is* her!"

Her eyes are as hard as buttons. Her jaw is sticking out, just like Susan's used to during arguments.

I stop, realising I'm doing Jones's work for him, driving her away from me.

"Okay," I relent. "Maybe it *is* her, but you can't be sure she's not being forced to write those letters. Mr Jones could be forcing her to write those words. You shouldn't necessarily trust what she's saying to you."

Her expression sags a little and her lower lip trembles. I feel like a vandal kicking in her carefully constructed sandcastle.

After lunch, we go and see the monkeys, the owls and parakeets, the pigs and the goats. Imogen doesn't say much. I try imitating the pig, but get no response. In the gift shop, I buy her a soft toy monkey just to see her smile again. She thanks me and hugs it tightly, but her face remains solemn. As we're heading out, we see the lady collecting for the red squirrel. I have change now and offer Imogen a pound coin to put in the bucket, but she doesn't take it. She just walks right past the lady, still cuddling her monkey.

I run to catch up. "Don't you want to help save the red squirrel?" I ask her.

"The lady could be lying," she mutters.

Some time later, we're driving along Forest Vale, a few minutes from home, when Imogen points out of the window and shouts: "Look, there's Theodora!"

I glance to my left and see her friend speeding her scooter along the pavement towards her house. Her mother is ahead of her, just approaching their front gate. I wonder if she's called the police yet, and it occurs to me, this could be my chance to talk her out of it. I pull up closer to the kerb, open my door (the window-opening mechanism being broken) and call out: "Hi Andy!"

She stops and looks at me, her body straightening in surprise.

"I just wanted to say sorry – about yesterday."

Without uttering a word in response, Androulla turns away, unlatches the gate and quickly ushers her daughter through it before hurrying down the path. My mouth is agape, just like the bearded dragon. I watch as she lets them both into the house, closing the door behind her.

"Why didn't Theo's mummy speak to you Daddy?"

"I don't know sweetie."

"Is she still cross with you for lying about what happened to me yesterday?"

I slam the car door, put the car back in gear and resume our journey home. "Maybe."

"Does this mean Theo can't be my friend any more?"

I glance at her and force a smile. "No, of course it doesn't."

It's early evening. Imogen is in the back garden, practising her somersaults on the trampoline. Taking my chance, I go into her room. Sure enough, I find the rib still there on the shelf in her wardrobe. The note isn't in the hollowed-out section – she must have hidden it somewhere.

The new toy monkey is on her bed, propped up on the pillow next to her other favourite, 'Giraffee', who is actually a dinosaur with a long neck, but I've never had the heart to tell her. The monkey's name is 'Bananas', christened on the drive home. I look for the note under her bed and on her little desk and in other nooks and crannies of her room, until I feel too guilty and ashamed to carry on.

When I come downstairs, Imogen's seated on the living room sofa watching *How To Train Your Dragon*. I cook us both vegetarian burgers, chips and peas. It doesn't feel appropriate, after our day at Paramount Wildlife Park, to eat meat.

After her bath, I put a new bandage on Imogen's knee. It's already healing well. She climbs into bed, cuddling Giraffee and Bananas, and I read her a chapter from *The House at Pooh Corner*, In Which It Is Shown That Tiggers Don't Climb Trees. She doesn't seem interested in talking about the weekend's events, not even her own misadventure in a tree, and I'm fine with that.

Downstairs, I turn to Netflix for something to distract me. I try a couple of new series and exit both after less than three minutes. I can hear the pipes settling in the basement. It sounds like the dull vibrato of old hinges. The weekend – Saturday, mainly – feels in retrospect like a sequence of small and large shocks, and the one I keep coming back to, even more than Imogen's fall, is finding Amy's number on the note from Jones. That's the one that keeps ringing like a cracked bell in my head. The coincidence is simply too great, especially after discovering just the night before that the girl I keep seeing in the park is her daughter. It gets me wondering who Amy really is. It feels like I'm only seeing a small part of a much bigger picture, much as I feel when beginning my investigations into a hard-to-explain crack in a wall, but with none of the usual anticipatory excitement, only a kind of deep-in-the-bones dread.

27

MONDAY 16 JULY 2018

IMOGEN GRUMBLES when I switch off the television before Peppa Pig comes on, and again when I whisk away her cereal bowl before she's quite finished. We have a fight over her ponytail – she wants a high one and I do a low one, and I refuse to change it because we're late.

"We're not late," she says.

It's a fair point, but what I can't tell her is that I want to get to school early so we don't run into Amy.

"Daddy has a busy day," I tell her. "Now stop whining and get your shoes on."

She takes an age over her shoes, and I end up kneeling on the floor and doing them for her.

Eventually, I get her out of the house. It's 8.20 and already warm, but I sense a change in the weather coming. The light is steel-bright, our shadows sharply stencilled on the pavement. Now and then a flurry of cooler air flaps at my shirt collar. The clouds are scrappy, like shreds of wool caught on barbed wire.

"I'll pick you up at three o'clock."

"Like you do every day," she says, hurrying to keep up with my big strides.

"Yes. Don't go home with anyone else, okay? Whoever they say they are."

She doesn't reply.

"Okay Midge?"

"Okay Daddy."

She stops to stroke Sid, who is in his usual place on the wall, like a fluffy ginger sentinel guarding the entrance to the park. I see the passing clouds reflected in his eyes. "We have to go Midge."

In Turnwood Park I catch her glancing up towards the gloomy corner of the park where the bushes conceal the derelict garden. She slows down again, and I take her hand and tug her forwards.

As we approach the green gates of East Halsted Primary School, I spot Androulla returning from dropping off Theo. I'm guessing she must have had the same idea of going in early, in her case to avoid *me*. I try to make friendly eye-contact as we approach each other, but she seems captivated by something in the near distance – a lamppost maybe.

"Morning Andy."

Not a glimmer from her, except for a slight but definite quickening of pace as she passes me. It's going to get seriously irritating if she decides to keep this up. I wonder if she's called the police yet.

After dropping off Imogen, I head back home by a different route, via Forest Dale, partly to avoid Amy and Alex coming the other way, but also because this will take me past Androulla's house. I don't want to be bothered with her – I have enough to deal with – but her rudeness, the way she's snubbed me twice now, has got under my skin. She might find it harder to ignore me when I'm on her doorstep.

Hers is a big house of dark brown, rustic bricks, a tiled bay, a garage tucked under the gable of a steep roof and a solid oak front door. She takes an age answering, as if, having guessed who it is, hopes I'll give up and go away. I press the bell button again. Eventually she opens the door. I glimpse a spacious entrance hall gleaming with ornaments, chandelier crystal prisms and marble tiles. Her husband's something in the City. A few years ago they hired a cricket club pavilion for Androulla's fortieth and invited the parents of every child in Theo's class. They hired a West End crooner and a DJ, and laid on platters of delicious Greek food and a free bar. She and Susan were good friends. They went on a jaunt to New York once. Susan wanted to hit the museums, but Androulla was only interested in one thing. She brought along empty suitcases, which she proceeded to fill with the clothes she purchased on Fifth Avenue.

This doorstep is as far as I've ever been, dropping off or picking up Imogen from parties and playdates. Androulla's friendship has never extended to me.

"Hi Ben," she says with an audible sigh. Beneath the irritation, she looks maybe just a little unnerved.

I decide to play it reasonable, conciliatory. "Andy, listen, I'm sorry to disturb you, but I feel we need to talk about yesterday. I may have said some things I shouldn't have. Of course you should call the police if you want to. I just don't think it's necessary. I think Midge exaggerated what happened."

"I agree," she says.

This stops me. I take a breath. "Sorry, what?"

"I thought about it later," she says, "and decided you must be right. You know Midge better than anyone and if you think she made it up then she probably did. I didn't call the police."

"Oh." I take a step back, missing my footing on the doorstep, so my foot lands with a jolt on the path. "Okay, well in that case, that's great. I'm glad we're in agreement."

Her composure has returned, and with it, a blankness. Her face is smooth, round, impermeable.

"Was there anything else?" she asks.

"No."

"Well then would you mind? I have to get ready for a gym session. Bye Ben."

She closes the door.

"Bye," I say to the doorknocker.

I should feel relieved, but I'm left confused and uncertain. There was nothing about that encounter that I found remotely reassuring. She agreed with me – at least her mouth did – but she spoke like a Stepford Wife, like someone with a gun pointing to their head. I think she just wanted to get rid of me, and said anything she needed to to do that. Something's happened to her since yesterday. Did the police tell her to steer clear of me or, if necessary, to placate me? Why would they do that? Am I under suspicion? For what? The dead tramp? The non-kidnap of Harriet Glass? What other crimes have been committed lately? Do they suddenly, after ten months, think I killed Susan?

Back at home, I wash up the breakfast things, tidy the kitchen, clean the toilet and tidy away the toys in the living room. When the house is restored to a semblance of order, I go into my study and seat myself at my computer. At one point I catch myself staring at a photo of Susan on my wall. It was from a weekend in Prague early in our marriage. She's standing on the Charles Bridge, a full-beam, effortless smile filling her face. *I can't* wait *till Devon.*

I turn back to the screen. It's 11.34. The time is ticking extremely slowly towards four o'clock.

Of course Mr Jones can't possibly expect me to allow Imogen to go anywhere near the wild garden. He must know it'll be me he'll find there if it's anyone. So what's his game? Does he want to kidnap or kill me? Let him try.

Susan goes on smiling from the wall. I was sitting here in this very chair on 9 September last year when I heard the front door slam. It was the last physical impression she ever made on my senses. I twist open the Venetian blinds and peer out the window. If I'd done this then, looked out of this window, watched her leave, what would I have seen? Would I have been able to discern anything at all in the way she walked down the path and out the gate?

Clouds are mustering in great platoons, covering half the sky. They look darker than anything I've seen in weeks, thickening like coils of muscle. I hope what comes won't be a brief shower. I want it Biblical – cleansing.

I go downstairs and boil up some spaghetti and make a sauce of chopped and fried courgettes, mushrooms, garlic and red pesto. I pour myself a glass of red wine. I'm not a heavy drinker, but I'm becoming a regular one: a glass at lunchtime and maybe another couple in the evening. It's okay though – it feels moderate, under control. The collapse in my hallway yesterday was weird, but no cause for alarm – most likely just a temporary effect of heat and stress.

After lunch I go for a walk. The blustery breeze is like a fresh facecloth after a long, sticky night. Avoiding Turnwood Park, Forest Vale and Daintree Gardens (Amy's neck of the woods), I head down Greenwood Lane and do a circuit of Holt Park. It's amazing how a change in the weather can help one's confidence. I feel ready for anything. *Bring it on*, I whisper to the clouds.

At five to three, I'm in the playground alongside the other parents, mostly mums, waiting for the classroom doors to open and our demob-happy darlings to race out to meet us. The rain is holding off for now, but the sky is fully grey with dark and silver patches, and now I fancy I feel a fleck of moisture on my arm, a warning gust of wind.

A moment later, someone touches my elbow, and I catch a whiff of something sweet and delicate. I recognise that scent – Susan used to wear it – and I still can't remember what it's called.

"Hi Ben."

It's not Susan, of course. It's Amy.

I want to pull away, but something in her expression holds me. She looks like a cat shielding a wound.

"Is Midge okay? I was worried after your call on Saturday. And then I didn't see you this morning."

Her voice is low and intense. There are wrinkles of concern around her eyes. But she also seems on the defensive. I get the impression she's losing faith in the world, or maybe just in me, though she's trying not to show it. I wish with a sudden and surprising urgency that it could be Friday evening again, in her front room, before I saw the photograph of Stephanie, before the call from Geoff Gunnell. If I could have that time again, I'm sure I'd kiss her.

"Midge is fine," I tell her. "I'm sorry I bothered you."

"It's okay. We're always here to help. Actually..." She gives a strange sort of laugh. "Alex and I happened to be passing your house a little while after you called and we saw Androulla and Theo going in." Seeing me take a breath, she hurries on. "Don't worry, I don't mind. I know kids. She probably wanted to see Theo because she's known her longer. Please don't feel bad. Alex wasn't bothered, or didn't seem to be. I just wanted to make sure she was okay, that's all... It was good, by the way. It went well."

"What did, sorry?"

"Our little ceremony yesterday – to mark a year since Steph went."

"Oh sorry, yes, I meant to ask you about that."

"I found a nice poem to read, and Alex drew a lovely picture of Steph in the Invisible World."

"I'm so glad."

The children have started emerging from their classrooms, an eruption of prepubescent energy barely constrained by the barking of teachers.

"Maybe see you at karate later?" says Amy, as we part.

"Oh, is Alex...?"

"Just starting, yes."

She gives me a bright, nervy smile. I watch her go to meet Alex, who is alone as usual. Imogen is chatting with Aisha. Theodora, I notice, is now keeping the company of Antonia and Kate. I hope my stand-off with her mother hasn't damaged her friendship with Imogen.

"How was school, Midge?" I ask as we start up the long sweep of Leafy Wood Lane.

"It was okay." She stops to salute a lonely magpie. "One for sorrow."

"Indeed. And what about Theo? Is everything okay between you two?"

"Yup." She looks at her hand. "Is it going to rain Daddy?"

The sky is a mixed picture – charcoal-coloured in the east, but the clouds have started breaking up elsewhere, admitting bright sunshine.

"I don't think the weather knows what to do."

"The *weather* doesn't know *whether* to rain or shine," she says in a piece of wordplay that would have made her granddad proud. Her laughter is brittle and nervous. I'm nervous, too. My stomach is a tight ball, because I know what's coming. As we approach Turnwood Park, she makes her request: "Daddy, can I skip karate this afternoon?"

My answer is already prepared: "No, you absolutely cannot. You have your grading in two weeks, and you want to get your green belt, don't you?"

"But I know the kata really well and I really want to go for a bike ride."

"You can go for a bike ride afterwards."

"But it might be raining by then."

An admirable bit of improvisation I'm thinking, as I hold the park gate open for her. "It might be. It might not be. But it makes no difference to my decision."

She gazes forlornly up the slope towards the bushes and the broken fence in the darkest corner of the park, and I put my arm around her shoulder. "Look!" I point east, where a rainbow has formed against the dark sky. It gleams like something magical that's broken through from another world.

"Oh it's beautiful! Take a photograph Daddy."

I reach in my pocket for my phone, but discover I don't have it with me, so I take a pretend photograph with my hands. "There! I've captured it in my memory."

Imogen snaps her own imaginary photo. "I've captured it too!"

28

BACK AT HOME, I hunt around for my phone in all the usual places, but it's nowhere. I wonder if I'm losing my grip. Blackouts, memory lapses, misplacing things. As the time closes in on four o'clock, I can feel the knot getting tighter in my stomach. The loss of the phone has chipped away at my confidence when I need it firing on all cylinders. I find an old phone in my desk drawer and put it on charge. It doesn't have a sim card, but I can at least connect to the Internet using wifi. Imogen comes downstairs in her gi, tying and then retying her orange belt.

"We'll take the car," I tell her.

"Do we *have* to?"

"Yes – or we'll be late."

More to the point, *I'll* be late for my appointment with Mr Jones.

"Can't we walk Daddy? Walking is more healthy."

I wonder now if she'd been planning to give me the slip while we were in the park. A gust of rain rattles the living-room window. The timing couldn't have been better.

"Look, it's starting to rain, Midge. Now we *have* to take the car."

By the time we get to the church hall, it's pelting down. I don't have an umbrella with me, so we dash into the hall in a crouching run, me holding one side of my jacket over her head like a bird's wing.

In the annex, the other students have congregated, both big and small, expressing their status obliquely by belt colour. Some of the black and brown belts are practising their strikes, defences and kicks in a solemn, staccato dance. Among the very smallest of those waiting is an anxious, white-belted Alex being given a pep talk by Amy. He looks up and manages a smile when he sees Imogen.

"You'll look out for him won't you Midge?" says Amy.

I hand Imogen five pounds to pay the instructor, and we watch the two of them file in.

"Poor Alex is so nervous," Amy laughs. "I think I'll stay and watch. What about you?"

I check my watch. It's three minutes to four. "I have to be somewhere unfortunately."

She hides what looks like disappointment behind another sunny smile. I flash her an apologetic one, then run out, hunched against the teeming rain. It's so dark now, I need head-lights. My windscreen wipers, even switched to manic speed, are about as effective as a bucket in a sinking yacht, but somehow I manage to steer my way back to Turnwood Park, parking at the top of Leafy Wood Lane. It's torrential out there, thundering through the canopy of plane trees as if something in the sky has burst. Mr Jones cannot possibly be expecting a little girl, or anyone for that matter, to visit his garden in this weather. Still, I'm here now, and I should see it through to the brittle end, as Dad used to say. I wish I'd brought a weapon – like the mallet or kitchen knife I'd brought on previous excursions. But I'd been too concerned with getting Imogen to karate and it slipped my mind – another instance, like the phone, of not being at the top of my mental game.

One final check on my watch – it's now a couple of minutes past four – and I open the door, into the warm, wet hail of sky bullets. Battered and slightly giddy, I hurry to the park, turn left and up the bank of bright green grass that bounces and flickers in the drenched light. Once you're wet through, rain is just motion. If I wasn't so tight with nerves, I'd almost enjoy the surrender to the soft pummelling on my head and face. Less so the cataracts down my neck and the cold bog inside my socks. I won't stay long. I don't want to get sick. Five minutes tops, just to confirm what I already suspect – that no one will be there. Then I'll head home and get dry.

Progress gets harder as I approach the overgrown upper corner of the park. My feet get caught in wiry, snaking brambles and soft, squelching mud. The diseased apple tree in the garden leans tipsily against the fence, drooping under the weight of the sky. Last time I came here, I pulled a couple of slats free of the upper rail to add to the already broken-off one, creating a gap big enough for me to squeeze through. Moving carefully now – I don't want to alert Mr Jones to my presence, if he's there – I claw my way into the garden, taking shelter under the tree's sagging limbs. The garden and its crumbling house appear less anomalous in this downpour – no longer a suburban eyesore so much as a lush corner of rainforest growing into the ruins of a primitive temple. Standing like a statue in the middle of what was once the lawn, is a man.

He's thigh-deep in the feral grass, gazing absently into a wild bramble thicket a yard or two off my left shoulder. My first instinct is to back away. He's no more than four strides from where I'm standing, and it can only have been the din of the rain and the shadow of the tree that's prevented him from noticing me. At the sight of him, my mouth becomes the driest place in this garden. He's big with a dark mass of beard and a tall, columnar body sheathed in a long black rubber raincoat that seems to have grown out of the churning sea of grass. What's alarming is how still he is, how uncaring of the torrents cascading onto his bare head.

There's something else though: I think I know this man. I don't mean I know him to talk to or anything, but I'm sure I've seen him around and about, maybe at the gym or the local shop, possibly at the school gates.

Seeing him is such a shock that I can't move, can't even think properly. Why is he just standing there? What's he doing? Long seconds go by with no movement from either of us – just the ceaseless rain. I know I must step out and confront him, but first – first I want to capture him in a photo. This seems to me more important than anything.

Very slowly I probe the pocket of my sodden trousers for the phone. It's slippery and I'm not confident it'll even work – I didn't have time to charge it up more than 25 percent, and phones often fail in the wet. I pull it out and hold it one-handed against my thigh, screen towards me, and press the home button. The screen lights up a patch of soaked denim. Keeping the screen shielded behind my hand, I bring it to my chest and press the camera icon. A time-stamped photo of the man in this place, along with the note to Imogen arranging the meet-up. That might be enough to get him arrested.

The man – he's almost a giant – doesn't look like someone watching for anyone, seems more to be thinking than seeing. His eyes are quiescent, yet primed, like silver balls in a pinball machine ready to spring to life.

I raise the phone just a little, so I can check the screen to be sure he's fully visible within it. He must have noticed this, because that's when his eyes quicken and he swivels to face me. The rain turns to ice on my skin. My thumb tightens on the camera button and everything pulses briefly white.

On the screen and in real life, the man smiles. It creases up his cheeks and forehead, splits the dark shroud of his beard with a bright crescent of teeth, and causes his eyes to shimmer like hot stars.

Panicked, I jam the phone back into my pocket.

"It's Ben, isn't it? Why did you just take a photo?"

His voice has a warm, cavernous depth, like gentle thunder.

And he knows who I am.

I step out from under the tree. The rain has softened, and the light in the garden has turned a waxy yellow. Without the rain's cocooning violence, I feel exposed, and also increasingly cold and wet. My clothes are stiff, heavy encumbrances.

"Do I know you?" I ask him.

He comes closer, his legs swishing invisibly through the high, trembling grass. Every muscle in me stiffens. But he offers nothing more aggressive than a hand for me to shake – a hand big enough to strangle a dog. "I don't think we've properly met yet, Ben. But I've seen you around and about. You live in the downstairs flat, is that right? I'm Luke, your upstairs neighbour."

Possible responses to this insanity flicker weakly through my mind, like a damaged moth trying to discern light where there is none. Something is clearly awry with this man. Or perhaps it's this garden, this house. It's like a warped and faulty imitation of the real world.

Assuming for the moment that it's real, I home in on two other possibilities: he's trying to gaslight me, or he's confused.

"I'm not a tenant here. I don't think anyone is."

Mr Jones

Disturbingly, he now throws his head back and starts to laugh. Deep and gutteral, it chugs out of him like a train in a tunnel. As he laughs, he closes his eyes and nods to himself as if acknowledging a legitimate misunderstanding. "Obviously not this place," he manages to say between gusts of mirth. "I'm talking about next door. Number 25."

I raise myself onto my toes to see what I can of the neighbouring house. The fence is broken in one place – probably his access route to this garden. The house looks in reasonable nick. There's a flat-roofed extension on the ground floor onto which a satellite dish has fallen face down. The upper storey has a mainly brick facade and curtained windows. The dark, tiled roof is interrupted by a small dormer.

"You think I live in there? Well, you've been misinformed."

"Oh," he says, his evident surprise not sufficient to shroud that white moon of a smile. "So then maybe you're just looking after the place?"

"I've never been there in my life. You've got me mixed up with someone else."

The smile loses a few watts. He draws back his head and squints at me as one might an optical illusion. "Do you have an identical twin, Ben?"

"No, you've just made a mistake, that's all."

Craning my neck to talk to him has sent fresh rivulets beneath my collar. The chill is seeping into my bones. I want to go home and get dry. But I can't leave this now. The man is *here*, at the stated time, as per the message. *If it smells like a duck and tastes like a duck*, as my old man used to say... And yet his manner and the things he's saying are so strange and unexpected, I no longer know what to think.

"Why are you here, Luke?"

"I could ask the same of you," he responds with a sharpening

189

of the eyes. "Perhaps you saw the police here on Friday. Did you hear about the dead body? Are you just a sad old rubbernecker like me?" There's a grubby comradeliness in the way he's nodding at me, hoping to find a kindred spirit in his own morbid curiosity. When I don't respond, his look becomes a touch more sly. "Or did something else bring you here, my friend?"

A thin beam of sunlight crests a cloud, bejewelling the shivering grass. Drizzle patters and gurgles through the bushes. I imagine slitherings of wet life emerging around me – slugs, frogs, worms.

Avoiding his question, and his stare, I try to move things on. "Luke, have you ever seen a child in this garden? She would have been about nine years old."

He looks at me for a long time without answering, a ridge of suspicion building on his forehead as if trying to discern some subtext to my question that could trap him. Then he shakes his head. "I've seen nothing here but squirrels, cats and the odd fox."

"What about a woman? Early forties. About five-eight. Fair hair."

"Pretty, was she? I'm not saying beautiful. Mouth a little too big. Eyes a touch too small. But most definitely pretty."

This description jerks all my strings at once. Carefully, I answer: "Yes, I suppose that kind of sums her up."

"I saw her," he says. "She had blonde hair with kind of reddish-brown streaks. She was going into your flat. But that was a while ago."

I can no longer feel the cold or wet. I can barely feel anything, just this soft fluttering in my chest. Blonde with auburn highlights. That was Susan's hair. "How long ago exactly?" I ask.

He makes a prolonged nasal hum. "Last year around autumn time. Maybe October, September. Not sure. Why, who is she?"

"My wife. She disappeared last autumn."

Luke's forehead sinks. "I'm sorry."

"It's alright. You may have helped."

My God! I'm thinking. *You may just have given me the first solid hint that she's still alive!*

"Do you have any idea where she is?" he asks.

I shake my head, and he doesn't meet my eye at first. I think again about the way he described her – the unflattering exactness of it.

"Do *you*, Luke?"

I say it mildly, but I don't blink as I stare him down, alert to the tiniest slippage of a mask.

He offers me a puzzled frown, nothing more than that. "Sorry Ben. I don't know where your wife is."

My body has begun to shiver, a real deep bone-shaker, and it's not just because of the temperature – barely at all because of that.

29

WEDNESDAY 14 OCTOBER 2015

"So YEAH," said Roy, seated in his usual throne by the brick hearth in Ye Olde Pear Tree. "Turns out she basically hood-winked me. She doesn't actually love horror at all and never did. She didn't even love my book, though she pretended to. She admitted she heard an interview with me on local radio, saw my picture in a magazine I write for, and decided I was the one, the bloke she'd been looking for, and she very deliberately went after me. First, she sent in this splendacious audition tape, which got her the job of narrating my book, which gave her an excuse to call me up and wangle herself an invite to the launch party, where she proceeded to seduce me over canapés and wine in plastic cups.

"Ten years later, here I am, living in a three-bedroom house in West Halsted with a wife, a mortgage and a couple of kids, and I don't know who I bloody am anymore. This wasn't the way my life was supposed to go. Okay, so the book wasn't a success – that's on me. But she never gave me the chance to have another crack. I had to be the breadwinner. She's never believed in me, that's the trouble. She's never believed I have what it takes. And now all her love and devotion goes into the kids and I'm just the occasional fuck buddy and payer of bills. She doesn't give a rat's arse if I never write another word.

"Which is why it'll be a matter of supreme indifference to her that I've decided to write another book set in the *Turnwood* universe. Not a sequel. It's better than that. It's the part of the story I didn't have the guts to include first time round. In the first book I talked about the thing that came out of the pond, but not about what happened after. I talked about the terror I felt when it climbed up the bank towards me and how my brain seemed to melt. I talked about how I collapsed into a paralysed stupor that was a kind of death. But I didn't mention the dream I had while I was in this stupor. It's that dream that will form the basis of my new book."

Roy took a long swallow of his beer, draining it. The firelight gleamed on the empty, foam-flecked glass as he gently rocked it. "When I woke up, the thing was gone – at least physically – although I heard it speak to me. I was just waking, in that giddy moment before my senses had fully reattuned themselves to the world, and I remember a cold, wet voice dripping words into my brain. It warned me never to speak or write of what I'd dreamt. That voice scared me so much, I kept the dream out of my book. Now, looking back, I'm not sure I even heard it. I think it may have been a hallucination. If I'd had the balls to include the dream in my first book, it would have done a lot better, I'm sure of it.

"Not that I'd get any support from the wife. I'd start on it today if I could, but of course that's not an option. I keep hitting the brick wall of my present reality, and I'm telling you the truth now Jean, I'm getting sick of it."

Roy slumped in his chair, and Jean leaned forward from the other side of the table and squeezed his arm. She picked up Roy's empty beer glass. "Let me get you another. I want to hear more about this dream."

30

MONDAY 16 JULY 2018

THE RAINSTORM TURNS OUT TO be brief. Forty minutes later, the dark clouds are in full retreat, leaving gaps of deep blue and flashes of blinding sunlight on the wet roads. I've been home, changed into dry clothing. Now I'm back in the Renault, bright needles spraying from my tires as I speed back to the church hall to pick up Imogen. I'm thinking about Luke. What am I to make of him? That odd, rock-like stillness at the start – and his still odder insistence that I am his downstairs neighbour. It would be easy to dismiss him as a lunatic, but he didn't seem like one. And his sighting of Susan last autumn feels significant – deeply so. As soon as I get back home, I'll do a land registry search on the neighbouring house and find out who the owner is. The thought sends a small throb of excitement through me. This could be my first genuine lead in ten months of searching, and what a mad and random way of stumbling on it.

Yet it does deal a slight blow to the Luke-is-Mr-Jones theory. If he's responsible for Susan's disappearance, why would he tell me he'd seen her there? On the other hand, if he isn't Mr Jones, why was he there, in the appointed place at the appointed time? *If it smells like a duck, and tastes like a duck...*

Steering carefully around a swimming-pool-size puddle, I turn into the forecourt of the church hall and slide into a parking spot. I have the full complement of spaces to choose from. It's about six minutes past five and I'm late, but not so late that all the cars would be gone by now. This sets off a distant alarm inside me. As I get out of the car, I'm struck by the desolate quietness. The only sound is the steady drip-drip from the beech trees bordering the car park, and the only living thing aside from me is a large crow picking at a worm or a slug on the puddled asphalt. Before I reach the hall, I can already see the place is closed. The windows in the doors are dark. I try pulling at one. It's locked.

My inner alarm is ringing at top volume now. Just over an hour ago, this place was humming with activity. The instructor was here, along with more than a dozen students. They couldn't all have dispersed so quickly after the class. It takes me a moment to see the piece of paper floating in the puddle by my feet. Its sticky-taped borders that must have affixed it to the window are grey and curled with moisture. Using my fingers as pincers, I retrieve the sopping-wet sheet and turn it over. The felt-tip scrawl is smudged almost beyond legibility, but the message is clear enough: "Sorry. Adrian is ill. Had to cancel... Full refund... See...next week"

Try sticking it on the inside of the window next time, idiot! I silently curse. But this fleeting irritation is flapped aside by a far weightier and more worrying thought. Why am I the only one standing here annoyed and mystified? Where are the other parents? And the kids they came to pick up? *Where...* is Imogen?

I reach instinctively for my phone to search for messages, then clock the generic screen background of planet Earth from space where I should be seeing Imogen's face snuggled up next to Giraffee.

I missed the karate group Whatsapp message because I lost my damn phone!

But it's okay. Amy was there at the class watching Alex. When it ended prematurely and I didn't show up and failed to respond to her calls, she must have done the sensible thing and taken Imogen back to her place. Breathing hard with relief, I hurry back to the Megane. As I'm doing up my seatbelt, my fingers tighten in sudden alarm around the strap.

Amy took her! Amy, whose phone number was imprinted on that note from Mr Jones – Amy, whose daughter keeps appearing in the park...

I finish strapping myself in and start backing out of the parking space.

What does that prove? I ask myself. It proves she may be as much a victim of all this as me.

My left front wheel sends up a rainbow arc of spray from the giant puddle as I take the curve too sharply onto the main road. I force myself to slow down. Of course I can trust Amy. Imogen will be fine.

And then, out of nowhere the name of the scent comes to me. *Gardenia.* Susan used to wear it, and now so does Amy. I smelled it on her in the playground, and when she and I were listening outside Imogen's bedroom door. She wears the same perfume. So what? And what about just before I smelled it in the playground, before she touched my elbow, I felt something, like a soft tug on my clothing. I thought it was a breath of pre-storm wind, but...

But nothing. It *was* the wind. She didn't steal my phone. I left it at home, probably on the shoe rack by the front door, for the same reason that I forgot to bring a weapon – because I'm getting careless, most likely due to a lack of sleep.

By now I'm on Sylvan Drive, about to take a right into Forest Vale. A few more minutes and Imogen will be in my arms.

And yet I'm pretty sure I picked up the phone from the top of the shoe rack before I went out. Could Amy have stolen it so I wouldn't get the message about the cancelled karate class, so she'd be able to take her to Him.

This is paranoia. Forget the phone. The phone doesn't matter. The important thing is I kept Imogen safe. I kept her away from the derelict garden. Wherever she was at 4 o'clock, she wasn't there, the time it said on the note to...

The time it said on MY note. I never saw Imogen's note.

Icy pearls of sweat break out of my forehead. I have to brake hard as a couple of teenage boys emerge between parked cars and pass in front of me.

My note could have been a decoy, sending me to the derelict garden at that time to keep me out of the way so...

With a small screech, I continue, crossing Greenwood Lane into Daintree Gardens, just seconds away now.

Why did she suddenly decide to send Alex to karate today?

I park the car and for a second I can only stare at Amy's house, impaled on a spike of paralysing fear. Then, like a galvanised frog, I jerk back to life and climb out of the Renault. Her gate bangs behind me as I hurry down the path and push my thumb hard on the bell. As the two-note chime fades I can hear my heart like a clock on a time bomb ticking downwards.

Amy opens the door, and her face cracks into a relieved smile. "You're here, thank God! I've been trying to get hold of you. You didn't answer your phone."

"Imogen is..."

"Here, yes. I'm sorry Ben, I didn't know what else to do as you weren't at home. Come in."

Imogen is sitting on the floor of Amy's messy, homely front room, playing a game of Connect 4 with Alex. There's a half-eaten platter of mozzarella cheese slices and carrot sticks on the coffee table. The scene couldn't be more normal – just your average after-school playdate.

Imogen looks up when I come in.

"Where *were* you Daddy? Why didn't you come and pick me up?"

I kneel down and hug her, breathing in her scent, feeling the rough fabric of her gi against my neck. It's not what she wants, and I can sense her restlessness, but I can't help myself.

"I'm so sorry Midge. I won't let that happen again."

I turn to Amy. "Thank you and I'm sorry. I lost my phone."

"Don't worry, I'm just glad I was able to help." She offers a smiling sort of frown. "You look so pale Ben, but you mustn't ever worry. I love Midge. I'd never have left her there."

"I know." I sigh, lost in my little girl's presence. The relief is almost physical. Tears feel very close.

"The kettle's just boiled," says Amy. "Let me make you some tea."

I climb to my feet, touch the top of Imogen's head, and follow Amy to the kitchen.

"What's wrong?" she asks me as soon as we're alone.

"Nothing."

"Come on Ben. You look terrified. Did something just happen?"

I lean back against the counter, check out the view of her small garden – deflated paddling pool, faded plastic playhouse, timber furniture – all beaded with raindrops from the recent downpour, which came too late for the drooping, dessicated plant in the big pot near her kitchen door. Its wilted leaves look like twisted brown paper.

I swallow some salty spit. "I thought something had happened to Midge."

"I go through those moments at least ten times a day," says Amy, handing me a cup of tea with a spoon and bag in the cup. She sets a saucer, milk and sugar on the counter nearby. "I know I'm over-protective, but I can't help it. It's hard enough leaving him at the school gate each morning."

"It's understandable," I mutter, stirring the bag, watching the tea darken.

"I guess we have to just learn to believe that they'll be safe. This is a safe neighbourhood."

I squeeze the bag hard against the side of the cup, watch the milk swirl like a mysterious fog under the action of my spoon.

"I've been receiving messages," I mutter.

"Messages from whom?"

"They're actually written to Midge, supposedly from Susan."

I can tell from her look of utter fascination that she won't be satisfied unless I tell her everything. Perhaps I need to anyway. I could do with an ally, and right now, despite my earlier doubts, no one seems more trustworthy than Amy.

So while the children entertain each other in the next room – and from the cartoon voices it sounds like images on a screen rather than toys are occupying them now – I narrate recent events to her: the rib, the notes, my night in the park, finding Imogen in the derelict garden, finding the tramp's body in the house, Imogen's version of how she fell out of the tree, and finally my encounter with Luke one hour ago. I don't mention my sightings of Stephanie – telling her about those would, I realise, instantly blot out everything else. It would be like trying to show someone a strand of hair while shining a torch in their eyes. Besides, I'm still not entirely sure the sightings were real. I don't tell her about finding her phone number on the note either. I'm less sure about my reasons for omitting that part.

Amy listens attentively from the other side of the room, arms folded, her back to the counter as the dishwasher behind her rumbles through its programme. When I finish, she's quiet for a moment, staring at the fridge to my right, as if trying to draw inspiration from some magnetic aphorism stuck there. Then she chuckles. She laughs often and not always at appropriate moments. It's a reactive sound, more akin to surprise than amusement.

"So you think this Luke fellow is Mr Jones and he's trying to kidnap Midge by posing as her mother? Even as I'm saying it I sound like I'm in a crime novel with an overly convoluted plot. I should know, I've narrated a few."

"You don't believe me."

"No I do, I do. There's clearly a madman on the loose, and it could well be Luke. You should go to the police with the notes and the rib and that photo you took."

"He threatened to hurt Midge if I do."

She glances towards the half-open door to the living room. From her vantage she can see the children. I picture them sitting on the floor next to each other, backs to the sofa, eyes big and shiny as they lap up the bright, fast-moving imagery on the screen.

Amy chews thoughtfully on her lower lip. I wonder what's going on in her head.

"You can't take him on by yourself, Ben. If you explain to the police he's threatening you, maybe they can give you some protection."

She can tell I'm not convinced. I don't even need to ask what she'd do in my shoes.

"Can I see the photo of Luke?" she asks.

I take out my phone and click on it. This is the first time I've looked at it myself, and the image I captured is unnerving. I wasn't holding the camera straight, and he looks like some looming monolith leaning at a crazy angle against a deep grey sky. The smile is a slash of white ripped out of the black night of his beard. His eyes are half-buried brown beads in the big prominences of his face.

I hand it to Amy, and something happens to her when she looks at it very similar to an electric shock. It starts as a flash in her eyes and spreads faster than splintering ice through her face. Her hand jerks as if the phone has turned into a giant venomous insect. It drops from her hand and cracks loudly on the tiles.

"I'm so sorry!" She's gasping, eyes wide, her hand pressed hard to her chest.

I rush to her, seize her shoulders. "Amy! What happened? What's wrong?"

She won't meet my eyes. "Your phone. I probably broke it. I'm so sorry."

Alex comes in. "Mama, what happened? Why do you look scared?"

I let go of her, embarrassed to be nearly embracing her in front of her son. I take a step or two back just as Imogen arrives.

"I'm fine," says Amy, striving for a smile. "It's nothing Alex. Mummy's fine. Go back to your television programme." She waits for the children to leave, then stoops and picks up the phone, which is now dark, and hands it to me. The screen is chipped. "I'll pay for the repair," she says.

"Don't worry about the phone. Just tell me why you reacted like that?"

"I don't know." Her hand has gone to her face, veiling her eyes.

"Did you recognise him?"

She doesn't respond.

"*I* recognised him," I tell her. "At least I think I did." I'm hoping this might prompt her to open up, but still she says nothing. "Amy. You have to tell me if you know this man. I have to know!"

I wait, but she remains still and silent, her hand continuing to mask her eyes, her forefinger and thumb slowly massaging her forehead.

So I seek a new line of attack: Thinking about the impression of her phone number on the message: "Do you know Mr Jones, Amy?"

Her hand drops and finally she looks at me. Her gaze is bright, her smile rickety. It looks like something held together with piano wire and hope. "I don't know Mr Jones, and I don't know Luke. I'm sorry I broke your phone. Please send me the bill. Now if you don't mind, I have to get Alex's supper ready."

31

So Imogen and I go home, both of us in our own ways confused, mystified and hungry to know more.

"What happened in the kitchen Daddy? Why did Alex's mummy drop your phone?"

I'd love to know, I'm tempted to reply, but I just smile and tell her it was a silly accident and would she prefer mac n' cheese or margherita pizza tonight.

Later, while I'm waiting for the pizza to heat up, I go onto the Land Registry website and pay £3 to request the title register for 25 Oakfield Crescent, the house next door to the derelict one. If I can trace the owner, I might be able to find out who really lives in the downstairs flat, and what the hell Susan was doing there last autumn.

"Theodora didn't talk to me today," says Imogen. She's at the kitchen table, making a colourful bracelet with her rainbow loom kit.

"I'm sorry Midge. I'm sure things will be better between you two very soon."

"I think she's going to be friends with Antonia and Kate from now on. Is my pizza nearly ready?"

I check the window of the oven. "Nearly. I'm just waiting for the cheese to get a bit more melted."

"I'm making her a friendship bracelet. I'll give it to her tomorrow."

"That's a great idea!"

I take out the pizza, place it on the big breadboard and slice it into eight segments using the pizza wheel.

"Here you go."

She puts down her loom with its complex arrangement of elastic bands, and picks up the first slice. She flinches slightly at the heat in her mouth.

"Careful darling."

She blows on it and tries again.

I sit down next to her. My wine glass is full. This is my second of the day and it's not even six o'clock. But it's been a strange afternoon.

"What time did your teacher end the karate class?" I ask her.

She says something through a mouthful of hot pizza, then repeats herself once she's swallowed it. "It was just after we started. Daddy, can I have some water."

I get up and take a glass from the drying rack. As I'm filling it, I spot my phone on the little shelf above the sink. I squeeze my eyes shut with relief. It was nothing sinister then – just me going mad.

Still, it's an odd place to leave it. I try to retrace my movements earlier in the day. I must have had the phone on me during my post-lunch walk because I was listening to the Happy Urbanist, a podcast about inner-city architecture. I would have got back here by around two o'clock. And then what? The next thing I remember was the walk to school to pick up Imogen. That would have been about forty-five minutes later.

"The water's spilling Daddy!"

I open my eyes. The water is indeed spilling out of the glass and over my hand. Quickly, I switch off the tap, tip out a little water from the glass and hand it to Imogen.

"Sorry Midge. I got a little bit distracted."

She slurps some water. "What's distructed?"

"My mind went away somewhere for a moment."

"Like it did before."

I take a gulp of my wine. "Like when sweetie?"

She carefully pulls apart a long string of molten mozzarella, watching how far it will stretch before it breaks. "Like yesterday in the entrance hall, but that was for longer."

"I've been a bit tired lately. Probably not getting enough sleep."

"And on Saturday when Mr Jones chased me up the tree and you didn't even wake up."

I take another sip of wine. She's right. That may have been another moment. And just a few hours ago, I had forty-five minutes of complete blankness. I got back from the park, and the next thing I knew I was walking to school to pick her up. Somehow, during that missing time, I put the phone on the shelf behind the sink.

Maybe I should make an appointment with my GP. I click on the phone, thinking I'll do just that, but my eye is immediately caught by the red circle indicating 13 new messages on the green Whatsapp icon. Adrian, the karate instructor, sent out his original message at 16.08 – said he felt woozy, and maybe he'd caught a bug, and he definitely didn't feel able to teach. This was followed by a flurry of responses from parents.

I pick up my wine glass.

"Maybe you shouldn't have any more wine Daddy."

I narrow my eyes at her.

"It makes you tired. That's why you keep getting distructed."

I'm unsettled by this from my daughter, yet can't help smiling – partly at her mispronunciation, but also because her hard little face reminds me so much of Susan, who had her own issues with my alcohol consumption.

"Your..."

"I'm what?" she asks.

I was about to tell her that her mother used to go on at me about drinking too much wine, but I stop myself. Her granny mentions Susan too much already, and now with these fake notes the whole topic has become way too fraught and is probably best avoided.

Instead I just say: "You're right my girl. I shouldn't drink so much."

She watches my hand carefully as I twirl the stem of the glass. I feel the need to subtly remind her of our relative standings in the household, and reach for an obvious formula. "Have you got any homework tonight Midge?"

"Just spellings to learn for tomorrow."

"Well, when you've learned them, I'll test you."

"Okay."

She goes on staring at my hand and the wine.

I glance through the patio door. "The foxes are out," I say.

She looks, and her face brightens. We both watch the vixen and her cub scratching their fleas and generally enjoying the late afternoon sunshine – a perfect example of a single-parent family.

With Imogen safely *distructed*, I sneak in a quick glug of wine.

I'm half an hour into episode one of a Netflix crime drama, and a lot has happened. It opened with a night-time chase and murder in which you see the victim, a woman, but not her killer. Now the police are investigating, talking to people who knew the victim, checking alibis. There is a fairly gross scene where they attend the autopsy. There's some sort of sexual tension going on between the two lead detectives, both of whom are attractive.

It ought to be absorbing. Yet I keep drifting off, watching the screen, seeing the protagonists' mouths moving, and not taking in a word of what they're saying. I know that if Susan was here, I'd be into it – she'd make damn sure I was. Susan was never a passive watcher of TV dramas. She was always passing comment on the quality of the story and the acting, making bitchy remarks about the actors' looks, trying to second-guess what would happen next. A big part of the entertainment for me was listening to her interactions with the TV. Without her here it feels flat and tepid, like day-old Coke, and not even any Bacardi to wash it down.

The woman the cops are interviewing now, a work colleague of the victim, reminds me somewhat of Amy. Not so much her appearance – the actress is a flame-haired, corn-fed, Midwestern girl with perfect teeth – but her manner. She laughs easily, and has a bold, strong voice, just like Amy, but she's also hiding something, some kind of pain. It gets me wondering about Amy, about the way she interposed herself in my life through Imogen's friendship with her son. Never before had Imogen shown any interest in befriending a boy. I understand he was lonely and my daughter has a compassionate heart. Even so, I'd love to know how it happened exactly. Did she approach him, or was it the other way around? Did his mother say, "Go to that little girl over there, she'll be your friend if you ask her"?

I think of Amy in her kitchen: the electric shock that ran through her when she saw the photo, and the change that came over her when I questioned her about it – how the walls came up behind those laughing eyes. *I'm sorry I broke your phone. Please send me the bill. Now if you don't mind...*

Amy. Luke. Susan. Something connects them, and it's not just Mr Jones, it's also me and Imogen and Stephanie, the derelict house and the house next door. Stephanie was there. Luke was there. Mr Jones, posing as Susan, tried to draw Imogen there. I think Amy knows Mr Jones. I think she knows Luke, too. Maybe they're the same person. And that person – Luke or Mr Jones – thinks I'm his downstairs neighbour. It's like a strange, circular riddle with lots of connections but no overall meaning or sense.

On the TV, the male detective smacks his forehead as an idea suddenly hits him. He makes a mental connection, and a witness is transformed into a suspect. He and his partner dive into their car and roar away.

I wish I could make connections like that, but I feel out of my depth. I'm an engineer, trained to be rigorous and methodical rather than creative or intuitive like an architect. When I do a site inspection, I work through my checklist in linear fashion, according to established guidelines. I start from the foundations and move upwards. But there's no order to this mystery, no established guidelines, no methodical way of solving it. It's going to need imagination – a smack-on-the-forehead leap of intuition.

The background music on the TV is getting more frenetic. There are sweaty close-ups of the cops at an apartment entrance, their gun muzzles pressed to their cheeks in the manner of all TV cops. They race in to find the suspect leaping out of a window. Shots are fired. They chase him up an external iron stairway and onto a rooftop. There are dramatic tumbles down sloping roofs, death-defying leaps across gaps between buildings.

It's exciting, but I can't concentrate. My attention keeps slithering away into the corners of the room – towards the moth reposing on the bright shade of the floor lamp, and the books on the shelf above it that I'll probably never read, to the framed mantelpiece selfies of Imogen, Susan and I on barely remembered holidays. Would the Ben in those pictures even recognise the hollow-cheeked, dull-eyed man sitting here now? When I next turn to the TV, the episode has ended. I switch it off, pleased to have got through a show in the same way an anorexic might be pleased to get through a meal. It feels like progress. I may even watch another one tomorrow.

Out of the silence, other sounds reemerge like pebbles in the sand when the tide goes out: the hiss of traffic on Forest Vale, the yapping of Mrs Gilbert's Pomeranian. And I can hear the pipes settling in the basement. Always the pipes. Tonight they sound like whalesong and rain dripping on a tin roof. I should go down there tomorrow and take a look at them. It's way past time.

32

TUESDAY 17 JULY 2018

THE REPLY from the Land Registry lands in my email inbox the following morning at just a little after ten o'clock. For several long minutes I stare at the name of the owner of 25 Oakfield Crescent, keeping very still, swallowing now and again to suppress the upwelling of emotion in my gut. Finally, I stand up, go out of the room and start walking down the stairs. My heart is beating faster than is probably healthy. What I'm feeling right now isn't anger, fear or excitement, but something ill-defined at the intersection of all three. I need to go out, get some air, try to calm myself down. Only with a clear head can I assess what this means.

I open the front door, and look outside. After yesterday's storm, the weather has reverted to type, though it's not quite as hot as on previous days, and the air carries the sweet, ripe aroma of bin collection day. The refuse men are late. Colour-coded wheelie bins stand outside each house. Flies are buzzing around the overflowing bags of Mrs Gilbert's black bin – she's mixed her food waste with her general waste again. I check out my own green, black and blue-topped bins standing in a neat line at the bottom of my front path. Somewhere in the middle of one of the bags in my black bin will be the pink shirt I threw out the other day – the one with the coffee stain and the frayed collar. I did like that shirt, and it's not too late to retrieve it. But what a mucky business, and what would be the point?

My feet, when not consciously directed otherwise, will always tend towards Turnwood Park, but this morning I head there with a clear purpose in mind: I have to go back to that house. The sky is a faded denim, and the shadows are faint, leaving everything looking as flat as a daguerrotype. Turning into Oakfield Crescent, I see signs of apathy and neglect, as if the park has spread its entropy, like Mrs Gilbert's brambles, into the surrounding street. A veil of dust lies over the cars parked in their driveways. I can smell sweet vanilla from the privet hedges run wild with little white flowers. Sid, the fluffy ginger icon of the Crescent, lies sprawled across the pavement, barely raising his head as I pass. The lawnmowers, hedge-trimmers and sprinklers are all asleep this morning. The only sound is the desultory warble of a dunnock.

I saw an optical illusion once in which a duck, looked at another way, became a rabbit. It took an effort of concentration to discern the alternate image because one's eyes and brain tend to select one interpretation of what they're seeing and stick with that. I always thought my marriage to Susan was a duck – not perfect, but perfectly decent – until the day I found out about Richard Landry, and I was forced to adjust my focus and accept that our marriage was in fact a rabbit. I was married to someone I wouldn't ever be able to fully trust. She simply wasn't the person I thought she was. Still, I loved her, and I was prepared to give it another go, because deep down I was convinced that she loved me. Our rabbit marriage may have been flawed, but in the end it was salvageable, so long as we both wanted it to be.

Unlike Karl Marx's take on capitalism, our relationship did not contain the seeds of its own destruction. Its destruction was caused, in the end, by an external force – a random psychopath.

That, at least, was how I saw things until this morning. But after the email from the Land Registry, I'm finding it harder to sustain that view. I'm finding it harder to believe that I ever knew anything about the nature of our marriage. It probably wasn't a duck or a rabbit, but something else entirely.

Now I'm standing on the pavement opposite 25 Oakfield Crescent, and it looks in every sense a normal, lived-in sort of house, at least compared to the disaster zone next door. Number 27, the derelict house, is as unprepossessing from the front as it is from the back. It's dark and ramshackle, with rust-coloured gang tags sprayed on the chipboard covering its windows, and a front garden that's a riot of rampant weeds, broken glass and litter. It doesn't belong here in the Forest Estate, and it almost seems to know it, the way it skulks in the shadows of the tall plane trees on its western border.

Number 25, on the other hand, very much belongs in this neighbourhood. It is a perfectly respectable-looking house. And yet, to me at least, it has a far more mysterious and troubling aspect than its decrepit neighbour. That's because, according to the email from the Land Registry, its owner is Richard Landry.

I don't know what I feel about this exactly, except overwhelmed and a little sick. Richard Landry was my wife's lover. She promised the affair was over in January last year. And when she disappeared the following September, and the police investigated him, they found no one fitting his profile. That's not to say they found no one at all. It's not that uncommon a name.

They even, now I think about it, found a Richard Landry who owned a house near ours – but he was a retired civil servant in his early seventies and had been living in Australia since 2012, so was quickly crossed off the list. This must have been his house, and at the time I can see how perfectly justified they were in treating it as just one of those odd coincidences. But if Luke is right and Susan was here last autumn, that throws a completely new light on the matter. This could be the first credible hint we've had in nearly a year that Susan is alive. I should be over-joyed, and part of me is, admittedly, excited, but equal parts are shocked and disgusted, because it can only mean that Susan walked out on us without a word of goodbye and is currently living a new life – quite possibly down under with her septuage-narian lover. If so, I can forget all about ducks and rabbits: I married a monster.

Standing here now, opposite 25 Oakfield Crescent, I cast around for alternative explanations. It's clear their affair continued after January, perhaps on some encrypted platform like WhatsApp. It must have grown more serious, and last September maybe Landry flew to the UK to meet her physically for the first time, probably here in this house. In one possible scenario, when she set eyes on him, she was less than impressed – especially when compared to his buff and youthful online avatar – and decided to call it off. He wouldn't let her, there was a fight, and he killed her.

It's a horrible idea, yet feels more plausible because it tallies with the Susan I thought I knew. It does, admittedly, leave the rabbit theory of our marriage as dead as the duck one. It means she broke her promise about ending the affair – there's no getting around that one – and I have to accept our marriage would probably have been over even if she hadn't disappeared. But at least it keeps her human.

There is another even more disturbing scenario, in which Susan is still alive, but trapped. I'm thinking now about the messages to Imogen. Perhaps she really is sending them. Could she be a prisoner in this house like some latter-day, suburban Rapunzel? It sounds absurd – impossible. Though occasionally you do hear stories, like that Austrian fellow who kept his daughter captive in his cellar.

I take out my phone and, after a bit of googling, find his name – Josef Fritzl. He was an electrical engineer who built a concealed extension in the basement of his home where he held his daughter Elisabeth captive for twenty-four years, repeatedly raping her, resulting in the birth of seven children. One of the kids died. Three were raised by Fritzl and his wife, while the other three remained in the underground prison with their mother. It all eventually came to light in 2008. The family was rescued, and Fritzl went to prison. He never showed any remorse for what he did. He just kept saying, "look into the cellars of other people, you might find other families and girls down there".

I look again at 25 Oakfield Crescent, standing modestly behind its paved forecourt, the quiet, mild-mannered sibling of the degenerate house next door, and I wonder what secrets it has in its cellar. A stash of porn mags? A collection of vintage wines? Susan? The thought makes me feel faint, and for a few seconds I think I may collapse. I reach out and grip the corner of a car's bonnet, keeping my hand on the warm metal until I'm steady again.

Oakfield Crescent, indeed the entire Forest Estate, was built around 1910, and number 25 has the typical traits of an Edwardian house: wide and roomy, with walls of deep, brownish-red bricks, large windows and a steep-pitched roof. Net curtains veil its ground-floor bay window. The upstairs bay is uncurtained but dark, as is the triangular oriel window next to it. The porch has a white-painted, ornamental trim, but it's restrained. There's nothing about the house that shouts, *look at me!* And perhaps that's the point. I'm sure the Fritzl residence looked very ordinary from the outside. I swallow and touch the warm car bonnet once again, as if for good luck, then launch myself slowly across the road.

The front door, shaded by the large porch, is a pale, greyish-green, simultaneously reminding me of my mother's abstract painting and the scummy surface of Turnwood pond. It's the kind of colour that only post-war designers of hospital interiors ever found appealing. There are two bells on the intercom system attached to the door's red-brick surround. The impersonal signs felt-tipped beneath them read 'GFF' and 'FLAT 1'

According to Luke, I'm a regular visitor to the GFF, and may even be its tenant. The idea is, of course, absurd, and he is either deluded or lying. Certainly, nothing about this entrance seems familiar. I ring the bell marked GFF and wait. After a minute, I try again. Two further minutes go by without response, so I try ringing Flat 1. After a much shorter pause, I hear static on the speaker beneath the bell and Luke's rumbled greeting. His voice is even deeper than before, and gruff at the edges, as if I've woken him from a hangover-induced lie-in.

"Hi Luke. It's Ben."

"Forgot your key, did you Ben?" he asks, his speech rising to a more friendly register.

I don't repeat that I've never been here before, as I don't want to risk dissuading him from granting me access. "Can you let me in please?"

"Sure."

At the buzz, I push open the door to a swish of draught-excluders on tile. The entrance hall is cool with white walls and a monochrome patterned floor. It's as plain and understated as the exterior, and as I run my eye over it, and breathe in the prissy odours of lavender and bleach, not even the faintest bell of familiarity chimes. I note almost immediately the door beneath the staircase. If the house has a cellar, that would be the entrance. The door has a roller spring catch, and a small tug opens it. The steps twist sharply down to the right and descend steeply into darkness. A dizzying wave of something like vertigo sweeps through me. I take a steadying breath. I don't want to go down there quite yet.

I go instead into the front room, which has the same bland, impersonal feel as the hallway. The curtains, cushions, lamp-shades and upholstery are in neutral shades and the place is immaculately tidy, like an upmarket hotel suite, lacking only the complimentary fruit basket. The books on the shelves to either side of the fireplace are mostly paperback novels. Checking more closely, I see they are of the lurid, sensational kind, many with dark spines and foil lettering – works of horror and the supernatural, of worlds out of joint. Something vaguely anom-alous flashes across my retina as I survey the hundreds of spines, but when I look again more carefully, I can't see it, whatever it was.

I pull a couple of the books from the shelf at random. The cover of the first features a Gothic castle, the second a cemetery and a cloaked figure emerging from green mist. With a grim, inward smile, I think of Turnwood Park and what a fine setting it would make for one of these tales. The subject matter of the books seems incongruous in this prim, determinedly inoffensive house. Then again, I remind myself, I haven't yet seen the cellar.

The bedroom has an obvious theme. The wall above the double bed is dominated by a large print of the famous Australian sandstone formation known as Uluru in its most dramatic sunset colours. On the opposite wall, above a chest of drawers, is an equally commanding map of Australia. Dotted about the room and mounted on the other walls are various artifacts: a polished wooden boomerang, a bark shield, an animal-skin drum, a long didgeridoo. I think of Richard Landry, stealer of cultural artifacts and men's wives, and I realise it's high time (I can't put it off any longer) that I looked at what he's keeping in his cellar.

Bracing myself at the top of the steps, I switch on the light and head down the six or seven steps. At the bottom, a bare light bulb illuminates a modest space with a flagstone floor and exposed beams on the low ceiling. The air is cool down here and smells of varnished oak and damp earth overlaid with the vinegary tang of wine. The wall opposite the staircase is filled with a floor-to-ceiling rack containing row upon row of gleaming wine bottles.

Apart from the wine, there's nothing else down here. My fantasy of finding a Fritzl-style concealed annex seems laughable now. The walls are, as I can tell from the briefest examination, solid. A waterproof render has recently been applied to what must have been the original brickwork, and behind that, I'm sure, is nothing but good, honest Halsted clay. There's nothing beneath the floor either except, ultimately, Australia.

I don't feel relief about this exactly. I'm still wound up as tight as that Aboriginal drum upstairs, but I find I can breathe more easily. I slide one of the wine bottles from its diamond-shaped alcove and cradle it in my palm. It's a Penfolds Bin 389 Cabernet Shiraz. I don't know much about wine, but there's something about the understated label that looks classy. It's not even midday, and I could happily down a glass of this right now. It would certainly help steady my nerves. Who could object if I opened it? Certainly not Luke, who probably thinks all this is mine anyway. But no, I have to keep a clear head. Reluctantly, I return it to its slot.

I don't know if I wanted to find Susan down here. I'm sure I dreaded it. Yet not finding her brings me no comfort. Moved by a strange impulse, I say her name. I rarely pronounce it out loud these days, and it sounds intimate, fragile even, in this small, underground space. And then, inexplicably, I find myself talking to her. "I got you wrong my love. In some ways I hope you're dead. I don't want to think of you alive and living free – a sun-tanned beauty on some Australian beach. I can't bear that idea, because of what it says about you and what it says about me. I wish I knew if we ever stood a chance. If I'd acted differently, or if you had. Or was it all impossible from the start? I'm sure you loved me once. So what changed? Was it you? Or was it me? Where did you go to that day? Did you come here, to this house? What did you find here that you couldn't find with me?"

33

BEFORE I LEAVE THE HOUSE, I pay a visit to Luke. I press the buzzer on the door at the top of the stairs. A shadow appears at the frosted glass and the door opens. Luke towers above me, yet he seems less intimidating this time in plaid pygama bottoms, a stained grey T-shirt and bare feet.

"Everything alright, Ben?"

He looks down at me from beneath hooded, hung-over eyes. Even in his current state, his height lends him an automatic status, as it must with almost everyone he meets. He has this elevated, godlike perspective on the world, while we who interact with him must always hurt our necks.

"Fine," I assure him. "Luke, can you tell me anything more about that woman you mentioned – the one you saw here last autumn? Was she with anyone?"

He squints and scratches a thickly bearded cheek, then shakes his head. "No, she was alone, and I only saw her the once."

"Where was she exactly?"

"Coming into the house. I was looking out of my window and I saw her."

His expression is solemn, and the overhead light casts strong shadows on the mounds and ridges of his face, reminding me of the carving of Abraham Lincoln on Mount Rushmore.

"Did you see who let her in?"

"She let herself in."

"She had a key?"

"That's right. I'd only recently moved in myself, and I just assumed she was my downstairs neighbour. But I never saw her after that one time."

"At what point did you start to see me coming here?"

He ponders this. "It was very soon after I saw *her*. You don't come too often though. I see you maybe once a week at most. That's why I wasn't sure if you were renting the place or just keeping an eye on it for someone."

"Did we ever speak?"

"You and me? No." He flashes his teeth in a twitchy, nervous smile. "You talk about yourself like you're another person. Don't you remember coming here?"

"No. That's the puzzling thing. But if you never spoke to me, how do you know my name?"

"Jean told me. I have no idea how she knew."

"Jean?"

"My sister. She lives here with me."

"Is she in now?"

Luke shakes his head. "I can tell her to give you a call if you like?"

"That would be good. Thanks."

"Give me a minute."

He disappears to fetch his phone. In one of the rooms off the landing, I can see part of a sofa, a scrunched up tissue on the carpet, a DVD of a movie, its cover obscured by a milky wash of sunlight. The place has a bachelor-pad odour of beer, sweat and sweet, oily Chinese takeaway. Leaning a little further through the doorway, something odd catches my eye: a pair of bathroom taps lying on the hallway carpet. The taps look rather too small for a typical bathroom, certainly for someone the size of Luke. They look more suited to the kind of small sink you'd find in a toilet.

Luke returns with his phone and I give him my number, which he keys in with stubby yet surprisingly dextrous fingers.

"Have you ever seen or met the owner of the house by any chance?" I ask.

"Nope. I pay my rent via direct debit. If there are problems, I contact the agent. I believe the owner lives in Australia."

I nod. "What about Amy Parker? Does that name mean anything to you?"

He hesitates slightly, for less than a second, then shakes his head. "Sorry, 'fraid not."

I thank him and return downstairs. I'm thinking: *he definitely knows her.*

Before I leave, I make a final return visit to the front room. There was something about the books in there that struck an odd note with me the first time I looked at them. I survey them again and try to work out what it was.

I recognise some of the author names: the famous ones that appear on the bestseller lists. Many of the spines are seamed and concave from eager and careless use. Some, however, aren't. On the second shelf to the right of the hearth are three pristine copies of the same book, all with attractive dark green spines and swirly white lettering. That was it, I realise now – the odd note. Why have three copies of the same book, all evidently unread? Next to these three slim volumes is a CD case with the same dark green spine and identical white lettering.

I move close enough to read the words on the spine in their charming font, and feel an abrupt and clammy chill, as if a pretty bird's egg has broken open to reveal the dead embryo within. The book's title is *Turnwood*. Printed in smaller lettering underneath is the name of the author: Roy Parker. Wasn't that Amy's husband?

"Turnwood. Roy Parker." I say these words out loud.

Then I slide out the middle volume, and it flops heavily into my hand. I absorb the cover illustration. The light in the room seems to fade, and everything goes very still. The only thing left moving is my heart, which I can feel as a distant thudding in my ears. The illustration shows a pond, almost identical to the one in Turnwood Park. Reaching out of the green, slimy surface is a grey hand.

I remember the day Amy told me about losing Stephanie. *I drove my husband mad*, she said. *It wasn't enough that he had to cope with losing a daughter, he had to cope with a crazy wife as well. He left in the end. Just walked out one day. I don't blame him. He couldn't understand what I was going through.*

A voice, my own, starts to whisper: "Amy's been lying to me all this time. She knew about this park, about Mr Jones. Her husband wrote about it."

My fingers, feeling as thick and clumsy as pigs' trotters, try to open the book. I fumble my way to the copyright page and check the publication date: 2005 – thirteen years ago. It's dedicated to his mother and father. No mention of Amy.

In a weak daze, I turn the page and start reading. The book starts like this:

．　．　．

No one intended Turnwood Park. It was an accident – the consequence of a dispute between the council and the developer to whom they sold the land. Perhaps this is why the park has no shape you could put a name to. It is what artists would call 'negative space' – the space between things. I lie here on the bank above the pond, in the shade of an ancient oak. You'll find me in this place every year around this time, the time my Laura disappeared. The tree has long, vertical cracks in its bark that weep black fluid during the early summer months. I look at these cracks and I think of her. I mourn her as I breathe the scent of musk mallow and corn marigold and watch the dragonflies hover and dart. She's still here, I believe, floating in some bosky hollow or beneath the pond's pale weeds. Ask the dragonflies. They know.

Some say the park is cursed. Lie long enough in the cottongrass that grows on the shady banks and you can almost smell the swamp. There's been no swamp here since at least 1926, but some smells linger. In the early years of the last century, when this suburb was built, the council and the developer could not agree on what to do with the foul-smelling Turnwood Bog. For nearly twenty years they argued, during which time the streets and houses went up around it, and the proud new middle-class occupants screened off the foetid mire behind tall evergreens and sweet-scented shrubs. In time, a compromise was reached, the swamp was drained, and a park hurriedly and thought-lessly laid out in its place, its shape defined by the surrounding streets.

Today, Turnwood Park is what conservationists like to call a 'wild' or 'natural' space, though it's far from picturesque. It is quiet certainly, but no one could call it restful. Nature is unstable here, prone to chaotic surges of knotweed and goosegrass, and sudden plagues of frogs and flying ants that disappear as quickly as they arrive. And something moves beneath the pond's pale green mantle. Some say the bog spirit never left. I don't know about that, but whatever that entity is, it took my Laura. Ask the dragonflies. They know.

I snap the book shut. It makes a dry, dusty clap in the quietness. Roy Parker feels as I do about that place. He's seen what I've seen. He understands – perhaps the first one who did. I wonder if Mr Raynerson has read this book. I should send him a copy. I turn it over and read the blurb:

Richard Land was no fool. He'd listened to all the gossip about his local park, and he didn't believe a word of it.

True, Turnwood Park was a little wilder and more overgrown than your average public garden. And some of its insect life could be a trifle exotic. But when people started telling Richard stories about a demon living in the pond, he had to laugh.

He stopped laughing the day his wife Laura vanished while walking by the pond. Could there be some truth to the legends after all?

In his determination to solve the mystery of Laura's disappearance, Richard would stumble upon an evil more deadly and terrifying than anything he could ever have imagined...

It reads in the exuberant style of a publisher's blurb. Yet it contains hints of things that seem to parallel my own experience: the wife who disappeared; exotic insect life, recalling that monster centipede; and the demon in the pond, reminding me of the occasions when I myself have seen something shift beneath the algae. Then there's the hero's name – Richard Land – which is too similar to Richard Landry to be a coincidence. The book is, after all, here in Landry's house. So Roy Parker and Richard Landry must be connected, and that means Amy and Richard are also connected, which, in turn, links Amy to Susan. Amy knows Luke, too. They all know each other. Amy has been lying. She didn't simply arrive in my life by chance – she inserted herself there for a reason. She has an agenda, and I need to find out what it is.

Placing the book on a coffee table, I slide out the companion CD case from the shelf. As I suspected, it's an audio recording of the book, with the same swirly calligraphy on the front cover:

TURNWOOD
   Roy Parker

Read by Amy Price
   4 CDs • Complete & Unabridged

On the back of the case is a black-and-white photo of the author – a ruggedly handsome dude – and below that, a monochrome mugshot of the book's reader. It's Amy alright, looking poised, pensively beautiful, and more than a decade younger.

~

I leave the house with the book and the CD pack. At the front gate, I pause and glance back at Luke's living room window, then at the porch roof just below it and to the left, and the front door below that. I remember Luke's words: *I happened to be looking out of my living-room window at the time, and I saw her... She let herself in.*

But he couldn't have seen Susan do that. The porch roof would have been blocking his view. It's possible he heard her key in the lock, but that's a quiet sound, and it's a noisy door, with the draft excluders scraping against the tile floor. Why would he say she let herself in if he didn't know it for sure? It can only be because he's trying to deceive me, just like his friend Amy. He wants me to think that I'm a regular visitor to this house, and that Susan used to be.

Glancing up at his window again, I gasp. Luke is standing there looking down at me. He's not smiling this time.

Nervously I raise my hand in a little wave, then turn and hurry back along Oakfield Crescent.

34

TUESDAY 12 SEPTEMBER 2017

Dear Amy

By the time you read this, I'll be gone. Sorry my darling, but I can't do this any more. God knows I've tried these past few months, but each day I only seem to drive you further into despair. It wasn't supposed to be this way. Losing Steph. The grief is way beyond the power of words to express. We're like two drowning souls, unable to help each other. I've come to realise that sticking around is only making things worse for you. You need positive uplift. Ronnie and Amber can give you some of that. Your therapist, too. But me? I don't think so. Not any more.

Losing our daughter wasn't the start of it. It's been obvious for a long time that we're no good for each other. I can be intense and moody at the best of times, and you thrive on light and laughter. We inhabit different worlds, and you've made it abundantly clear you're not interested in mine. For you, the priorities, aside from the children, have always been a nice home, nights out drinking and dancing, podcasts, foreign holidays. And there's nothing wrong with any of that. You wanted me to be a decent provider, and that's not an unreasonable desire either. But for me those things are all much less important. I cherish writing, reading, long walks. Conversation yes, but also periods of solitude and reflection. I'm interested in the world of dreams and nightmares, of the things below the surface.

Maybe if 2003 had never happened I'd have found it easier to be the man you wanted me to be. But it did happen, whether we like it or not, and you don't ever fully come back from something like that. It's part of who I am. In many ways I'm still there by that billabong in the hot sun, seeing what I saw, what I *know* I saw. It's changed my perspective. While you like to look up at the heavens and hope, I look down at the ground and shudder. I've tried to rid myself of this bug in my system. I tried to write it out. And maybe if the novel had been a success and I could have written full-time, I might have found some measure of peace. Maybe if you'd given me a little more support and shown some faith in my abilities, things could have been different. But after we bought the house, your priorities changed, and I had no choice but to give up on my dream. None of that matters now anyway. I doubt I'll ever write another word.

I'm not running away Ames, just removing the shadow of my existence from your life, to give you (and me) a chance to heal. Maybe in the distant future, if the raw wound ever turns to scar tissue, we could be friends. Right now, all I know is that being apart is the best thing for both of us.

Yours in love and hope
  Roy

35

TUESDAY 17 JULY 2018

AFTER A HOT, fifteen-minute hike, I get to Amy's house in Daintree Gardens. I wipe some of the sweat from my face and run fingers through my hair so it doesn't lie too flat against my head. I ring her doorbell and mutter to myself, trying to assemble my thoughts into some kind of order. If she denies everything or feeds me more lies, I don't know how I'll react, but it won't be pretty.

Amy looks strung out and over-caffeinated when she greets me. There are dark circles under her over-bright eyes, and a small yellow stain on her top that could be egg. She's holding her phone tightly. I wonder if she's been speaking to Luke.

"Hello Amy Price." I try to keep my manner light – amused even. I show her the book and the CD case.

"Well!" she says, her eyebrows and voice pitched higher than normal. "You've been digging around in my shady past."

"I'm guessing you met your husband while doing the audio of his novel."

She gives one of her odd laughs. "Come in, Ben. I don't want the neighbours thinking we're having an affair."

I follow her into the front room, stepping over the usual mess of toys and games, and sit down on the sofa where I once – bizarre as it now seems – nearly kissed her. She offers me tea or coffee, and I ask for a glass of water. After returning from the kitchen and handing it to me, she goes and hovers restlessly near the window.

"It's not usual," she says, "meeting the author, but there were one or two aspects to the novel I wasn't sure about and wanted to discuss."

"Like what?"

"Well, er, for instance, how to pronounce certain names. At one point, the main character researches swamp monsters from around the world, and, uh, I remember one from the Congo that I had particular difficulty with..."

"Or perhaps you just wanted to meet the dashing Mr Parker." I angle the CD case with its author mugshot so she can see it.

She gives a short laugh. Then her phone pings with a text, and she glances down at it. Her eyes flit to the window.

"Is this a bad time?" I ask.

Amy sits down in a chair facing me and makes an effort to meet my eyes. "I'm sorry Ben, it's been an odd sort of morning."

"Would that have anything to do with Luke?"

"What?" Her voice comes out almost as a squeak. She shifts uncomfortably.

"You know – the guy whose photo I took in the derelict garden. The one you reacted so strangely to. Is that him texting you now?"

"Look, I've just been busy, that's all."

I pick up the book, flicking slowly through the pages. "Why didn't you tell me your husband had written a novel about Turnwood Park?"

"I don't see what reason I would have to–"

"We walked through the park together. Don't you remember? It would have seemed an obvious thing to mention."

"You mean that wild fantasy place near your house? The one Midge called a fairy garden? *That's* Turnwood Park?"

"Of course it is. Don't tell me you didn't know that!"

She shakes her head. "I honestly didn't. I'm new to this area."

"The derelict house backs onto it." I point out the illustration on the book's cover. "This is the pond. It's identical – apart from the zombie hand."

Leaning back in her seat, she breathes heavily. "I had no idea. I assumed Turnwood Park was fictional." Her perplexity appears genuine, but I know it can't be. I notice her eyes have gone wandering again.

"Maybe it's time you stopped lying." I try to say this gently, but my jaws have clamped shut from nerves and it comes out in a hiss through my teeth. "I've just been over at 25 Oakfield Crescent. That's where I found these." I nod at the book and CD case. "I spoke to Luke, who lives in the upstairs flat. He looked about as shifty as you do right now when I asked him if he knew you. Roy, you and Susan are all connected to that house, am I right? It's no coincidence you moved here, is it? You wanted to be near 25 Oakfield Crescent."

Amy is looking hard at her hands, which are clamped between her knees. Her mouth is as tight as a frost-bitten flower bud.

"I need you to tell me what's going on, Amy. Right now!"

"It's not because of the house," she says quietly, still looking at her hands. "I knew nothing about the house."

"What then?" When she doesn't respond, I repeat the question with added volume.

"She wasn't his first." She blurts this out quickly, like a child admitting to breaking a window.

"Sorry, who wasn't whose first?"

"Susan. He'd had other flings before her."

"You mean... Roy?" My hand tightens around the glass of water.

She nods. "But with your wife it was different. He fell in love."

"But the guy she had an affair with was called Richard Landry."

"That was the name Roy used on confidential.com. It was a fake name."

"But Richard Landry exists. He owns 25 Oakfield Crescent."

Amy gives a start. Her mouth opens. "Landry owns that house? Roy always told me his uncle lived in Australia."

Uncle.

Nothing is clear yet, but I feel like I'm starting to make out shapes in the mist.

"So Roy used his uncle's name on the dating website?"

"That's right. And he must have used his uncle's house as a place to meet his women." She looks sullen, defeated – too used to betrayal to get worked up about it.

The headshot of Roy Parker smiles back at me from the CD case, with his smouldering eyes, strong jaw and designer stubble. I can see why Amy called him up for a chat about pronunciations, and I can see why Susan, ten years later, got hooked on those same damn eyes.

"He would have known..." Amy murmurs.

"Known what?"

She sighs and gets to her feet. "I need a coffee. What about you?"

I follow her into the kitchen, still messy with the remains of her and Alex's breakfast, and watch as she clatters about busily with cups, and the kettle steam rises around her.

"Roy would have known what?" I try again as she hands me my mug.

"I'm not talking about Roy," she says. "I mean Luke – the giant you met. He and Roy go way back. I became friends with him, too, but he dropped out of sight around the same time Roy did. I was shocked to see him in that photo you showed me yesterday – and to find out he was living nearby. I went round there after your visit. I dropped Alex off for a sleepover at Ronnie's. I was prepared for anything – even violence. I wanted to find out if he knew anything."

"Knew anything about what?"

"About Roy and Susan and where they went."

I put down the coffee. It's boiling hot, and I can't be too sure I won't spill it in the next few seconds.

"Did he?"

I wait on the precipice of her lips.

"No," she says.

A weight drops in my stomach. I tell myself, this is not a dead end – it's only the beginning. I just need to probe a little more.

"Why do you care where Roy went? Do you still love him?"

She blows gently on her coffee. "No I certainly don't. Not any more. But I have this feeling..."

"What feeling?"

I follow her gaze to the back garden – to the deflated paddling pool and faded plastic playhouse, the dead plant on the patio.

"What feeling?"

"I think Roy may have had something to do with Stephanie's disappearance – or at least he knows more than he's saying."

"Do you have any evidence of that?"

"No, it's just an intuition. But I didn't get a chance to ask him about it because he walked out on me. That was last September. He wrote me a letter before he left, and something he said in it has stayed with me. He said 'It wasn't supposed to be this way' – talking about Stephanie. That makes me think he did know something... I've not seen him since."

"You think he went off with Susan?"

She glances at me. "Yes. Yes I do. I knew all about her by then. I'd known for months, ever since I read his messages to her. He was so bad at covering his tracks. I cracked his password on the dating site first go. He'd used Alex's birthday would you believe? I found out her name, where she lived. He swore he'd stopped seeing her, but I knew..."

Her face in the sunlight looks old, and as hard as stone.

"That's why you moved here, right? You wanted to be near him and Susan. So..." I scratch my head – hurt, confused, but still wanting to give her the benefit of the doubt. "Why weren't you straight with me about this? Why didn't you tell me you knew about Roy and Susan. It would have saved us both so much time."

She chucks what's left of her coffee in the sink and starts to clear up the breakfast things. I have to move closer to hear her over the sound of washing up.

"I don't know why I moved here," she says. "Maybe that was one reason, but I didn't hold out much hope of finding him. I thought *you* might know something though. I admit I took advantage of Alex's friendship with Midge to become matey with you." She twists and briefly meets my eyes before going back to scrubbing a frying pan. "I'm sorry I didn't tell you about any of this before, Ben. I didn't want you to think me deranged. Ronnie thinks I am, and she's almost certainly right."

She's after my sympathy, but the taste all this leaves is cold and bitter. I think of the way she suggested a play date and then invited me out to dinner. What a mug I was.

"So all along I was just a source of information to you. I told you about Devon. What else? The messages. Luke..."

She keeps her back to me, but stops scrubbing. "You're more to me than that. A lot more." When she turns, her eyes are glittering. "You've been a friend, and I don't have many of those."

Right now I don't know whether to kiss her or walk out of here. I can't walk out yet – there's more I need to know.

"I was going to tell you, Ben, I promise. But first I wanted to get you to trust me."

"Do you think Roy and Susan are living somewhere around here?"

She shrugs.

"What happened when you went over to Luke's last night?"

"We got drunk."

"You..." I can't go on.

"He didn't know anything, or said he didn't. Now I realise he must have been lying. He's living in Roy's uncle's house according to you, and he must have known about Roy's trysts with his lovers. Probably heard them going at it through the floorboards. Oh God!" Her head drops. She covers her eyes with the side of her hand.

"Why the hell did you get drunk with him?" For some reason I can't get past this part.

She folds her arms across her chest, hugging herself, her eyes somewhere up and to the left. Her hands are red from the hot water.

"We started reminiscing. Luke used to come over and do odd jobs around our old house in West Halsted. He was a dab hand at plumbing, carpentry, gardening, you name it. That's when I first got to know him. He's got some great memories of Stephanie when she was little. It was good hearing him talk about those days. Just being there with him felt good, like old times. It almost felt, in some ways, as if Stephanie was there with us." She flushes. "I can't believe he lied to me."

"Did you spend the night there?"

Her eyes climb down from the ceiling and settle on me. "What's that got to do with anything?" Her cloud of confusion is tinged with thunder.

But I'm angry too – at her recklessness and stupidity. "He was standing in that garden in the pouring rain at four o'clock yesterday afternoon – the exact time and place Imogen was supposed to meet her mother. He's also an old pal of your husband's. How could you have possibly believed he isn't connected to all this?"

"I asked him about that meeting with you in the garden. He said he loves gardens and gardening and had been thinking about tidying up the old place, even though he knows he's got no right to go in here. He didn't think anyone would mind. It's such a frustration to him every time he looks at it from his bedroom window. That's how he explained it to me."

"And what do you think now you know he's a proven liar? Does that still sound like a convincing story to you? He wasn't gardening when I saw him – he was staring at the back fence."

She frowns, pushes some hair from her eyes, then looks at me in a stupefied daze as if she's just noticed I have green skin. "How do I know *you're* not lying, Ben?"

"What are you talking about?"

"There was something else Luke said last night: he told me

he's seen you going in there regularly – to the ground floor flat. It didn't make any sense at the time, and maybe I'd drunk a bit too much to make sense of anything. But now... Now I'm wondering: is there something you're not telling me about that house? About Roy?"

I shake my head, concerned by the way she's looking at me. "Luke said the same to me, too – said he'd seen me around. But it's not true. I promise you, today was my first visit."

"And why should I believe you rather than Luke, who I've known for so much longer?"

"Because you know Luke lied to you about not having seen Roy, when Roy's obviously been using that place as a lovenest. Look, I don't know why Luke said that. Maybe he's trying to gaslight me. Maybe he's confusing me with someone else. But I swear I've never been to that house before."

She no longer looks accusing, but her expression remains stony and unreadable. The barricades have gone up behind her eyes.

"I've never lied to you about anything, Amy, and that's the truth."

As I say this, I think of those sightings of Stephanie in Turnwood Park, which I still haven't told Amy about, and feel a twist of guilt.

She softens a little. "I want to believe you, Ben. I'm not sure if I should, but I want to. You swear you found that book and CD in that house?"

"I swear."

She returns to the washing up, and I pick up a tea towel and start drying up the plates, pans and dishes piling up on the rack.

She smiles her gratitude at me. "What else was on those bookshelves at the house?" she asks.

"Horror books. Hundreds of them."

She nods. "That sounds like Roy's collection. He reviewed horror novels for a living. His own novel was a one-off. He had an experience – in the summer of 2003. He originally told me it happened while he was on holiday in Australia. Later, he admitted it happened here. Roy often lied about stuff, as I came to discover. Something came out of a pond. Something that couldn't be. He never really described what it was."

"This experience, whatever it was, must have happened at Turnwood Pond. Think about the book's title, the location of his uncle's house, the name of his hero."

"You're right, I see that now."

"How did the book do?"

"It got some decent reviews – mainly from authors he'd been kind to in the past – but sales were fairly low. The publishers didn't exactly beat a path to his door asking for a sequel. Roy was disappointed. He had dreams of becoming a full-time writer. He started on another novel, but couldn't finish it. When the kids came along, I told him he had to give up on his writing hobby and focus on earning a living. He really resented me for that." She watches the dirty water swirl down the plughole. "I don't know what he was like when he was younger – I only met him after his experience in 2003 – but he definitely had issues that man. There were probably reasons for his obsession with horror."

I nod along to all this, though I can't feign much sympathy for Roy Parker's struggles with his inner demons, nor for his failed career as an author. The man walked off with my wife. He is not the injured party here. I try to steer Amy's thoughts back to practicalities – and right now, Luke is our only lead. Luke, and maybe his sister...

"Was there anyone else in Luke's flat last night?"

"No, it was just us." She's finished the washing up and is in the process of cleaning out the sink.

"You didn't see Jean, his sister?"

Amy pauses in the act of scooping filtered scraps of food into the organic bin, and turns to me. "Luke had a sister. He *did* have a brother called Tom, but he's dead. Took his own life a few years ago. It was a tough time for Luke. Roy helped him through it."

"He told me Jean lives with him in the upstairs flat. It was Jean who knew who I was."

She looks blank – mystified.

"You didn't see any signs of anyone living there besides Luke?"

She ponders a moment, then shakes her head. "No – none."

"I think we should pay Luke another visit," I suggest.

Amy nods, then looks away and starts washing her hands. "Yes, let's go together this time. But not today. I have some thinking to do."

36

Tonight, the pipes in the basement are groaning, and sometimes they creak like twisting leather straps. I think of horses straining at the bridle, or something trapped that's struggling to free itself. The images on the TV screen flicker and dance before my eyes. I've been watching these images for a while now without taking in any of the plot, and I have no idea what's going on.

My attention has drifted, on currents I don't understand and cannot control, back to Amy and our conversation this morning. I've been wondering why she didn't want to go straight over to Luke's with me. She had some doubts, I could tell. "I have some thinking to do," she said. She could have said, "I have some *things* to do". That's what most people would have said in those circumstances. But she said *thinking*, and the choice of word was significant. Some of that thinking, I dare say, was about whether or not to trust me. She's still unsure, despite what she said, who the liar is – me or Luke.

There was something else she said to me just before that. I meant to ask her about it at the time because it struck me as odd or significant in some way, but I never got around to it, and now I've forgotten what it was. This isn't too surprising, given the poor state of my memory these days, but it's frustrating that I can't recall it. I know there's no point in wracking my brains because that's not how memory works. I have to just wait and hope that something will trigger it.

~

All this reminds me of the thing I've been meaning to do since this morning. I switch off the TV and blow dust from the old CD player. It was last used at Christmas, when Imogen and I hummed along to the crooners – Bing Crosby, Frank Sinatra, Nat King Cole, et al – while decorating the tree. I take out the Christmas Crooner CD and replace it with the first disk of *Turnwood*. After taking a sip of my wine, I press play, then lie down on the sofa with my head on a cushion and close my eyes.

I'm soon immersed in the deep, melted gold of Amy's voice as she narrates her future husband's story. *Turnwood* alternates between two different points in the life of its protagonist, a journalist and broadcaster called Richard Land. Some of it is set before Land's girlfriend Laura disappeared, and some of it is set afterwards. In the "before" sections, Land is happy, confident and uber-rational. A professional skeptic, he writes and presents magazine and radio exposés of everything from spiritual cults to homeopathy, and he is especially dismissive of cryptids, such as the Loch Ness Monster and Bigfoot, not to mention the infamous bog-demon of Turnwood Park. In the sections after Laura's disappearance, Land seems like a shell of the man he was. His confidence is shot and he is unable to move on with his life. He's lost faith in reason as a tool for explaining reality and seems to have lost his way. It turns out that Laura's was the first in a spate of vanishings, all in the vicinity of Turnwood Pond. Each incident is described in chilling, atmospheric detail, while keeping the identity of whatever's doing the snatching obscure. Land connects with other victim families and forms a friendship with a woman, Clare, who lost her daughter. Clare encourages him to open his mind to the possibilities of a paranormal explanation. Together, they start researching swamp demons.

Amy reads the story beautifully, inhabiting each character so you always know who's speaking, almost like a radio play. There are no sound effects – her voice and Parker's words supply all the necessary atmosphere. After half an hour, I'm hooked. Yet I also feel a touch of queasiness at the parallels between the unfolding story and my own life – even more so when I think of the role the writer and the narrator would, in their different ways, go on to play in it. Roy has become my bog-demon. Amy has become my Clare. It all seems very incestuous, or like that snake that eats its own tail. Eventually, it becomes too much. The queasiness interferes with my enjoyment of the story and I have to switch it off.

There's something else that's been bothering me: the pipes aren't settling in the way they usually do after the hot water goes off. They're squeaking and rubbing like something ensnared that wants to escape. It's high time I went down to the basement to check on them. I've been putting it off for far too long.

Oddly, I have an impression that I *did* go down there recently. It may even have been yesterday, but I don't have a concrete memory of it. I suppose it could have been a dream. I may have heard the pipes in my sleep and dreamed I went down there to check up on them. I wish I could remember my dreams when I wake up from them. Traces of them sneak up on me sometimes days later, and by then I can't remember if they're dreams or memories.

There is one thing I *can* check though, before I'm forced to go down there. I drain my wine and struggle to my feet. In the cupboard in the laundry room I find my Flow Doctor water pressure gauge and attach it to the tap in the sink. The pressure, after turning the tap on full, is comfortably less than 80 psi. That's eliminated one possible source of the problem – excessive water pressure – which is annoying because it means I no longer have an excuse not to go down and make a physical inspection of the pipes.

I don't know why I'm so reluctant to venture into my own basement. Surely it can't be fear. This very morning I descended into Landry's cellar, which is surely a scarier proposition than my own. There are no demons below this house, and definitely no trapped women or girls. And I am the man, after all, who slept rough in Turnwood Park one night, and may even have witnessed the swamp thing. I smile at the thought. That shape I saw moving beneath the algae can only have been the breeze. Nothing could be alive under all that scum. Except that the air, as I recall, had been very still that night. It makes me think of Roy's alleged inspiration for his novel – the thing he saw coming out of this pond in the summer of 2003.

The pipes, which had been peaceful these last few minutes, give a sudden, loud belch, making me flinch. This is followed by an impatient sort of ticking sound, like a station clock or an old man's tutting. I feel them beckoning to me. I can think of no more excuses to delay going down there.

~

In the entrance hall, I open the door beneath the staircase, switch on the light and clunk down the eight wooden steps into the chilly basement. I do so loudly in a manner suggesting that

I am the master of this house and I shall go where so ever I please. Reaching the bottom of the steps, much of my fear dissolves, replaced by a profound despondency. I remember now why I hate coming down here. The small room smells of dust, mouldy drywall and neglect. At one time we had plans to turn it into a homely den for Imogen and maybe a future sibling or two. The white plasterboard panelling, now darkly splotched with mould spores, was as far as we got. In the middle of the bare, concrete floor is a five-station home gymnasium. Its steel tubes and cables, hard seat and iron weights look like a torture machine in the bleak glow of the single naked lightbulb. After the den idea died, we used this space briefly for exercise. And after Susan disappeared, I stopped doing even that.

The basement is basically a storage place of my abandoned dreams, of futures now long consigned to the past. But I didn't come down here to get maudlin. I came to check out those damn noises, which, for the time being at least, have ceased. In the corner of the room is the wall-mounted boiler and cylindrical water tank with copper pipes leading off them. Pipe noises can occur when the heated metal expands and then rubs against structural features. I examine the pipes and ensure they're all firmly secured to the wall. I inspect the boiler thermostat: 65 degrees. Not too high.

I wait for the noises to start up again, but now I'm down here the pipes are, of course, as quiet as sleeping lambs. I could try resetting the system's air chambers, which would mean draining the pipes. It's a pain to do, and I'm not at all convinced it'll solve the problem. If there isn't enough air in the system, it can cause a hammering sound when water slams against the piping. I've heard a few knockings and hammerings over the past few nights, it's true, but also a lot of other sounds, including creak-

ing, rattling, groaning and ticking, which makes me think it's
something else I haven't yet thought of.

The silence continues, and everything seems calm and
smoothly functional. It's strange, but now I'm down here I have a
strong hunch that I won't be hearing any more noises tonight.
It's as if this was all the house wanted – for me to come down
into the basement. The pipes summoned me, and now I've
come, everything is going to be just fine. Why they summoned
me, I have no idea. But it feels very much as though they did,
and that I'm now exactly where they want me.

This is all perfect nonsense of course. No one summoned
me. Even so, I look around just to check if anything is amiss that,
while I'm here, I can put right. The home gym stands large and
redundant in the middle of the room, reproaching me with its
very presence. I sidle up to the pull-down bar dangling from its
chain and push it so it swings gently, along with its shadow on
the concrete floor. On a whim, I sit myself down on the seat,
reach up to the bar and do five pull-downs as far as my chin,
sending spasms of semi-pleasurable pain through my under-
exercised latissimus dorsi.

But if the pipes summoned me to the basement for anything
(which of course they didn't), it certainly wasn't to build muscles
or burn calories. I'm in the middle of wondering what it might
be, and whether I'm crazy for even giving this idea headroom,
when I spot something tucked almost all the way into the
hollow beneath the steps. It's a two-drawer filing cabinet. If I
hadn't been sitting here on this seat, I would never have seen it. I
remember now that Susan and I used the cabinet as overflow
storage for our paperwork.

The top drawer, I notice, isn't fully closed. It's overhanging its
lower twin by about an inch. I go up to it and pull on the handle.
The drawer is heavy, but slides smoothly open, revealing a

succession of green hanging files, each one identified by a white-card label inside a clear plastic tab. There are files here for mortgages, pensions, bank accounts, child benefit, school matters, medical matters, phone contracts, tax and insurance. It looks like a lot of old stuff that could have been chucked out years ago if I could have been bothered. Near the back, my eye falls on a file that's newer and slimmer than the rest. The file's label, written in blue biro block capitals, is "25 OAKFIELD CRESCENT".

For a moment, I just stare at it, trying to make sense of what I'm looking at. Then I reach for the top of the file and grasp it, meaning to pull it out. My hand freezes. I can't do this, or I don't want to. There is no scenario in which reading this file will turn out to be good news. Why would Susan – it had to be Susan – have kept a file on that house? It was one thing Luke saying he'd seen her there. He could have been mistaken, just as he was mistaken, or deluded, about seeing *me* there. But *this* – there can be no mistake about the existence of this file.

My mouth has gone very dry, and for the first time I feel the chill of this subterranean room. It's like a coldness under my clothes, touching my skin. I'm trapped: I have to read what's in the file, and at the same time I really don't want to. I don't want to know that Susan was a tenant there, or a co-owner of the house. And I don't want to know what it will reveal to me about her affair with Roy Parker.

But I can't just squat here forever with my benumbed fingers clamped to the metal strips at the top of the file. I have to make a decision. I could close the drawer, return upstairs and try to pretend I never saw it. Of course that won't be sustainable as a long- or even short-term strategy. I know I won't sleep a wink tonight knowing it's down here. However much I wish I could undo these last few minutes, I have no choice. I have to look inside the file.

I pull it out, keeping it pinned together between my fingers. My knees creak painfully as I rise to my feet – I've been squatting here longer than I realised. I kick the drawer shut, walk up the stairs, switch off the light and close the door. Standing in the warmth of the hallway, back pressed against the wall, I briefly close my eyes.

I have to do this. But first I need wine. I go into the kitchen and pour myself a fresh glass – a big one – then carry the glass and the file back to the living room where I sit down on the sofa. The house is silent now. The pipes have done their job. All the hammering and rattling is contained right here inside this green folder.

It's time to open it.

~

There's a single document inside, and beneath that a brown manila A5 envelope. The document, several typewritten pages in length and stapled at the top left-hand corner, is an assured shorthold tenancy agreement. The property in question is Ground Floor Flat, 25 Oakfield Crescent, East Halsted, N23 4DX. The landlord is named as Mr Richard Landry. The tenant is – and this is where my eyes almost leap clear of their sockets – Mr Ben Rose. Not Susan then. Me!

Underneath my name is the commencement date of the tenancy: 12 September 2017, the day Susan disappeared. The expiry date is 11 September 2018, a little under two months from now. So according to this document, I am the current tenant of the downstairs flat at 25 Oakfield Crescent. The rent is, according to this, £250 per calendar month – a ludicrously low amount for a flat of that size and in such a location. I would have expected it to be four times that at least. The remainder of the document comprises a set of clauses that look like the standard legalese one finds in all tenancy agreements. On the final page is my signature alongside Landry's.

Feeling numb both outside and in, I turn to the manila envelope. It's heavy, and unmarked except for six numbers with dashes between them scrawled in biro on the back: 6-4-3-9-1-7. I fumble it open – it's not stuck down – and pull out a set of keys: a standard Chubb and Yale on a keyring with a yellow plastic tag. I have no doubt they'll prove to be the keys for 25 Oakfield Crescent.

I return to the opening page of the tenancy agreement and stare for a long time at my typewritten name, my mind groping around for rational explanations – escape routes from this insane new reality. Then I flip to the back page and examine the signature: B. Rose, with the lower curl of the 'e' extended and a flourish beneath – an underline that curves twice back on itself like a flattened 's'. It's my signature alright, or a very good forgery. It could have been lifted from somewhere else I suppose, but a close inspection reveals that the biro has dented the paper. I don't think I'll need Geoff Gunnell to confirm its authenticity.

I grope in my pocket for my phone and open my banking app. Among the recent direct debits on my current account, I spot one for £250 to "RL25OC rent" that went out on the 12th of this month – less than a week ago. Scrolling back further, I find another of these payments on 12th June, and again on all the months going back to September of last year, when the payments began.

As I take this in, I feel as if the floor beneath me has cracked open to reveal a basement far deeper than the one I've just visited. Is there something wrong with my head? I resist the pull of this direction of thought, knowing it can only lead to madness. This is a fraud perpetrated on me by others. It could have been Landry, Roy or Susan, or any combination of those three. Whoever it was, they took advantage of me at a very vulnerable moment. Last autumn I was barely able to look after myself and Imogen, let alone look out for any fraudulent activity on my current account. And the amount – £250 a month – is just low enough for me to have remained unaware of it, even when I began to get mentally back on track in the spring.

But the signature is mine, and Luke says he's seen me going into that flat...

I glug some more wine, squeeze my eyes shut, press the heel of my hand to my forehead. I can't go there. Not now. Not ever. The door to *that* basement will never be opened, because it doesn't exist.

PART III

37

WEDNESDAY 18 JULY 2018

WE'RE WALKING TO SCHOOL, Imogen and I, and a breeze is gusting unenthusiastically through Turnwood Park, setting the dandelion seeds afloat and mussing the dead grass stalks and the feathers of the few remaining ducks. Now and then I'll catch a faint odour of charred grease from another day's barbecue wafting in from the neighbouring gardens. In the distance, a metal gate is slowly creaking and banging on its hinges

"How much longer until the holidays Daddy?" Imogen asks.

"Three more days including this one," I inform her.

"Three more days of school, three more days of sorrow!" she sings. "Three more days of this old dump and we'll be home tomorrow."

"I should never have taught you that song," I say with an inward grimace. "Your school is definitely not an 'old dump'."

"The words don't work anyway," she says. "I should really have sung *and we'll be home the day after the day after tomorrow*, but that doesn't sound so good."

"No it doesn't," I agree as I steer her around a dog turd.

The pond in Turnwood Park lies as still and dead as a slab of pale green concrete. There can be nothing under there – nothing alive anyway. But something is lying on the surface. It looks like part of a child's doll. A leg and both arms are missing. It makes me think of a shark attack victim. Imogen is dawdling, and I have to hurry her on.

"I can't wait for school to be over," she says.

"I'm sure you're not alone in feeling that way," I tell her. "The teachers probably can't wait to be shot of you lot either."

"Daddy, I don't think Theodora likes me any more."

I'm used to Imogen's abrupt switches of topic – only this one doesn't exactly feel like such a big switch.

"Why is that, sweetie?"

"Because when I gave her the friendship bracelet I made for her, she wouldn't put it on."

"I'm sure she appreciated it Midge. Just give her a bit of time."

She stops walking. I turn to see what the matter is. She cuts a lonely figure on the path with her little hand curled above her eyes. At first I think she's saluting a magpie, but then I see she's squinting at something. I look to see what's caught her attention. The sun is dazzling up in the top corner of the park. Even so, I'm sure I can see something there besides the trees and bushes. Someone is standing there in the long grass – a small, solitary figure. It looks like Stephanie. The world falls very still and quiet, except for the creaking and banging of that distant gate. She's watching us, her neatly brushed hair shining in the light. But as my eyes start adapting to the gleam, I lose sight of her.

Imogen starts forward as if to give chase. "Did you see her Daddy? Did you see the girl?"

I blink a few times and look again. There's no one there now

– I'm not sure there ever was, and I don't want to give Imogen any reason to go near that garden.

"I didn't see anybody sweetie."

"But you *must* have seen her."

I pluck a dandelion from the grassy bank. "Blow," I tell her, and she blows. We watch the feathery seeds scatter to the wind.

"See, they're everywhere," I point out. "A cloud of these, when the sun shines on them from a certain angle, can look exactly like a little girl."

Imogen wrinkles her nose doubtfully. "Really?"

"Really."

"Do they never look like little boys?"

I shake my head. "Clouds of midges look like little boys."

We continue on our way, and I feel relief as we leave the park, ducking under the hedge to enter the long, downward-sloping curve of Leafy Wood Lane. This stretch of our daily walk, taking us from here to school, always feels like a return to normality. There are more people about. The roads are busier with traffic. The light is clear and sharp and doesn't play tricks on our minds. For the first time since that descent into the basement last night, I feel *myself* again. Deleting that mysterious direct debit from my bank account didn't do it. Neither did banishing the tenancy agreement and the set of keys to the bottom drawer of my desk alongside the doll's head. However much I tried to dismiss it all as part of some bizarre plot against me, the doubts kept rising. What if I did those things myself and just forgot? This question, with its implication stretching out behind it like a long, scary shadow *(if I did those things, then what else might I have done?)* ensured I got no restful sleep last night. It's only now, on this bright and bustling thoroughfare, jostling alongside the other parents and their charges, saying good morning to Rose, the

257

lollipop lady, that I can see it for the nonsense it really is. I did *not* sign that agreement. I am not a tenant of the flat at 25 Oakfield Road. I have been hacked. The question is, by who, and why?

We're approaching the school gates when Imogen stops me and says: "After I gave the bracelet to Theodora and she wouldn't put it on, Antonia laughed at me."

She looks like someone who's stumbled into a dark tunnel and can't find her way out. Poor thing! I want to hug her, but there are lots of people around and she always recoils from public displays of affection.

"Wait a minute... Are you saying Antonia was there?" I smack my forehead like the detective I saw on TV the other night. "That explains everything. Theo didn't put the bracelet on because she didn't want to make her new friend jealous. You need to get Theo on her own. Then you'll find out how she really feels, and I bet she still likes you."

Imogen, hardbitten veteran of playground politics, shakes her head with a forlorn kind of wisdom. "I don't think so Daddy. Antonia said something after she laughed, and that's when I knew I can't be friends with Theo any more."

"What did she say?"

"It must have been Theo who told her. That's the only way Antonia could have known."

A pulse of protective concern clambers through my ribs and squeezes on my heart. "What did she say?"

"She said that you weren't a good daddy because you didn't even notice when Mr Jones chased me up the tree. She said you don't look after me properly."

I open my mouth to respond, but the words get stuck in my throat. Then Aisha runs up. Imogen looks at me one more time – a very serious look. I try to smile. I mouth the words *I love you!*

but by that time she's turned away and the girls are walking through the school gates together.

Shortly after returning home, I call Amy. She sounds a touch wary when she answers. "Have you done your *thinking*," I ask. "Are you ready to go and see Luke?"

"Yes," she says with a nervy sort of conviction, as if still in the process of persuading herself. "I can be at yours by ten, then we can walk over there together. Did you say you had proof that Landry owns the house?"

"I do."

"I want to see it when I come over."

"Okay. See you at ten."

I make some coffee and toast while I wait for her, and watch the fox cub dozing on one of the many bare patches on the lawn, its healthy red coat glistening in the morning sun. I have questions of my own for Amy – like what she said to me near the end of our conversation yesterday – the thing I wanted to come back to, but then forgot about. Maybe she can help me with that.

The doorbell goes while I'm brushing my teeth. I spit and glug and wipe my mouth with a towel, then hurry downstairs to let her in.

Amy is in close-fitting jeans and a stripy T-shirt. Her sandy brown hair is tied in a knot at the back, although a few gently coiling wisps have fallen loose. There's a light sheen of sweat on her face and dark patches on her T-shirt around the armpits. I'm guessing she walked here.

Her smile, once so freely given, is now guarded and makes only a brief appearance as she greets me. She seems keen to keep this businesslike.

"Do you want a drink?" I ask.

"Just some water, thanks."

I take a bottle from the fridge. She declines my offer of a tumbler and drinks straight from the bottle, wiping her mouth with the back of her hand.

I lead her upstairs. The last time we did this, she led the way with the intention of spying on our children. That was the moment – just eight days ago – when I first learned about Stephanie, and things started to change between us. I wonder now if she'd planned it, or hoped for it, knowing the conversation Imogen and Alex were likely to have. She'd wanted to get me to open up about Susan, thinking she might learn something about Roy, and maybe she used the children as a catalyst for that.

On that occasion we had a weirdly intimate moment outside Imogen's bedroom door. This time there's no sense of intimacy as we turn the other way and enter the box room that serves as my study. I see it as an outsider might, as a rather dull work room. On the desk is a computer, phone, calculator, jar of pencils and a tray full of papers. On the wall next to a small bookshelf of box files and reference books is a 2018 planner, a framed certificate and a photo of Susan smiling in Prague.

This last item is the first thing Amy notices. I think I glimpse curiosity waging a brief fight with jealousy before both are supplanted by an expression of bland politeness. "Nice picture," she mutters.

"Yes, I've always liked that one."

I pull open the bottom drawer, take out the email from the Land Registry, which I'd printed off earlier, and hand it to her.

She studies it for a few seconds before giving it back. "It looks authentic, although what do I know?" An odd, disjointed laugh bubbles out of her.

I shake my head, disappointed by her attitude. "What reason would I have for lying about this? You can check the email if you want."

"No, that's okay. I believe you. We really need to straighten all this out with Luke. Shall we go there now?"

"Before we do, there's something else I should show you."

"What?" I look at her puzzled frown and wonder I'm going mad. She's just starting to trust me. Do I really need to do this? I think I do. Luke is almost certainly involved in this conspiracy of deceit that's being spun around me. Before we confront him, Amy needs to know the full extent of it. I reach into the drawer again, this time for the tenancy agreement and the manila envelope containing the keys. I hand them to her, saying: "I found these in my basement last night. They back up what Luke was telling us about seeing me around that place."

She stares at the front page of the tenancy agreement, showing the address of the property, the dates of the tenancy, and my name, then glances at me, alarm flaring in her eyes.

"It's bogus," I tell her before she can say anything. "Susan must have put it there – she's the only person who could have. And I'm sure these are keys to the house. She, Roy and Luke must have wanted some documentary proof I was renting that flat. I've no idea why. I don't know if maybe a crime was committed there that they want to frame me for."

"A... crime?" Amy takes a horrified breath.

I reach out and touch her arm. "I really don't know, I'm just speculating."

Then her eyes fall on the final object in the drawer. She reaches in and pulls out the doll's head.

I squeeze my eyes shut, silently cursing myself for letting her see it. When I open them again, she's rotating the bald, filthy thing in her hand, peering at it from different angles, but there's no terror on her face. "Is this one of Imogen's?" she asks.

I start breathing again, blessing my luck that she doesn't recognise it.

"It's just some sentimental thing. She found it somewhere, and won't let me throw it out. Kids, eh?"

Amy gives a brief, tight smile, and tosses the head back in the drawer. "Shall we go?"

38

TUESDAY 7 FEBRUARY 2017

"YOU DON'T LOOK like your photo," were Susan's first words to Roy as he approached her in Halsted Town Park. She was sitting on a bench between the duck pond, covered in a fragile window of ice, and the old village stocks. She had chosen the location, saying it would allow her to punish him if he was late. She wore a white winter coat and a green bobble hat. Her nose was pink from the cold. She looked nervous. Roy offered the dimpled smile that he'd been charming women with since he was six, and went for a teasing response.

"I'm sorry, madam. Do I know you?"

She laughed. "Black suit jacket, jeans, grey scarf. Check. Writer's paunch. Check. Dog-eared copy of what I believe is *Below* by Bram Hill stuffed in his pocket. Check. Do I need to go on? If you're not Roy Parker, I'll go jump in that pond."

"Or I could push you in." He came closer, and she rose to her feet to step into his embrace. The first sensation, as her cheek touched his and her arms closed around him, was of warmth like a carefully nurtured candle flame, and an earthy scent of gardenia. The coincidence of the perfume bothered him only briefly. The differences between Susan and Amy were substantial enough. Susan was just an inch or two shorter than him, a far smaller height difference than with Amy, and it felt splendacious and right. He drew back a little so he could look at her. Her lips were full, her eyes small and brown. There was a teasing humour in their dark centres.

"If you were referring to the photo on the jacket of my book, that was taken thirteen years ago," he said. "Are you disappointed in what you see now?"

"Not at all. The greying hair suits you. You know you're completely out of my league."

"Don't be stupid. You look bloody beautiful."

She didn't – if he was honest. Her photo had flattered her. Not that he cared. What mattered was that he wanted her and no one else. This was the real deal – he was almost sure of it. But since they were on the subject of the physical, she had one feature he didn't have to lie about or exaggerate. "Your hair," he said. "In the winter sun it's incredible. It contains so many colours, from the palest blond to brown via every shade of auburn and flaming gold."

"Mr Writer! I'm not a girl from one of your stories." Her tone was admonitory but the pleasure he'd kindled was written all over her face.

"If you didn't exist," said Roy, "someone would have to make you up, and he'd be a miles better writer than me."

"You're definitely nicer-looking than Sailor Boy anyway," she said.

"Sailor Boy?"

"It's my private name for the photo you used on your profile."

"I felt like such a bloody fraud doing that. I didn't think I could risk using my real name and mugshot."

"You're just too well known, Mr Celebrity Author!" There was mocking laughter in her eyes.

"It's true. I was worried that one of the three people who read my book might stumble on there."

"I never believed in Sailor Boy anyway," she said. "I couldn't imagine him writing the words you wrote. He's not who I dreamed about when I... you know."

Roy shook his head and tutted. "Not five minutes in, and is that our first reference to self-pleasuring?"

She laughed, and he kissed her. The kiss became more intense. Their arms tightened around each other. To Roy, it felt a bit like melting.

"It's so strange seeing you," she said when they broke away. "Are you real?"

"Is anything?"

"Don't start with the philosophy or I shall put you in those stocks over there and pelt you with rotten leaves."

"Sounds like an idea for our second date."

This time she initiated the kiss.

"Let's walk," she said eventually, and they wandered hand in hand past the pond with its black-mirror surface.

"So?" he asked.

"So what?"

"I'm dying to know. Did you read my book?"

"I did."

"And?"

His lunch was now doing somersaults inside him. His skin felt hot in spite of the chilly air. Her opinion about this meant everything to him.

"Some of it read as if written in a dream," she said. "Other parts read as if written in a library. I preferred the dream parts."

"The dream parts? You mean the chapters set in the park?"

They were walking past a bed of daffodils, and they looked to Roy like yellow-bonneted girls all nodding along.

"When the characters entered the park," said Susan, "they went into a different kind of universe where nothing made sense. It was a bit like Alice in Wonderland. They tried to make sense of it – I really liked the way they tried to explain to themselves why time was flowing differently and why the geography of the park kept changing. I loved all that. But there were other parts of the book that seemed to come straight out of Wikipedia – all the research into swamp things from around the world. It slowed it down and took away some of the mystery. I kept wanting them to get back to the park."

Roy nodded and swallowed back the bitter-tasting muck from his stomach. They were walking near a big patch stinging nettles, their leaves rimed with frost. He wouldn't react. Not yet.

"But did you like it overall?" he asked. "Did you think it worked as a novel?"

"I didn't want to stop reading it, so I suppose that's a good sign. You're a talented writer and know how to hold the attention. But overall, no, I don't think it quite worked. You have a better book in you, Roy, I'm sure of it."

When he failed to respond she stopped and turned to him. "Are you upset?"

He tried to smile, but he looked and felt like someone with lockjaw. Eventually the words came out in a strangled sigh: "Everything you just said – I knew it at the time. But they all said they loved it – my agent, my editor, Amy. I let my ego get the better of me. God I wish I'd known you fifteen years ago, Susan! You could have saved me a fuckload of pain."

She kissed him on the cheek. "You have to write another book. The book you were meant to write. This life you're leading is killing you. I'm not saying that because I want you to be with me. Of course I want that, but even if things don't work out between us, I would still say it, because I care so much about you..."

More than ever, he felt like she was the one – the real deal. "I do have a book I want to write," he said. "It's based on a dream I had that same summer, not long after I saw what I saw come out of the mire."

"It sounds amazing. We have to make it happen. What's it about?"

They were standing by a children's playground with swings, climbing frames and slides, the colourful paintwork cocooned by frost.

"The central character's a little girl," said Roy. "She's been taken prisoner, placed in an underground cell. She knows almost nothing about her captor. He always wears a mask when he visits her, so she never sees his face."

"What kind of mask?"

"I can't remember. Some kind of animal. I'll know it when I see it. The only thing the girl knows about this man is his name, or the name he's given her. He calls himself Mr Jones."

39

WEDNESDAY 18 JULY 2018

ON OUR WALK to the house, I ask Amy about the thing that's been bugging me. "It was near the end of my visit yesterday," I say to her. "We'd been talking about Roy's book, and then I changed the subject to something else – call it *Subject X*, because I don't remember what it was. When we were finished with Subject X, we agreed that we should go and see Luke again, and then I left. But while we were talking about Subject X, you said something that intrigued me – something that I wanted to ask you to elaborate on, but I didn't get around to it. If I could remember what Subject X was, I'm sure I'd also remember what this thing was I wanted to ask you." I turn to her hopefully. "Do you have any idea what I'm talking about?"

She shrugs. "Was it about Roy's experience in 2003? Because I can't tell you any more about that than I've already said. He never really described it."

"No, it wasn't that – although that is also something that interests me. It wasn't about Roy's book. I think it was about Luke – some other anomaly in his story that we need to get straight. I wish I could remember what it was before we speak to him."

"Well," she says, "maybe it'll come up during the conversation. Maybe you'll remember then."

"I hope so."

I've brought a few items with me in a briefcase for our confrontation with Luke – physical evidence of this strange campaign being waged against me and my family. These include the tenancy agreement, the manila envelope containing the keys and the second message from Mr Jones. I would have brought all three messages, but I destroyed the third, and Imogen has hidden the first somewhere. When we get to the house, I fish out the keys from the envelope in my briefcase and try the Yale one in the lock. The door opens smoothly, as I expected it to. Amy glances at me but says nothing, her face unreadable.

I step over the junk mail and pizza leaflets on the mat and start to head up the stairs, but Amy veers into the front room. I double back and join her there. She's staring at the book-laden shelves, her face pale, her lips dry. "My God!" she whispers.

"These are Roy's books?"

She nods. "Publishers sent them to him for review. Our house heaved with the damn things. He wasn't sentimental about them, except for one. He'd have gladly left the rest behind, along with me and the kids. But I made him box them up and take them all away. He must have brought them here, but..." She trails away, her eyes suddenly full of urgency as they scan the shelves.

"What is it?"

"He had a favourite book. It went everywhere with him. It

was called *Below* by someone called Bram Hill. He said it had "gone into his blood", whatever that means. I can't see it here, can you?

After a few minutes search, I have to agree: "It's not here."

"Then neither is he," says Amy. There are spots of fire in her cheeks.

"Maybe we'll learn something from Luke," I suggest.

She doesn't respond, but follows as I leave the room and head up the stairs.

I press Luke's door buzzer and wait for his looming shadow to appear at the frosted glass. It doesn't. I check my watch – it's gone eleven o'clock. I try the doorbell again.

"Maybe he's out," says Amy after another minute has gone by. She takes out her phone and starts flicking through her recent calls.

"You've got his number?" I narrow my eyes at her. "It was him texting you yesterday, wasn't it?"

She puts the phone to her ear, seemingly unfazed by my accusatory glare. While waiting for Luke to answer, she says to me: "Just before you turned up, I texted him about Devon. I'd forgotten to ask him about it when I saw him the night before. That text I got was his reply."

"What did he say?"

"Roy never mentioned anything to him about Devon." She sighs. "He's not picking up and it's not going to voicemail either." She types a quick text to him, then gives an irritated tut. "Bloody thing didn't go through." She starts down the stairs. "Looks like we might have to do this the old-fashioned way, with a paper and pen."

~

After searching in vain for writing tools in the living room and bedroom, Amy turns to me with hands on hips. "Come on, Mr Tenant, you must know where the stationery is stored in this house." She's wearing a smile, but it's thin and doesn't reach her eyes, and there's an undertone of testiness in her voice. I get a strong feeling she's just going through the motions of trusting me. Showing her the tenancy agreement was probably a mistake. It's altered her perception of the situation. I'm now as much a suspect in her eyes as Luke.

Without saying a word, I open a set of double doors at the far end of the bedroom. It takes us into a large kitchen – a rear extension to the original Edwardian structure. Amy rummages through the drawers of the country-style kitchen units while I check out the view through the French window doors. Luke has done a good job on the garden – it's lush with dark soil and greenery, despite the drought, and with shade nets protecting the vegetable patch. I can see how the deranged boscage of thorn bushes and trees on the right must disturb him. Beyond the back fence are the taller trees of Turnwood Park, including the big oak where Mr Jones buried his pig-bone messages.

Amy finds no stationery in the kitchen, so our search moves on through a laundry area into a small room containing a desk. The books in here are more eclectic than in the front room and include several handsome-looking photographic volumes on Mr Landry's beloved Australia, but there's no sign of the Bram Hill one.

From the middle drawer of the desk, Amy pulls out a small pad of square-format, unlined paper, and a blue biro. The sight of it rings a loud, clanging bell in my memory. She's about to start writing her note when I tell her to stop. From my briefcase I excavate the note – the second message from Mr Jones – and toss it down next to the pad on the desk. There's no need for me to point out the similarities. Amy raises her eyebrows. "So this is where the notes were written?"

"Looks like it. And most probably with that pen you're holding."

She looks at the pen, and then starts examining everything on and around the desk more carefully. Her gaze stops at the sight of something in the wastepaper basket next to the desk. She reaches in, picks out a slightly crumpled piece of paper clearly torn from the same pad, and places this on the desk alongside the second message. The penmanship is identical. The paper is creased and the writing's been crossed through by two diagonal lines, but it's still perfectly readable – and recognisable...

Dear Midge, I live close to you. Sometimes I watch you go to school, but I can't speak to you. Mr Jones won't let me. Mr Jones says Daddy is being naughty. He's sticking his nose into things that are none of his business. But I'm beginning to think he's just pretending to be angry with Daddy. I'm beginning to think that Daddy and Mr Jones are secret friends. And they worked together to steal me away from you. If I try to leave here, I'm scared they'll catch me and hurt me really badly. So I must stay where I am. But I so want to see you Midge. And I have a plan for how we can meet. Mr Jones goes out every afternoon at five

That's where it stops, quite abruptly. It's the third message from Mr Jones – or a first attempt at it – and finding it here in this flat is both exciting and unsettling. I shouldn't be surprised. This house is the source of every mysterious thing that's happened to me lately. This is Mr Jones's house – whoever Mr Jones is – and it's only natural that I should find this here. Yet I feel unready for it, like a card player handed too many cards at once. They're falling from my hands before I can properly grasp them, before I can find the matching suits and the sequences.

"This is an earlier draft of the third message," I say to Amy. "They must have decided four o'clock would be a better time for the meeting than five..."

"The notes to Imogen were written on this desk," she says again, in an oddly flat voice. "And you are the tenant here, so..."

"Wait a minute! No I'm not, I keep telling you. And don't tell me you think I wrote this."

"I'm just stating the facts, Ben." She avoids my scalding stare, turning her attention to the note instead. There's a coldness to her. She sounds like a prosecuting attorney in a courtroom, as she reads out a sentence: "*Daddy and Mr Jones are actually secret friends, and they worked together to steal me away from you.*"

I grip the edge of the desk, angered and unnerved by the direction towards which her mind is steering. "It's a lie, don't you see? They were trying to turn Midge against me."

"*They?*" says Amy, with infuriating calmness. "Who is *they*?"

"I don't know... Luke. Susan. Roy. Maybe Richard Landry."

She's looking at me as if I was a stranger yelling random names in the street. The vertiginous feeling has intensified. It's like last night when I discovered those direct debits going out of my account, when the floor started to soften and crack. This time the subsidence is much worse – it's as if a great sinkhole has suddenly opened up beneath me.

"Luke is an old family friend," says Amy. "He's a big, friendly lummox, and no disrespect to him, but I doubt he'd have the brains to scheme against you like this. Also, what would be his motive? He doesn't know you. Neither does Roy. And Richard Landry is in Australia. As for Susan, I don't know what kind of relationship you two had, or why she'd want to do this to you, but... she's got what she wanted. She's got my husband. So, again I have to ask, what's her motive?" She waves the note at me. "The only person who could have written this is you, Ben."

"Why? Why would I *do* that?"

She shrugs. "I don't know." Then she gives a sigh and the shields lift a tiny fraction and I see a light in her eyes. This gives me some hope, until I realise it's the light of compassion, which is far worse than her earlier coldness. "I think..." She stumbles. "I don't know how to say this, Ben, but I think, maybe, you ought to see a doctor."

I can't let her go there. She's wrong, and I have to make her see that. I will not be pushed into the sinkhole. "Luke *lied* to you!" I snap, uncomfortably aware of the rising pitch of my voice compared to the calm steadiness of hers. "You asked him for information about your husband and he didn't say anything about Roy using this flat as a place to meet his women..."

"Maybe Roy never did use this flat," responds Amy. "I just assumed he did – it would have been very convenient." She frowns as another thought strikes her. "Maybe he believed it was too risky, because Luke and I were friends and I might hear about it – so he just left his books here. He could have come here one day while Luke was out and dumped his books on these shelves and then left. Luke would never have known."

She's shifting everything around – reinterpreting the evidence to suit her new narrative. But I can't let her. She has to see... "For God's sake, Amy! He was waiting in that garden at exactly the time the note told Imogen to go there! He was just standing there, stock still, in the pouring rain. He wasn't gardening."

Amy tilts her head at me, her eyes filled with pity. "Oh Ben, you may think that's what you saw, but how can we really be

sure. It was raining hard. You were in a very wound-up state."
She touches my arm like a kindly vicar reaching out to a troubled member of her flock. "This is actually good news. If you're
Mr Jones, it means Imogen isn't in danger. But you really do
need to get some help. For your own sake."

I snatch my arm away. "Don't *touch* me!" My face is tight and
brittle, and I feel it may crumble at any moment. But I'm not
going to break in front of her. I turn away before she can see the
tears in the corner of my eyes. In a sudden rage, I tug at the
drawer – pull it right out of the desk. Then I turn it over and
shake all its contents onto the carpet. Amy has to step back
sharply to avoid the shower of pens, dust, paperclips, staples,
pencil sharpenings and fluttering papers. Tossing the drawer
aside, I crouch down and peer at the papers, picking each one
up and examining it. One of them is Midge's response to the first
message:

*Dear Mummy. I was so happy to get the stick for my present. Thank
you! It was lovely to recieve your note, so hear I am writing back to
you like you asked. I havent told Daddy, but I think he is suspicius. I
hope you are safe. I don't want Mr Jones to hurt you. When can you
come back? I miss you. Love your Midge xxx*

I blink away a tear, tuck it into my pocket, and go on searching,
I'm not even sure what for. There's a book of matches with a logo
on the front consisting of a rhinoceros and "TM Construction"
underneath. Some digits have been scribbled on the inside flap
– 6-4-3-9-1-7 – the same numbers that were written on the
manilla envelope containing the keys. They could be a burglar
alarm code – or something else. I pocket it, just in case it's signif-

icant. Another of the papers – a yellowing sheet ripped from a wire-bound notebook – is a shopping list: oranges, broccoli, prosciutto ham, soya milk, curly kale, falafel, hummus, pitta bread, chocolate (90% cocoa). The specific nature of the items, and the hand that wrote them, give me a small, surprisingly sweet pang. It also gives me hope. Susan wrote this – no one else ever could, or would.

Still crouching, and without looking up, I say quietly: "I don't think Susan is involved. This is what they used to copy her handwriting."

"Or what *you* used," says Amy.

40

SHE WRITES a note for Luke and returns upstairs to slip it under his door, while I brood in the entrance hall. I'm trying desperately to think of ways I might convince her she's wrong. There's still the anomaly of her phone number impressed upon the second message. That could suggest the possibility of a deeper mystery – except I know what she'll say: that I jotted it down myself. If anything, the appearance of her phone number on the message strengthens the case against me. I'd best keep quiet about that.

She reappears, skipping lightly down the stairs. "I think I'll head off now." The clear implication: our investigative partnership is over, possibly our friendship, too.

"Hopefully Luke will call me when he gets back from wherever he's gone," she adds. "I'll definitely quiz him about Roy. But I honestly don't think he had anything to do with those messages. If I learn anything from him, I'll call you." Again, I see that ghastly compassion in the tilt of her head as she looks at me. "Go see a doctor, Ben. I mean it."

I can't let her go like this. "Wait."

She sighs. "What is it?"

"Think about it logically. How the hell could I be paying two-fifty a month for a place like this? It doesn't make any sense."

"Maybe you struck up some arrangement with him. A low rent for, I don't know, keeping the place maintained. You're obviously only using it some of the time."

She turns to leave. I watch her pull open the front door to the hiss of the draught excluder, as a shaft of sunlight transforms the crest of her sandy brown hair to burnished gold. I suddenly know she's not going to call me. I no longer even figure in her life. Unless...

"I saw Stephanie," I hear myself say.

She spins around, her mouth a dark hollow of shock. "What are you talking about?"

I feel out of control. What did I just do? Where am I going? I only know that I can't stop.

"I saw her in Turnwood Park about a month ago. Twice. And then again this morning. Three times in all. Imogen also saw her a couple of times."

Amy lets go of the door and runs at me. I think she's going to hit me, and I step back. She grabs me by the front of my shirt, near the collar, pulling the material up almost to my chin with her fist. The ridges of her knuckles are white, as is her face. "Don't fuck around with me, Ben. Is this more of your madness?"

"Let me go, and I'll tell you everything."

Breathing like a pressure cooker, she releases me. "I'm waiting."

So I tell her about the girl in the Hello Kitty t-shirt and jeans with the pink butterfly design on the pocket. I explain exactly where I saw her and when – the first time on the 18th of June, the second encounter four days later. I describe her in every detail, privately marvelling at how clearly I can still see her in my mind, when my memory of most things has become so shaky.

Amy listens with furious intensity, wide eyes fastened on me, lips parted. Even the hairs on her forearms are standing up as if every part of her is in super-sensing mode.

I explain how I saw the girl run into the derelict garden, awakening my interest in it, and how I found the head of the doll she'd been holding in the long grass.

"The doll's head in your desk drawer?"

"Yes."

Her hand goes to her mouth, while her eyes burn into me like pits of molten tar. "You saw the photo of her when you came to my house – when was it? – last Friday. You've known about this for FIVE DAYS. Yet you said nothing!"

"I thought... I thought I must have been seeing things. How could she still look like she did in that photo, in the same clothes, after ten months? It makes no sense."

"But you said Imogen saw her too."

"I know. It makes no sense..."

"You should have told me Ben. You should have bloody told me."

My mouth curls in resentment at her hypocrisy. "You remember what you said to me yesterday? When you were explaining to me why you kept quiet about your reasons for moving to the Forest Estate? You said you didn't want me to think you were deranged..."

"Yes, but my silence wasn't threatening a child's life!"

She brushes past me as if I'm not there, pushes open the door at the end of the entrance hall that leads into the little study.

"Where are you going?"

"To that house."

I go after her, catching the door as it's closing. "There's no one there," I call to her. "The place is a ruin. The police went in, I told you, after I found the body of the tramp. They'd have found her if she was there."

"The police weren't looking for a little girl," says Amy, striding through the kitchen. She fights with the lock on the French window doors, then pushes it open and runs out into the garden. I watch through the window as she charges through Luke's vegetable patch, knocking over part of a bamboo trellis before crushing herself through a gap in the fence and disappearing into the jungle of Number 27. I wonder if she might have a point. The police weren't looking for a little girl...

I go out into the heat of midday and squeeze myself through the same gap in the fence. In the wild garden the brambles tear at my knees. I wade through thickets of crackling brown heather and tall yellow grass, and mount the patio, where clumps of tough, purple-flowering buddleia are growing out of the cracks. Ahead of me, Amy is disappearing through the same broken back door I entered five days ago.

Coming into the house I'm once more confronted by the depressing smell of mildew and old furniture. At least the stench of putrefaction has gone with the removal of the corpse. The murky windows admit enough light to make out the black tracery of mould on the walls, the exposed entrails of a dead sofa, and the dim figure of Amy picking her way through the rubble. "Steph!" she calls out, her voice a mournful whine. "Steph! Are you there my darling? It's Mum."

I follow her into the dining room and then the kitchen,

where it's as dark as a cave. Her voice calls continually for her daughter, and I can hear her feet on the dusty tiles, and the scrape of a table leg as she bumps against it, and a scuffling sound that may be rats or something else. I fumble in my pocket for the matchbook with the rhino on the cover. I tear off a flimsy match and strike it against the back. White light flares, steadying to a dim yellow flame. In its glow I see Amy twisted around to stare in my direction. Her surprise and fear is mingled with a dawning of hope. When she sees it's me, her expression flattens out. "Why are *you* here?"

"I want to help you look for your daughter."

"And I want to kill you for not telling me about this sooner."

She scans the kitchen – shadowy but just about visible in the feeble light. She takes in the foul black ooze in the sink, the charred utensils, the rusted cooker, the filth, the stains, and I know she's thinking what I thought the first time I came here – that no one has lived in this place in a long, long time. No one sane or human, that is. Amy stifles a gasp by biting down on her fist. We're being watched by a pair of shiny black eyes.

"Rat," I wince, taking in the snout and pink ears. "Big fucker."

The rodent is the size of a kitten, but scrawnier. It's standing on its hind legs on the kitchen worktop, its fur gleaming with grease, a long grey worm of a tail coiling down over the lip of the counter. Its motionless eyes never leave us. There's something in its front paws – something long and pinkish-grey and bent in the middle. I move a little closer.

"Oh shit, it's a finger," says Amy, and she retches.

I drop the match. Luckily, it stays alight. But by the time I pick it up again, the rat has gone.

Amy starts babbling: "What the...? Where...? Whose...?" She's gasping, and looks on the verge of collapse.

"The tramp," I tell her sharply, "– was missing a couple."

This calms her down, but only a little. She starts stumbling towards the corridor on the far side of the kitchen, wailing, "I have to find my baby."

I call after her: "That leads to the entrance hall. There's a staircase there to the upstairs but it's partly collapsed and is unsafe. There's another room off the hall, which is where I found the tramp, and I'm guessing there's a ground-floor toilet somewhere. I don't think there's anywhere else that's accessible."

I don't mention the disturbing graffiti on the entrance hall wall – I WILL COME FOR THE ONE YOU LOVE THE MOST – but that's another reason I don't want her going there.

"What about in there?" she says, pointing to a door in the corner of the kitchen, almost obscured by a large cupboard. I edge my way around the table to get a better look. The door is small and easily overlooked – still, I'm cross with myself for not spotting it on my first visit, when I had the benefit of a torch. I grab the handle, turn and push. Cold air hits my face, carrying a smell of coal dust.

"A cellar," says Amy.

"Another one!" I mutter.

Amy pushes past me and starts down the wooden steps. "Stephanie?" she calls. "Stephanie? Are you there?"

The blackness of the cellar feels almost solid, and the glow of my match can penetrate only a few feet. "Be careful, I call after her. Let me go first."

"Steph?" she cries.

I grab her arm. "Stop! You don't know what you're walking into. The steps may be broken."

She relents and lets me go ahead of her. I move down slowly, checking each step for cracks before entrusting my foot to it. I feel the heat of the dying match flame biting at my fingers and shake it out. I have to stop to light another.

At the bottom of the steps, my feet find stone floor. I walk a few paces forward and hold up the flame. Amy stops at the foot of the steps and looks around. We're in a small, brick-lined cellar – no more than five feet by nine. It's empty, apart from a small pile of coal in the far corner.

Amy strides past me and kicks at the coal. Some of the pieces tumble to the floor with a harsh clinking.

"Bring your match closer," she says.

I do so, and she points out a thin, crescent-shaped hollow in the wall, exposed by the dislodged coal. Amy squats down and starts shoving the remainder of the coal aside, raising dust and lots of clatter. The crescent quickly reveals itself to be a circular concavity, maybe a foot and a half wide. She puts her arm all the way in. Then she bends very low and inserts her whole head. She emerges a second later. Her eyes are big, excited. "Give me the match."

I hand it over, and she puts her head in again, this time holding the match out in front of her.

"What is it?" I ask.

When she reappears, her coal-dust-smeared face is grinning. A strange laugh hiccups out of her. "It's a tunnel, Ben. A girl-sized tunnel."

There's something not altogether sane about Amy's grin, especially with the match so close to her face, deepening its shadows and making her eyes glitter. She's too excited. Finding a tunnel doesn't mean finding Stephanie, but I suppose it's something, when before we had nothing, and I can't help smiling too. The question is, where does it lead?

Amy puts her head back inside the opening as far as her shoulders will allow, and I hear her voice, muffled and echoey, shouting her daughter's name. There's no response, so she tries again, several times. Eventually, I touch her arm. "I don't think she's there."

Amy struggles back out. Her initial joy has been replaced with pouting defiance. "Maybe she's unconscious, or she can't hear us. But she made this tunnel, I know she did, and I think she's at the other end – wherever that is."

"I've been thinking about that." I crouch down and pat the bricks above the tunnel. "This is the eastern external wall, and the tunnel is some eight or ten feet, I reckon, from the front of the property, so it can only lead to one place, and that's the cellar of Number 25. The thing is I searched that cellar yesterday and it was empty, apart from..." I leap up, knocking my head on the low ceiling and dropping the match, which sputters and goes out, submersing us in complete darkness.

Pain explodes in my head.

"Apart from what?" I hear Amy ask.

"A wine rack," I grimace, rubbing the sore area. "The entrance must be behind it. Come on." I reach out and find her elbow with my other hand and pull her back towards where I think the steps are. My knee collides painfully with the diagonal beam supporting them. "Dammit!"

Then her voice, which now has a smile in it, says: "It's okay Ben. I've found the steps. This way." Her hand closes around mine.

41

WE GET out of the house without further mishap, and a few minutes later, we're in the cellar at Number 25, contemplating the wine rack.

I imagine she's thinking what I'm thinking, which is that there's no way an adult, let alone, a child, could move this rack aside to reach a tunnel behind. It's simply too big and heavy.

"If she took out every bottle, she could have dragged it aside," suggests Amy. "She could have dug through the brickwork behind and built her tunnel to the other cellar."

I can't help my look of bemusement. "Just to clarify: you're saying that she was held prisoner down here, in this bare cellar, and then escaped?"

"Escaped into the ruined house next door, yes. That's how she must have got out into the park."

I think Amy's making a leap here. In fact, the more I consider the Stephanie-building-a-tunnel theory, the less sense it makes. "Isn't all this just a little... *fantastical?*" I try to say this in a mildly self-doubting tone so as not to offend her. "If she did do that – escape from here – how come the rack is now back in position with all the bottles in their cubby holes? Did her captor do that? And who, by the way, *is* her captor?"

Amy's looking up at me from beneath hooded eyes in a way I don't much care for. I put a hand to my chest, and shake my head. I feel heavy and sick inside.

"I don't know who did it," she says, turning away from me and dropping onto her haunches. She starts pulling the lowest bottles out of the rack and standing them in a haphazard line on the flagstone floor. "Right now all I care about is finding her."

Once she's removed most of the lowest row of bottles, she bends right down so her head is level with the floor, and she examines the wall behind.

"What can you see?" Vaguely, I notice her bottom sticking up, which in another world, and at a different time, I might have thought looked very nice in those tight jeans.

"Nothing but wall," she groans, and sits up. "Are you sure this is where the tunnel comes out?"

"Pretty sure, except..." I pause. In the professional compartment of my brain, far away from the part that thinks about bottoms, I've constructed a sketchy floor plan of the two houses and their cellars.

"Except what?" she prompts.

"I've just realised the distance is too great. The tunnel would have to extend right under the living room."

"Isn't there a space under the living-room floor?"

I shake my head. "Houses of this era have pretty shallow foundations. The walls are supported by stepped brick footings. There may be a crawl space between them, but if so, it's no more than a foot deep." I do a quick mental calculation. "Anyone tunnelling from this cellar to the one next door would have to dig through at least twelve feet of solid earth.

Amy's shoulders slump and she shakes her head in weary bafflement. "But I saw a tunnel there..."

"How far did it extend?"

"I couldn't tell. As far as the match light penetrated. A few feet at least."

"Well, it may just have been a small hollow – a place to hide something. It could have been decades old."

She starts to get up, then staggers as she loses balance. I try to grab her, but she's falling away from me and I miss. Her hand reaches out instinctively for something solid and her palm lands hard, with all the weight of her body behind it, on one of the bottles poking out of the wine rack. Fortunately, the bottle doesn't slide away or break, and provides surprisingly solid support.

"Are you okay?" I ask her.

"Yes," she says, blinking a few times. "I'm fine. It's very lucky that bottle didn't move."

She turns to look at it, touching the red wax seal covering the cork. The bottle is one column in from the right-hand edge of the rack, and about halfway between floor and ceiling. She grasps its neck and tries pulling it out. It doesn't budge a millimetre.

"There's no label on it," she says, peering into the alcove. "And I'll swear there's no wine in it either. Why would anyone put a fake bottle in here?"

"To make his collection seem bigger maybe? I'll bet there are others." I try testing bottles at random, sliding them out and back in. Every one of them is genuine.

"Not that then," says Amy, still caressing the neck of the fake bottle and muttering to herself: "Look at its position, here on the right about halfway up. It's where you'd put a – put a door handle, if the rack..." – she tugs on it, harder this time, and we both hear a soft click – "...was a door."

I stare like a spectator at an awesome magic show as Amy pulls on the bottle and the entire wine rack swings slowly open on a silent hinge. Behind it is more wall. Thin lines in the wall mark the edges of a rectangular door. On the righthand side of the door is a steel handle with a keypad above it.

For a moment, we can only stand and stare. I'm barely aware of Amy's response. Mine is simple horror. All I can think of is Josef Fritzl. Amy grips the handle and tries to turn it. Of course, the door is locked. She starts bashing on the door, screaming her daughter's name.

"Wait!" I pull her back. "I think I have the code." I take the matchbook from my pocket. "The number here." I point to the six scrawled digits on the inside flap. "It's the same one I saw on the envelope containing the keys to this house."

"Try it," she breathes. "Quickly!"

So I punch in the numbers: 6-4-3-9-1-7. We hear a hissing, grinding sound and something metallic unbolts inside the door. I grasp the handle, and this time it turns. Amy clasps her hands to her chest and closes her eyes, as if in prayer. I push open the door.

A big part (perhaps most) of me doesn't want to see what's on the other side. My imagination is like a rampaging torrent at this moment, and it's flowing into the darkest places the mind can travel. I step quickly into the room, ahead of Amy, so I can block her view in case it's something awful. On the interior wall to the right, my hand searches for and locates a lightswitch. I take a breath – a deep, steadying one – and press it. An LED striplight flickers on.

What I find is just a very simple room. There's no maggot-infested corpse – only poorly whitewashed breeze-block walls, a stained pink carpet, a child's bed, a table and a stool. Amy pushes me aside and goes in. There's a doorway in the far wall, leading to another room. She looks in there briefly, then returns to the bed, which is covered with a yellow duvet patterned with unicorns. There's a teddy bear on the duvet with a red heart on its chest. It looks new and untouched. Amy picks up the pale yellow pillow. With exceptional care, like a pilgrim handling a relic, she removes a strand of dark hair from its surface. Her face shines for a moment in a kind of awe. Then she collapses onto the bed. She looks broken, her limbs spread awkwardly on the small bed, her head bent forward as she holds the pillow close, nursing it like a baby. She makes a moaning, keening sound, and then, throatily: "Oh my God! She was here. She was here."

I go and check the other room. It's a tiny bathroom, barely big enough to fit a toilet, sink and shower. I'm struggling to believe that I'm not in some waking nightmare. Could a child – could Stephanie – have been kept here? What monster did this? Could Susan have been involved? I don't want even start entertaining that idea. And where is Stephanie now?

The sink with its taps are tiny – child size. Something briefly flutters into my mind when I look at those taps, but it's gone before I can grab hold of it. I try turning one of them. Nothing. The water's been cut off. Was that a punishment, I wonder, or because the cell's young occupant has now gone? Below the sink is a cupboard. There's barely space for me to crouch down to look inside. I have to squash myself between the bathroom wall and the cupboard door. Beneath the cupboard's single shelf, behind some towels, I find what I'm looking for. The wall below the sink is made of plasterboard with a hole cut into it for the drainpipe. Stephanie must have used a knife or something to cut herself a much bigger hole. There's a space beyond this for pipework, and then there's the brick wall lining the cellar at Number 27. Stephanie removed enough of these bricks to allow herself to escape. It must have taken her months with the tools she had. Amy's "tunnel" was essentially the width of the wall between the two houses and the short space beyond it. If her match flame had been a little brighter, she'd have seen the towels in this bathroom cupboard.

I emerge from the cupboard to find Amy watching me from the bathroom entrance. "I've found Stephanie's escape route," I tell her. She looks at me and the pain in her eyes is almost unbearable. "Where is she? Where's my baby gone?"

"I don't know."

"How long was she in here?"

I hesitate, thinking about my sightings of Stephanie in the park, wondering if I should cushion the truth and then deciding not to. "Around a year, I guess."

"Oh my God." She leans heavily against the doorframe. "This tiny place..."

Amy looks ready to collapse. I wish I could offer her something to calm her nerves. I check the upper shelf of the cupboard. There's toothpaste, soap, shampoo, even some Neurofen for children, but no sleeping pills or sedatives. "Maybe we should go back home. Talk about what to do next."

"She was eight," says Amy. "Eight! Who would do this? What monster...?"

I get to my feet. "Come on." I try to coax her out of the bathroom, out of the cell. She follows reluctantly.

As we emerge from the cellar into the clear daylight of the hallway, I notice she's got some things in her hands. One of these is the naked body of the doll – the one whose head is in my desk drawer.

"Where did you find that?"

"Under the bed," Amy replies, her voice hollow.

The other thing she's holding looks to me at first like a pale pink rag. Looking closer, I see it's a shirt. I hear a dull click, and realise it's my throat making a dry swallow. I take the shirt from Amy and examine it. There's a coffee stain on the front, and the collar is frayed. It's my shirt, the one I threw in the bin four days ago.

"Where did you find this?" I ask her.

"Under the bed," says Amy in the same zombie-like tone. "It doesn't smell of Stephanie though." And then she looks at me and her eyes suddenly sharpen. "It smells of *you*."

I shake my head. "No, Amy."

Frightened now, she takes a backwards step, bumping into the bannister rail. She's looking at me as if I'm some kind of monster.

"Amy, someone planted this here. I threw it out days ago. I put it in the bin."

Her lips have gone white. "I'm going to call the police," she says, and she turns and runs towards the door.

I catch her before she can open it, and spin her around so she's facing me. I hate the way she's cowering as though I'm about to hit her.

"Amy please. If you tell the police about this, they'll take Imogen away. I can't let that happen. Look, let's talk about this before we do anything – anything that can't be undone."

She's wriggling, trying to free herself from my grip, forcing me to restrain her with my whole body in a weird, unnatural embrace. I don't want it to be this way. I like her, dammit. Who knows, maybe what I feel is more than just *like*. But at the same time I know that I'll do anything – I'll even hurt her – to stop her going to the police.

She struggles more fiercely, digging the headless doll into my chest and shrieking in my ear: "Let me *go!*"

"I can't. I'm sorry. I'm so sorry. You'll have to stay with me until we sort this out – until we find out who's really responsible."

I drag her away from the door and out of the hall into the Australia-themed bedroom where there are no windows onto the street. I push her down so she's seated on the bed, her arms pinned to her sides, and I put my face close to hers, trying to make her look at me. I want to sound calm, rational. "Amy, you have to believe me, I had nothing to do with your daughter's kidnapping..." But it's hard to keep my voice steady when I have to strain every muscle just to keep her from bolting.

"What did you *do* with her?" Her eyes are crazy now. Spit has flecked the corners of her mouth. "You mad bastard! You mad sick fucker! Do you even remember?"

She's making me anxious. I want to hit her just to calm her down, but I know that will only make things worse. Watching her scream at me, I can almost see Susan in her place, and I wonder, have I been here before? How do I know that hitting will only make things worse?

"Mad Mr Jones!" Her voice has a taunting, sing-song tone. I want to gag her mouth to make it stop talking. "You kidnapped Steph. You wrote those notes pretending you were Susan. You frightened Midge out of the tree. What else did you do? Did you kill Susan and Roy?"

"Shut up!" I snap. "Please! Just... stop talking."

She stops, and appears to calm down.

I let out a relieved breath. "If I let you go..." I begin. But then I have to break off as she tries to bite my face. "Amy, stop that!"

She's like a wild animal, snapping at my nose. "Listen to me a minute. If I let you go, do you promise not to run?"

"Fuck you!" She spits in my face.

My hands are getting tired. I can't hold her for much longer. I *hate* this. I hate *myself* for what I'm about to do, but what choice do I have? We saw no rope or cord during our earlier search, so I can't tie her up. But the house does have one very secure location. I pull her to her feet, drag her out into the hall and then back down into the cellar. She resists every step, clasping onto door frames as we pass through them.

"Oh no! You're not putting me in there. Ben. Please!"

"You're not giving me any choice."

I feel for the phone in her jeans pocket and wrestle it out. She tries to grab it back and I have to rip it from her fingers. Then I duck as she tries to push the neck stump of the decapitated doll into my eye. I shove her into the cell, using more force than I intended, and she crashes onto the bed, hitting her head against the wall.

I wince. "I'm so sorry! I'll come back soon when you're... in a better mood."

She struggles to her feet as I start to pull the door closed. "Ben, don't do this, pl..."

The door locks shut, cutting off her voice. Her fist starts banging against it. I mutter an apology, which almost sounds like a prayer, and run back upstairs.

42

IT's after one o'clock when I step out of 25 Oakfield Crescent. A little over two hours have elapsed since Amy and I entered the house, yet it feels more like two days. I stumble along the pavement like a refugee from a dark world, squinting against the spears of sunlight. The heat has turned the air to shimmering glass. Plane trees and pylons tremble under a searingly blue sky. The streets are silent and deserted. Even the ever-present Sid must have retreated into some shady nook – or is he, like everything else, shunning my presence? The wretched pink shirt, I discover, is still in my fist, clutched like a ragdoll won from a funfair sideshow.

It was bad, that cellar. Bad stuff happened down there. A little girl was imprisoned for nearly a year. But that wasn't my doing, whatever Amy may think – whatever the evidence shows. I stare at the shirt, checking once again that it's really mine (it is). I'll burn it before Amy can use it against me. She must understand, I had to protect myself. I was reasonable and restrained. That's what I tell myself. But the painful scratches on my arm, the dull ache in my chest where she jabbed me with that headless doll, suggest a different story. I perpetrated a brutal event. Every few seconds I recoil, as if a dark bird has flapped its wings in my face, but what I'm seeing is Amy stuck in that cell.

But she was mad. She believes I kidnapped her daughter. She was going to tell the police. I'd have lost everything – my house, my job, my reputation. Maybe I'm not even so bothered about any of those things, but I'd have lost Imogen, and next to her everything else fades into the brown horizon. Amy might as well have put a gun to my head and shot me – what she was threatening was no worse. I had no choice.

And now? What do I do now?

I must find the real culprit – the one who planted false evidence: the tenancy agreement and this shirt, the one who pretended to be Susan in those notes to Imogen and then attacked her when she was climbing the tree. I have to find Mr Jones. I only have a few hours. Soon Amy is going to be missed. Her friend Ronnie will call. And Alex will need picking up from school...

That's when I stop, suddenly breathless. I sit down heavily on a brick pedestal – part of someone's front wall – and mop my brow. I'd forgotten about Alex. He'll be stepping out of his classroom in just two hours, looking around for his mum. Amy will have to write a note for the teacher, giving me permission to pick him up. She won't do that of course. Why should she? I'll have to forge it. A sickly sigh leaks out of me. Is this what it's come to? And assuming they accept the forged note and release Alex to me, what then? What's the next step in your brilliant plan, Ben?

I know I'm in a bad way as I let myself into the house. I feel exhausted at a bone-deep level, and demoralised. I know I can't leave Amy in that cell for the whole day. She'll go demented. The bathroom isn't even plumbed in. I'll have to bring her water at least, and let her know Alex is okay.

I toss the shirt onto the kitchen table, thinking I'll deal with it later. Then I crack open a beer and drink almost half of it in one gulp. I make myself a sandwich – tuna (a pretty dry experience, as we've run out of mayo) – and take the bottle and the remains of the sarnie into the front room. On my laptop, the emails have been marching in. I have to arrange a site visit to Mrs Mattinson's house in Pine Walk (another basement!); Mr Porter of Elm Close requires an urgent inspection of an expanding crack in his external front wall; and I've been commissioned to write a report on the stability of a fire-damaged house in The Larches.

I close my eyes, too tired to focus on any of this.

When I next look at my watch, it's twenty past two. I must have slept because I have a little more energy now, but time has crept on and soon I'll need to go and pick up Imogen – and Alex. I cringe at the thought of lying to the teacher. What am I doing? Have I fallen completely out of my tree? Amy's been in that cell for nearly an hour and a half. I should let her out and end this madness. To hell with the consequences. Even while I'm thinking this, I know I'm never going to do it. My best course is to leave her in there for the rest of the day – let her understand I'm serious. Maybe by early evening she'll have calmed down, or she'll be desperate enough to negotiate.

I check her phone for messages, hoping to find one from Luke. There's a text from her dentist telling her she's due for a check-up, and another from DHL saying they tried to deliver a parcel, and one from Ronnie. Unfortunately, there's nothing from Luke. Before I can read Ronnie's text, the phone's battery dies. With a sigh I get off the sofa and plug it into the charger. The phone lights up, but asks for a password. I fling it aside, irritated and maybe – no, definitely – a little worried. Ronnie strikes me as the proactive type. If she doesn't get a response by the end of the day, she'll likely go over to Amy's to check up on her. My room for manouevre is becoming compressed. The walls are closing in.

I need to think. Who's doing this? Who is my enemy?

I desperately wish I could recall that remark Amy made during our conversation yesterday. She said something about Luke, I'm sure of it, and I'm sure it was important. But trying to remember it is like trying to crack open an egg by staring at it – a complete waste of time and energy.

Needing air, I open the window. Sounds of someone practising the piano drift in from a neighbouring house. The hesitant notes, with their frequent pauses, seem to match my own state of mind. I'm in the dark, fumbling around in search of solid facts about my enemy. It's not entirely dark though. I can discern vague shapes here and there – semi-solid facts I suppose I could call them. For example, I know for certain that Richard Landry is in Australia. The police tracked him to a town in Victoria, so I can be pretty sure he isn't the one writing notes to Imogen and stealing shirts out of rubbish bins. He may be a signatory on that false tenancy agreement, but signatures can be forged. Landry can be crossed off my list of suspects.

As for Luke, I know he lives in the house where Stephanie was imprisoned, and that he was in the derelict garden at the appointed hour of four o'clock yesterday afternoon, looking very suspicious.

And what about Roy? I know he's Stephanie's father, which gives him a clearer motive than anyone for kidnapping her. And he has his demons, according to Amy. *He had issues*, she told me. *There were reasons for his obsession with horror.* He wrote a book set in Turnwood Park, and had a bad experience there during the long hot summer of 2003. Could he have developed Josef Fritzl tendencies then, which later emerged during his marriage to Amy? It's possible. He could have forced Susan to write those notes to her daughter, hoping to kidnap her, too.

Roy, I've decided, is my number one suspect.

But Amy is sure he isn't living in that house. Her reason? A book. A book that had "gone into his blood" and "went everywhere with him". The book wasn't in the house, so neither was Roy. That was her conclusion. But can we be certain the book isn't somewhere there. We didn't search the place *that* thoroughly. I remember the title: *Below*. And the author? Bram Hill. I fire up the laptop and check Amazon for details. It was published in 2003 (a big year in Roy's life, it seems). As far as I can see, it was the only book ever written by Mr Hill.

For centuries (the blurb reads), *the Nyx reigned over the dark silence of her underground citadel, feeding on the spiders, bats and eyeless centipedes that wandered the prehistoric passageways.*

The Nyx knew nothing of human civilisation – until, one day, they came: on the land above her cavern, they built a grand hotel, shattering her age-old peace with pulverising light and noise.

The Nyx shook, she quaked, she very nearly perished. But in the end she survived, and by the time she had regained her former strength, her entire being had become distilled into one irresistible mass of destructive fury.

She would have her revenge.

The front cover is impressive. It shows a giant, rather frightening hand reaching up through the earth towards the foundations of a tall, top-heavy building – a little reminiscent of the famous poster of the shark movie, *Jaws*. I'm starting to see a pattern with Roy: his obsession – his fear – appears to be about dangerous things living below the surface. The bog-demon from his own book has this much in common with the Nyx. This makes me think of Stephanie living for a year in that room below the ground. I wonder if Roy's bog-demon is also female. Does he see all girls and women as belonging to the underworld? It seems to me increasingly obvious that Roy is my persecutor. Roy is Mr Jones. Which means he must be living nearby – with Susan.

But what about Devon? my internal doubter asks. *I can't WAIT till Devon,* she said just days before she disappeared.

The clock in the corner of the screen shows the time is two-forty-five. I'm already running late for the school pick-up and I haven't even forged a note for the teacher. I slam shut the laptop and run upstairs for some paper and a pen.

"Alex's mum has a toothache," I tell Miss Hardacre, struggling to catch my breath after my mad dash to East Halsted Primary. "She had to arrange an emergency appointment with the dentist. It was a last minute thing and she asked if I could pick them both up."

The teacher barely glances at the note I've shoved into her hand – just passes it back saying "well I do hope she feels better soon." Her attention has already been captured by a crying child.

So there I am, walking out of the school with both Alex and

Imogen in tow, while they excitedly celebrate this unanticipated playdate.

"Has my mummy got a *very* bad toothache?" asks Alex.

"I'm afraid so," I tell him.

"How did she get it?"

"I'm not sure."

I hadn't expected this level of questioning from the normally taciturn boy.

"Maybe she cracked a tooth," suggests Imogen.

"Or her tooth came out when she ate a sweetie," says Alex.

They both giggle at this idea.

"I'm sure she'll tell you all about it when she sees you," I say in an attempt to end the speculation.

After the shady climb up Leafy Wood Lane, we enter the unfiltered sun of Turnwood Park. The heat of the day seems to collect in its rounded slopes and hollows and on the baking tarmac of its path. It smoulders like fire on the dry grass. I glance to my left, towards the back of Number 25. The roof of the house is just visible beyond a screen of trees. I think of Amy in her cell. It'll be cooler down there, I hope. But she must be thirsty, and scared as hell. She doesn't trust me to pick up her boy and keep him safe – wouldn't want me to anyway. To her I'm now a monster.

The heat licks at my face and sears my lungs. Sweat trickles down my neck and back like warm tea. I wipe it from my eyes and the bridge of my nose. She doesn't understand I'd sooner walk through fire than hurt a hair on Alex's head. Up ahead, the children walk side by side. They look beautiful in the light, like a pair of angels. They almost seem to glow. I have never so loved nor envied their innocence.

A muggy breeze dries the sweat on my cheek and whispers through the trees, creating a shifting mosaic of light and shade upon the ground. I look up at the towering oak and its millions of leaves, which have darkened over the summer to the colour of winter kale.

Imogen and Alex have left the path and are stepping between and over the oak's roots that coil through the dust like petrified snakes. There is no rib buried there today, which brings me some relief – and Imogen isn't looking for one either, which brings me more. Briefly, the park becomes an almost benign place, until Alex gives a shout. He's pointing at the pond. "I saw it ripple!" he cries. "There's something in there."

When I turn to look, the water is still – unnaturally so beneath its thick green lamina. Imogen runs down to the bank and picks up a piece of fallen branch. Alex, more cautiously, follows her to the edge of the water, watching as she leans in with the branch to prod at the algae cap.

"Come away from there!"

Imogen looks back, surprised by the forcefulness of my tone. "We have to go," I add in a calmer, if still harsh, voice. It's a struggle keeping a lid on my nerves when everything feels like it's unravelling, but I must – at least in front of the children. They return to the path and we resume our walk home.

"My daddy once saw a hand come out of a pond," says Alex. "It tried to grab him but he ran away."

"Eugghhh!" shrieks Imogen in an ecstasy of disgust.

I stare at the boy. The sense of hopelessness recedes, at least for now, as my curiosity is pricked. "He told you that?"

"Yes."

"When did this happen?"

"Before I was born."

The famous incident from 2003. He didn't tell anyone about it, according to Amy – except, it turns out, his son.

43

THURSDAY 9 MARCH 2017

ROY SAT naked in bed apart from the panda mask on his face. Beside him, Susan was sleeping. Now and then she'd shift about and her head would roll against the pillow as if she was stuck inside a troubled dream. She often slept during their afternoon liaisons. He didn't begrudge her this, since it was only to catch up on the sleep she'd missed while sexting him the night before. Ever since her husband Ben got wise to their online affair, they'd been forced to use burner phones in late-opening cafés – her in East Halsted, him in West.

During the day, they operated on different shifts. Susan, like Amy, did breakfasts and got the kids to school, whereas Roy, like Ben, did the afternoon pick-ups and made the tea. That meant Roy could catch up on his missing zeds by sleeping late. After-noons were Susan's chance to do the same. And it wasn't so bad, as it gave Roy a little extra writing time while she snoozed. For writing, read planning. He hadn't yet committed actual words to paper.

Propped against Roy's duvet-covered knees was a notebook.

He knocked his pen rhythmically against the panda's shiny white cheek as he read through his scrawl. The outline of his novel was shaping up splendaciously. It was based on a dream he'd had during that pivotal summer of 2003. He'd dreamed of a man called Jones who lived in an old, semi-ruined house and wore a bear mask. He stole children and imprisoned them in his earthen cellar. In the end, the people of the community took their revenge and drowned him in a swamp. Roy sensed all this had happened a very long time ago – maybe hundreds of years. He would set his novel in the present day, and it would be written from the point of view of one of his young captives. Roy had mapped out the crucial scenes and sketched quite a detailed background for his female protagonist. The sole remaining blank – admittedly a big one – was the main man, the bad dude Mr Jones. Who was he? What was his motivation? What were his plans for the girl?

The dream had told him nothing about that.

Roy had hoped that physically donning the mask might help. But even looking at the world through Mr Jones's disturbingly round eyeholes gave him no particular insights into the fellow's experience (besides a stuffy feeling of confinement and a limited field of vision). Perhaps his enigmatic quality didn't matter – or rather, perhaps it was the whole point. The very absence of a personality could make Mr Jones all the more frightening. He was a baleful emptiness, a lacuna at the heart of the book. Readers could interpret him as they pleased, or just be chilled by his creepy anonymity. Even so, Roy thought that he at least, as the author, ought to have some notion of who his chief antagonist was, even if he didn't disclose any of this in the book.

If the man behind the mask remained a troubling void, the mask itself was a splendacious success. He'd trawled Amazon for bear masks, but none were quite right, being either too friendly or too scary. What he needed was a touch of both. Purely by chance, one of his searches turned up a panda in the "customers also bought" section, and he knew immediately that this was what he'd been searching for. If pandas had been known of in medieval Halsted, he felt sure Mr Jones would have worn such a face. Roy recalled him as a slender fellow in the smart grey tunic of an upwardly mobile merchant. Roy would place his version in the modern-day equivalent of a grey suit. When combined with the panda face, it produced an effect that was inexpressibly sinister.

Susan stirred and opened her eyes. She looked up at Roy, and immediately recoiled. "Shit! You scared me!"

"Really?" said Roy, moving closer to her. "Are you saying this doesn't do it for you?"

She smiled, stretched out a bare arm from under the bedclothes and pushed the mask up off his face. "Appearances can be contraceptive," she said.

That made him cackle. "One of Ben's dad's witticisms, I presume?"

Susan nodded and glanced at her watch, then back to Roy. "Gimme a kiss, Mister Panda. I just had a very weird dream and I need you to tell me I'm not evil or insane."

Roy obliged her with the kiss, not just on her mouth but also her neck, her shoulder and both breasts. "What was your dream?" he asked.

"I don't want to think about it. Please just kiss me."

He did so, and placed a hand between her legs. She moaned and closed her eyes, then flipped them open and slapped his hand away.

"Shit, I'm supposed to be giving a lecture in Global Digital

Culture in less than an hour." She gave him a terminating smacker on the lips. "Sorry my little Love Panda. Can we continue this next week?"

After her shower, while he watched her dress, he thought: *I love her. I really do. This is the real deal.* He asked her again about her dream. She said nothing as she clipped on her bra and then pulled on her skirt. He noticed her eyes were red.

"What's wrong?" he asked. "Come and tell Uncle Roy all about it." He patted the bed next to where he lay.

Susan ignored him. She shrugged on her blouse and was in the middle of doing up the buttons when she suddenly stopped and looked at him. Her eyes had lost all their humour. They were wet with tears, but their gleam also struck him as oddly cold.

"You and I were living together somewhere, I'm not sure where. It was a big house with a big, fuck-off pool in some sunny part of the world."

"I'm loving it so far."

"The thing is, it was just us. Imogen wasn't there. I always imagined, if we ever did move in together, that Midge would be with us. I mean she's my daughter, my own flesh and blood. I can't just leave her."

Susan came and sat on the bed, her shirt still half open. Roy's notebook fell away as she twisted towards him and collapsed onto his chest.

He stroked her hair, wanting to believe with all his heart that he loved her and wishing he knew what to say. "You don't know what'll happen Sue," he eventually murmured. "You may win custody." He had no idea if this was true – he certainly didn't want it to be true – but it sounded like something she would want to hear him say, and that was all that mattered.

She sat up and stared at him, her eyes like chips of broken glass. "You don't understand, do you?"

And he thought: *Oh no!* "Understand what?" he asked.

"Roy, what I'm saying is that I was happy in the dream. I was happy she wasn't around."

44

WEDNESDAY 18 JULY 2018

"Have you seen this book before?" I ask Alex, showing him the copy of *Turnwood* I'd taken from 25 Oakfield Crescent. We're at home now, in the kitchen. The children are chugging down big glasses of iced water.

"That's my daddy's book," says Alex. "Why is it here?"

"I came by a copy," I tell him.

"Look, Immy!" Proudly, he shows her the picture on the front, with the hand emerging from the swampy pond.

"Eww! That's ghastly!" she screams, suitably impressed. "Did your daddy really write that book?"

"Yes."

"Is it about a monster in the pond?"

"Yes." He's nodding and grinning, flushed with delight.

"Where is your Daddy now?" she asks.

The grin wavers. "I don't know. But I get messages from him, like you get messages from your Mummy."

I was about to interrogate Alex about his dad's experience with the swamp monster, but this latest revelation from the ever-surprising boy is so much more interesting.

"You get messages from him?"

"Yes. They don't always make sense, but I try to work them out by jiggling around the words. It's like a puzzle."

I shake my head, confused. "Where do the messages come from?"

"From there." He points at the book.

"From *this book*?"

"Yes. I'll show you." Putting down his water, he takes the book from my unresisting grasp and flicks the bottom corner with his thumb, riffling through the pages to the end. He shows us the final folio. "It's got two hundred and twenty-four pages, see?"

"Uh-huh," I murmur, dumbly fascinated about where this is going.

Alex hands the book to Imogen, takes out his phone and clicks on an app called Random Number Generator. A screen opens with boxes for minimum and maximum number. He inserts the numbers 1 and 224 in the relevant boxes and hits 'Generate'. The number 95 comes up. "Turn to page ninety-five in the book," he instructs Imogen.

She does so.

"Each page," says Alex, "has thirty-five lines. I counted them."

He inputs 1 and 35 into the minimum and maximum boxes, and it generates the number 10, so he asks Imogen to read out the tenth line of the page.

She quickly counts off the lines under her breath, then clears her throat dramatically and reads: "*in this very park, so thickly covered by plant life that will...* That's where the line ends."

"How many words is that?" asks Alex.

Imogen counts. "Twelve words."

Alex recalibrates his number generator. "What's the twelfth word, Immy?"

"Will."

A rising excitement swims in the boy's eyes. "That's the start of the message. It sounds like it could be a question."

"This is *amazing!*" says Imogen. "Let's carry on."

With a disappointed shake of the head, I leave them to it. For a brief moment I thought Alex had shone a lamp – maybe even a floodlight – on the dark pit I've been scrabbling about in these past few days. Instead, it turns out the poor kid is just playing a game to give himself the illusion of contact with his father. Well, I suppose it's no worse than the fantasies my mother feeds to Imogen. I just hope they don't chance on an unpleasant word.

I go and fetch my laptop and Amy's phone from the front room and take them through to the playroom with its connecting door to the kitchen, so I can keep an ear on the children. The time is now twenty to four. Amy's been locked in her cell for more than two and a half hours. Soon Alex is going to start wondering what's happened to his mum. A hollow note of despair seeps from my throat, and I bash my forehead a few times with the heel of my hand. *What have I done?*

I can't get into Amy's phone, but any messages she's received flash up briefly on her home screen. There have been no more since I last checked. My own phone shows two missed calls from a new client, John Porter. I call him to set up an appointment. It turns into a longer conversation.

"I had my house underpinned five years ago," he tells me in a reedy voice, "and the crack in my front wall appeared last year. I've been measuring it each week and it's definitely getting bigger.

"Who did the underpinning?" I ask.

"It was a builder called Thomas Macey," Porter replies.

I give a sympathetic sigh.

"You know of him?" asks Porter.

"I gave evidence against him in court four years ago after a house he'd been working on collapsed. He failed to support the foundations properly during a cellar conversion. The judge ordered his company to pay a quarter of a million pounds in damages. Put him out of business."

"Really?" says Porter. "So there wouldn't be any point in suing him, if it comes to that?"

"No. Especially not as he's dead. He took his own life a few months after the court case."

"How awful! Well, hopefully my buildings insurance will cover any remedial work. Or Mr Macey's will."

"Hopefully."

Privately, I have my doubts. In the case I worked on, Macey's insurer refused to pay out after my testimony proved his incompetence. And the owner's insurer claimed they weren't liable if the house fell down of its own accord – ridiculous, but true. As far as I know, the owners are still chasing them through the courts. I don't tell Porter any of this, not wishing to depress him. Also, something is nagging at a corner of my mind – something about Thomas Macey.

"Mr Rose?"

"Hm?"

"I asked when you'd be able to come and take a look at the crack?"

"Ah, well let me see..."

I've locked a woman in a basement to stop her telling the police that I kidnapped her daughter. Oh yes, and I have her son in the next room and he thinks she's at the dentist.

"My diary's pretty clear, Mr Porter. How about tomorrow morning at 11?"

As I end the call, Imogen gives a shout from next door, and the word she utters makes my neck hairs stand up.

"Devon!"

I hurry through to the kitchen and find them both sitting at the table, Imogen holding open the book, Alex with his phone in one hand and a pencil in the other. He's writing down the word she's just shouted on the pad I use to write shopping lists.

"It's spelled *D-e-v-o-n* , not *D-e-v-e-n*," I tell him.

"So far we have *will, see, I* and *Devon*," says Imogen. "It doesn't make any sense yet – *but this is so exciting!*"

"Can I have a quick look?" I ask, taking the book from her. "Which page was it on?"

"One-nine-two," she says. "It's on the sixteenth line."

I quickly read the page, trying to get a sense of the context. In the scene, Richard Land and his friend Clare are busy researching bog-demons in the library – possibly because Wikipedia wasn't very big in 2003...

"There's a bunyip legend in a town called Devon in Victoria," said Clare. "Aborigines carved this image of it into the bank of a nearby billabong. Look at the hand, Rich." She passed the book to him and he studied it. It was an ugly thing, like a long, flaccid-skinned dog with an elongated head, but it had oddly human arms – and hands. Yes, it could be the same, he thought. Maybe. But this was Australia, the other side of the world.

"Can we have it back now Daddy?"

"Of course," I say, absently returning the book to her. It hadn't occurred to me that Devon could be anything other than the English county. I suppose I didn't want to believe that Susan had travelled any further from me than that. So did Roy and Susan go to Devon, Australia, to research a bunyip legend? What the hell is a bunyip anyway? Or a billabong for that matter? Richard Landry lives somewhere in Victoria. Not Devon, or it would have definitely rung bells with me, but maybe close to Devon.

It's another piece of the jigsaw, possibly, or it's a red herring – a slimy, bloated red herring living in a billabong. I boil the kettle for some tea, suddenly and painfully aware of Amy and her dry throat less than a quarter of a mile away.

From the table, Imogen exclaims another word – *in* – and the children start attempting a possible word order for Roy's evolving message:

"Will I see in Devon?"

"I will see in Devon."

"I see Will in Devon."

"The next word will be *you* – most definitely!" predicts Alex.

But the next word isn't *you*, it's *window*, which doesn't help them at all in terms of sense.

I prepare some celery sticks and carrot batons with hummus for their afternoon snack. Soon after that, Imogen suggests they go outside and play on the trampoline. It's five o'clock, and the heat is ebbing from the day.

I watch them from the window as I tidy up the kitchen. My thoughts circle back to that conversation with Porter about Thomas Macey. Why does that name nag at me? The builder killed himself in early September 2016. That was when I started getting all the abuse because of my testimony in the court case – anonymous death threats by email and post, even a dog turd through the letter box. I called the police. They questioned Macey's friends and family but weren't able find the culprit – and it did seem to be coming from one person. The police were sure about that, because the writer exhibited what they called "idiosyncratic traits" in their messages. The short sentences was one, and the capitalization of certain words. They also used the word "just" a lot.

It's the only time in my life I've ever felt truly hated, and it was horrible: a daily barrage of foul-mouthed hostility that went on for eight weeks. It caused real strain between me and Susan, and may even have prompted her to embark on her affair with the man who turned out to be Roy Parker.

Then, one day, the messages stopped. After the silence had maintained itself for about a month, I heaved a big sigh of relief and got on with my life. Yet a part of me did wonder: loathing that visceral doesn't just switch off like a tap. It might go underground, find new channels of expression. Or it could sit and fester and mutate into something else – maybe something worse. It's like water leaking into a building. It might find its way in through some cracked grouting on a balcony, or a corroded piece of guttering, or an inadequate flashing on a roof. Then weeks or months or even years later, a stain will show up on a ceiling, and it could be in a completely different part of the building, far from the original ingress. Water is horribly patient and relentless like that.

Eventually, this niggling anxiety faded. Other preoccupations arose to take its place, like Susan's affair, and then her disappearance. But hearing Macey's name again in the midst of this current crisis makes me wonder: could the two be connected? Could the person trying to frame me for the kidnapping of Stephanie Parker be the same one who waged that campaign against me two years ago? I have no evidence for this – it's just a hunch. Water will find a way, and will always make you pay.

On the counter is a half-full bottle of supermarket Merlot.

My wine glass is upside down on the draining board. I want a drink, but it's only quarter past five. I should go to Amy now, let her out, apologise. She can go to the police if she wants. I'll explain the whole thing. They'll understand. It's this madman who's been hating me these past two years. It started with emails and letters and a dog turd, and now he's writing messages to my daughter through a pig's rib, pretending to be her mother, and trying to get me blamed for the kidnap of this other girl. He hates me, you see, and when someone hates you that much, they'll never stop. It's like water, Officer – they'll always get you in the end.

When I look down, I see the long-stemmed glass is in my hand and there's wine in it, most of it gone. I'm not sure when or how that happened. Outside, the children are jumping on the trampoline, practising somersaults. The shadows are lengthening on the yellow grass. It's nearly six o'clock.

45

I open my eyes and find myself slumped on the kitchen tiles, leaning against the cupboard where we keep the cereals. Something is glittering on the floor near where I'm sitting. It looks like a tiny shard of broken glass. The digital clock on the oven reads 7:04. I grunt in surprise, and push myself to my feet. A wave of giddiness nearly causes me to tumble back down. I catch hold of the counter for support until it passes. Looking through the window, the light outside has turned golden. The trampoline is still. The garden is empty. Where are the children? What happened to me? Where is my wine?

I become aware of a soft, jerky noise coming from somewhere in the house. It sounds like a child snivelling. I rush into the playroom and find Alex there, curled up as tightly as a boy can be, in the little gap between the upright piano and the sofa. He has a big red bruise on his face. When he sees me, he jumps up and runs to me, throwing his arms around my waist and hugging me tight.

"Alex, what happened? Where's Midge?"

"I c-c-c-c..."

His tongue paralysis is scaring me. "Alex, please. Speak to me."

He makes a jagged, animal noise. He's staring up at me with huge, wet eyes. I want to shake the words out of him, but he looks petrified – incapable of speech. I'm holding him up by his arms, probably too tight.

"Breathe, my boy. Just breathe and tell me everything."

"I w-want my m-mummy."

"I'm sorry Alex but she's still – she's still at the dentist. Just tell me what happened."

"I t-tried to f-find you but..."

"But what? Where's Imogen?"

"He took her. M-Mr Jones took her."

A trapdoor drops out from under me then. My breath – and all the rest of me – falls away into space and I'm left swinging. I let the boy go and he slumps to the floor like a ragdoll. Fear is like a noose around my neck. *My girl. He has my little girl.* I watch myself from a cold, frightened place as I start rampaging around the house, flying into each room, shouting her name, and all the while knowing in the dark well of my heart – the part that knows everything I will never admit to knowing – that I'm not going to find her.

"Midge! Where are you?"

I scream this to her bedroom, to my study, to the street from my window. And the answer is always silence. Soon I've checked every room in the house and am contemplating extending the search into the streets, when I remember one more place. My shoes thunder down the stairs. I yank open the cellar door and switch on the light. "Midge?"

Silence.

I clatter down the wooden steps – and there, in the half-light, my little flare of hope dies. She's not in the cellar. It's just the same pathetic, sad-smelling place that it was last night.

Except.

In the dim corner beyond the exercise machine, there's a pile of clothing on the floor. That definitely wasn't here last night. I go over and pick up the first item. It's a pair of trousers from a suit – a smart, grey crêpe men's suit. Underneath the trousers is a matching jacket, a white shirt and dark tie – all of them casually discarded on the concrete floor. I pick up each one in turn – and then immediately drop them when I see what's lying at the bottom of the pile.

A panda mask.

I snatch it up, anger and distress rising within me, my fingers itching to crush it. It's a cheap, ugly thing – white but for the black ears, nose and eye patches – the plastic moulded to give the impression of fur. The effect of the smile, especially when coupled with those hollow circles for eyes, is sinister rather than friendly.

Mr Jones took my Imogen. The thought is unbearable. I'm so terrified by it I can barely breathe, let alone think straight. Every day, every hour, every minute that passes, the less likely you are to ever see her alive again. Gooberman told me that after Susan disappeared.

I have to think.

I should call the police. The search needs to begin now. *NOW!*

But can I really do that? They'll ask questions. Where was I while all this was happening? I'll say I had a blackout – I fell unconscious in the kitchen. But Alex said he didn't see me there. And what happened to my wine? They won't need to know about that. But they'll find this outfit in the basement. They'll ask about Alex's mother, and then...

I can see how it will look.

I'll have to keep searching for her myself, at least until I can get my own part in it straight – until I can find out where the hell I was when it happened. I'll start with Alex. He must tell me everything.

~

"Alex. Start from the beginning. What exactly happened?"

We're sitting at the kitchen table. Roy's book is still there next to us. So is the notepad with Imogen's neat handwriting. I've given Alex a smoothie. The boy is a little calmer now, but his hand is trembling as it holds the carton.

"We were jumping on the trampoline," he says. "Then Mr Jones came into the garden."

"Where did he come from?"

"From the house. He came out of the kitchen door."

"And then what happened?"

"He came straight towards us. He reached through the netting and grabbed Immy by her hair. Sh-Sh..."

"Go on."

Alex makes a whining sound in his throat, like a scared dog.

"You have to tell me Alex, or I'll never be able to find her."

"She screamed! He pulled her off the trampoline by her hair and dragged her across the grass."

My hand has gone to my mouth. I'm biting my finger hard as I picture this.

"I ran after them," Alex says. "I tried to pull her free, but he hit me on the face and then I can't remember anything until I woke up and Immy and Mr Jones were gone. I ran inside and looked for you. I looked all over the house, but I couldn't find you. I wanted my mummy. I was so scared. I was crying. I went and sat in the playroom for ages. And then you came."

"Are you sure I wasn't in the kitchen when you were looking for me?"

"Yes." He nods for emphasis.

For a moment, I'm silenced, unable or unwilling to contemplate the next question. All I can hear is the boy's unsteady breathing. He's waiting. I have to push on, go to places I'd rather not.

"Alex, I don't want you to be scared when I ask you this next question. I have to ask it because the police will ask it and I want to know what you'll tell them. Are you ready?"

"Yes."

"Alex, do you think that I could have been Mr Jones?"

His eyes, fixed on mine, swell up, and his chest and Adam's apple rise as if he's about to scream, but no sound comes out. He's trembling badly now and I place a hand on his to reassure him. His hand – his whole arm – tenses up when I touch him.

"It's not true, Alex. I'm *not* Mr Jones. I just want to know if... Look, I'll put it another way. Was Mr Jones the same sort of size and shape as me?"

He hesitates, his eyes never leaving mine. Then he gives a very slight nod.

I can't help the grimace – and he sees it. I had been praying Jones would be smaller, bigger, thinner or fatter. Now I'm getting desperate. I can feel it.

Madness is approaching. It appears as a dark fog. In my mind I'm standing in Turnwood Park on the bank above the path, and the fog is rolling up the bank towards me from the pond. I'm so scared and as the darkness closes around me, I can no longer see which way to turn. I can't go to the police or Amy. But I have to.

I have to confront a possibility – one I've been resisting for far too long. But the evidence keeps stacking up and I can no longer ignore it. There's the shirt and the suit and the mask. There are the blackouts – especially the blackouts. What happens when you start to lose trust in yourself? Where do you go when the enemy is no longer out there but inside?

Maybe I do things during the blackouts.

Where did my wine go? What was that little chip of glass on the floor when I woke up?

For some time I've been aware of my unreliability as a narrator of my life. No one can ever see themselves with perfect objectivity. I know I have memory lapses, and that I can some-times be an imperfect judge of my own motivations. I probably see myself as a lot calmer and more rational and even-tempered than I actually am. But these are like cracks in plaster or drywall. They're superficial, not structural. My understanding of the basic realities of my life and of who I am are, I've always assumed, sound.

But now more serious anomalies are appearing. Why couldn't Alex find me when Mr Jones came? Why couldn't Imogen see me that day when she was chased by the same Mr Jones. Me and Mr Jones – why are we never seen together? That has to make me wonder! Did I write those messages in the pig bone? When Stephanie saw me in the park, why did she run away?

Do I do things during the blackouts?

These aren't like cracks in plaster or drywall. They're like cracks in concrete, and they're getting wider. But a house can't analyse itself. If it's my own mind that's cracking up, what can I do about it? If I'm doing these things, how can I trust myself to...?

I find myself in my bedroom, dressed in the grey crepe suit from the basement. Looking in the mirror, I see it fits me perfectly. There's something in my hand. It's the panda mask. I place it on my face, pulling the elastic over the back of my head. It feels confining. The air smells of plastic. The circular eyes are like tiny portholes. I stare at myself as Mr Jones in the mirror – try and imagine myself coming into the garden and dragging Imogen off the trampoline by her hair, striking Alex across the face when he tries to intervene. I feel sick when I think about doing those things.

"What did you do with her? What did I do with her?"

From behind me comes a scream. I turn to see Alex staring at me from the landing. The front of his shorts is wet. I rip off the mask.

"Alex. It's me. Please don't be scared."

As I move closer, he backs away until the heels of his school shoes are hanging out beyond the edge of the top step. I rush out and grab him to stop him falling. He screams again, and struggles to free himself.

"I want my mummy! I want my mummy!"

As soon as he says it, I know he's right.

"Of course," I nod, letting him go. "We'll go there this very minute."

It's the only place that Imogen can possibly be. Because if I'm Jones, that's where I'll have taken her – the same place I took Stephanie.

"Alex, I promise you we'll go straight to your mummy. You

don't need to be frightened any more. I'm going to take these clothes off now. I was just checking them to see if you were right and Mr Jones was my size. Now I'll be able to tell the police exactly how big he is and they'll be able to catch him, okay?"

He nods, while still trembling in terror. "Please can we go to mummy now."

"Absolutely." I coax him into the bathroom with a pair of Imogen's tracksuit bottoms to change into, while I hastily change back into my normal clothes and go and fetch a bottle of water from the fridge. Excitement and renewed hope is filling me up like sweet wine. As Alex and I set off, I'm beaming from ear to ear.

"Is this the dentist's house?" Alex asks ten minutes later, as I usher him into 25 Oakfield Crescent. He looks exhausted. I must have walked him at a jet-fuelled pace.

"Yes. Now wait in here." I prod him into the living room. "I'll bring her up in just a moment."

He wanders over to the bookshelf. "Those look like my daddy's books."

"They do, don't they? Don't move from this room, Alex. I'll be back very soon with your mother." And, please God, with someone else, too, I nearly add.

I exit the room while he's still absorbed in the books – before he becomes aware of being left alone in a strange house and starts to get scared again. Hurriedly, I descend to the basement, where the wine-rack door is still open, just as I left it. Now I must be careful. When they see me, they'll think I'm the other fellow – the bad one. I have to convince them to trust me.

I take the matchbook from my pocket, but I'm so nervous I

drop it. My eye falls briefly on the rhinoceros logo on the front with the name of the business beneath. I pick it up and am about to flip it open to get the door code when I stop and check that name again: TM Construction. Could that stand for Thomas Macey by any chance? Yes of course it could. It could also stand for Tobias Marwood or Travis Murphy. Probably just a coincidence. No time to worry about that now. I return my attention to the numbers, pressing them out very carefully on the keypad.

My anxiety is almost overwhelming as I press the final digit. I'll have to beg for their forgiveness. I'll turn myself into the police, get myself committed to a psychiatric hospital. I'll do everything and anything. Just please God, let Imogen be okay.

Very slowly, I twist the handle and open the door.

46

SATURDAY 8 APRIL 2017

"My, you're getting to be such a big girl!" said Luke. "How old are you now, Stephie."

"Seven and three-quarters," she answered, peeking out from behind her mother.

"That's pretty old, isn't it?" gasped Luke, lifting his gaze and winking at Amy.

Roy, standing in the entrance to the kitchen, observed this little scene playing out in the hallway. Luke, he thought, must appear like a fairytale giant to the little girl, towering over her in his endless blue overalls, the big grin parting that bushy black beard.

"Good of you to come at such short notice, Luke," said Amy. "It's the upstairs toilet this time I'm afraid."

"Hi Luke!" Roy called. "Come say hello when you're done upstairs."

"I will be sure to do that my friend."

Roy listened to the heavy tread of Luke's feet as they followed Amy's lighter ones up the stairs.

Stephanie ran to her father. "He's going to see my poo in there," she whispered in a mortified voice.

"Luke sees that sort of thing every day," Roy said. "If a toilet is blocked, the poos won't go down. It's not your fault."

"Will he know it's mine?"

"I should think so. If you've seen as many poos as Luke has, you get to know what sort of person made them."

"It could be Alex's."

"No, I definitely think that one looks like one of yours."

The girl's shoulders slumped in despair. She went out into their conservatory and from there into the garden. Roy watched her run all the way to the back and sit on the tree stump in the corner, as if trying to get as far away from her shame as possible.

Roy hated inflicting these casual cruelties on his daughter. He hated himself for it, and he hated its effect on her. He only knew it was necessary, like an adjustment on a seatbelt; a gradual loosening of bonds.

In his hand was the notebook, every page of it now filled with jottings about the new novel, provisionally entitled *Mr Jones*. He fingered the edges like a priest handling a battered old Bible, or a child a comfort blanket. He went into the little conservatory – an extension built for them by Luke a few years ago – and sat and flicked through his notes. A biro tapped against one cheek, now and then swooping to underline a passage or add a few extra words.

Twenty minutes later, Luke appeared at the entrance to the conservatory. "All running smoothly now," he reported. "Except I broke my plunger" With a sad grin, he held up the snapped stick.

"A bad workman maims his tools," said Roy.

"What's that?"

"It's just something..." he began, then stopped. He'd been

about to say it was something Susan's late father-in-law used to say, but then he remembered: that was a part of his other life – the life he wasn't supposed to mention here.

Besides, right now he had more important matters to focus on. "Where's Amy?" he asked Luke.

"I think I heard her go into your bedroom."

"Okay, that's good," said Roy, closing the conservatory door and ushering Luke to a chair. He glanced outside and saw Stephanie watching them from her tree stump. She wouldn't dare come any closer while Luke was here.

"We have a few minutes," Roy said. "I want to talk to you about 25 Oakfield Crescent."

"If you want me and Jean out, that's fine. Just let me know when."

"It's not that. You can stay there for as long as you want. I wanted to talk to you about a job I need doing there. I wrote to my uncle recently asking for his permission to expand the basement, and he's said yes. Even better, he's agreed to pay for it."

"You want to expand the basement?"

"That's right. I want to excavate beneath the front room. I think there should be space there for a little bedroom and bathroom."

"May I ask why you want to do this?"

Roy squeezed hard on his notebook. "It's personal," he said. "I just want to know if it's something you could do."

Luke looked out of the window, bathing his face in the early summer sun. He smiled and waved at Stephanie, then put on a clownishly sad expression and wiped away an imaginary tear when she failed to respond.

"I've never excavated under a basement before," he said. "It makes me nervous, particularly with such an old house. I'd need to consult a structural engineer."

"Consult whoever you like. But Luke, if you do take this on, you must bill my uncle directly for the work. Richard Landry is the client. Do you understand? Amy can never know about my connection to that house. And another thing: it needs to be ready by the beginning of July."

47

WEDNESDAY 18 JULY 2018

As I STEP inside the cell, the first thing I notice is that no one is there. Almost at the same time, I perceive a flutter of movement in my peripheral vision, way off to my right. Instinctively, I dodge left just as a cannonball slams into my right shoulder, making me stagger. Pain bursts there like a bright rocket, making me yell. Twisting right, I see Amy just as she's hurling her right arm at my head like someone throwing a spear, but there's no spear in her hand. I fall back, at the same time reaching out to try and catch her wrist as she flings it forward. I miss, and her hand crashes against my sternum. More pain – far more than could be inflicted by a fist. Again, I hear a scream fly out of me as my back crashes into some item of furniture, making it rock. I slide down a smooth, vertical surface until my bottom hits the hard floor. Above me, Amy, like a witch, hair flying, lips white, has her hand raised to crush my skull like a cockroach. I kick outwards and my foot connects with her shin, unbalancing her. Using the chest of drawers (or whatever it is) behind me as a lever, I spring up and my elbow connects with her chin. She totters backwards, falling awkwardly against the side of the bed. Something black skitters from her hand onto the pink carpet: a piece of coal. My shoulder and chest are throbbing, but I barely notice. I kick the coal away and seize her by the shoulders, drag her onto the bed with its unicorn-patterned duvet.

"Amy, for fuck's sake calm down! Where's Imogen?"

Her eyes look unfocused. I think she may have hit her head when she fell.

"Where. Is. Imogen?" I ask again with painstaking slowness.

"Imogen?" she croaks. There's dry spit around her mouth. "How would I know? Where's Alex?"

"He's upstairs. He's safe, don't worry."

She tries to get up, but I shove her back down. "Not yet. Are you telling me I didn't bring Imogen here?"

Amy shakes her head.

I feel the life and strength – everything that has kept me going these past twenty minutes – leak out of me. The pain I'd been ignoring comes back tenfold. I grit my teeth against rising despair. *What next? What next?*

"Mummy?" A small voice from the cell doorway.

I turn around. Alex is standing there, looking at me with fear and something close to revulsion. I immediately release Amy and back away to the far side of the room. Amy struggles to sit up. She puts out her arms to Alex. "Come here, my darling!"

He runs to her and they hug. Tears form in the creases of my eyes as I think of Imogen, wanting nothing more than to hug her and tell her I'm sorry.

"Mummy why are you here? This isn't a dentist."

Amy struggles to speak through chapped lips. "A dentist? What are you talking about?"

"I told him you were at the dentist," I tell her, handing her the bottle of water.

Alex cowers at my approach, his dark eyes tracking me from his mother's arms like a puppy watching the swoop of an eagle.

Amy unfastens the lid and takes a swig. I notice her hand on the bottle is brown with brick dust. Her nails are chipped and broken.

"You need to let me go now Ben," she says, wiping her mouth.

I sit heavily on the bed beside her, bending forwards, elbows on knees and sliding my hands through my hair. Everything is hurting and I feel like screaming until all my breath is gone. "Then go," I say to her. "Go to the police. Tell them everything. Imogen's gone now, so what does it matter?"

"Where is she?" Amy asks.

"I don't know. I must have taken her somewhere. I'm Mr Jones. I'm Mr fucking Jones and I took her somewhere, only I don't know where." I bang the heel of my hand repeatedly into my forehead. "I don't [bang] know [bang] where! [bang]"

"You've got no memory of this?"

I shake my head. "Not the faintest shred of a memory. Kidnapping Stephanie, writing those notes, wearing that stupid mask. I have blackouts. I must do these things during blackouts. There seems to be this other me who takes over. Some kind of Jeckyll and Hyde thing, I don't know."

Amy stands up and moves to the cell doorway, pulling Alex with her. She's clasping his shoulder protectively. He's leaning into her hip, sucking his thumb. Something is clutched in her free hand – some sheets of paper. "I don't care," she says, her voice a little clearer than before, and as hard as that piece of coal she just hit me with. "I don't give a shit how insane you are, Ben. I will see you punished for this. I will work to see you behind bars. But first I want the truth. All of it. As soon as it surfaces from that cesspool in your head, I want to know what you did with my daughter and what's happened to her. Maybe this will jog your memory." She hands me the sheets of paper.

"Where did you find these?"

She points to the item of furniture I fell against earlier. What I thought was a chest of drawers turns out to be a child's pink desk with a matching chair. The desk has a single drawer, slid half open. The papers in my hand are warped and crinkly and covered in dense, dark pictures, clearly drawn by a child – Stephanie, I can only assume. The first 'drawing' is little more than a mindless black scribble covering most of the paper. At the top, in a crude, juvenile script, are the words *MY DARK DREAM*. The next artwork is also a dense scribble, but there's a vaguely human shape to it, with recognisable arms, legs, torso and head. I flick to the third drawing. The colour green is introduced here, along with the black, and the outline of the figure is a little sharper. It looks slender and long-limbed. When I reach the fourth drawing, I freeze. At the top, in the same wobbly script, are the words *MR JONES*. Underneath is a big green face with a wide, downturned mouth and round eyes. The eyes are pure black crayon, so intensely scribbled that it's warped the paper, creating two shiny little craters. Is that how she saw me? *Mr Jones?* It's a horrible face – nothing like mine, but not wholly unfamiliar either. I wonder if I might have seen a face like it in some spooky picture book I once read to Imogen. The next drawing is a rudimentary sketch of Turnwood Park, as seen from the top corner. The big oak tree is there, and the path and the pond below that. The colours are gloomy greens, blacks, browns and blues and there's a crescent moon and stars in the sky. The final drawing shows the pond with a little girl standing beside it. The girl is little more than a stick figure with brown hair. She's wearing a pink top and blue jeans. She can only be Stephanie.

"Well?" asks Amy.

I shrug, tenderly rubbing my chest. "I have no idea what they signify, if anything. It seems to me that when I'm Mr Jones, a completely different person takes over. None of this – this cell, these drawings – mean anything."

Amy's mouth tightens. "It seems to me..." she parodies. "Fuck you, Ben. I'm going to the police. They'll wring the truth out of you."

"That's fine. I'm ready. And I'll try and remember, I promise. I *have* to remember, for Imogen as well as Stephanie. I can't tell you how sorry I am."

Some of the fire goes out of her cheeks. "Okay," she says. "Now give me back my phone."

I extricate it from my jeans pocket and hand it to her, along with the drawings. Then she tosses the bottle of water onto the bed. "I'm going to lock you in here – in case you turn into Jones while I'm gone."

We both hear a muffled ping. "Is that yours?" I ask.

She checks her phone's screen and shakes her head.

I pull my own phone from inside my jacket. There's a message there from my mother. My heart stops – everything stops – as I read the opening line.

Hello Darling. Imogen is safe here with Susan.

This is all I can read, because immediately the tears start and they smear out the rest. Amy grabs the phone from me before I can wipe my eyes. I glimpse an awakening surprise and consternation in her face, then she flings it back on the bed, grabs Alex's hand and leaves, shoving the door closed behind her.

. . .

Imogen is safe here with Susan.

I can't get past that opening sentence, and don't want to. There are whole books of meaning that could be teased out from those six words, and I could spend happy years contemplating them. I could eat and drink and die on those words, and if I never get out of this cell, it will have been a price worth paying, because Imogen is safe with Susan. But of course I read on. I have to. What else is there to do? The full message reads as follows:

Hello Darling. Imogen is safe here with Susan. She's told me EVERYTHING. She begged me not to text you but I just had to. I just want you to do the right thing my darling. You're BEN, not Mr Jones. REMEMBER that. But Mr Jones lives inside you. He's DANGEROUS. Please don't try to visit. You will only upset them if you do. Just do the right thing and turn yourself in. You need treatment. I love you. Mum.

My brain is still too fuzzy and hot with relief to take in all this new information on first reading. But by the time I've read it through for the fourth time, the implications start to penetrate. I, as Mr Jones, must have been keeping Susan prisoner. But where? Surely not here with Stephanie. This cell is too small for one person, let alone two. And there would have been at least some sign of her presence here.

So I must have kept her somewhere else – probably the same place I took Imogen, before the two of them escaped together. If I did that, then I don't need Mum or Susan to tell me to keep away from them. I'll make sure I never go near them again. And when another blackout comes and I change? I'm just glad Mr Jones will be trapped in here. Amy must have gone to Mum's house. She'll talk to Susan, reassure Imogen that I can't harm her. Then they'll tell the police everything and I'll be placed safely behind bars where I can't hurt anyone else. That's good. That's how it should be.

But even as I'm thinking all this, a rebel voice inside me is protesting: *Listen to yourself. This is preposterous. How could you have kept Susan imprisoned for ten months? This is Halsted in 2018, not 1980s Beirut.* But I dismiss the voice as the old me still refusing to accept the truth. Worse, it could be Mr Jones who's wormed his way into the Ben Rose part of me, trying to under- mine my new self-awareness and sow seeds of doubt. I won't listen to the voice. There's too much evidence now to ignore the truth of who I am, however hard that may be for me to accept: this message from Mum is just the latest.

But look at the message, the voice continues in its irritatingly insistent tone. *Look at it really closely. Don't you see something there? Something that doesn't quite fit your narrative?*

To humour the voice, I look at the message again.

Does it really sound like Mum? Is that how she writes?

Sure that's her. Why not?

Look at those short sentences, the frequent capitalised words, the overuse of the word 'just'. Doesn't it remind you of someone?

I know where the voice is going with this. It's comparing this message to those nasty emails I received back in 2016 in the wake of the Macey suicide – trying to persuade me that it's from the same source. And I have to admit there are some striking similarities, and it's really not like one of Mum's rambling, barely punctuated texts. Has she ever even used caps lock, except accidentally when the whole message comes out in shouty block capitals?

But if she didn't write this message, then who did?

There I go again, getting seduced by the siren voice, wanting so much to believe that I've been set up here – the innocent victim of some big conspiracy. I have to shut the voice up, and the only way I can do that is to test its theory against the evidence and watch it crumble.

To start with, how did my shirt get in this cell? And how did the panda mask and suit get in my basement?

A third party – the real *Mr Jones, let's say – planted them there.*

Okay. I can just about buy that. But what about the tenancy agreement and the rent going out of my account each month?

The agreement was faked, and Mr Jones must have hacked your bank account.

So he's a computer expert. I suppose that could also explain why he's so familiar with Imogen's schedule and Susan's writing style. But what about the fact that he and I never appear in the same place. Why do I always disappear when Jones shows up?

By always you mean on two occasions – no need to exaggerate. The first time Jones appeared, when he chased Imogen up the tree, she was in a complete panic. There may have been foliage blocking her view. It's possible she just didn't see you. Your absence during his second appearance is harder to explain but not impossible. Jones could have temporarily hidden you behind a curtain or sofa, or in a wardrobe, so Alex didn't see you when he searched the house. He could have cleared up your spilled wine before going out into the garden to drag Imogen away.

Okay, that's just about feasible. But wasn't it convenient that I happened to have those blackouts at exactly the time Jones decided to strike? Surely that proves, if nothing else does, that Jones is me and I'm Jones.

Perhaps. Perhaps not. Have you considered the possibility that Jones caused the blackouts? He could have spiked your wine this after-

noon? Think about it. Every time you've had a blackout, you had a drink beforehand.

Oh hell!

I turn back to the message from Mum, this time with a more sceptical eye, and the more I look at it, the more obvious it is that it's fake, and I wonder how I could ever have been taken in by it. The power of an idea – the idea of my guilt – had taken hold of me. I'd become passive, weak-willed, a follower of the prevailing narrative – exactly what my professional training warns against. My job is always to be led by the evidence, not the reassuring words of the client, architect or contractor.

The voice was right, dammit! It wasn't Mr Jones, it was me, the *real* me, rational and clear-eyed, trying to break through this fug of despair and passivity. The message came from Mum's phone, so whoever sent it must have stolen it, or – and the hairs on the back of my head bristle at this thought – they have Mum. And Amy is going over there right now with Alex, her defences down and with no conception of what she might be walking into. As far as she's concerned, the monster is safely caged down here.

Oh crap!

I have to get out of here. I check out the cell door. It's a rectangular slab of steel at least an inch thick – there may be unicorns on the duvet cover, but the door makes no pretence as to what this place really is. I obviously can't escape that way, but maybe I can try the backdoor route by expanding on Stephanie's work.

48

CRAMMING myself into the tiny space between bathroom wall and cupboard, I check the hole again. There's been recent work on it. The towels have been removed from the lower part of the cupboard, which is now covered in fresh dust and fragments of brick and cement. The hole in the wall is a little bigger than before – bricks have been dislodged. I remember Amy's broken fingernails. She, too, had escape in mind. And when she heard me arriving, she must have reached across the twelve-inch gap behind the plasterboard, and through a further twelve inches of wall, to obtain the piece of coal she tried to brain me with.

Although wider than before, the gap is still too narrow for Amy to have crawled through, let alone me. Still, expanding it, even without tools, might not be as big a job as I'd feared. I lay myself flat on my side to give my arm maximum reach and begin bashing at the exposed brickwork with the palm of my hand. There is some movement, but not a lot. After twenty or more blows, my hand is sore and bleeding and I've made zero progress. I groan and cough up some dust.

In terms of bricks, Amy has already picked off the low-hanging fruit. To make the hole any bigger, I'll need a different strategy. Rearranging my body so I'm seated on the floor with my legs inside the cupboard, I attempt to bash at the bricks with my heels. But with the limited space and the drywall and pipework in the way, I can't get much power behind each kick. The bricks hold firm.

There's only one thing for it. I wriggle out of the cupboard and get back on my feet. Then I take a firm grip of the sink surround, wincing at the pain in my injured palm, and heave upwards. Nothing happens. The surround won't budge. So I turn my attention to one of the cupboard doors, ripping, tearing and kicking at it. Here at last I meet with success. The furnishings are cheap and the MDF tears easily enough from the metal hinges. Once both doors are off, I pull again at the sink surround, this time managing to prise it away from the sink. The noise, the dust, the violence is intense, but also satisfying. I feel, in my small way, I'm inching towards the bigger goal of escape. For the next while I lose myself and all track of time, entering a dark and quite pleasurable zone of pure destruction. My sole focus is on removing this obstacle. With each minor success, more of my confidence returns, and I gain new tools along the way: a sharp blade of wood broken off a cupboard door, a P-trap from under the sink, a pair of child-size taps. The bathroom becomes a war zone as I fling away the smashed debris of my demolition work.

At last, with cupboard, sink and most of the pipework removed, I stand before the naked wall. The plasterboard has been stoved in and partially wrenched away, exposing the brick lining of the cellar at Number 27. Kneeling down, I try using one of the tiny taps as a hammer, bashing at the loose bricks, but it's too small to get a decent grip on. When I lose patience with this, I sit on the floor, with my back braced against the bathroom wall, and give the opposite wall the full force of my heels. A brick falls, and soon after it another. The hole is getting bigger, but I'm getting tired.

My burst of destructive energy now ebbing, pain is returning to my shoulder, my chest and the palm of my hand. I don't want to stop now with freedom so close, but my body is reaching its limits. And I'm hungry. The last thing I ate was that dry tuna sandwich for lunch. It's ten past nine. Imogen disappeared at around seven, but it feels much longer ago. I've been functioning on fear and adrenaline ever since. I'll rest here a while amid the dust and shattered pieces of cupboard and sink, and carry on when I've got a bit more energy. My eyes close, and a moment later it seems, I'm in the park, beneath the oak tree...

Imogen is in the pond. She's sinking, crying out to me for help. I hear her terrified screams, "Daddy! Daddy!" and I run towards her, but Amy is standing on the path, blocking my way. She folds her arms around my neck and starts kissing me. I have to go and rescue Imogen, but I can't free myself from Amy and her fierce embraces. I can see Imogen is now up to her neck in the swamp. Her arms are reaching out to me, fingers clawing at the air. I struggle, but Amy is strong, and it's not just Amy. Susan is there too, trying to smother me in kisses. Through strands of her auburn hair I catch sight of Imogen as her face falls beneath the surface. Then Susan and Amy fade away, and I'm on the bank watching Imogen looking up at me from under-neath the black water. Deeper she falls, her arms and hands too, the green mat closes over her and the swamp falls still. She's gone and it's as if she was never there.

. . .

I wake with a start, my heart battering like a mad fish against my ribs. For a moment, I don't know where I am. Something is gleaming at me from the floor. I blink a few times and it comes into focus. A tap – a baby chrome tap. Absently, I pick it up and turn it over in my hand as after-images from the dream pulse through my head.

Slowly, understanding of my situation returns. I know I have to continue digging my way out of here. I must reach Imogen – rescue her from the monster who did all this. And Susan, too. There's no time to waste. But this little tap – something about it is clawing at me, snatching at a dangling thread of memory. I saw it somewhere recently – and not down here. It's getting depressingly familiar this feeling of nearly but not quite making a connection, as the faulty synapses of my memory fail to spark. Yet this time, to my delight, I catch the thread.

It was upstairs in Luke's flat – this little tap and its twin were lying on the beige hallway carpet. What were they doing there? If Luke fitted these taps, then he knows about this cell. He may even have built it. Like a falling domino, this memory trips another one: when I saw the taps, I was waiting for Luke to come back to me with his phone. He was planning to take my number to pass on to his sister and flatmate, Jean. And this in turn reminds me of a moment yesterday in Amy's kitchen, when Amy said: "Luke had a sister. He *did* have a brother called Tom, but he's dead. Took his own life a few years ago." Here, finally, was the so-called *Subject X* that I'd been so frustrated about forgetting.

And now I know why it was so important, because suddenly, everything falls into place: Luke's brother Tom was Thomas Macey. That explains the matchbook I found upstairs with the rhinoceros logo and "TM Construction", and the message from Mum's phone, written in the style of those hateful emails sent following Macey's suicide, must have been written by Luke. Luke, who built this cell, blamed me for his brother's death, and has been the author of this entire vicious campaign. He didn't destroy me the first time, but water will find a way, and will always make you pay.

These connections come to me in a sudden rush and a new image of Luke rapidly assembles itself in my head. It's exhilarating but also terrifying, because all I can think about is the sheer size of the man and the fury of those emails he sent. *His bark is so much worse than his height*, as my Dad may or may not have said.

I think of that man, that vengeful giant, and Imogen under his control. Susan, too, maybe, if he wasn't lying about her, and my mother – but mainly Imogen. The thought tips me into a kind of frenzy. I start kicking at the bricks with my heels, showering my shoes and ankles with dust. Fear lends me strength and a frantic energy. Cement fractures and crumbles, more bricks start loosening. My trainers are getting torn to shreds, the sole of one coming away from its upper, but what do I care? All I can think of is Luke. Luke with Imogen.

Bricks tumble. I choke and cough up dust. The hole is getting to look man-size now. I try to squeeze through but get caught at the shoulders, tearing my jacket. So I reverse and put my back to the wall for another round of kicking, and dust and falling bricks. Before making a second attempt, I strip down to my boxers and throw all my clothes through the hole, along with the sharp blade of wood from the smashed cupboard, which I'm thinking might just serve some purpose as a weapon. Then I launch myself to freedom. After a lot of painful wriggling and squirming, I get through, landing caked in dust and sweat and with scratches all over my shoulders and torso, on the cold floor of the cave-dark cellar of Number 27.

49

I WILL COME FOR THE ONE YOU LOVE THE MOST

Those words, hysterically daubed on the wall in dark red paint are caught in my phone's silvery light as I stumble through the ruined house. They make me think of Luke standing motionless in the rain, waiting for my daughter. He would have taken her on Monday if she'd shown up. In his mind, I killed his brother; now he has my daughter.

I have to get there as fast as I can – but I don't want him to know I'm coming. The quickest, least conspicuous route to my mother's house is via Turnwood Park, so I go out the back way, through the kitchen, trying not to think about the rat we spotted there earlier snacking on a human finger like a chicken drumstick.

Outside it's fully dark. The time is twenty-five to ten. My phonelight shines shakily on nettles, ferns and thick couch grass as I tramp a path through the back garden. I walk in an odd, high-stepping gait to avoid catching my broken shoe on the tangled undergrowth. Approaching the back fence, I use my long wooden blade to push aside the brambles. The moon is weak, swathed in smoky drifts of cloud, its light a gun-metal gleam on the tops of trees. The only other illumination, as I wrestle my way through the gap in the back fence, is the splintered yellow light from houses backing onto Oakfield Crescent. I descend the slope to the path as quickly as my flapping trainer will allow.

My mother's house backs onto the southern flank of the park on the far side of the pond, which glistens under the feeble moon like pale green wax. I give it a wide berth, I don't know why – certainly not because of that ridiculous ghoul's hand on the cover of Roy's book. I pass through a grove of small trees and reach the fenced border. Among the set of keys I dig from my jacket pocket is a brass yale that opens Mum's front door and also the wooden door in her back fence. As quietly as I can, I slip it into the lock and ease the door open. It whines on its hinges, thankfully with no more volume than the average barn owl or a feral cat.

The back garden is long and narrow. Up at the house, lights are burning in the kitchen-dining room. It's the first sign that something is wrong. Mum is usually in her parlour by this time, or in bed. The rear ground-floor lights should be off by now. If Luke's watching for me from that room, he'll see me coming up the garden path, so I keep to the shadowy strip of lawn that runs between the path and the flowerbed. I feel very awake now, pumped with adrenaline and a healthy dose of fear. My various aches are no more than background music, but my right shoe is becoming a liability. More of its stitching ripped coming through the undergrowth, separating the sole almost completely from its upper. I kick it off, along with the other one, and bend to pull off my socks. The turf is warm against the soles of my feet, and comforting in some primal way, but in the half-light my feet look pale and vulnerable, and my wooden blade looks no sturdier than a child's sword.

I have to fight against morbid premonitions of what I'm going to find inside the house. Blood on the kitchen tiles. My mother dead, her throat slashed – the first part of Luke's vengeance. Part Two will be Susan. Part Three, Imogen. A cold trembling in my neck passes down my spine. I quicken my pace.

Halfway up the garden, I pass the big, darkened window of Mum's studio, where Imogen has spent countless happy hours since she was an infant splatting paper with hand prints. It's unbearable to think about normal stuff like that now. In the light from the house I can make out the wind-sculpted beach boulders my mother has placed at the studio entrance, and the statuette of a Buddha sitting atop one of them.

At the top of the lawn I consider making a quick dash up the steps onto the patio, but decide against it – I'd be too exposed. Instead I clamber awkwardly over a wooden trough filled with flowers. I manage it, but my head brushes the lower branch of a fir tree, setting off a wooden windchime. I fall into a frozen crouch and wait for the melodic clanking to cease. My bruised sternum aches with every thud of my heart.

No one appears at the windows, and I start breathing again. I edge forwards in a virtual crawl until I'm pressed against the wall, side on to the French window door and hopefully out of sight of anyone inside. My feet feel wet. Looking down I notice I'm crouched in a puddle from a leaky hosepipe reel mounted on the wall behind me. Mum must have been watering the garden earlier. I lean closer to the door until I can see inside the dining area. No one's there. The kitchen looks empty, too – what I can see of it.

Reaching up very slowly, I pull on the door handle. It swings open – a second sign that something is wrong. Mum is always careful to keep the back door locked – nervous that teenagers high on skunk will break into her house from the park one night. I stare at the point of my child's wooden sword and imagine trying to thrust it into Luke. I can't.

I close my eyes. My lips tremble with words I want to say – words of prayer, maybe, but I have no religion. The thing I cling onto at this moment in the dark, crouched on a wet patio, is my odd belief in destiny. It doesn't sit comfortably with my Godless rationality, yet it's been there for me at times of fear. It has to do with the way, in retrospect, everything that happens makes sense. The past follows a line of inevitability, like classical architecture. It's only the present that appears wobbly and chaotic, but that's an illusion because we're caught in the middle of it. All that I'm going through now will one day be in the past, and it will make sense.

I stand, nudge open the door, and walk into the house. The kitchen is as empty as the dining area. There's a watery smell of vegetable stew and the ever-present fug of cigarettes. The door to the hallway is closed, blocking any view of other rooms. Granny's abstract painting – her "swirly bit of nonsense" – is still propped against the kitchen wall where I saw it a week ago. Its pale greenish-grey is the same colour as the pond when I saw it just now under the anaemic moonlight. And the face that only Imogen could properly see is there, in the top left corner. It gapes at me with its wide, downturned mouth, and its round, blank eyes that seem to bleed evil. Imogen's right, it's a bad, bad face. What's more, it's virtually identical to the face Stephanie drew in her cell – the one she labelled 'Mr Jones'. How that could be and what it means, I have no idea – and I have no room in my head to think about it right now.

The kitchen is tidy – just a single plate, a wine glass and

some cutlery left to dry by the sink. Mum's ugly fish-mouth ashtray is filled with fags. Everything is normal, yet everything is wrong. The lights, the unlocked French window doors. And why is the door to the hallway shut?

"What the hell is going on?" I mutter under my breath, mainly to release tension and hear the sane tone of my own voice.

My question is purely rhetorical, yet I get a reply – sort of – and from an unexpected direction: a muffled shout from behind me. I spin around, a scream very nearly breaking out of my throat. I can't see anyone, but the shadows are large and deep. I step back out onto the patio, accidentally scraping my toe on a broken tile. I compress my yelp into a hiss, and silently curse my lack of shoes.

The garden, or what I can see of it, is a sleeping corridor of deep greens and shadows. Yet I definitely heard something coming from there. And now I see something, too – something I missed earlier, being so fixated on reaching the house undetected. Extending beyond the puddle of water created by the dripping hosepipe are several sets of footprints heading across the patio. They go down the steps and onto the flagstone path, where they are fainter but still visible. Where the path forks, the footprints turn right onto the branch leading to the studio.

The studio.

So that's where they are. Luke, Mum, Susan and Imogen, sitting there quietly in the dark. When I walked up the garden just now, I passed within a few feet of them. They must have been there, watching me from the window. But why? What are they doing in there in the dark?

I wonder vaguely when everything will start to make sense. Will it be at the end of this path? Behind the door of my mother's studio? Sense feels right now like something that will always be just out of reach, protected behind a membranous wall that stretches and stretches on the point of a pin, but refuses to burst. It began a month ago, with a rib buried in the ground, and here I still am, still forcing the pin further into the membrane. But surely there can't be any more mysteries behind this one. What are they doing in there in the dark? For better or worse – almost certainly worse – I'll soon find out.

I walk slowly down the garden path, feeling the cool, sticky wetness of those footprints under my soles, and I halt before the studio entrance, a barefoot soldier with a child's weapon in his hand. The Buddha, seated atop his boulder, looks serene. *This will all make sense*, he says. *The future will soon become the past.* I wish I had his confidence. The windows in the door are black and opaque, reflecting the house lights and, dimly, my exhausted, unshaven face. I reach forward, turn the handle, probe the membrane a little further. This does, finally, feel like the end.

But the door is locked. I didn't really expect it to open, did I? Perhaps I hoped for a happy ending. A surprise party. A room filled with guests, balloons, streamers, horns, glitter. Susan standing there, with Imogen and Mum, their arms open in welcome. *"We wanted to say sorry, and to thank you for caring! Have some cake dear. Take the weight off your feet. You don't have to be scared any more."*

The door is locked and the studio appears to be empty, but the footprints tell a different story. So did that muffled shout I heard just now. I rattle the handle. Sick of the games, I shout: "Is there anyone in there? Imogen? Susan? Mum? Please stop all this and tell me what's going on."

Silence. Nobody there. The footprints lied.

And then, a voice out of the dark: "Please don't come in Ben."

It's my mother. She's trying to sound calm, in control, but I can hear the tremble of fear in every word.

"Mum, what's going on? I know you didn't write that text. Is Imogen there?"

"Yes."

"Is she okay?"

"She's fine. Please just go..."

"What about Susan?"

This gets no reply.

"Susan! Are you in there? Speak to me!"

Nothing.

I rattle the handle. "I'm coming in! I'm breaking down this door!"

And then I hear Imogen. "Run away Daddy! It's a trap!"

50

MONDAY 11 JULY 2016

ROY STARED at the crack in the ceiling above his bed, eyes as wide as they could go, but he didn't see it. He didn't see anything. His mind was still fully immersed in the dream. *Immersed* was the wrong word. *Saturated* might be better, if the liquid saturating it was some kind of acid perhaps. The dream was eating him alive, and it was still here. The smell, the voice...

He turned to his right and observed Amy asleep beside him. He reached out and touched her shoulder, hoping the reality of her warmth and solidity might dispel the lingering after-effects of whatever was infecting his mind. She shrugged his hand away, as one might a fly, and went on sleeping.

The first part of the dream hadn't been so strange. He had, after all, been thinking about Mr Jones on and off for nearly a year in preparation for his new novel. In the dream, Roy had been a child, playing in the park in East Halsted. Mr Jones approached him, wearing his panda mask and a light grey summer suit. He smelled of sweet almond paste and Roy fancied he saw a friendly twinkle in those round panda eyes (although really he saw nothing in them – nothing at all). Mr Jones gave

Roy a doll, and the doll smiled up at him with her cupid-bow lips. Roy wanted nothing more than to look after her and brush her silky blonde hair. But even at this stage of the dream, he had suspected there might be something wrong. The doll seemed too heavy and she moved strangely in his hand, as if there was something inside her – something alive.

Mr Jones told Roy that he lived in a castle backing onto the park and he asked Roy if he wanted to come and live with him there. He would live like a prince and have as much cake as he could eat. He could look after the doll and she would have a different outfit for every day of the year. Roy nodded and took Mr Jones's hand and the two of them went to live in the castle, which backed onto the park – except the closer they got to it, the more the castle looked like an old ruined house, and once he was in there Mr Jones changed. He flung Roy into a cellar, which wasn't like a cellar but more like a cave.

Roy never got to eat any cake. He survived by eating whatever slimy creatures he could find living in the puddles of the cave floor. His beloved doll became naked and filthy, and Roy, in his sadness and frustration, ripped off her head. That was a mistake, because then the thing that had been living inside the doll slithered out. It was the same thing that had climbed out of the swamp. It stank of sweetness and rot and pain. Its skin was the colour and texture of pond slime and its hair was lank, dark weeds. It opened its toothless fish-mouth and looked at him with round black eyes that leaked at their edges – not tears but pain – pure dark liquid pain. Roy had the feeling that this tormented, ugly thing was the real Mr Jones, and the Mr Jones he met in the park was a ghost.

Even now, having woken up, he could still smell the bloody thing. It overlaid the real-world aromas of warm, slept-in bedding. How could that be? How could a smell outlast its own dream? It reminded him of an incident from his boyhood. He'd been searching for snacks in the kitchen cupboard when he found a container that had been shoved right to the back of the top shelf – an old-fashioned biscuit tin. He pulled it out and opened it. Inside was something wedge-shaped and covered in white hairy circles with dark green spots. It took him a while to understand that the hairy thing in the tin was a slice of his parents' wedding cake. That was a horrible thought, since his parents had been married for at least ten years. But the thing he remembered most was the smell when he first opened the tin. It was the smell of sweetness gone bad. Things that ought to be delicious – like fruit and icing and almond paste – now making him feel sick. In later life, especially in times of stress, that smell had sometimes crawled back into his nostrils unbidden.

Whatever had slithered out of the doll and the swamp had the same smell, the smell of sweetness gone bad, and it was still here. But it wasn't just the smell that was lingering, it was also the creature's voice. The thing had spoken to him right at the end of the dream. In a voice that reminded Roy of water seeping into a blocked drain, it had said: "In one year, I will come for the one you love the most."

Roy had heard a similar declaration once before. At the end of his dream of 2003, the same voice had warned him, "If you tell the story of this dream, I will come for the one you love the most."

The voice, like the smell, continued to vibrate in his head, and it scared him more than anything, because it proved the creature was real – he hadn't imagined the warning in 2003. And if the creature was real, then so was the threat. It knew that Roy planned to tell the world about Mr Jones, and because he hadn't heeded its warning, it would have its revenge. It would come for the one he loved the most.

But who did Roy love the most? Was it Amy, Stephanie or Alex? Roy wasn't going to let the creature take any of them. And he wasn't going to give up on the book either. What would be the point? Unlike last time, this was no ultimatum, merely a promise.

I will come for the one you love the most.

Roy opened his laptop. "Then have it your way," he murmured, and he began searching for dating sites.

51

WEDNESDAY 18 JULY 2018

I HAVE no time to react to the sound of my daughter's voice. It's immediately followed by the snap of a lock being turned and then the door flies open. Luke steps out onto the path, eyes shining, lips red and wet within his beard. He looks like a giant boy about to pull the wings off a fly. Sounding almost amiable, he says: "You should have turned yourself in like your mother told you to Ben, or done everyone a favour and hung yourself, you miserable piece of shit."

"I just want Imog..."

That's as far as I get before his fist – I suppose it's his fist – comes out of nowhere and catches me on the side of my chin. For a moment I'm weightless, flying. Then with a thump I'm on my back, breath knocked from my lungs, my jaw hot and bright as if attached to a live electric wire.

Luke's form hangs over me, blocking out most of the night. The blinking red lights of a plane seem to fly into the thick black mass of his hair. I'm trying to suck in air and can hear myself groaning – a high, thin sound, like a child. I hope Imogen isn't seeing this – her Dad turned into a snivelling prey animal.

Somehow, the weapon is still in my hand. I raise it slowly so it's pointing towards his leg. It looks like a pencil trying to threaten a tree trunk. Luke swings a boot and a new, shattering pain transforms my hand. My little wooden toy goes tumbling.

His face is now just inches from mine, his breath thick with spiced meat and beer. Tears trickle from my eyes. My hand is a throbbing claw. My jaw is a hot mess. "I'm not allowed to kill you," he rumbles, "but that doesn't mean I can't beat you to shit, you sly, slick fuck, murdering with your lies."

The other side of my face explodes. I can feel teeth crack as a taste of copper fills my mouth. I try to get up, but he kicks me hard in the ribs. It feels like steel smashing into balsa wood.

Then, from above, I hear a soft grunt. I twist around to see what's happened, and nearly scream from the pain. My ribs are like knives turned onto my flesh. But I can now see why Luke's stopped hitting me. His hand is clamped to the crown of his head, his face full of hurt surprise. Amy's there, next to him, holding the statue of Buddha like a nervous aunt holding a baby – up and out from her body.

"Why did you do that?" Luke asks her.

"Why are you hurting him?" she responds.

"He killed my brother."

Her face turns to blank stupefaction.

I want to break in here, explain to her that what he's saying is rubbish, but even opening my mouth is agony. I think he may have broken my jaw and maybe my cheekbone, too.

"His lies to the court ruined Tom's life and broke his will," says Luke. "My brother killed himself because of that fucker down there."

"I didn't know about any of that," says Amy. "What concerns me is what happened to Stephanie. Do you know if he took my daughter?"

I try to get up, but the pain in my side rips me apart, so I attempt to slip away by using my legs and my good hand. Like a worm, I slide myself slowly into the shadows behind the studio.

"If he did, I can't let you kill him," I can hear Amy saying. "He has to tell me where she is."

I can smell warm compost. It feels safe. I can hide out here, get my strength back.

"Are you saying that fucker killed Stephanie too?" screams Luke.

I hear the thump of his approaching boots reverberating in the earth and wait despondently for the next assault. This one comes hard in the thigh. The force of it rolls me onto my back. It's bad, but it barely registers in the pain charts when compared to my ribs, hand, jaw and cheek. My left hand – the unhurt one – falls on something in the leaf litter. It's my sharp stick. Luke closes in, crouches over me, pulls me up by my jacket lapels ready to give my face another pummelling. I ram the stick into his neck.

Or I try to, but my aim is poor and instead it goes into his shoulder – three or maybe four inches into it.

Luke's mouth becomes a red tunnel. He rises to his full height and howls. Staggering backwards, he bounces off the studio wall, his hand clamped around the stick, his pale shirt flowering red at its base. He howls a second time, and someone comes running out of the studio – a tall, slender figure. A woman, I think, but not Susan. She's holding Imogen, one arm clamped around my daughter's neck. In her other hand is a gun.

Imogen is trying to turn her head to look at me, but it's impossible – she's being held too tightly. I start crying at the sight of her. She's okay – my girl looks okay, and so calm and brave. But she's in terrible danger.

Her captor is staring at Luke, and seeing the two of them

together I suddenly know who she must be. I suppose there's a family resemblance in their heavy foreheads and beady eyes – Luke's brown, hers black. But there's also evidence of a sisterly devotion in the tightening lines of her face when she sees his wound. So this is the mysterious Jean. It hadn't occurred to me until now that they might be accomplices.

My mother follows them out. She's in her night dress, her long grey hair disshevelled. There's a big bruise on her face. I sob with relief that she, too, looks okay. Mum rushes to me and helps me to my feet. My ribs scream at the effort and my head pulses with giddiness. For a woozy moment I'm sure I'm going to pass out. Amy is watching all this with a strangely deadpan expression. She must be able to see the gun trained on my daughter, but if this has prompted her to reevaluate the situation, she's not yet showing it.

Jean, if it's her, is drawing the stick very slowly out of Luke while he bellows and weeps and pushes back on her hand to make the extraction process slower. With the two of them thus diverted, I limp over to Imogen and try to pull her free, but the woman, without even interrupting her delicate operation, bashes my broken cheek with the back of her hand. The detonation of pain in my face makes me scream. When I manage to open my eyes, the muzzle of her gun is pointing at my head.

"Ben, please don't provoke her," Mum whines.

I stumble back, swallowing blood.

Jean jerks Imogen closer to her. She prods Luke with her elbow to start walking along the overgrown path behind the studio. He shambles away, still skewered, and she follows him, dragging Imogen with her. Her upper body is half turned so she can keep her gun trained on me until they're out of sight.

"What the hell is going on?" asks Amy once they're gone.

Even if I was physically able to talk, I wouldn't have the words – not now, not with Imogen stuck in that woman's grasp.

"They made me send that text," Mum says, half crying as she wipes the tears from my eyes. "None of it's true. Susan's not here. And I know you're not Mr Jones, Ben."

I nod and turn from both of them, staggering off in the direction in which Imogen was taken. Did I really believe Susan would be here? If I did, I was a fool. Once I knew that text wasn't from my mother, why would I believe a single word it contained? Only because I wanted to. I know now that the message was designed for one purpose: to draw me here so they could carry out their mad, delusional act of revenge. What I cling to are Luke's words from earlier – *I'm not allowed to kill you.* They offer just a fragment of hope that Imogen and I will survive the night. Maybe I can persuade Luke that beating the living shit out of me was enough. Honour has been satisfied.

The path ends in a flower bed where a series of stepping stones have been laid to give access to the rear of the garden. The door in the back fence stands open, swinging limply in the night breeze.

They've gone into the park. I hobble over to the door as fast as I can. The bones in my head feel hot and misshapen. Every step, every breath, sends a fresh bolt of pain through my side. My right hand, at least, is feeling slightly better. I can flex the fingers without too much discomfort.

I push through the door and enter the park. About ten yards ahead of me, down a gentle slope thickly covered in sedge and bordered by wild goat willow and rowan, is the pond, looking as lifeless as a slab of green stone. Luke is crouched near its bank, head down, his hand still clamped to the stick I plunged into him. To his left is Imogen. She's gazing at me with a sad, solemn expression, the same one she wore when we buried Shelley the snail last year. I'm desperate to take her in my arms and carry her away from this hell. The reason I can't is the gun muzzle pushing through her dark golden locks. The sight of it is an abomination. It's unbearable. Holding the weapon is the she-devil I think of as Jean.

I wonder why they've brought me here to this hateful place, this teeming, decaying jungle on the banks of a barren pond. There's a whisper of leaves behind me, and Amy arrives. "Your mother's calling the police," she murmurs in my ear. "The woman's name is Jean. She's Luke's sister and your mum says she's very dangerous, so please don't provoke her. Let the police deal with them." In an even softer voice, she adds: "I'm so sorry for earlier, Ben."

I spit out some blood along with half a tooth. It seems an eloquent enough response.

Amy raises her voice so she can be heard by Luke and Jean. "Where's Roy?"

"In Australia – with Susan," mutters Luke, not looking up.

Most probably Devon, Victoria, I think to myself. *How could she?* But my anger is more like a reflex. It feels muted like the ache in my leg, not sharp like the pain in my ribs or mouth, or like the gun pointed at my daughter's head.

"Why didn't you tell me, Luke?" demands Amy.

In response, he gives a roar and pulls the spear out of his shoulder in a single, wild jerk. Then raising his head, he screams at the sky. He twists his body and hurls the stick at the pond. There's a hollow plop, and the stick briefly disappears before bobbing to the surface. The perfection of the green mat has been broken, disfigured by a dark smile.

"And what about Stephanie?" asks Amy, her voice now hesitant and quavering.

Luke is crying from the pain and doesn't reply.

"She's dead," says Jean, speaking for the first time in a low, flat voice.

Amy screams. "No! No! No! No! No!" She pulls at her hair. Her body crumples like paper set on fire.

"Mr Jones took her," says Jean.

"What?"

"Give me back my child!" I try to break in. It comes out of my battered mouth as *Gim-bah-mah-chah*.

Jean ignores me. She has a thin mouth, not exactly made for smiling, but I can hear a smile in her voice, as she speaks. "Mr Jones came to me in my dream. He told me to take Roy's daughter and put her underground, and when she was ready, when she got the dreams, she would go to him."

"What does that mean?" Amy has fallen on her side, cheek pressed to the earth, fist pulling at a tuft of grass.. "What happened to my child?"

Like someone in a trance, Jean seems barely aware of our existence, but the hand holding the gun to my daughter's head remains taut and steady. "I didn't know what he meant by putting her underground," she continues. "But then, one day, Roy asked Lukey to build the room behind his cellar, and I knew that Roy must have also been visited by Mr Jones. It was all part of the plan. So me and Lukey snatched the girl and we put her in the underground room. And sure enough, when she was down there, she got the dreams and she went to Mr Jones, and he took her."

Now Jean looks at me. Her black eyes seem depthless, reflecting no light. They're not like eyes at all, more like holes. I remember Imogen saying: *I couldn't see anything through the eye holes Daddy... under the mask there's nothing there.*

"And now it's this one's turn," she says, tugging Imogen's hair and pulling her head hard against the muzzle of the gun. I flinch, wanting more than ever to charge over there, but I know I couldn't manage more than a few steps before....

"She has to die," says Jean, "because it's the only way to make things square between us, Ben Rose. A life for a life."

"Pl...Pl..." I can't form the word. Tears start from my eyes. I fall to my knees. Hands raised in surrender. "Plees..."

Imogen's face is creased and stretched in a way I've never seen before, her head pulled into her shoulder, her whole body straining from that confining, encircling grip.

"I'd have killed her already, only I got the dream again," says Jean. "Mr Jones told me he wants her, too, and you can't deny him when he's hungry. He took Roy's daughter, and now he wants yours. I don't personally care how she dies, just so long as she does. And I'm glad you're here Ben Rose, so you can witness the closing of the circle that opened on Monday the fifth of September Twenty-Sixteen. That was the day my brother hanged himself after you obliterated his life, and I'm going to enjoy watching as Mr Jones obliterates yours."

"No! Plees! I'll do anythi... Kill me!"

"Killing you wouldn't do any good though, would it? I wouldn't see your pain when Mr Jones takes your daughter. That's when I'll know you suffered like I did. That's when we'll be even."

Through my tears, the colours are starting to blur: the jade green of the pond bleeds into the deeper shadows beyond, which spill into the twinkling gold of distant attic windows, all of which seems inconsequential next to the endless black of Jean Macey's eyes and the white knuckle of her trigger finger. I long for the blue of an approaching police light, but I know it won't come in time.

Yet time, at this moment, seems to elongate. The three of them fall still, like a tableau under the dead glow of the moon:

Luke, head down, collapsed in his sunken hollow of private suffering; Jean, cold and alert, preparing to drink in my pain; Imogen between them, head cocked in a frozen cringe from Jean's gun. The only motion is sound: the night breeze, and Amy's quiet keening. And then, minutely, the picture moves. The pond surface shivers, wrinkling like neck skin blown upon by a cold breath.

"He's coming," says Jean. "Say goodbye to your little Midge."

Luke raises his head. "I'm scared, Jean. I don't know if..."

Jean turns briefly to her brother, and that's when I start my headlong charge across the yards that divide us, ignoring all the protests from my injured body. But before I can reach them, my body is halted – stopped as if a plug has been ripped from its socket.

52

SATURDAY 15 JULY 2017

So in the end it was a dream! A year and three days had passed since the watery-voiced demon uttered its prophecy, and nothing had happened. The curse had gone unfulfilled. The fiend turned out to be a fantasy – rotten fruit of Roy's diseased imagination. All the horror he'd read over the years must have leached into his subconscious like toxic waste to produce this foul emanation. And the resulting stress he'd suffered these past twelve months, the casual cruelty he'd inflicted on his daughter, had been for nothing.

He should have been angry with himself, yet all he could feel right now was relief – and joy. Relief that the demon didn't exist, and joy that he'd found Susan. The damp fiend may have failed in its core mission, but it had played a blinder as cupid. *I will come for the one you love the most* it had warned. *But you didn't specify who that should be, did you, you stupid green gargoyle?* So naturally, to protect his family from the creature's slimy clutches, he'd visited a dating site.

The creature had spoken to him again last March, giving more explicit instructions: *Prepare a place for the one you love the most. Make it underground. And when the time comes, I will come for her.* Roy had done exactly as he'd been told. He built a secret annex behind the cellar at 25 Oakfield Crescent and had every intention, when the time came, of drugging Susan and depositing her there while she slept.

He didn't go through with it in the end because, dammit, that was the flaw at the heart of his plan. If she's the one you love the most, you're not going to sacrifice her to a monster, are you? Not even to save your own family, because you love her more than them – that's the whole fucking point! *And I do*, he thought. *I love her more than Amy, more than Alex, more than...*

But none of that matters now, because nothing has happened. The fiend didn't come for anyone, not even for Sally, next door's friendly pug, for whom Roy nursed a serious soft spot. He could hear her right now, yapping for joy with all the breath her little lungs could muster.

He'd spoken to Susan the morning after the anniversary of the curse, and every morning since, and she was fine. His family was fine, too. This morning, a Saturday, Alex went off on a play date, and Amy and Stephanie headed into town to buy Steph some new shoes, leaving Roy to get on with his book. Alex came back half an hour ago and was happily playing in the garden.

A shadow had lifted from Roy's life these past few days, and the rest of it now stretched out before him with the warmth and clarity of a sunlit road. In a month or two, he would leave Amy and move in with Susan. It wouldn't need to be messy – she would probably be quite relieved. With Susan's support and encouragement, Roy would finish his novel *Mr Jones*, his follow-up to *Turnwood*. He had a good feeling about this one. It had the smell of a commercial success. It was also that wonderful thing – *catharsis*: the cleansing and purgation of fear through art. He'd faced down the demon (the *inner* demon, as it turned out) and defeated it.

He and Susan would stay in the neighbourhood, so he could see the kids on weekends. The children had to be part of his future, especially Stephanie. No parent should have a favourite, and of course he loved Alex to bits, but he and Steph had always had a special bond. He remembered holding her in the hospital room on the day she was born, when she looked up at him with her inquisitive dark eyes, testing the air with her tiny tongue. He had trembled at her fragility – dressing her in that white babygro while the nurses were attending to Amy, terrified of breaking those little bones.

He had a lot to make up for. These past twelve months he'd said some cruel things to Steph in an effort to protect her from the demon. He'd seen the misery and confusion in her eyes, forcing himself to remain aloof and remote as she played alone in the garden or her room. Time was on their side, though. He would repair the damage. What was twelve months in a lifetime?

Roy checked his watch, wondering vaguely where Amy and Steph were. Four hours was a long time to be shopping for a pair of shoes. He switched on his phone to see if there were any messages.

53

JEAN, momentarily distracted by her brother, senses my rush towards her and swings her gun ninety degrees so it's pointing at me. For the first time I see expression in her empty eyes. It may be hesitation or calculation. She has a dilemma: she has to stop me, but she doesn't want to kill me. Seeing me pull up short makes her smile. I suppose she must think I stopped because of the gun trained on me when the truth is I'd welcome a bullet if it could save my daughter. Jean starts to swivel the gun back towards Imogen, but never manages to complete the turn.

Something is climbing out of the pond behind her. The sight of it instantly cuts the power supply to every muscle in my body and flattens every thought in my head. How can I describe what I'm seeing? My first impression is that part of the pond has climbed out of itself. Something with the same bilious green colour and smooth, waxy texture has risen from the surface in a kind of branching column more than six feet tall. In the dull metal light of the moon the emerging mass quickly resolves itself into a figure with limbs, a torso and a head. The limbs and torso are long and slender, with the head disproportionately large and round, like a pumpkin perched in the branches of a sapling. A face emerges from the head's smooth surface. It has a wide, downturned mouth, a small lump of a nose and round eyes as black as Jean's, but somehow even flatter in expression and more insectile. The horror and fascination of it is that I've seen this exact face twice in the past few hours, in pictures created by Stephanie and my mother.

Jean has just started to turn her gun arm back towards Imogen when the green entity seizes her from behind with both its long arms. A thin cold smile greets its touch. "You're here," she sighs. "I have the girl for you. Here she is." She tries to pull Imogen closer to the thing, but it's a struggle with her upper arms squashed tight against her torso. A small frown of puzzlement clouds her smile.

"Jeanie," mutters Luke, his shiny brown gaze riveted by the pond creature. "Jeanie, are you sure this is right? This doesn't seem right."

His sister again tries to move her arms. "Mr Jones," she says, the calmness of her voice now sounding a little forced. "I've brought you the Rose girl, just as you asked. I have her right here, do you see?"

But her discreet, tugging efforts to free herself achieve nothing. Her smile intensifies into a thin-lipped grin, and she emits a sustained, guttural grunt as she tries, with more concentrated force this time, to tear herself from the pond thing's sticky grip. "What are you *doing?*" she eventually exclaims, frustration sending her voice close to a shriek. She embarks on a series of sudden, violent yanking motions with her arms. During one of these, the gun flies from her hand, but she maintains her tight grip on Imogen.

Luke, now openly terrified, grabs her free wrist and tries to pull her out, but he can only apply one hand to the task – his other arm, disabled by the shoulder wound, hangs uselessly by his side. "Jeanie!" he wails. "Jeanie, what's happening?"

His sister refuses to succumb to panic, but her grin is now a manic rictus. "It's not me you came for Master, it's the girl. Let... Me... Go!" She starts hurling herself from side to side and in doing so, her grip on Imogen finally loosens. Imogen sprints up the bank to me. I fall to my knees and hug her tight, wincing only slightly at the stabbing pain in my ribs. She relaxes heavily in my embrace like she once did as a baby, but neither of us can enjoy the moment. Our attention is inevitably drawn back to the spectacle playing out by the pond.

I can't understand the source of the pond-thing's strength. It has no discernible muscles or flesh. Its body is watery and seems to slosh around and even splash as its victim squirms and threshes, with tiny green globules flying out from its surface. Yet even with Luke's help, Jean can't free herself from its embrace, and the more she flails, the more she seems to become enveloped by it.

"She's sinking into it," Imogen whispers. And she's right. Either that or the thing is growing into her – it's hard to work out which. Luke finally abandons the struggle. Jean reaches out her arms towards him, pleading with him to keep pulling, but he appears paralysed with horror at the sight of his sister's slow submergence.

With most of her body and the back of her head gone, the motion of her limbs gets weaker, like a tiring insect caught in a spider web. In desperation, Luke picks up the gun and fires into the pond-thing. The report is very loud, like a firecracker, and a jet of liquid erupts from the back of the thing's head. It makes no difference. As the entity grows through her, Jean herself seems to transform into something less fleshy and more pondlike. Even her screams start to sound like mucous gurgles.

I don't know how long it takes for Jean to disappear – less time, I suspect, than it takes to describe. And when she's gone, the creature doesn't linger, but quietly sinks back into the water, reincorporating itself into the pond. A hoarse, grinding moan comes from deep inside Luke's chest as he watches the surface fall still once more and become as lifeless as a slab of pale green stone.

In the distance, a police siren wails, and Luke starts to run. I can make out his giant form stumbling up the bank on the far side of the pond, heading back towards his flat on the north side of Oakfield Crescent.

Arms fold around me and Imogen – a comforting scent of white spirit and cigarettes. "Did you see it?" I ask my mother.

"I don't know what I saw," she says.

"The pond ate Mr Jones," says Imogen. "I don't think she's ever coming back."

I kiss her hair.

Amy crawls closer to us and Mum embraces her, too. "I'm so sorry my dear." Amy sobs and says nothing. She takes Imogen's hand, holds it to her cheek and kisses it.

PART IV

18 NOVEMBER – 2 DECEMBER 2018

54

SUNDAY 18 NOVEMBER 2018

LUKE WAS ARRESTED LATER that night in his flat. He didn't resist. His confession, given in the early hours of 19th July, was, as far as I can tell, a full and honest one, and was of course immediately dismissed as lies and delusion. Two days later, I was visited in hospital (where I was being treated for two broken ribs and hairline fractures in my jaw and cheek) by Detective Constable Dave Adler. He asked me to corroborate aspects of Luke's statement, which I did. Adler managed, at first, to retain his composure. He asked me to go through it again, and then a third time, at which point he became angry, reminding me that wasting police time was a punishable offence that could land me with a six-month jail term. Clearly exhibiting signs of strain, he went on to admit that Amy, Imogen and my mother had all given similar accounts to mine and Luke's. More interviews followed with other police officers and brain doctors. Our stories didn't change, and we began to hear mutterings from behind cupped hands – terms like shared delusional disorder and *folie à plusieurs*. The pond was dredged and no bodies were found. That didn't surprise us.

The fate of Jean Macey and Stephanie Parker remains, as of this date, a mystery.

For my own part, I couldn't let it rest. I've spent months now trying to piece together the story of that night, probing that membrane with my pin. It has yielded in some places, but not all. Unanswerable questions remain. The events of 18 July 2018 were the culmination of a long campaign of criminal activity by the Maceys involving trespass, fraud, drink spiking, abduction, false imprisonment and aiding and abetting in murder. Jean Macey's hatred of me and desire for revenge was all-consuming. Luke shared these feelings to some extent, but he was always the follower – Jean was the instigator. It was she who wrote those abusive letters and emails to me in 2016, and it was she who later attempted to frame me for the disappearance of Stephanie Parker.

Of course there was more to it than that – a lot more – and this is where the story starts to get murky. Something happened to Jean in 2017. The brain doctors would call it a psychotic episode. I think demonic possession would be more accurate. I'm going to use this language, even though it makes me, and I'm sure many readers, uncomfortable, because to do otherwise would be to deny what I witnessed on the night of 18 July. What came out of that pond doesn't fit into any category of natural animal. There may well be a better word for it than *demon*, but I don't know what it is.

In early 2017, Jean became possessed by a demon known as Mr Jones. He told her to kidnap young Stephanie Parker and imprison the girl underground. At first, Jean was confused by the command, but in March of that year Luke was commissioned to build an annex behind the cellar at 25 Oakfield Crescent, and that's when Jean understood where Mr Jones wished her to place Stephanie.

There is some dispute concerning the origins of the annex project. Luke claims Roy hired him to build it, but Roy, when he was interviewed by police at his home in Devon, Australia, last August, denied all knowledge of it. He admitted to a vague acquaintance with Luke, but said he'd never commissioned such a work and wouldn't have had any right to do so as he wasn't the owner at that stage. His lawyer supplied documentation proving that Roy only inherited the property from his uncle, Richard Landry, in March 2018, eight months after the annex had been completed.

Even so, none of this smells right to me. Landry had been suffering from dementia for some years before his death in November 2017. It seems perfectly possible to me that Roy commissioned it in Landry's name. For what purpose, I have no idea, but from what Amy told me, Roy's acquaintance with Luke was a lot more than "vague". Might he have been involved in his own daughter's sacrifice to Mr Jones? I could go to Australia and confront him about this, but perhaps there are some parts of the membrane that are best not probed.

Luke completed the annex in early July of 2017. On the 15th of that month, he and Jean kidnapped Stephanie Parker. The plan was simple and well-executed. That morning, Amy and Stephanie went shopping in Halsted Town. They parked in a multistorey car park and Amy went to purchase a ticket, leaving Stephanie alone in the car. Jean, ahead of Amy in the queue, pretended to struggle with the ticket machine, delaying Amy so that Luke could snatch Stephanie.

While she was in the annex, Stephanie was apparently visited by Mr Jones in her dreams. This part of the story is all speculation. Why he wanted her underground and how he imbued her with the desire to escape her prison and meet him at the pond in Turnwood Park, I have no idea. The pin probes and the membrane stretches, but it remains intact.

Stephanie was killed – Luke wasn't too clear on the dates – some time in early August 2017. She spent a few weeks at most in the annex before escaping into the park where she was taken by the demon. So the girl I occasionally glimpsed in the park last summer was a ghost – again, maybe not the best word for it, but the only one we have. She could have been nothing more than a visual echo of Stephanie, except I know she was cognisant of me, and each time I saw her she tried to lead me back through the garden and into the derelict house, maybe to show me where she had been held.

Jean may have been possessed, but she remained herself and still burned with the old revenge fever, which is why, when she needed someone to frame for Stephanie's disappearance, she chose me. With the downstairs flat at 25 Oakfield Crescent standing empty and the owner overseas, it was easy enough for her to fake a tenancy agreement and make me the official tenant of the flat, thereby putting me on the scene of Stephanie's incarceration. In September 2017, a few days after Roy and Susan's departure to Australia, Jean entered my house, most probably with a key copied or stolen from Susan. I was at my lowest ebb at this point, and no doubt in a drunken slumber when she used my thumbprint and phone to set up a monthly direct debit on my bank account for the rent.

The following June, she made a mock attempt to kidnap young Harriet Glass, the school gossip, thereby kickstarting a rumour around East Halsted Primary School about a creepy fellow named 'Mr Jones'. Despite her use of his name, I very much doubt the demon had anything to do with old panda-face. This was Jean, in avenging mode, acting alone.

But framing me for Stephanie's abduction was clearly not

enough for her – she was also going to abduct and kill my daughter. She began by placing a note in Imogen's book bag, purportedly from Susan, telling Imogen that she (Susan) had been kidnapped by Mr Jones and to check for a "stick" under the oak tree in the park. "It will be our way of talking," she had promised. And so the pig-rib messages began. She hoped the messages would destroy Imogen's trust in me, and make her more susceptible to a meeting with her "mother". But when Imogen failed to show up in the derelict garden at the appointed time, the plan changed to straightforward abduction.

At some point during the days leading up to 18 July, the demon stirred back to life within Jean and commanded her to bring him Imogen. She was happy to oblige. All that mattered to her was that my daughter should die and, ideally, she wanted me to witness it. The text she sent from my mother's phone was intended to draw me to Mum's house. It was my invitation to the evening's sacrificial rite.

According to my mother, Luke had turned up that evening posing as a government environmental officer offering advice on how to make her house more energy efficient. As soon as he was in the house, he struck Mum in the face and tied her up. Then Jean came in with Imogen. After Jean sent the text from Mum's phone, the Macey siblings spent the subsequent hour arguing. Luke had wanted to go on the run. Jean was determined to wait for me to arrive.

At 9.15 pm, fifty-five minutes after the text was sent, Amy arrived at my mother's house – she'd have been there earlier but had struggled to find a babysitter. Amy knocked and rang the bell for about ten minutes, then proceeded to break into the house by smashing the parlour window. This prompted Luke and Jean to move their prisoners into Mum's studio. Ten minutes later, I showed up.

55

WEDNESDAY 21 NOVEMBER 2018

ROY AND SUSAN sat beneath their arbour in the shade of a faded bougainvillaea and sipped their wine. It was a warm, breezy afternoon and they were working their way through a case of Yarra Valley Chardonnay. *Gentle melon and citrus notes*, Roy had observed on first tasting. That had been at lunchtime – two hours and three bottles ago.

On the cedarwood table between them sat an unopened letter from Luke Macey, stamped "HMP Halsted North". Susan, who was as usual out-pacing Roy on the drink front, asked blearily when he was going to stop messing about and open the fucking thing.

"Why look under the rock when all I'll find there is woodlice?" he answered, his handsome face, craggy and brown from the sun, creasing into a humourless smile. He cracked a salted cashew from its shell, tossed it into his mouth and chewed without registering the taste. Above them, the eucalyptus trees whispered. The shadows would never go away, not even in the brightest Australian sun, but the wine could send him into a pleasant daze. Susan's nagging could be ignored, like the bush flies. The deeper nagging, too, the ghost of Stephanie, had dulled to a faint tug. The veiling was temporary, alas. Tonight, in his dreams, or with the morning hangover, she would return, silently watching him from her grassy knoll, killing him with her eyes.

"If you don't open it, I will," said Susan, reaching for the letter. Roy slapped her hand away.

"Fuck you!" she said. Then, after a moment: "I'm going in." She stood up, or tried to. Her balance was off, and there was an ugly scrape of wood against stone as she toppled against the chair.

He waited impatiently for her to stagger away, but she didn't. She just stood there, leaning against the back of her chair.

"What is it?" he eventually snapped.

"When are you going to start writing again?" she asked. There was a fixedness to her gaze that he didn't think was all down to insobriety.

"I don't know. When the inspiration strikes."

Inspiration was never going to strike, he knew that. His inner landscape was all dust and scorched earth. He would continue to type orders to his local bottle-o and maybe one day get round to making a will. Other than that, not another word would he write.

"What are we doing, Roy?"

He didn't answer.

Eventually, she wove and stumbled her way back into the house, giving the concrete patch in the patio a wide berth as she went. They both avoided it, even though it was no longer a pond. The very first thing Roy did after they moved in, even before fixing the leaking roof, was drain the pond, line the pit with a waterproof membrane and then fill it with concrete. The elongated oval patch was level and flush with the patio – Roy had made sure about that. Despite this, after heavy rainfall like they had last February, water always seemed to puddle there and when it eventually dried a faint greenish stain remained that took hours of scrubbing with a wire brush to remove.

Roy stared at the letter over the rim of his wineglass. What could it tell him that he didn't already know? He had played with fire, gambled for glory, and lost the one he loved the most. Everything else was secondary. Jean was dead. Luke was in jail. Ben and Imogen were okay. That Jean had been taken and Imogen spared pleased but did not surprise him. The demon never took kindly to those who told his story. Roy had tried it in fictional form; Jean as a piece of performance art, wearing panda-face to scare the kids. Both had been brutally punished.

Roy was pleased at her comeuppance. In terms of compensation, it was like finding a five-cent piece in the charred remains of his house, but it was something to hold onto during long, sleepless nights. However much he blamed himself for Stephanie's death, Jean was the one who had done the deed. She had taken his daughter to Mr Jones. Luke had never described the moment of Jean's death, but that didn't stop Roy from trying to visualise it – the surprise, the dawning horror. Imagining it got him through the nights. Wine got him through the days.

"He may know something important," Susan had said of Luke's letter. "Something he didn't tell the police, something that didn't make the news…"

Sure, like Stephanie didn't really die. Like she's been found living in the North Pole or Timbuktoo, dazed but okay…

Something like that maybe.

He refilled his glass and lit a John Player Special.

What are we doing, Roy?

Everything was contained in that question. Now he was no longer writing, what *was* he doing apart from drinking his way through his uncle's inheritance? Susan had burned her bridges for him. She couldn't go back. They'd cut themselves adrift and had nothing to look forward to but bridge nights with their neighbours, Tom and Sheila, and the next case from Yarra Valley. Sometimes at night, he heard Susan crying. She did it softly so he wouldn't hear, but he heard.

Almost angrily, Roy reached for the letter and tore it from its paper skin. He skipped the opening pleasantries and went straight for the meat, which was contained in a single paragraph. He read it three times before flicking open his Zippo and burning it to ashes. Then he reached for another bottle.

I never told you, Roy, about Stephanie, and how brave she was in those few weeks she spent as our cellar guest. The thing about Mr Jones, he doesn't take all of you. He didn't take all of Jean, and he didn't take all of your little girl either. She was there to the end, and sometimes I could hear her crying at night. She cried for her mum and her brother, but mostly she cried for you. But the next morning, when I brought in her breakfast, she always had a smile and a good morning and how are you Mr Macey. I couldn't believe it was the same girl. Of course I wasn't to know she was busy digging a tunnel behind the bathroom and was just putting on a show. But still, you could easily forget she was only eight years old. Her composure in those circumstances was quite something. On the last evening, the evening of her escape, she wore that same friendly smile and said, nice to see you Mr Macey, and I hope you had a good day. Then, as I was leaving, she said: if you ever happen to see my parents and my brother, tell them I love them and I think about them all the time. Tell them I'm sorry if they're sad. I'm sad too, but life can take some funny turns and this is just the way things are. Tell them to love each other as best they can and to spare me a thought from time to time, because wherever I end up I'll be thinking of them. Will you do that for me Mr Macey? Will you tell them that?

56

SUNDAY 2 DECEMBER 2018

ON 8 AUGUST, I went to Stephanie's memorial service and listened to the eulogies from her "aunties", Ronnie and Amber. There was a display of photos of Stephanie from babyhood to the final one, taken in the back garden on the day she was taken, wearing the iconic (to me anyway) Hello Kitty T-shirt and jeans. The display also contained some of her artwork – unicorns, elephants and castles – though none of the annex drawings. Alex contributed a work of his own showing his sister surrounded by flowers. Amy did not speak, but she acknowledged with smiles the consoling words of others. Throughout, she clutched the pale yellow pillow she had found in Stephanie's cell. Her eyes had shadows under them, but she seemed calm. *I'd like a grave to put flowers on*, she once told me. I'm sorry she never got her wish.

Amy and I have talked only a little since then about the events of 18 July. We were, we openly acknowledge, victims of a grand deception. This has made it easier to forgive both ourselves and each other for the things we did that day, almost as if Mr Jones and the Maceys had temporarily turned us into monsters and our actions weren't our own. Of course this isn't really the truth, and we know it, but it's our way of dealing with the truth.

On the surface, we remain friends, and are often at each other's houses, though only for our children's playdates – I don't think there will be any more adult dates for Amy and me. At a deeper level, there remains an unspoken miasma between us that may never be fully cleared. I will always struggle to forgive her for not telling me about Susan and Roy, and for befriending me on a false pretext. She may never forgive me for not telling her about my sightings of Stephanie – even though they turned out to be spectral. We each have our internal justifications for acting as we did, but we'll never convince the other, so we don't talk about it and our friendship remains superficial, and maybe that's for the best.

We don't talk about what happened to Jean Macey by the pond either. None of us who witnessed it do. Even Imogen seems to have consigned the episode to a taboo corner of her mind. Was that thing the demon that took Stephanie? Was it the same entity that Roy saw in 2003? Why did it take Jean and not Imogen? And how the hell did its face show up in my mother's painting? More questions – more probing at that unbreakable membrane.

And what of Susan? I'm still dealing with my feelings about her. I want to view her as a monster. How else can I explain the actions of a woman who walks out on her husband and seven-year-old daughter without even a goodbye? It seems evil and inhuman, yet these are simply words we use to describe behaviours that we don't understand and would perhaps prefer not to. I have to be humble. On 18th July 2018, I locked up a woman in a cell for over seven hours. In extremis, we sometimes do bad things. Susan may have been in extremis – hating me, or loving

Roy, so much she was prepared to abandon her own child. Or maybe she just didn't love Imogen that much. That is always possible. There is no iron law of the universe that says a mother has to love her child.

I want to understand her. I want to see her as something more complex than a monster. I've seen real monsters now, and I'm not only talking about the thing that came out of the pond. Real monsters, like the Maceys, aren't that interesting – they're quite banal actually. But I can't put Susan in that category, not the Susan I knew. She was never banal. I'm not saying I can forgive her, but she's not dead to me either. Let's just say I've put her in a box marked *In Limbo*, which may not be so different from the box my mother and Imogen put her in after she left us, the one marked *Disappeared*. A person can come out of either of those boxes if she chooses to – if we let her.

When Luke told us by the pond that Susan was in Australia, Imogen didn't pick up on it. She had a gun pointing at her head at the time, and her mind was probably on other things. She still asks after her mother, but not quite so often these days. I haven't told her the truth. On this issue, Granny and I are in complete agreement. In time, when she's older, she'll find out and will hopefully by then have the inner strength and maturity to deal with it. For now, I let her persist with the idea that her mother is living in a magical place where the disappeared people go, and maybe one day, if we're lucky, she'll come back.

The weather has turned colder lately. The foxes have grown their thick winter coats, but we don't see much of them these days. Imogen and I have finished *The House at Pooh Corner* and are now reading *Tom's Midnight Garden*. In the evenings, after Imogen has gone to sleep, I watch Netflix and drink wine. I still miss Susan's presence next to me and often wonder what she'd make of this or that show. My concentration has improved since the summer, but I still drift off sometimes and find myself listening to the pipes settling in the basement.

Next weekend we'll put up the Christmas decorations. I wanted to put my old crooners CD on the stereo yesterday, to get into the yuletide spirit, and found Roy Parker's audio book in there. I took it out and threw it in the bin. The heatwave and all the madness of last summer seems a long time ago. The sun, when it occasionally shows itself, no longer blazes or oppresses, but is a comfort, welcome on the skin like the touch of an old friend. Turnwood Park remains a disgrace, but it bothers me far less now that winter has deadened and concealed its excesses. There's often a pretty coating of frost on its shaggy slopes in the mornings as Imogen and I, dressed in our scarves and hats, make our way along the path towards school. The big old oak sleeps in the amber glow of the low sun, and Imogen doesn't stop to look for anything in the iron-hard earth beneath its bare branches. The pond is still a stagnant green swamp. On some mornings a thin layer of ice appears on its scummy surface, and children throw stones to make the ice splinter and crack. Imogen and I will sometimes watch them, though never for long. Neither of us feel any desire to linger there.

THE END

ACKNOWLEDGMENTS

I would like to thank all the members of the Conway Writing Group – especially Dan, Martin, John, Christy, Debs, Nandarane and Maire – for their insightful feedback on this and other stories, and for giving me the motivation to keep going with this writing lark. Particular thanks must go to my good friend Dan Brotzel for his brilliant comments and for encouraging me to send this one out there.

Thanks to my parents Anita and Emile, my wife Paola, my children Michael and Maya, my sisters Kelly and Gabi and their families, and my brothers Matt and Carl for all their love and support. I'm especially indebted to Maya, whose company on our walks to her primary school was the original inspiration for this novel.

I am hugely grateful to the team at Indie Novella for their faith in the book and for their editorial suggestions, in particular Damien Mosley, Emily De Vogele, Lydia Jones and Matthew Gowans. Thanks also to Callum Hood and Melissa Junttila for their fantastic cover designs.

i

n

Indie Novella

www.indienovella.co.uk